Relentless Target

By R.W. Barton

Relentless Target is Dedicated

To Brad

Chapter One
Night Attack

Wednesday/Thursday—November 17/18
Stronghold—Southeastern Iranian Desert

It was a calm, quiet evening and Ayatollah Abdul Sarhardi had turned in early. A breeze provided a welcome respite from the hot sun of the day and his room was quite comfortable. He was satisfied that his quest was on track and that Allah was pleased with his work so far. The western powers were in some turmoil, and he was very pleased with that status. His movement was on track to create the political base of New Persia and become a world power in the Middle East. Combining Iraq, Iran, and Saudi Arabia into one, powerful, oil-dominant state was to be fulfilled. His well-placed agents of change in each of these countries were working their way up the various management levels of the governments and were getting close to where he wanted them before beginning an effort to combine the countries politically. He was sure it would result in some bloodshed, with discontent and riots on both sides, but sometimes those sacrifices needed to be made for the overall good of mankind and the Islamic religion and way of life. His demands on the western nations had been rebuffed, but his religious and political support had never been higher, including from some of the nations in the so-called "Third World."

Allah's will would be done.

It was 3:00 a.m. and the ayatollah and most of his immediate staff were asleep in their quarters within the underground stronghold. The quiet and peaceful early morning was suddenly disturbed as the ayatollah's main assistant, Khatib Al Daye, came rapidly down the corridor and shouted, "Get up, get up. We must leave immediately. Get up. All of you, get up. We must evacuate immediately."

The ayatollah, irritated that his sleep had been interrupted, pulled the curtain back on his quarters and nearly ran into Khatib. "What is happening?" he asked. "Why are you waking us so?"

"Abdul-Hakim has said to implement the emergency evacuation plans. An American warplane has gotten through our defenses and is coming to attack us. We need to get out of here," Khatib said with great urgency, bordering on panic, in his voice.

The ayatollah shook his head rapidly as others rushed by him. "What? How can that be? The Americans have all been bluster and don't have the courage to actually attack us. They don't even know where we are," he said with puzzled incredulity.

The six-foot-tall Khatib shook his head rapidly and continued with a great deal of urgency, "Nonetheless, Defense Minister Abdul-Hakim has said they are coming and we need to leave immediately. The American warplane will be here in just a few minutes. Hurry. I fear for your safety."

The ayatollah looked around quickly at the rough-hewn walls carved into the dirt and deposits of the Iranian mountain desert cliffs. It had been home to him for some time, and to leave it would be very difficult. His simple bed, his work desk, and the small rug covering the dirt floor; items he would miss. Glancing over at the small balcony that overlooked the valley, he could see a few stars in the black of the night. Many hours had been spent on that balcony planning and discussing the future with his immediate staff members. He looked over at his desk and study area and realized there was no way to take several of his documents with him. He would have to hope they survived whatever was coming and that he could retrieve them later. It was several years of planning that he would have to abandon. Heart wrenching. But he had to go. He turned, picked up his personal copy of the Koran and a small flash drive with some of his documents, and followed the others toward the evacuation point.

They immediately, along with several members of the staff, ran for the evacuation room. They pulled on black robes as they ran and put black hoods over their heads. In the space of just a few minutes, fourteen of them arrived at the emergency escape room and looked out at the base of the far cliff where the power generation equipment was located. The room they were in was the terminus of the power cables for the stronghold coming up from the power station.

One cable was different. It was a zip line for emergency use and for evacuation in case of attack. Abdul-Hakim's planning was accurate. One at a time they mounted a platform, put a sling and harness around their shoulders, legs, and waist, grabbed the speed controller on the zip-line clamp, and pushed off. They moved as quickly as possible down the twelve-hundred-foot steel cable. Several of them were on the zip line at the same time. Just before they hit the power station they braked and dismounted onto another platform and quickly headed down to the base of the cliff.

The thin, bearded, six-foot ayatollah had not done this before, and was petrified of the process. He had to be coaxed into climbing up onto the terminus platform and finally heading down the zip line to the power station. As he went, multiple surges in the zip line occurred as people got on and off. The zip line was bouncing a bit, causing reflections and the flickering of moonlight to occur off the steel cable. It was not a smooth ride.

Once at the power station, they got off the platform and Khatib led the way, following the cliff base for nearly one hundred meters, to a large boulder under an overhang. Dressed in black, they were nearly invisible against the dark cliff background, sandals and footwear slapping on the rocks as they raced along. While they were walking and stumbling along, they could hear a tremendous roaring sound building in their ears. As they went, they looked up, frightened, as the low-pitched, thunderous sound got louder and louder.

What was it? Fear on their faces as realization hit. A very large aircraft was coming in low and fast, the engine sounds racing before it. In the face of the cliff was a small concrete reinforced opening, and Khatib herded all the people through the opening as fast as he could. Following the last member, Khatib ducked into the entrance, the dim light from inside revealing his intense dark eyes and a full beard. He was followed by Abdul-Hakim. Abdul-Hakim hesitated for a moment at the entrance. Dropping his head cover, he turned and watched. He saw the barely visible camouflaged B-52 and a ghostly gray KC-46 refueling tanker fly overhead. He watched as the ground on top of the adjacent mesa, where the stronghold was located, lifted up in a huge wave as the sides of the stronghold blew out. A huge underground explosion had taken place within the stronghold and the ground shook with the impact. Instead of a cliff, the entire stronghold mesa became an airborne dust cloud and steep, rubble-strewn slope. And a huge grave for hundreds of New Persia people.

3

With extreme grief, his eyes misting over and his shoulders slumping on his thirty-four-year-old, five-foot-ten-inch frame, he turned quickly and went inside. Inside the opening was a corridor that ran twenty yards into the cliff and through another narrow doorway with a secure lock. It was open, and he hurried into a small room lit with several feeble electric lights. Some small sand and pebbles fell inside the man-made cavern from the impact and shock wave of the bomb. But they were safe.

The room was long and narrow. Simply a wide tunnel dug into the cliff. He shooed several stragglers as they continued on and passed through two more sharp turns in the tunnel, and came to a small timber-reinforced room that contained storage facilities for emergency rations and living materials. Sleeping blankets and bedrolls, food packets, water containers, and several copies of survival information, along with copies of the Koran, were on the dugout shelves. A gentle breeze brushed their faces, and they realized it was from a small ventilation fan.

Still confused and in shock, the survivors gathered in the middle of the room not knowing quite what to do next. Abdul-Hakim was the last to arrive in the room. He had stayed at the entrance and emotionally watched the utter destruction of the stronghold. Still shaking in shock and grief, he addressed them and explained that there were enough rations for twenty people for two weeks and that this was a hidden place safe from the enemy.

In a barely controlled voice, he continued, "The American commandos have arrived and knocked out our self-defense systems. We don't know how many are here, but all the close-in radar vans have been destroyed or severely damaged. The sound you heard a few moments ago was a bomber that got through, and it has destroyed the rest of the stronghold. We are probably the only survivors." There was no motion, just absolute stillness and total disbelief as the news sank in. They just stood there. Heads shook, and several ministers turned to the walls and leaned for support, overwhelmed.

The ayatollah was completely stunned. This could not be happening! He turned to Khatib with a beseeching look, eyebrows furrowed downward and mouth half open. Khatib looked back at him and then looked at the floor, slowly shaking his head from side to side.

4

Khatib thought for several difficult moments and then said, "We didn't think this was possible, but it has happened, and we need to survive to continue our work. It is too important for our people and our children. We will persevere."

The ayatollah responded, "Yes ... yes, of course. But so much destroyed and so many of our people just gone. It cannot be ... but it is." He turned and looked at each of the survivors in the dusty room. Some looked back at him; others looked away. None showed fear. All were stunned. Many began to quietly weep as the reality of what had happened became apparent.

After a moment the ayatollah turned to Abdul-Hakim with resolve coming back into his voice and said, "We must continue. What are your suggestions for the immediate time? Can we leave soon or should we stay here?"

Abdul-Hakim, drawing on a strong personal reserve of strength, stood tall and responded, "We are safe for the time being. I don't think the Americans know of this shelter. We need to stay here until the American commandos, and I'm sure that's what are here, have left. As I said earlier, we have two weeks' worth of supplies right now. Our dispersed radar trucks will be returning soon and we can use them to get some more supplies. But right now, we need to stay here until we are sure the Americans have left. Then we can begin to recover."

The ayatollah, with intense eyes over a thin and trimmed beard, nodded his understanding. He thought for a moment, and then said, "We have suffered a grievous blow tonight, and this will live in our memories for centuries. When we are free to move about, we need to tend to anyone on the surface who might have survived. And then perhaps we need to consider moving to our alternate center."

Several in the crowd of selected staff and support personnel, stunned over the past several minutes of activity, nodded quietly in agreement. It was obvious that they could not remain here for very long. In shock, they sat on the earthen floor, some praying, and all waiting for further instructions. What if the Americans came back? Not a good thought!

Abdul-Hakim waited for twenty minutes, then, putting the black robe and head cover back on, departed through the entrance. He wanted to see what the situation was and see if there was anything that could be done in the darkness. After carefully going behind the boulder at the entrance, he slowly walked very cautiously down the base of the cliff toward the power station. His men manning the power station had either escaped or been killed by the Americans; he didn't know which. He stopped and listened. He could hear voices. Foreign voices—speaking English.

He, very carefully, eased around and under a boulder, listening. The Americans had discovered the zip line and were discussing what it meant. After several minutes, the officer in charge told them to blow the electric plant up and rejoin the other commandos at "Charlie." Abdul-Hakim quietly crawled back toward the safe cavern. He got halfway there when there was another large explosion and dirt and small debris rained down on him. The Americans had destroyed the power plant.

He waited in the darkness and dirt for another twenty minutes and then worked his way silently back to the power plant. It was essentially gone. Just a shell of some walls and debris of electrical equipment. The diesel fuel tanks had been destroyed and the fuel was burning fiercely on the ground surrounding the tanks. It provided only a very dim light to see the devastation. It appeared that the Americans had gone, but he wasn't absolutely sure. He looked up at what had been solid walls of the adjacent cliff where the stronghold had been and saw nothing but ruin and piles of bricks and rocks. The stronghold was now just a steep slope of dirt and rock. No sign of life.

He began to hear emotional wailing from right above him. Families of the men buried in the stronghold were beginning to move around on the cliff-top above. It had been quiet until the Americans left ... now it was beginning. Of the over twenty-four hundred people in the stronghold and family complex, over seven hundred were in the actual stronghold when it was hit. They didn't know the exact number, but would have to determine that as best they could from surviving family members. The remaining seventeen hundred or so were in the family quarters on the adjacent cliff above him. There were significant survivors. About nine hundred were members of the New Persia movement and the remainder were family members. Abdul-Hakim looked at the devastation and heard the families and men who had escaped. Many of them were beginning to climb about in the rubble, using flashlights to find any survivors.

The movement would survive. They needed to move, though, and it would take a major effort to accomplish that.

Moving all these surviving people from the Iranian desert to the alternate center would be difficult.

He looked across at the rock-rubble slope again. His eyes teared up a little and he told himself that this was all Allah's plan and to follow His wishes. He made his way back, following the base of the cliff, and entered the safe cavern again. He went to one of the shelves holding water and took several swallows from a bottle. He could feel their eyes on him. He looked around. All had become very quiet. The sixteen total survivors in the cavern were all looking at him. He looked at the floor and then over at the ayatollah sitting on a bedroll. He said, "I think the Americans are gone. The stronghold is no more. We have people in the family areas that are just now coming out to see the results. To be safe, I think we need to stay here until it is light. That's only a couple of hours from now. Then I'll check again. If the Americans have gone, then we can go out and see the results of the raid. And we need to begin to plan on our next actions."

The ayatollah responded, "Very well. We will wait until first light before venturing out. Then our first action should be to tend to any survivors in the stronghold. After all of you have a chance to look things over, we will meet and discuss what the next actions should be." He looked around the room and all were nodding in approval. Most, though not all, of his senior staff had made it out, including the recently assigned local Chinese program manager, Zhang Qiang. Many of the lower-level people had not. And there were some of his men who had been off-shift sleeping in the still-intact family quarters. He quickly realized he had a core capability once he was able to get it together again.

The B-52 strike was a major blow, and one designed to remove him from the world, but it had not done that. He would be back. He again looked around at all the ragged remains of his loyal staff. His eyes lowered, his head drooped slightly, then he looked back up to the ceiling and softly whispered, "We will be back."

Two hours later, Abdul-Hakim carefully departed the cavern and made his way slowly to the power plant. The sun was barely up and much of the dust had settled or blown away. As he walked, he listened closely and intently. He did not want to be surprised by the American commandos. But all he could hear was the impassioned crying of relatives of the people killed in the stronghold.

Walking around at the base of the cliff, he saw no sign of the Americans. He climbed the rubble-strewn slope, looked around at the various family members, and saw no Americans. He thought they were gone.

Retracing his steps, he went back to the cavern and told them all that they could leave now. If there was no food or water, they were welcome to come back and eat and rest if they wished. But for now, they were free to look at the destruction and define what they needed to do next. Khatib interrupted to let them know that there would be a meeting scheduled for the afternoon and he would let them know where and a specific time. His comment registered, but it was blank stares of shock he saw on their faces. A very quiet group of people filed out of the cavern and into the early light of morning.

They were about to witness what they had wrought.

Over Iran, the satellite does not blink. Its stare is constant and unwavering. The lens automatically adjusts for cloud cover and light conditions. It sees what it is looking at. Then it transmits that image across the darkness of space to another satellite in a double hop to a receiving station at Schriever AFB in Colorado Springs. A young Air Force lieutenant is at the console, watching the stronghold. It's been several hours since the strike occurred, and she is seeing quite a few people coming from the family quarters on the adjacent cliff to work in the wreckage of the stronghold. It's a ragtag group with no organization to it at all. They are searching for any survivors and hoping to find a few. They do find some, but many more are buried too deep and will never be recovered. She sees this and feels sorry for them. She can see the crying of the women and the collapse of some of the men. It is pitiful.

Shortly after daylight, she sees a small parade of individuals, organized, watchful, with dark clothing and dark hoods, not keffiyeh. They come from the base of the adjacent cliff and walk across the small, rubble-strewn expanse to the foot of the slope. Due to the boulders and rubble she can't see where they really came from. They just appeared. They look up at the slope as a group. The lieutenant isn't sure what she's seeing. She calls the squadron commander over. He looks at it and she runs a replay of the "parade." He doesn't know what to make of it either. He directs her to put it in an electronic file for the detailed analysts to review later in the day. In the meantime, they keep monitoring for any other unusual activities.

Later that same day, several military analysts looked at the digital file and all came to the same conclusion. It was a group of respected men who were reviewing the damage to the stronghold. Possibly some leaders in the movement, but that was speculation, since they couldn't see their faces or determine other means of identification.

Thursday—November 18
On Board *USS Kennedy* in the Gulf of Oman

Ryan McKenzie, watching the returning action from the bridge of the aircraft carrier *USS Kennedy*, looked down on the flight deck in amazement. They had accomplished the mission and the ayatollah's stronghold had been destroyed. As far as they knew, the ayatollah was in the stronghold and was now dead. His New Persia movement would have died with him.

It was still dark in the very early morning, and the SEAL team was back on board, having just exited the still-running Osprey aircraft. They were high-fiving each other as they made their way to the debriefing facility below decks. Word had been received that the two damaged B-52s, along with the two KC-46s, were still en route to Diego Garcia, but they expected to be on the ground in a few hours.

Ryan, a retired Navy commander, SEAL, and the president's personal representative to this mission, moved down the passageways to the debriefing room. He sat toward the back as Lieutenant Jackson Rider, the leader of the SEAL team, who had provided critical on-site intel and watched the strike unfold, went through his detailed debrief of the seven days they had spent in the southeastern Iranian desert. Never discovered until it was too late, the team had been able to pinpoint the stronghold location and provide the laser designation signal to the GBU-57 bunker buster dropped from the attacking B-52. There were only minor injuries that happened to two members of his team, and all were able to extract from the remote site without incident.

Ryan listened with both enjoyment and envy. Had it not been for a gunshot wound in his leg two months earlier, suffered at the hands of a New Persia terrorist, he would have been on that mission. But to have been associated with the mission in such an important manner—well, he really appreciated it. He continued to listen until the briefing was complete and then retired to his quarters. It would be a long day tomorrow as he headed back to Washington, D.C. and then on to his home in Freeport, Texas.

That evening, Major Corrine Callaway, the B-52 mission commander, couldn't buy a drink in the Diego officers' club, and she had been called directly by President Martinez to congratulate her on the mission success. He also notified her that she was to be promoted to lieutenant colonel, and she and her crew, along with the tanker crews, would be receiving the Air Force Cross, second only to the Medal of Honor, for their actions. It had been quite a show.

In the morning, Ryan said goodbye to the fleet commander, Admiral Link, and boarded the C-2AR Greyhound Carrier On-Board Delivery (COD) aircraft for his flight back to Diego Garcia and then on to the United States. It would be a long flight across the Pacific "pond." Lots of time to think about the events of the past few days and what might lie ahead.

Chapter Two
Stronghold Rubble

Thursday—November 18
Stronghold—Southeastern Iranian Desert

The ayatollah was standing in distressed amazement and wonder outside the stronghold rubble. The devastation was nearly complete. He was quietly weeping, tears flowing down his cheeks, as he surveyed the destruction of so much of his movement. He moved around at the base of the slope of rubble that had been his home for the past two years. Everywhere he looked was devastation and ruin. He coughed at the dirt and covered his face with his hands.

His soldiers and support people, and their families, had found several people alive in the rubble. However, only a few that would recover from the blast. As best they could, under the primitive conditions, they cared for those injured. The ayatollah had a devoted group of followers, and, as word of the strike passed into the neighboring areas and other parts of the Middle East, new volunteers would arrive. He was sure of it. It was just in the nature of people in that part of the world, especially the young. The loss of manpower and expertise was significant, but he was completely convinced they would return; his movement would return stronger than ever.

As he was standing there, he heard the distinctive sound of a helicopter in the distance approaching from the north. He turned toward the sound and saw a small blip on the horizon getting larger as it approached. He climbed to the top of the mesa to see what this visit was all about. He watched the helicopter carefully as it slowed down, circled for a landing, picked out an intact, barren place on the top of the mesa, and landed. Camouflaged in desert sand color, it had military markings of the Iranian Army on its side and carried several heavily armed soldiers, along with a primary passenger. The soldiers immediately deployed around the helicopter in a defensive posture, which the ayatollah found to be ridiculous given the circumstances. After the pilot shut down the engines and the rotors stopped turning, a small man in traditional Arab clothing stepped out, looked around with some disdain at the smoldering ruins and distasteful smells, spotted the ayatollah, and stepped smartly toward him. As he approached, the ayatollah recognized the Iranian minister of the interior, Amad Essa. He was a small man, no more than five foot four inches tall, but carried himself with confidence and an air of arrogance. The ayatollah internally grimaced, because Essa was not a pleasant man to deal with, and this interruption was not welcome. But he also understood the politics, and forced a polite welcome. The ayatollah moved toward Essa, bowed slightly as they met, and said, "I welcome you. While I was not expecting your visit, and we have no form of refreshments at this time, I would hope that you will understand. We are in the very first parts of recovery from the events of last night and earlier this morning."

Amad nodded and said with some condescension, "I understand. And the reason I came was to see the damage myself and to be able to report back to Tehran on the results of the Americans' 'visit.' We can provide some humanitarian assistance to you during your time of need. And I am here to assess that need. So ..." He looked around, shaking his head slowly at the damage. "Can you tell me what you think you may need in the way of assistance?"

The ayatollah looked around at the devastated stronghold and said, "Not yet. We are just now looking at the situation to define what we have lost and what we may need. I would estimate that it will take us another day or two to figure out the damage, what needs to be done, and how we might begin the recovery."

As he wrapped his robes tightly around himself, Amad said, "I see. Well, let me look around a bit and see for myself what the task may entail. Then we can talk again before I depart."

"That would be fine. I'll have one of my people accompany you." The ayatollah turned and said to Khatib, "Get Abdul-Hakim over here to help the minister and to answer any questions he may have."

The twenty-eight-year-old Khatib, who had been shadowing the ayatollah, nodded and rapidly went to do his bidding.

Turning back to Amad, the ayatollah said, "I think it will be obvious that we would like to have assistance in food, water, medical help, and medical supplies. That much would be a given, and any help with those items would certainly be welcome."

Amad nodded in understanding, saying, "Yes ... that would make sense," and started to move toward the edge of the rubble and the steep slope. The ayatollah immediately cautioned him that it would be dangerous near the edge because of unstable rock and dirt. Amad hesitated and began looking around at other areas, nodded, backed away from the edge, and waited for Abdul-Hakim to arrive.

A few moments later, Abdul-Hakim took the minister on an informal guided tour of the site. As they walked, they went by people pulling victims from the rubble and placing the dead in wraps. The wrapped bodies were being placed in a line on top of the mesa. At some point in the process, a photographer who had accompanied the minister took a series of digital pictures and video.

While the minister was on his tour, the ayatollah and Khatib began an initial assessment of the situation. All the communications were down. Their water supply was damaged but still partially serviceable. Food in the family areas was adequate for several days. Grieving families would need to be consoled and comforted. There had been absolutely no consideration on the part of the family members that this could happen. People were in deep shock and would need time to recover.

And a graveyard for the heroes would need to be quickly established. Marid, the logistics planner, quickly assumed this task and began work on an adjacent mesa. He also began a count of the dead as best they could.

After tending to several of his people at the destroyed stronghold location, the ayatollah made a determination that he and some of his immediate staff would have to move on. There was a lot of work to be done to get the movement back on its feet and functioning again. They would move to the alternate center, reassess the situation, and determine what their path forward would be. It would be hard, but necessary, to the future of the movement.

Abdul-Hakim returned with the minister after an hour of looking around and viewing the damaged areas, from the basic stronghold to the destroyed power plant. Amad went into a short discussion with one of his staff that had been along, and said to the ayatollah, "We will be leaving now. I have a good understanding of your needs and will expect to hear from you tomorrow or the next day regarding your assessment. I agree that you need immediate medical help, and supplies of food and water will be needed in the next day or two. I will get those items moving right away. We will helicopter in some critical medical items and personnel—however, with the primitive roads, it will take a few days to get some more supplies in to you. I would be prepared to last for several days if I were in your position."

The ayatollah bowed slightly, nodded, and said, "I appreciate your generosity and your visit. I will contact you regarding our assessment as soon as possible. We will look forward to help in the next few days for those initial needs. Allah be praised, and be with you." He turned to go about his other business as the minister headed back to his helicopter. A few minutes later, the helicopter lifted off in a large dust cloud and slowly disappeared to the north.

In the later morning hours of daylight, the radar trucks that had been placed out in the desert two hundred miles to the south, and succeeded in preventing one B-52 from attacking the stronghold, arrived back at the stronghold. The deployed men came in, shocked expressions on their faces; shocked at the devastation and sorrow they faced in their people. The radar truck satellite radios survived and the ayatollah directed them to contact Kadar on *Persian Wind,* tell Kadar what had happened, and direct him to return to harbor at Chah Bahar as soon as possible. His mission to attack the Alaskan pipeline with the yacht and mini-submarine would have to wait.

It was very early morning, with dawn an hour away. Kadar al Sabah, the ayatollah's Pacific Ocean mission commander, and his crew were cruising in the two-hundred-fifty-foot oceangoing yacht *Persian Wind* across the Gulf of Oman, heading east for his next mission assignment in the northern Pacific. They had left on schedule the previous evening from Bandar-e Abbas and were now well underway. He looked off to the right and saw an American task force, with the *USS Kennedy* as the lead ship. His jaw tightened. It was a formidable group of ships and certainly projected strength and power for the American Navy. They were several miles off to his right as he continued his course at a moderate cruise toward the horizon.

He could see several aircraft in a landing pattern around the huge ship. They must be conducting some form of nighttime exercises, he thought.

It was now several hours since they had passed the *Kennedy*. The sun was up on a bright day when their radio, which had been silent for many hours now, suddenly came to life. They were being contacted by one of the antiaircraft launch trucks, not the stronghold operations center! Puzzled, Kadar responded to the call with his call sign, "Launch 1. *Persian Wind*. Read you."

"*Persian Wind*. Launch 1. This message is for mission leader Kadar. The ayatollah is directing you to return to Chah Bahar immediately. The stronghold has been destroyed by the Americans and we need to evacuate some of our senior people to the alternate center. Repeat, return to Chah Bahar as fast as possible for an evacuation of senior personnel. All other communications channels are down. Please acknowledge."

Kadar almost dropped the microphone and stared at the radio, completely stunned. The stronghold destroyed! The Americans managed to find it and destroy it! How? His mind reeled! It couldn't be! He must have misunderstood.

"Launch 1. *Persian Wind*. Please repeat."

"*Persian Wind*. Launch 1. Per instructions from the ayatollah, you are to return immediately to Chah Bahar for evacuation of senior New Persia personnel. Destination is the alternate center. Is that clear?"

Kadar shook his head in dismay and brought the mike to his lips with shaking hands. "Launch 1..." He hesitated, and then continued, "Destination is Chah Bahar for evacuation. *Persian Wind* out." He still couldn't believe it. He sat for several moments gathering his thoughts. He turned to his navigator and directed a course change with a destination of Chah Bahar. He then directed the engine room to make a maximum effort to come up to full speed. As the helm and engines responded, the *Persian Wind* did a 180-degree turn. They lowered the hydrofoils into the water and felt the surge of power as the twin-turbine engines went to near maximum capacity. They began to fly across the water, heading in the direction from which they had come. He wondered how bad it was and what the situation would be when he got to port. No telling at this point. He was still in shock.

Chapter Three
Evacuation

Thursday—November 18
Stronghold—Southeastern Iranian Desert

     Khatib went out into the rubble, found the senior staff members, and told them to meet with the ayatollah in the safety of the cavern at 3:00 p.m. As the hour approached, the various staff members began to work their way back to the cavern. Many were reluctant to leave the people in the rubble; others, with just the opposite feelings, were anxious to leave the devastation, even for a few hours. While they said nothing, it both sickened them and made them extremely angry at the infidels who caused this devastation. Jaws were tight and drawn, shoulders hunched over. Finally, they were all gathered in the cavern, sitting on the bedrolls, and sipping water from bottles.

     The ayatollah reviewed the situation with each of them. They each provided what they had seen and done for the past several hours. It was pretty much what he expected. Total devastation. No communications except what was on the returning trucks, damaged water supply, food stocks enough for a few days, and the loss of roughly one-third of his men. He looked at Marid, his logistics lead, and told him, "I want you to stay here and manage the total recovery efforts, not just the burial details. I, and others, will be going to our alternate site to assess our situation and continue our mission through Allah's will. Eventually, we will move people from this location, but that is some time off. After we have a chance to assess, you will be notified of the planned actions and put together a list of our needs to be sent to Minister Essa. We need to provide him with that information by tomorrow. Is that understood?"

     Marid nodded and responded, "Yes, sir. It will be done."

     The ayatollah looked over at Salah, his technical lead, and asked, "Can any of the close-in radar vans be repaired?"

     Salah responded, "We may be able to get one of them back in operating order, but the others have been too badly damaged to repair."

The ayatollah nodded and said, "Very well. Do what you can with them. And then prepare to move down to Chah Bahar for transport to another location."

Salah bowed his head in acknowledgement.

"Khatib, is the alternate center capable of supporting us at this time? It wasn't finished the last time I was informed."

Khatib responded, "Yes, sir. It can handle some of us, but not the whole staff. It does have communications capabilities, though not as extensive as we have been used to. We will have to be selective about who goes until we can expand the facility. People can certainly sleep outdoors if they wish, but to have a fully capable facility that houses all functions will take, at the minimum, several more months." He looked around and continued, "Given our circumstances, I think we can continue our efforts, but we should delay them for several weeks until we can reconstitute. We need to select and train some new people to replace those lost last night, and that will take some time. A quiet delay will have the added benefit of fooling the infidel world into thinking they have totally destroyed us. Their guard will be reduced and they will become more vulnerable."

The ayatollah teepeed his fingers in front of his chest, nodded slightly, and said, "How many of our people should we take with us?"

Khatib blinked and said, "I would think the maximum for now would be no more than forty-five people. We have food and water enough to support that many. And, Allah willing, we can bring more in as the facility is modified."

The ayatollah announced to the group that the *Persian Wind* had been recalled from its mission in the northern Pacific and was returning to pick them up at Chah Bahar. The yacht should arrive in another day or two and be ready to pick them up. Therefore, they were to board the trucks tomorrow and begin the trip down to the coast. Since it was well over four hundred miles, Allah willing, it would take at least two days to get there. By then, *Persian Wind* should be there and they would be taken to the alternate location.

"I want you to draw up a list of suggested people. Obviously, I want all my immediate staff that survived to move. Additional support people are up to you. But I do want to be able to continue our efforts. I can certainly see the reason for your suggested delay and agree, but I think we should limit that delay to no more than three months. By then we should be able to let the world know that their efforts were in vain and that we are back. Until then, however, I think we should be very quiet and pursue our goals in secret. The fewer that know about this, the better."

Khatib bowed his head and quietly said, "I totally agree." He went to implement the ayatollah's desires.

Friday—November 19
Stronghold—Southeastern Iranian Desert

By the following morning, the racks with the antiaircraft missiles and generators and other support equipment had been removed from the back of the trucks to make room for the ayatollah and his people. After careful consideration, thirty-eight people would make the trip, and, with their necessary belongings, filled the four trucks and trailers completely. It would not be a comfortable ride, but it was better than walking or riding camels ... and quicker.

To avoid raising suspicion from the U.S. satellites positioned above, using an arbitrary set of departure intervals from the stronghold, they headed east through the desert toward the north-south highway connecting Birjand and Zahedan. After the first day they stopped just south of Zahedan, set up temporary camp in the desert, and spent the night. Early the next morning, they broke camp, and at midday passed through the town of Iranshahr. Several hours later they arrived at the small port town of Chah Bahar, where the *Persian Wind* was waiting. It had been a tiring two-day journey, and they were all anticipating a rest aboard the yacht. And better food.

Overhead, the ever-seeing satellite captured the activities at the stronghold site and transmitted them in near real time to the operations center at Schriever AFB in Colorado. Continuously monitored, and analyzed every day, the activities were of considerable interest to the senior military personnel all the way up to the top. Colonel McMichaels, the 50th Space Wing commander, came in shortly after noon and asked for a quick status. The duty officer, a stern and ambitious Captain Marcus Carver, gave him a quick rundown. "Nothing apparently significant, sir. Some Iranian government officials have visited via helicopter, and we think they are getting ready to send in some supplies and help. Several trucks with trailers departed, heading south, a little while ago, in what looks to be some form of supply run. Again, it doesn't appear to have any consequence given the circumstances they are going through. I'm sure they are trying their best to just recover from that B-52 raid." The colonel nodded and said, "Thank you, captain. If something develops, make sure I know about it right away."

"Yes, sir. Will do."

The colonel quietly looked around the operations center, nodded at several people manning the consoles, and made his way out of the center though the secure doors. Back in his office, he composed a short status message and sent it forward to the Air Force Space Command headquarters at Peterson AFB in Colorado Springs.

Saturday—November 20
Chah Bahar—Gulf of Oman

In the early evening, Kadar and his crew welcomed them on the yacht, which was large enough to hold them quite comfortably. After making sure all of his guests were properly attended to, Kadar coordinated with the harbor personnel, and, with full tanks of fuel and water, along with additional food, backed the ship away from the pier. Turning in the harbor, he slowly moved forward and out through the breakwater with only a very small bow wave. It would be a three- or four-day trip to the alternate, depending on weather, and, while he could certainly make the trip significantly shorter, he wanted to make the journey as smooth as possible. He also did not want to draw unnecessary attention to their departure. They came up to a comfortable cruise of eighteen knots with the hydrofoils retracted and the turbines running quietly. The planned route took them southeast through the Gulf of Oman and into the Arabian Sea. Then he would make a course correction to take them to their destination. It would not be a direct course. He was wary of being tracked and did not want to make it easy for the infidels.

Soon after they got underway, and after they had a chance to rest for a few hours, the various ministers and staff met in the main conference room and had their evening meal. All were quite subdued and thoughtful as they ate. It was very sobering to think of losing over a third of their personnel at the stronghold, and many of those lost were the cream of the crop.

It was a devastating loss and they would require some time to recover.

Zhang Qiang went to see the ayatollah with a mix of respect and dread. He knocked and was bidden to enter the ayatollah's cabin. The ayatollah was looking at him as he entered.

Zhang bowed slightly then said, "You have suffered a grievous loss, and I want to express the condolences of my government. We also wish to convey our hope for your future and wish your endeavors go well in spite of this setback."

The ayatollah just bowed his head slightly and said, "Thank you for your concerns and your assistance to us in the past. Can I assume that you will continue with that assistance?"

"Yes. I have been in contact with my government, and they wish to remain a hidden partner in your efforts. Once you have determined a course of action, and the requirements to accomplish that course, we will continue with the assistance. But we must know what you intend to do before we can assist. We will wait until you have a chance to regroup, and then work with you as required."

The ayatollah smiled slightly and said, "Thank you for your assistance and assurances. I can assure you that it will not go unrewarded." Zhang then bowed slightly and departed the cabin.

After the meal and evening prayers were over, several of the ayatollah's ministers informally got together to discuss what had happened and what their next activities should be. Khatib, though one of the youngest, took a strong role in defining their meeting's purpose and required outcome. Along with Abdul-Hakim, they organized a series of meetings with specific goals and desired results.

Ministers for finance, logistics, personnel, facilities, security, communications, and operations had all survived, and, with a few key staff members, were on board *Persian Wind*. Following Khatib and Abdul-Hakim's lead, the next day, Sunday, a series of meetings in each area of support were held and actions from those meetings agreed to.

At the end of two days at sea, a meeting was held, with all in attendance, with the ayatollah. With some minor exceptions, he blessed the planning they had accomplished and directed limited funding to begin implementing the plans.

While very little could be accomplished while they were still in transit, a much clearer focus on future activities and needs became very apparent. They were using this forced idle time for good purpose.

Sunday—November 21
Washington, D.C.

After a very long flight back to Washington, D.C. from Diego Garcia, Ryan joined his good friends Jasper and Dave at the Ritz for an evening of talk and recounting the events of the past few days. Jackie Conover, Ryan's girlfriend and the president's primary scheduler, joined them for a good meal.

The next afternoon, they were driven to the White House for a meeting with the president and several members of his staff, to include General Foley, the chairman of the Joint Chiefs of Staff. They were all in a good mood as they were escorted into the Oval Office. President Martinez greeted them with handshakes and a smile on his face. A significant problem to his administration had been eliminated.

President Alberto Martinez, a former senator from Arizona, and a graduate of the Naval Academy at Annapolis, Maryland, looked trim from playing tennis and golf. He had a quick mind and capacity for absorbing information rapidly. While very friendly in a social environment, he could also be very short and direct in a business or government meeting. A former Navy engineer, he had met and worked with Ryan while both were on active duty. He was in a good mood and glad to see Ryan and his friends.

"Ryan," he started, "I want to thank you and your team for the job they did in locating and eliminating the threat of New Persia. The teamwork and effort you displayed was simply wonderful. Please accept my appreciation for a job well done."

"Well," said Ryan, "the location was really through the expertise of some of the military and all we did was follow up on some of the details. But I appreciate the comments and am very glad things worked out the way they did. Now maybe we can all get back to our daily lives."

The president nodded and they all sat down for a few moments of conversation. After fifteen minutes, Maria, the president's secretary, interrupted and said the president had a follow-on meeting to attend to. They stood up, shook hands all around again, and Ryan and friends all left.

Wednesday—November 24
Alternate Operations Center, Socotra Island

After four days of meandering cruising, they entered the artificial harbor on the southern coast of Socotra Island that had been constructed to allow their various patrol boats and sea vessels to come and go from the alternate center with minimum notice. They approached the main pier and quickly tied up. Immediately several vehicles approached the yacht, and the ayatollah, and his party, left the *Persian Wind* and boarded the vehicles for the five-minute ride to the center. It was the first time many of the ministers had seen the new quarters, and they were quite pleased. While it was not as big as the stronghold, it was also not buried underground, at least the part they could see. They had some beautiful views of the surrounding ocean waters, and the overall effect was of spaciousness and being one with nature. The planning had been completed over a year before, and a decision made to place the new facility above ground, with some secure facilities below. While there were some security concerns over this decision, they felt they would be best protected by electronic means and maintaining the secrecy of the location.

Khatib walked down the gangplank to the dock and awaiting vehicles. It had been some time since he had been here, and the construction progress was quite satisfactory. The harbor area and the piers were complete, with the road up to the center completed also.

In the distance he could see the center complex of buildings. They were low, single-story buildings with roofs that overhung the walls a significant distance. The buildings were set into the ground three steps down, which lowered their silhouette and made them less susceptible to tropical storms. Rainwater was caught by a collection system and routed to underground cisterns. Jalousie windows were installed for ventilation, and the roof overhang helped keep temperatures down in the office and living complexes. The complex was designed for both living and office functions for the more senior staff. It was more efficient and a better use of the space in the buildings, with covered walkways connecting the three buildings. In the center of the complex was the only part that was underground, and that held the primary control center and communications systems. In that complex there were also quarters for a security response team, along with their vehicles.

Khatib marveled at the progress that had been made, and was pleased. The foreign workers had done quite well. All the materials for the construction had to be imported, and the French construction company had performed admirably. There had been some hiring of local workers to augment the French team, but the construction expertise and primary efforts had been imported.

Glancing up the hill, he looked at the latest major addition to the complex, not operational at this point. Two thirty-meter satellite communications antennas were installed on their pedestals and currently pointed straight up. The necessary operational electronics had not arrived and would not be available for several months. But it was an impressive sight.

The ayatollah went immediately to his quarters, and Abdul-Hakim, along with Khatib, made quarters' assignments for the rest of the council ministers and leads. They were further instructed that there would be a meeting for everyone in the main conference center tomorrow. In the meantime, they should get acquainted with the facility and review the past two days of planning work to start the recovery process.

Wandering the halls of the new operations complex, several of the leaders found their way to the dining area, the outside conference facility, and the indoor conference facility. The center was first rate, and, when complete, would accommodate many more people than were present now. However, not as many as the stronghold could handle. Down a short outdoor winding path away from the harbor, they also found a large complex of apartments and single rooms. After some minor discussion with Abdul-Hakim, the ayatollah explained that these were the quarters for those with families or those who wished to live on their own outside the main center. While not plush, the quarters were comfortable, safe, and quite an improvement over the mesa quarters back at the stronghold.

Chapter Four
Ayatollah Musings

Thursday—November 25
Alternate Center, Socotra Island

In the early morning hours, after saying prayers, Ayatollah Sarhardi wandered around his new quarters with a certain lack of enthusiasm. With normally intensely burning eyes that had recently dimmed a bit, his New Persia movement had received a major blow from the Americans when his stronghold was destroyed along with close to seven hundred of his personnel killed. He still had close to two thousand people after the strike, and for many who were not sure of supporting his movement, the strike was a deciding factor. Even with the brief passage of time since the strike occurred, he had seen an increase in the numbers of followers and those willing to join his movement from the Middle East. It would not be long before he would be back up to the same strength he had enjoyed before the strike. And he was convinced his movement would continue to grow beyond that level. Eventually, he could see his movement taking over a significant portion of the current Middle East—Iraq, Iran, and Saudi Arabia, to form the core of New Persia—and that was his intent. He would head up the effort to bring Islam back to the forefront as a religion and the Middle East as a world power.

But for right now, at the low point in his movement's activities, he was feeling a certain internal shortage of commitment and uncertainty. He was committed to his cause, but the blow had had its effect on his internal reserves and sense of direction. Yes, his cause was just and proper, but oh, the cost! Cost in lives lost, financial setbacks, and schedule delays, with an estimated seven hundred dead and probably more deaths coming in the future, as his movement gained momentum and additional converts.

He stood quietly and looked through the large window that faced out over the newly constructed harbor where the *Persian Wind, Persian Storm,* and *Persian Desert* were tied up to their berths. Experimental trimarans of huge size, the *Persian Storm* and *Persian Desert* were over two hundred feet long, and very much adapted for ocean voyages. The *Persian Desert* would be departing to the northern Pacific as a replacement for the *Persian Wind*. The *Persian Wind*, the two-hundred-fifty-foot yacht that had brought them to Socotra, had been one of the early mission ships. She was due to depart for China now that *Persian Storm* and *Persian Desert* had arrived. In addition there were several patrol boats. Beyond the harbor was the hazy blue of the ocean stretching to the horizon, and, while he couldn't see it, eventually the east coast of Africa. Right now it was a peaceful time, and he resolved to make the best of it. It would take several months to recover from the infidels' strike, and he would use that time very effectively.

He looked around at the furnishings of the room and realized that he missed the rougher trappings of the stronghold. The air here was more pleasant, as they were adjacent to the sea, and the sounds of small local animals and the ocean were pleasurable to the ear. Overall, the environment was easier. But they were no longer near the center of action in the Persian Gulf or the Red Sea. There was significant shipping in the Arabian Sea, but the overall sense was one of remoteness. He would have to work through that.

The west was still not complying with his program of energy reductions and changes. He pulled out a copy of his speech, given to the United Nations several months ago through Iranian sponsorship, and reviewed it again. The requirements he had presented to the UN as a body were received with a mixture of disbelief and total rejection in the west, and partial acceptance in some governmental organizations in the Middle East. He looked at the items again.

1. *Iraq/Iran and Saudi Arabia join politically to form a New Persia with a theocratic government*
   a. *Temporary head of the New Persia interim government will be Ayatollah Sarhardi*
   b. *All assets of previous regimes to become part of New Persia to include funds held in foreign bank accounts*
   c. *All international agreements to be in abeyance until New Persia government can review them for applicability/modification/elimination*
   d. *Over a period of 180 days, all current embassy personnel will be recalled and new assignments made based on internal judgments*

    e. *Internal elections for New Persia to be held within 90 days without any outside influence from western "democracies" ... no monitoring of election processes*

2. *Worldwide production of oil to be cut to 25% of 2015 quantities*
    a. *It is Allah's resource and thus unbalanced use by western infidel powers must be stopped*
    b. *We need to extend life of oil reserves so Allah's people can share in the benefits*
    c. *The west needs to reduce its voracious use of oil and, if desired, develop alternative energy sources*

3. *Other sources of energy are available to world ... and to the world, I say, develop and use them*

4. *Oil funds in Arab countries are to be used for all Arabs and not for benefit of a few sheiks/leaders ... too much like infidel businesses in western world ... only the rich benefit; they will be impounded/confiscated*

5. *UN to sanction US for excessive oil use and for not containing oil use to what the US can produce internally*

6. *All foreign forces are to leave the New Persia territories within 30 days ... not even "advisors" allowed*

7. *All foreign forces are to leave the Middle East permanently within 90 days (Middle East defined as Turkey, Lebanon, Syria, Egypt, Jordan, Israel, Afghanistan, Pakistan, Iran, and Iraq*

8. *Western companies to train Arab personnel in oil well technical matters ... then out of the country ... within 1 year*

9. *All women/girls' schools to be shut down immediately; foreign teachers to leave within 15 days*

10. *All oil wells and associated equipment and pipelines will become the property of the New Persia government ... with no compensation to companies. They have already made enough profit over Allah's resources*

11. *All ports will be shut down for 60 days to allow time for production cuts to take effect*

12. *Any attempt to "freeze" New Persia funds will result in a total shutdown of oil production and stoppage of all shipping inbound or outbound*

13. *Other countries' oil production assets will be gradually disabled (as already demonstrated) if they refuse to cooperate*

       He reviewed the list of requirements and demands with deep satisfaction. They were good, and he was not about to give way on any of them. Even though the west had tried to negotiate on them, he had held firm. New Persia would eventually prevail, even with periodic setbacks such as they had just experienced at the stronghold.

These requirements met his desires to bring the world back into harmony with Allah's wishes. And the Allah-given black fluid would not be squandered on western infidel interests. Reducing the usage to a more reasonable twenty-five percent of 2015 quantities would help bring the western powers' energy needs into better alignment with the rest of the world. It was a good and just program.

His dictates would bring true Muhammadism back to the home of Islam, the land of their ancestors. His political reunification of Iraq, Iran, and Saudi Arabia, with others to follow later, into a New Persian religious and economic powerhouse would be fulfilled as Allah desired. And he would direct it as the recognized leader of this new movement. Women needed to be back in the home, raising and caring for the children, while the men were out working and furthering the work of Allah.

Then the precious fluid could be preserved and made to benefit his people for centuries to come. And he would be the one to do it through his movement. He would be revered for all time as the prophet who had brought Allah back to prominence and Muhammadism back as a major religion in the world. He would prevail.

It was obvious the western powers had no feeling about the future generations and what they might need to continue a reasonable and sustainable lifestyle. The Allah-given resource needed to be preserved and made to last, not wasted on large cities and transportation networks that provided nothing for his people. The west must be forced to reduce their oil usage and turn to alternative forms of energy, which were actually plentiful. Negotiations were useless, because they resulted in a less-than-desired outcome, and his goals, drawn from Allah, could not be compromised.

Looking out at the endless seas, he continued to think. The western world had been built on the backs of those less fortunate. In every country in Europe, and especially the United States, working people had broken their backs, both figuratively and literally, to build the nation. And they had succeeded beyond all hope. But they had also placed the bulk of the wealth associated with that success in the hands of just a few. And those few had held on to the wealth, not benefiting the rest of the populations, and thus those who had actually built the nations benefited the least. He was determined to break this mold in his native Middle Eastern countries. New Persia would be the core of the new world order, and he would lead it.

As he thought through these musings, he gained the inner strength he was looking for. His posture became more erect, his body and musculature regained their firmness, and the fire returned to his eyes. His demeanor changed and he became even more determined to see his life's mission carried out successfully. Allah willing, he would overcome his adversaries. The west, and others determined to waste this resource, would be put in their proper place. Allah's will would be felt throughout mankind.

He turned and went back to the small table that functioned as his desk. He sat down and began to plan for the next few days of activity. He had a lot on his mind and needed to get things clear before he issued any instructions. Within a couple of months, after crew training was complete, he would have a ship, the *Persian Desert*, in the northern waters of the Pacific Ocean, and it would soon be bringing the Eagle into compliance with his demands. Kadar, the designated captain of the *Persian Desert*, was one of the finest mission commanders he had, and he trusted him implicitly. But he needed to keep track on the progress of the mission and what problems, if any, Kadar might be facing. He also had planning activity underway for striking at the devils in his own area of the world, the Middle East. And, finally, there were plans to halt some of the oil production capabilities the British enjoyed in the North Sea.

In spite of his demands and entreaties, Saudi Arabia and Iraq were both still trading with the west and not curtailing their shipping activities at all. He needed to meet with both of them and convince them to stop their exports to the west. The oil resources needed to be retained for Arab use, and sales to the west would need to be significantly reduced. He needed to make sure they would feel the need to comply with his demands. If they did not comply, a strike on their shipping facilities would be planned in the near future. Iran had seen at least some of the light, and stopped trading with the U.S. Their shipments were all now being directed to the Far East, either China or India, depending upon market pricing of the crude.

But they had not reduced the exports to make them last. That still needed his attention.

Chapter Five
Directions

Thursday—November 25
Socotra Island Operations Center

Later in the morning, the ayatollah met with his surviving ministers in the main conference room of the alternate center. They had all gathered under the guidance of Khatib and Abdul-Hakim. It was a muted group with many things on their minds, and they were nearly overwhelmed by the intensity of the situation they had left behind. Each had contributed to the studies and briefings developed during their trip to Socotra, but all had their doubts over the course of actions that might be required to bring New Persia back to its former self.

They rose in respect as the ayatollah entered and sat down at the head of the table. He looked around at his primary advisors with intensity. He could see the uncertainty in several of their eyes, and the slumping posture of defeat. They needed leadership and a course to follow; after his private musings, he was prepared to give both.

He stated with firmness and a strong intensity, "We have an Allah-given task to perform in spite of this serious setback we have suffered. And we shall overcome this event. We still have the support of our friends in the various governments, and our forces shall become stronger in the coming weeks and months. Marid, our logistics manager at the stronghold, informs us that many willing volunteers are arriving every day to support us in defeating the infidels in the western world. And our cause is just. Since the western world refuses to agree to our demands and reduce their dependence on oil, we will continue to force our will upon them." He looked around the room again and saw a slight change in the posture of several of the men. They were feeling some hope. They were responding. There was less apparent defeat.

Khatib also looked around the room at the group of men. He nodded as the ayatollah made his remarks. They would continue to plan and carry out actions against the

29

western world, and their allies in the Middle East, until their stated demands were met. They would not negotiate, because negotiations were not possible with the infidels. Only force and unwavering strength of commitment would bring the rest of the world to a realization of the righteousness of their goals.

The ayatollah continued, "We will spend some time in gathering our remaining forces, training the new ones, and planning our next steps against the forces that hold us back. The suggestion was made several days ago that we take about three months to readjust to this new reality. And I accept that. In the meantime, you all met several times when we were on the high seas and developed a series of actions we need to take to become a viable and visible force for Allah once again."

Khatib listened intently and watched the various ministers as they absorbed what the ayatollah was saying. He too noticed the increase in positive posture as the words flowed. He felt the positive emotions emanating from several of the ministers as the message sank in. They were regaining their resolve.

The ayatollah resumed, "The plans you all briefed me on during our seaborne journey are to be implemented as soon as possible. We cannot delay in getting our capabilities back to normal. As this facility is expanded and made more capable, we will bring many more of our people here to support your efforts. You need to identify to Khatib who you would like to bring here and in what sequence. As I mentioned, we will take three months to get our capabilities re-established and plan for the immediate future after that." He looked over at Kadar and said, "Can you be ready in three months for your mission to the northern Pacific with the new ship?"

Kadar was a moderately tall person, especially for the Middle East. He had been a backup mission commander for the ayatollah and was responsible for the partially successful mission when the U.S. secretary of defense's aircraft was destroyed—but the man survived. With dark hair and very hairy arms and hands, combined with his dark complexion from the sun and desert where he was raised, he was intimidating to look at. His complexion was slightly wrinkled and showed both the desert and sea effects. In his thirty years he had spent a good time at sea and was well versed in navigation and naval combat techniques.

Kadar, now the mission commander for the northern Pacific mission, nodded and said, "Yes, sir. In about three months we should be ready, but could certainly use additional time to become more proficient. The new trimarans are quite different from the yachts, and take several sailing skills that we are just now getting some expertise on. But we can be ready to meet your timeline."

The ayatollah, leaning forward in his chair and folding his arms on the table, said, "Keep me informed of your progress. While we may take three months to gather our forces and continue planning, there could be a possibility of sending you out on the mission early."

Kadar responded with a slight head bow and said, "Yes, sir."

The ayatollah then turned to Ghanim, the operations planner, and said, "Are we able to implement the strike in Great Britain?"

Ghanim responded, "Yes, sir. Our man there is trained and equipped. We just need to get some additional information on the U.S. administration's schedule of flights into Heathrow. Once we have that information, we can proceed."

"Excellent. Let's continue with the planning, get the flight information we need, and proceed with the planned event. Again, this does not have to depend on our reconstitution efforts. We have the plans, equipment, and people all in place. Let's activate the plan."

Ghanim commented, "Sir. We will determine the flight schedules, but it may be some time before a worthy U.S. administration target flies into Heathrow. We just don't know yet, but will monitor the schedules until the time is right."

The ayatollah looked back and impatiently said, "Yes, yes. I understand that it may be several months. But I want to make sure we are alert to the schedules so we can take advantage of the first opportunity."

Ghanim looked back and just nodded slightly to the comment. He said nothing further, since he did not want to irritate the ayatollah.

Khatib was startled slightly at this direction. He felt they had enough to accomplish just to get reorganized and back up to strength. Given their current situation, he felt they were moving too fast. But he said nothing. In the meeting he did not wish to question the ayatollah's directions. And it actually was true for that particular mission. Assets were in place, plans finished, and the dry runs were complete. It could be done without affecting their rebuild efforts.

The ayatollah then recapped: "We will conduct the northern Pacific mission as soon as Kadar feels confident in accomplishing it. And we will activate our plans for the Great Britain action. And finally we will continue with the plans for the rebuild of our organization as you all defined them during our journey here."

The ayatollah then went around the room and asked each minister if there were any questions. There were none. Khatib then added, "We have preliminary information from Marid that, so far, his team has accounted for six hundred twenty-eight of our brothers killed in the stronghold disaster." The ayatollah nodded and continued to look around the room. There were no other questions or comments, and the meeting broke up.

Kadar, working with Ghanim, set up a schedule of training requirements he felt he needed to accomplish before he could take on the mission. He had stated that he could be ready in about three months, and, after looking at what he needed to train, he was not sure he could make that timeline. But he had made the statement in the meeting, so he was going to do his best to meet it. The operations manager was also dubious after looking at the requirements. But both agreed to try and make it.

Friday—November 26
Socotra Island Operations Center

The next morning, *Persian Desert* set out on the first of several training sessions with their Chinese instructor aboard. Working the sails on such a large vessel took a great deal of cooperation and no small amount of skill. The day was productive, and they managed to get in several hours at sea with full sails, tacking exercises, and furling activities. At the end, Kadar was encouraged that they might meet the schedule.

With the ayatollah's direction from the meeting, Khatib sent out a message to a cell in Great Britain letting him know that tasking would be coming soon and to be ready. Paddy McFarland received the message and prepared his truck and other supplies for the event that would, in his mind, bring the world to its senses on the oil issue. He again drove the old plumber's truck to the outskirts of Heathrow, parked, and went through all the procedures he had been taught. Then, once satisfied that all was ready, he drove back home to await word. He was excited in a calm manner. Finally some action.

Paddy was both anxious and pleased that they had decided to use him after the training he had gone through. The advanced rocket-propelled missile (ARPM)—with the latest in camera guidance capabilities—he had received from the New Persia group was ready. They needed a rich target. Although he knew that it could still be quite a while, he was ready when the tasking came through.

Wednesday—December 1
Socotra Island Operations Center

Khatib spent the better part of several days defining what support might be required of their silent partners, the Chinese, over the next few months. Zhang had said that they would continue with their support, though in a hidden manner. After coming up with a list, which contained most of the current support and a few additional ones, he called Zhang in for a discussion of the situation. They met in the main conference room with Salah and Ghanim.

Khatib began, "We want to express our gratitude to you and your country for assisting us so well in the past. I don't believe we could have made the progress we did without your critical help."

Zhang just looked back with a very neutral look on his face and nodded.

Khatib continued, "The assistance you have provided in the past for logistics items, ships, vehicles, missiles, parts, fuel, communications equipment, facilities, and food are certainly welcome, and we would like to see those continue. In addition, we will need support in transportation of people around various locations in the world, and your assistance in this would be very welcome. I recognize it is a new requirement to move people, since we have been doing it internally, but some of our plans are quite ambitious and require large numbers of people to move. An example is the movement of over a thousand people from the stronghold to here on Socotra. This can be done over a period of time, but it's an example of our needs."

Zhang looked over the list and nodded. He said, "As I mentioned to the ayatollah earlier, we will continue with the assistance we have provided in the past. I will look over these new needs and let you know. I see nothing here, though, that cannot be accommodated." He smiled as he stood up. Then, looking around the room, he said, "We consider ourselves to be your silent partners and will maintain that status." He then left the room.

Khatib looked over at Ghanim. "Looks good." Ghanim and Salah both agreed.

The support would continue.

Chapter Six
Called to Washington

Monday—December 6
Ryan's Marina, Freeport, Texas

Ryan was doing some work on one of the drain lines for his marina and thinking he probably would have to call a plumber. The stoppage seemed to be beyond what he normally could handle. But it did have to be fixed. He started back to the office and looked up as he was hailed by his administrative assistant, Betty. She was calling to him to hurry up, making motions that he had a phone call. He stepped up his pace and entered the office, where the phone was sitting on the counter. With a questioning look at Betty, he picked up the phone.

"Ryan. Can I help you?"

"Ryan. This is Maria. How are you?"

Ryan was a little surprised to be getting a phone call from the U.S. president's secretary, but responded, "Fine. Just doing some minor chores around here. How are you and what can I do for you?"

"We're great here, and thanks for asking. The president asked me to see if you can come up here this Wednesday, day after tomorrow, and meet with him and a few others. Can you do that?"

"Sure. What's going on?"

"He wants two things. One, you to be present when he personally pins lieutenant colonel leaves on Major Calloway, and two, it's been a few weeks now and he wants to do a final review of the strike and get your thoughts on how we might have done that better. We can make the usual travel arrangements for tomorrow morning for you. Can you make it?"

"Love to. I haven't met Major Calloway but I sure would like to. Her actions were just extraordinary. And I think a final review would be very useful. I'll get Jasper and Dave and we'll all be there."

"Sounds great, and I'll tell the president and set things up here. Have a good one, and bye for now."

Ryan sat down for a moment and smiled. It would be good to go through the information they had gathered after the raid and see what improvements could have been made. And he would be able to see Jackie again ... his smile broadened even more at that thought.

Tuesday—December 7
En route to Washington, D.C.

The next morning, Ryan, Dave, and Jasper were at the Galveston Coast Guard Station terminal waiting for the Gulfstream V C-37 aircraft to arrive. After engine shutdown and refresher coffee for the Air Force flight crew, they boarded and were seated comfortably. Taxi out and takeoff were uneventful, and they were soon winging their way northeast to Andrews AFB outside of Washington, D.C.

Ryan sat in one of the very comfortable seats and looked at his two very close friends. The six-foot-three, 250-pound Jack "Jasper" Charleston was a retired Navy master chief and deep-sea diver who now worked in the same field for civilian projects around harbors and oil wells. He was quite friendly, but a person you did not want to cross. Dave Carlson seemed just about the opposite. At five foot seven and a slim 150 pounds, he reminded one of Woody Allen. An internationally known naval engineer, he was good at just about everything he tackled, and had saved their previous missions in the service several times. He now worked as an underwater design engineer for Underwater Submersibles in Houston, Texas.

Ryan and Dave turned as Jasper said, "I think it will be good to review the results of the raid and the planning that went into it. There are probably some additional pieces of info that have been gathered now, and we may learn something useful."

They landed uneventfully at Andrews and were met by the normal black Suburban then driven to the Ritz-Carlton in downtown Washington. Their rooms were ready and there were short, unclassified briefing papers waiting for each of them in the assigned rooms. In all cases, the papers were just a summary of what had happened back in November, and the results of the strike. There was nothing new for them, since they had participated in the planning and execution of the strike. It was a good summary, however. Included was an agenda for the meeting tomorrow. Once settled in the hotel, they met at the bar and, after getting drinks, reviewed between them what they had found in the summary.

Ryan said, "I don't see anything new. Do either of you?"

Both Dave and Jasper just shook their heads and took a sip of their drinks.

Ryan nodded. "I'll call Admiral Watkins, the president's military aide, and see if the agenda has changed. According to the existing one, we are going to meet with the president at 10:00 a.m. in his executive conference room."

Both Jasper and Dave just nodded. They had seen the same information. Neither spoke.

Ryan dialed Vice Admiral Max Watkins' private cell phone, confirmed the meeting time, and told the admiral they would all be there. After a few more minor comments, they both hung up. The meeting was all set, and they would be picked up at 8:30 a.m. at the main hotel entrance.

Jasper set his beer on the cocktail table in front of him. He turned slightly to the right and said to Dave, "I suspect our glorious leader here"—nodding at Ryan—"probably wants to leave us peons and get on with his date. Jackie is waiting!"

Dave, pursing his lips slightly, furrowed his brow, and looked over at Ryan, then back to Jasper. He said, "Really? Would he be that rude? Leaving us on our own here in this great big city? I think that would be just terrible of him. He could at least have arranged for a couple of dates for us. Don't you think? I mean, Jackie must have some friends she could entice into joining us."

Ryan's eyes rolled up as he took a drink of his Beefeater martini. "It appears to me that you two are more than capable of finding your own companionship tonight. It wouldn't be the first time, now would it?" He raised his eyebrows, looking at the two of them.

Dave looked off in the distance, seeing nothing of particular interest, and turned his gaze on Jasper. "I guess we'll just have to fend for ourselves, Jasper. Seems cruel, but we just need to face facts. He's not interested in our evening, or how we might spend it."

Jasper feigned disappointment and said, "Yeah. I guess you're right." He sighed heavily, reached for his beer, and finished it in one long draft.

Dave and Jasper then broke out in big smiles, told Ryan to call Jackie, and left. As they departed, they shook their heads in exaggerated disappointment.

Jackie Conover was the president's primary scheduler. A petite five-foot-three, pixie-cut brunette, she was a widow due to the Gulf War and was a veteran herself, as an eight-year former Marine MP. She had helped with the president's last campaign and had stayed on as his scheduler. She and Ryan had met while he was doing previous work for the president in solving the problem of the ayatollah.

Ryan sat back and called Jackie. They arranged to have dinner together, and she spent the night with him at the hotel. She then rode in with them to the White House in the morning.

Wednesday—December 8
Washington, D.C.

They were standing in casual conversation the next morning. Jack Harrison, the president's chief of staff, Mike Detirro, the secretary of defense, Vice Admiral Watkins, General Newt Foley, the chairman of the Joint Chiefs, General Abe Fairchild, the Air Force chief of staff, Mark Allison, the CIA chief, Jerry Ocasio, the chief of Homeland Security, and Miriam Blacock, the national security advisor, were all present. Maria came in, followed by the president. He motioned them all to sit down as he went over to the coffee urn and poured himself a cup. He then sat down at the head of the table. Informal.

The president looked around the room briefly then began, "Welcome back Ryan, Dave, and Jasper. I appreciate you coming in for this little review."

Ryan, Dave, and Jasper all nodded in response but said nothing.

The president continued, "I think we need a short overview of what happened and then see if we have missed anything. I don't want a total rehash, but I also think we may learn something from what happened." He nodded at a young Air Force captain who had quietly slipped into the room. "Captain, please run through your overview."

The young captain, with a nametag that said "Jefferson," began with a barely perceptible click of a pointer. A small briefing chart was presented on a small screen behind him and in front of the president and the rest of the attendees. He did not even turn around to begin his presentation.

"As you all are aware, last year a new movement appeared in the Middle East called 'New Persia.' It was headed by Ayatollah Abdul Sarhardi. After damaging several of our oil wells in the Gulf of Mexico, and killing several divers who had been sent down the risers, they presented a series of demands before the United Nations, demands which were impossible to meet without total western economic collapse." The demands showed up on the briefing screen as he continued. "These demands are in the package in front of you and can be reviewed at your leisure." The briefing screen changed to a small list of recent events. "After presenting the demands, and seeing total rejection of those demands by the western world, the ayatollah's group began a series of attacks on western governments. Our own then-secretary of state, Mr. Sanford Billings, and his entire entourage were killed over the southern Caribbean Sea when his plane was shot down by this group. Attempts were made on the secretary of defense. While he and his people survived, his aircraft was destroyed. The vice president's plane was discovered to have an unauthorized modification, and the British and German governments foiled attempts on their ministers also."

The captain stopped for a moment and then, looking directly at the president, continued, "In spite of a plea before the United Nations by President Martinez, the United Nations refused to act, leaving the United States little alternative but to act on its own. This group was considered to be a criminal element, since they were not a recognized country on their own." The next chart showed a pinpoint spot on the mountains of southeastern Iran. "And since the country of Iran was unwilling to do anything about this New Persia group in their southeastern mountainous territory, it was decided to unilaterally eliminate them. A strike was planned and carried out against what New Persia called the 'stronghold.' This strike ..." A film of a B-52 with a KC-46 right above it began in slow motion. The large bomb was dropped and the entire mesa it penetrated erupted in a cloud of dust and debris. "... was carried out using a combination of U.S. forces, and succeeded in eliminating the stronghold as a viable threat to our economic world. Intelligence estimates put the casualties at something over seven hundred killed in the blast, to include many of the top leadership of New Persia." He stopped for a moment, then continued, "The B-52 and tanker support, the KC-46 you saw in the film, both staged out of Diego Garcia. They were assisted by a SEAL team that had been inserted a week before the strike and laser-designated the site for the bomb. While two B-52s were initially en route to the target, both were damaged by SAMs and only one was able to continue that mission. And it had one engine shot up." A slide showing a damaged B-52 appeared. The next slide came up showing a V-22 Osprey loading personnel. "All SEAL ground personnel were extracted using V-22 Osprey aircraft. There were some minor injuries but all personnel made it back safely." He paused as two more slides came up showing the *USS Kennedy* and the Diego Garcia complex. He continued, "The Ospreys, with the SEAL team aboard, recovered on the *Kennedy* and the B-52s and KC-46 safely recovered at Diego. That concludes my briefing. Are there any questions?" The lights came up as he looked around.

The president looked around the room then back at the captain. "Apparently not, captain. Thank you for the briefing." With that, and recognizing the polite dismissal, the captain departed quietly.

The president then looked around the room and said, "Okay. We've just had the cook's tour of the raid. Let me start with you, Newt. What do you think? Could we have done it better?"

General Newt Foley looked back and then quickly at each member in the room. "Yes, sir. We did succeed. But just barely. I can't fault the crews, but we missed the mobile antiaircraft missiles a couple of hundred miles south of the target. That mistake almost cost us the mission. Somehow we missed those missiles. And they were not normal missiles. We still don't know what kind of guidance system they had. Whatever it was, it was passive, because the B-52s never knew they were being targeted."

The president nodded and asked, "So they were hit by some form of new missile we haven't known about?"

General Fairchild then said, "That's right. We're still in the process of trying to find out what they are. Whatever they are, they had enough range and stealth to hit those B-52s at high altitude."

"Were the satellite images of any help?" asked Ryan.

General Foley shook his head as General Fairchild turned slightly to face Ryan and said, "No. The cameras, because of the anticipated strike, were all focused on the stronghold. Not two hundred miles south of it. So that was a dead end too."

The president and Ryan both just nodded in understanding.

General Fairchild continued, "The strike was just a few weeks ago and we have our missile experts looking at everything they can think of. The basic consensus of opinion is that, since it was passive, it must be some form of camera technology. At least that's the thinking right now. And we have our collective ears to the ground, with our British and German friends, to see if we can find out anything through the CIA and other intelligence channels." Mark Allison nodded in agreement. Continuing, the general said, "Until we can find out what is going on, we have a real hole in our offensive capabilities. We have to fix that. With that one major problem, the rest of the mission went off pretty well. And by the way, the SEALs did an outstanding job of locating and designating the target."

The president turned to Mark and asked, "Do you have anything to add to this? If there is a missile out there that we can't counter, we have a major problem."

Mark looked back at the president and then over to the generals. Then he said, "It's Chinese. We know that much from some sources in the Middle East. Just heard about it this morning before this meeting. What we don't know, at this point, is what its capabilities are. Obviously it can be truck mounted and is quite mobile. But its range and targeting capabilities and limitations are still a mystery. We're actively working on it and hope to have some more information that we can pass on soon." He looked back at the general and said, "We understand the criticality of this situation and are pouring a lot of resources into finding out what these missiles are."

Both the generals and the president just nodded.

Jasper then commented, "Since these are apparently truck mounted and capable of going across very rugged terrain, they have to be relatively small and therefore have limited range. I'd be willing to bet that our satellites saw them and they were just discounted as supply trucks or something of that sort. Assuming that we have recordings, I think someone ought to go back and look to see if they can be spotted. If they can, then perhaps some enhanced imaging techniques could be applied and we might find out a little more about them."

The president pushed his lips out in a kind of considered pursing motion and nodded. Before he said anything, Mark picked up on it right away, saying, "I'll have someone on that right away and get back to all of you soon." He stepped out of the room and made a phone call. Coming back in, he said, "It's underway."

The president then said, "Thank you for your comments, Abe. You too, Jasper. We'll have to see what

41

develops from Mark's investigation. I certainly agree with you that we need to find out what they are and how to counter them … and we need to do that very quickly."

He turned to Miriam Blacock and said, "Any thoughts from your perspective?"

The national security advisor, an attractive, mature career diplomat, said, "No, not really. The very low reaction we saw to the strike by the other countries in the region indicates that they are not going to create a fuss. I think it will blow over soon as other issues come up."

The president nodded, looked at the table briefly, and said, "I certainly hope so." Turning to the whole room, he asked, "Is there anything else any of you can think of that may help us in the future?"

General Foley moved slightly toward the edge of the table and said, "Yes, sir. From a tactical perspective, the Air Force guys have been burning the midnight oil trying to figure a way around this missile problem, at least temporarily until we can find out what's going on."

The president responded, "And what have they come up with? Anything?"

General Fairchild nodded as General Foley said, "Yes, sir. With the stealth and high-speed capabilities of the F-22, we think we can outrun whatever this missile is. Plus, if we have to penetrate foreign airspace, we do it on the ground at high speed so whatever their guidance system is, it won't have a chance to lock on. Now, I'm talking about some form of truck-mounted system that the F-22s would blast past before they hear them coming, and low enough that they can't see them until they are past. If they use some form of stationary, highly sensitive radar for an initial lock, we could have some problems, even with our jamming capabilities. But it's a start and becomes very situational dependent."

"Okay," said the president. "At least there's a possibility. I think Jasper's idea may be very helpful and we'll just have to wait and see. In the meantime, we need to be very quiet about this. I don't want the world to find out we have some form of vulnerability." Heads around the room were nodding very vigorously at this comment.

Ryan then spoke up: "Sir. Has there been any word or indication that the New Persia group is still viable or working on a comeback? The ayatollah had some very good staff people, and if they survived, there could be some activities leading to a resurgence of their movement."

Miriam, interrupting, responded, "We haven't heard of anything like that so far. At least, I haven't heard of anything yet."

Ryan and the others just nodded in response to her comments.

The president looked around again, then looked at his watch, and said, "We all have another meeting in a few minutes. If you think of something else we need to consider, please let Jack know and we'll schedule another meeting. I appreciate your time and comments. For now, let's enjoy ourselves for a few minutes. Follow me."

And with that he got up and left the room, heading into a slightly larger conference room with several people in it, including military. As the president entered the room, someone brought the room to attention. The president immediately, in the military manner, said, "As you were." He headed for the dais area where several military people were located. Walking up to Major Corrine Calloway, he reached out and shook her hand then moved down to shake several full colonels' hands. As he moved down the line, Admiral Watkins introduced the B-52 wing commander and others. The president then proceeded over to two civilians, Major Calloway's mother and father. He said something very quietly to them and they accompanied him back to the dais where Major Calloway was standing.

The president then turned to Major Calloway and they stood at attention as Admiral Watkins read a proclamation describing her outstanding actions as commander of the B-52 that destroyed the New Persia stronghold. At the completion of the reading, the president turned and was given lieutenant colonel leaves. He turned back to Major Calloway as Major Calloway's parents stepped up upon the president's hand motion. The president then handed each parent the leaves, and they pinned the leaves on their daughter's shoulders. This was not a normal process, since the president usually did the pin-on, but the president wanted to take to include her parents in the ceremony. A photographer stood by recording video and taking still pictures of the whole ceremony. Very moving. The president then shook hands with the new Lieutenant Colonel Calloway. The whole room erupted in clapping and laughter.

The president then led all in the room to a table for refreshment and drinks. A small informal line formed, including her entire crew, to congratulate her, and she, embarrassed and shaking a little at all the high-level attention, shook hands with her crew and the various colonels and generals present.

Ryan walked up to Lieutenant Colonel Calloway, introduced himself, and congratulated her on the promotion. He introduced Jasper and Dave and also expressed his appreciation for the way she had pressed on with the mission in spite of the damage to her aircraft. It hadn't been easy.

She looked back at him, knowing who he was and what role he had played, and thanked him for the comments. She then introduced him to her parents, and they continued with a short discussion of her mission and the promotion.

A return flight had been set up for Ryan's team for the following morning, since they had been unsure how long the meeting was going to last. So they had several hours and the evening to kill. Ryan talked with Jackie and arranged dinner for all of them for that evening. In the meantime, Ryan, Dave, and Jasper went back to the Ritz, had some lunch, and took seats in a grouping in the lobby. It was now 3:00 p.m. and they were all a bit tired and jumpy. While the B-52 missile problem certainly came up, there had to be other aspects of the mission that could have been improved. But they didn't know what. With soft drinks in hand, they discussed their concerns.

Ryan began the discussion: "Well, we did get the mission done. But there were several problems if we think about it. One of the B-52s got through and took out the stronghold. But what comes to mind for me is the attack on the two B-52s that nearly took out the mission. We don't know where those missiles came from or what their capabilities might be. They obviously got through the passive defenses of the bombers." He stopped and took a small sip of his ginger ale.

Dave took advantage of the short break and said, "Well, from today's meeting, our CIA fellows are certainly pursuing that issue. If there is something out there that will down the B-52s, and we can't determine what it is, and figure out a defense for it, our whole bomber fleet is at risk. And that's something we can't tolerate. A solution simply has to be found."

Jasper nodded in agreement. "It is a real puzzle, all right. I wouldn't want to be one of those crew members under that circumstance."

Ryan started again: "Judging from the level of attention this has, I'm sure they are putting in a lot of effort on that issue. What else did we learn out of this very real mission?"

Jasper said, "Well, we certainly blew the hell out of the stronghold with that GBU-57. I would be concerned over using just one of those bunker busters. It seems to me that one area of improvement would be to make sure at least two of them were used in any future strike. What if one's a dud?"

Dave said, "Well, I agree with the comment, but each B-52 had two on board and they were worried about overkill. If you drop them too close to each other, it's possible to have the first one destroy the second one. That was one reason for the two B-52s, so they could separate slightly on their run in. Of course, that's not what happened with one of the B-52s having to abort. We were just lucky that the primary B-52, with Lieutenant Colonel Calloway leading, was able to get through and finish the job. She and her crew had lots of guts, especially with one engine out and leaking fuel."

Ryan then commented, "Right. Was there anything that the SEALs did, or didn't do, that could have been improved?"

"I thought they did a real creditable job. Sitting there like that, watching the stronghold for close to a week and not getting spotted, would have been quite a chore," said Dave. He continued, "They were key to making sure we had the right target and illuminating it with lasers for the bomb run. I can't think of anything they did that could have been improved."

Jasper added, "I agree. They did a fine job. The only concern I have is that they didn't stick around a little longer to make sure we got the really bad guys. We think we got them, but it would have been good if they could have, somehow, confirmed it. But I understand their antsy need to bug out. I'd probably have done the same thing after a week in that desert and the mob of people still left."

Ryan said, "You know, if those refueling tankers hadn't come up country when they did, we might have had a totally different result. Linking up with both damaged B-52s and giving them much-needed gas actually saved the entire mission. That wasn't part of the planning. It was just the tanker crews responding to what they saw as an immediate need. Perhaps one improvement for any future missions of this type would be to have tankers closer to the action so it won't take as long to help a damaged aircraft."

Dave looked a bit dubious. "You can't have tankers too close, otherwise they might take fire, and I sure wouldn't want to see that."

"Well, they did it on this one and were fired on as they went over the target," Jasper responded.

"Yes," said Dave. "But they were high enough that the ground fire couldn't reach them. A better-prepared enemy would have downed that KC-46 in a heartbeat."

Jasper shrugged and nodded. "Probably."

Ryan agreed. "Well, it sounds like there were a few things about this mission that could have been improved, but not much. We have concerns over what kind of missile was used, the SEALs could have confirmed a kill, and the tankers, by their actions, really saved the day."

Dave nodded. "I'd say that about sums it up. Okay. What now?"

Ryan said, "I'm going to summarize this and send it to the president when we get back. Now that we sat through his review meeting and have had a chance to listen and think about it, I think he would like our viewpoints." He looked at his ginger ale and said, "I don't know about the rest of you, but since it is now going on 5:00 p.m., I'm going to get something a little stronger."

Dave and Jasper both agreed, and they all headed for the bar for a stronger bit of drink.

Chapter Seven
Ryan on the Gulf

Wednesday—December 29
Ryan's Marina—Freeport, Texas

Christmas was over, and Jackie, down for the holidays, had decided to go into town for a little bit of post-Christmas shopping. Ryan, fresh from his morning run five miles down the beach, which helped him maintain his 175 pound trim frame, walked down to the pier in his marina and his thirty-four-foot Hunter sailboat. He had found a replacement for his thirty-six footer that had been destroyed by the New Persia terrorist group. The "new" one was really a preowned boat he had located near New Orleans. It too was blue, and rigged for single-person sailing, which he did every chance he got. After locating it near New Orleans, he had sailed it down the Intracoastal Waterway to Freeport, Texas, where his marina was located.

Dressed in beige-colored Dockers and a light jacket, he boarded, stowed a few food and drink items for the day's sail, and looked over the cockpit and rigging. Then he moved to the bow. From there he slowly moved aft, checking all of the rigging, looking for any fraying of the lines, and also looked at the boat's decking for any corrosion. He did this routine once per week to assure himself that all was in readiness for sailing. He finally finished up at the platform just aft of the transom. The weather was clear but cool, with a slight breeze and no change forecast for several days. Everything was in order and he smiled inwardly. It was a good life.

He finished his pre-sail routine and radioed to the Coast Guard that he was departing his marina. They wished him a good sail. He bounded up onto the dock, quickly released the restraining ropes from the small bollards on the pier, and hopped back aboard. He powered the small electric motor, settled behind the wheel, and, with sails furled, slowly backed away from his pier. His head felt like it was on a swivel as he backed out into his main channel, then turned ninety degrees to line up with the marina exit. He quietly engaged the electric in forward gear and silently moved toward the exit and the main channel of the Brazos River. Once clear of the marina and into the river, he turned and quietly began a slow motoring cruise toward the Gulf of Mexico.

He looked at the morning sky, the small breeze ruffling his partially sun-bleached brown hair, and enjoyed the slow motion as he went downriver. It was a very calm morning, with several other boats taking advantage of the good weather and moving out for a day's sail on the gulf. He sipped some coffee from his thermos, turned, and looked at the marina receding in the distance, then turned back around and made a slight course correction to stay in the channel.

A few hours later, Ryan was out on the Gulf of Mexico enjoying the Wednesday morning. The sun was out and the day looked like it would meet the promise of the forecasters: cool, slight breeze, and cloudless. He was ready.

Ryan was busy with planning some modifications to his marina and also planning for the trip across the Gulf of Mexico to the Florida west coast. He had been working on his marina for almost a month now, since the B-52 raid on the ayatollah's stronghold. The Gulf of Mexico oil was again flowing unhindered as it should, and, as an aside, he and Jackie were really hitting it off well.

He made some adjustments in the course from the cockpit, went down to the frig, got some cold V-8 juice, spiked it a bit with vodka, and returned to the cockpit. The water only had a very slight chop to it, and the boat was sliding through it like a playful otter. Smooth as silk. He looked at the distant horizon and the Gulf Coast of Texas. His marina was finally beginning to turn a little profit, and he expected it to do better as the spring and summer arrived, especially after he finished with some significant upgrades that were to be underway soon. He stood up behind the wheel and felt the full breeze on his face as he took a drink from his frosty morning glass. Retired from the Navy two years before, his activities as a SEAL commander, and some deep-diving experience, had really helped in doing in the ayatollah. With his good friends Dave and Jasper, they had managed to stop the ayatollah and his group from holding the world hostage to their impossible demands. There had been a couple of close calls as they pursued the ayatollah, but all had worked out.

Ryan sat back down and began thinking about the raid and the aftermath. The lone surviving B-52 had made it through the ayatollah's defenses and destroyed the stronghold in the mountains of southeast Iran. But there had been a couple of anomalies in what he had heard, and seen, to make him suspicious. The night of the raid, from the bridge of the *USS Kennedy* in the Gulf of Oman, he had seen a suspicious yacht moving to the east at a reasonable pace. Suspicious in that it looked just like the one that had been captured by the Coast Guard in the Gulf of Mexico and proven to be the source of the oil well stoppages. The next day, just following the strike, the bridge crew informed him that the same yacht had been moving at a very high rate of speed back to the west toward the Gulf of Oman.

But he was constantly bothered by what he wasn't sure of. Did the ayatollah get away from their strike? Was he a survivor and continuing to plan for future mischief? He kept running two facts over in his mind: (1) from debriefings he had attended, there was a zip line for escape from the stronghold and it may have been used, and (2) the actions of the yacht he saw while on the bridge of the *Kennedy* may have been in response to the destruction of the stronghold.

The strike force might have missed the main target in this overall action.

Chapter Eight
Tracking

Monday—January 3
Socotra Island Operations Center

Abdul-Hakim was looking at some of the video he had taken of the stronghold shortly before they left Iran. A little over a month had passed since the Americans had struck. As he was reviewing the destruction that had occurred, he paused to think. It was obvious the Americans had known of their location before they struck. And the U.S. president was not the one finding this information. Someone in the U.S. administration was doing the running around for the president, and that person had to be stopped.

He approached the ayatollah with his concern and received approval to investigate further. Perhaps there would be a way to stop this menace to their mission and New Persia's goals. Abdul-Hakim called in his lead investigator/troubleshooter, who was knowledgeable of American culture and very good with the English language.

Ramiz Al Sahaf had studied at the University of Wisconsin-Madison, graduating with an engineering degree, and was very proficient in the English language. He was tall, slightly over six foot, and fairly thin, with an easy way about him that had gone over well with the other students in Madison, Wisconsin. He had a slight beard that was thin and wispy, and a moderate amount of dark hair. He had been radicalized by the waste and environmental damage he had seen in the U.S. After the bombing of the stronghold, which he fortunately missed due to some other travel arrangements, he was even more determined to help the cause. They met in Abdul-Hakim's office.

"Ramiz, I have an important task for you. I want you to go to the United States and see if you can determine who the person is that is basically running the resistance against us. Someone in the administration is the lead and we need to find out who that is. We know the military is involved because of the bombing, but there has to be someone in the background doing some, or all, of the planning and coordinating for the U.S. administration."

Ramiz nodded. He was sure this was something he could do well. He could go to the Washington, D.C. area and, through some contacts he still had from school, probably find out who this person was. At least he could get some leads and narrow it down. He said, "Yes. I certainly can do that, and am sure I can succeed. When would you like me to leave?"

"On the next flight to Sana'a, the Yemen capital. Then connect to somewhere in Europe and then on to the States. That way there is less chance of someone catching on to your actual mission. This whole thing needs to be kept secret. Understood?"

"Certainly. I will check the flight schedules and leave as soon as possible."

Abdul-Hakim nodded and smiled slightly.

With that, Ramiz departed the room and headed down the hall to his small one-room quarters. He was looking forward to going back to the States and seeing some of his old friends and, at the same time, contributing significantly to the New Persia movement. He recognized that he was functioning as a spy in the enemy's camp, but that did not matter to him. He was contributing.

He coordinated with their internal travel administrator to get tickets for the next day's flight to Sana'a, and was pleased at the quick response. Then he would transfer to a flight to London, where he would remain overnight. Then on to New York from London the next day. It would be tiring but worth the effort. He packed a few belongings, went to the food preparation facility, and got a bit to eat. He returned to his quarters, said evening prayers, and went to sleep.

The following morning he shaved off the slight beard and changed into western jeans and a sport shirt. Ramiz was then taken to the airport outside Hadibu, where he caught the commercial Felix Airlines 737 jet for Sana'a. He was on his way. He had a mixed feeling of both anxiety and anticipation as he made his way back to the United States.

Wednesday—January 5
Washington, D.C.

Two days later, Ramiz found himself in New York City. He spent the night there and caught a commuter flight to

Washington, D.C. After checking in to the Residence Inn in Arlington, he made a phone call to an old friend from the university who was now working in the U.S. State Department. Gerald Santos was a friend who had expressed some of the same feelings he had over the environmental damage being caused by the oil industry. While at the university they had met on several occasions and shared their distaste for big oil over cups of coffee at Whaley's coffee shop just off campus. He hoped Gerry could help shed some light on the person who headed up the anti-New Persia efforts. At least he would be a good start.

Gerry was surprised and pleased to hear from Ramiz, and agreed to meet with him. They arranged to meet at a restaurant nearby for an evening meal. Ramiz arrived early and found a place to sit. Due to his religious feelings, he turned down the waiter's offer of drinks, favoring just ice water. He was a bit nervous, because he hadn't seen Gerry in several years and wasn't sure how all this might play out.

Shortly after 6:00 p.m., Gerry showed up. A nervous individual, he was rail thin and did not look very healthy. A pale complexion, combined with his thin build, gave the impression of gauntness. His high-pitched voice just lent more to the overall impression of a sickly individual. But he was cheerful and greeted Ramiz warmly.

"Ramiz! How good to see you! I was very pleasantly surprised to hear from you earlier today."

As they shook hands, Ramiz bowed his head slightly and responded, "Gerry, it is good to see you also. We had some very good experiences in school. I had a chance to come to Washington and, of course, thought of you." He continued, "You look well." He was lying. "Washington must be to your liking!"

Gerry exclaimed back, "Well, when I had a chance to get into State, I figured I'd better jump on it. There aren't too many jobs like this, and I'm lucky to have one." He stopped for a minute, then asked, "What brings you to Washington?"

Ramiz responded, "Business. I'm with the big oil company, Aramco, in the Middle East, and we have some delicate negotiations going on with some of the oil companies here in the States."

"I see. Well, I hope the negotiations go to your liking. They can be very difficult at times."

"I think they will go reasonably well. They are for some contract renewals and shouldn't present too much of a problem. What are you up to these days? Do they keep you pretty busy in the State Department?"

"Yes, they keep us busy. But not always in a useful way. We have the usual organizational problems. Ever since we lost the secretary of state in that plane crash, we have had a temporary person running the show, and that isn't good. We need a real head of the organization, but President Martinez keeps putting it off. He's such an ass. I'd like to see him voted out at the next election and get someone in there that has some international experience."

Ramiz used this comment as an introduction to the subject he really needed to get at. "Well. I don't know about that. From an outsider's perspective, he did quite a job on that New Persia thing I read about in the papers. Bombed the hell out of that group."

Gerry chuckled and said, "Well, yes. He did, but if it hadn't been for the CIA, military, State, and nearly everybody else, he couldn't have pulled that off. He just got lucky that we didn't lose more than we did."

"I don't know, we all have to deal with large organizations in these kinds of things. Of course, I'm sure he had someone ramrodding the effort, but he still had the final say and approval. I'm sure he was pushing hard all the way."

"Yeah, well, he did have the Joint Chiefs heavily involved, since they had to do the strike planning. They were helped by a guy named Ryan McKenzie, and that's probably who you are referring to as the ramrodder. He was pretty effective in getting things done. We had several taskings that he was following, and it wasn't easy keeping up with him and his friends."

Ramiz intentionally looked startled. "You mean it wasn't one of the military doing all this coordinating?"

"Nope. Ryan is a Navy guy, but he's retired now and got into it quite by accident. He lives down on the Texas Gulf Coast at a marina, and, for some reason I don't know about, these characters destroyed his boat and nearly killed him. When the president found out about it, he asked Ryan to be the go-to guy."

"I see," said Ramiz. "How is it that you know all this detail?"

"I was the point guy for a couple of the actions that came down to the State Department. So I was briefed on what was going on and actually sat in on some of the briefings and meetings with the president where this was discussed. I can't talk about what went on in those meetings, but that's how I'm familiar with what went on."

Ramiz nodded in understanding. He had what he needed. Simple. And lucky.

"Anything still going on in that area? Since the bombing's over, I would guess not?" he asked.

"Not lately. I haven't heard of any activity. But then again, I'm normally not that close to the action. This one was a bit of a fluke, because they did tag me for the information."

"It's been a few years now since we left Madison and the Wisconsin Badger community. Have you been back there at all?" he asked. He was intentionally diverting the conversation to make it appear that he wasn't really that interested in Gerry's work requirements.

Gerry grinned and shook his head. "I haven't gone back there since we left. That last year really almost did me in. Talk about a party environment! I think I was in a daze most of the last year, and it took me a while to recover!"

Ramiz smiled in understanding. It was quite a party school, and he had been really challenged to avoid much of the frivolity. But he *had* managed, and was glad he had. His conscience was clear and his prayers to Allah were pure.

They continued to converse for another two hours, and finally Ramiz broke the meeting off, claiming that he had some early meetings to attend to. Gerry understood, and they shook hands as they parted. Gerry had, unknowingly, been extremely helpful.

After he got back to his hotel, Ramiz located the business work center, logged on to the internet, and looked up all the marinas on the Texas Gulf Coast. It wasn't really too hard, because there were quite a few marinas along with their associated advertising. It took him a little over a half-hour to locate a marina just south of Freeport, Texas that listed a Ryan McKenzie as the owner-operator. Quite simple, really. He wrote down the address and phone number for use the next day. Then he looked up airline schedules and booked himself out for the next morning. He would go to Atlanta and then on to Houston. He wanted to meet this Ryan McKenzie face to face.

The next morning Ramiz checked out of the hotel, drove to Reagan National Airport, turned in his rental car, and was dropped off by the shuttle at the main terminal. He easily went through security, got a bottle of water, and went to the gate, where he waited for the next hour. After changing planes in Atlanta, he arrived with no problems in Houston late that afternoon. He got a rental car and took airport road west to Highway 288, headed toward Freeport. It was a cool late afternoon and he enjoyed the drive south.

Checking the information from the internet ad, and using Map Quest on his computer, he was able to locate the marina without much difficulty just off Texas Highway 36. It was now fairly late in the afternoon, so he decided to find a hotel and finish his little investigative work in the morning. Checking the internet again, he found a Towne Place Suite in Clute, Texas only a few miles away just off Highway 288. Calling ahead, he booked a room for the night and arrived there with no difficulty.

Everything was working out quite well. Abdul-Hakim would be quite please at this detective work. He would pursue it further in the morning. He said his prayers, spent several minutes looking out the window thinking, and went to bed.

Chapter Nine
Contact with Ryan

Saturday—January 8
Freeport, Texas

In the morning, Ramiz faced east toward Mecca and did his morning prayers then got some toast, fruit, and orange juice for breakfast. He stepped outside and enjoyed the morning breeze that was coming in from the gulf. He checked out of the Towne Place Suites and reversed his path from last evening, heading back to the marina and a short—he hoped—meeting with this fellow Ryan. He found the marina with no difficulty and pulled into the parking lot off the county road. He got out of the car and stood for a moment looking at the facility. It had over one hundred slips and was being upgraded and renovated in several areas. Construction was just underway, and crews were busy at their work while still maintaining the boating activity of the marina.

Ramiz looked around a bit more and located the marina office on the bottom floor of the two-story structure. He walked over to the office door that looked out over the marina itself, opened it, and walked in. It was a typical marina office, with rental information, charts, and other navigation paraphernalia for sale, along with various nautical items of interest to the boating community. There were also some items of food available for the permanent residents of the marina.

A person was sitting at a computer behind the counter. She looked up as he approached, then glanced back down at the computer, hit a few keystrokes, and, satisfied with the results, looked up and said, "Can I help you, sir?"

He responded, "I hope so. I have a small sailboat up on the Neches River north of here. We're moving and I was wondering if I might meet the owner."

She responded, "Certainly, sir. His name is Ryan McKenzie and he is out on the construction area with one of the crews. I'll page him for you. It will take just a few minutes."

Ramiz nodded and said, "Thank you. No hurry."

Betty called out to Ryan on the local radio net. He responded that he would be back in shortly.

While waiting for Ryan, Ramiz, trying to be friendly, said to Betty, "You his wife?"

Betty looked back and said, "No. Ryan's wife died a couple of years ago."

Ramiz was looking out at the piers. He turned to Betty and asked, "How many slips are there?"

Betty responded, "We have one hundred and one slips right now."

"So this is being run by Ryan and you?"

"There are a couple of other employees. Ryan runs it by himself." Instead of being friendly, she was beginning to get a bit suspicious. He didn't feel right. *I need to be careful. This guy seems to be probing*, was her thinking.

Not sensing her hesitation, he continued, "Well, it seems to be a very nice marina. I'll have to seriously consider coming back here. Are all of the slips taken or are there some vacancies?"

"No, we're not full. We have some vacancies. It depends on what you are looking for in terms of size and amenities. For instance, some of the slips have fifty-amp power, the others are all at thirty amps. It depends on what you want."

"Well, I'm not real sure yet. That's part of the reason for checking it out."

Betty just nodded in acknowledgement of his comments and didn't say any more. She turned her attention back to her computer and began inputting data into a program.

He turned and went over to one of the chart racks and began perusing the materials there.

A few minutes later, Ryan came into the office with an expectant look on his face. He looked around for a moment and spotted Ramiz over by the nautical chart rack. Ryan walked over to Ramiz as he put a chart down, stuck out his hand, and said, "Hello. I'm Ryan McKenzie. I understand you may be interested in berthing your boat here."

Ramiz took Ryan's hand in a friendly manner, shook it once, and released it quickly. He responded, "Yes. I have a boat up on the Neches River up near Beaumont. My wife and I are moving down here due to a business change and I was wondering if there was room available and what the fees might be." He had a questioning look on his face.

Ryan was a little smaller than what Ramiz was expecting. While very trim, Ryan stood slightly shorter than Ramiz. For some reason Ramiz was expecting a much larger person. Ramiz listened closely as Ryan related the capabilities of the marina and explained the fee structure. Ramiz did not stare at Ryan, but did make good eye contact with him, and Ryan did not miss a beat—he looked right back. Ramiz asked a few questions regarding the policies and nodded thoughtfully as he heard the answers.

Ramiz's thoughts turned to how they might pull off eliminating Ryan. As Ryan was going through the policy explanations, Ramiz glanced around the room with an analytical eye on how they might hit the place. There were two doors into the marina office and a set of stairs in the back. One door came from the parking lot, the other door went out to the marina proper, and the stairs obviously went upstairs to something. He mentally concluded that it would take at least one more visit to figure out the details. He looked back at Ryan as Ryan finished his explanations. Ryan wasn't a pushover.

Ramiz thanked him and shook Ryan's hand as he said, "I appreciate your time and the explanation. The facility looks like it will work for me, but I have a couple more that I want to look at. I would appreciate your business card and will be in touch."

Ryan responded, "Fair enough. If I were you I would do the same thing." He handed Ramiz a business card and said, "I appreciate your considering us. I'll look forward to hearing from you. Thanks for coming by."

Ramiz nodded, turned around, and left through the parking lot door. He went out to the parking lot, opened his car door, got in, started the engine, and sat there for several moments. Had he gotten all the information he needed? Was there anything he had missed? What questions would Abdul-Hakim have for him? He wasn't certain.

He changed his mind about leaving that day. He went back to the Towne Place Suites and got another room for the night. He wanted to take a little bit of time and think it through. It would be better to not be in a hurry, to get the information, even if it meant going back to the marina before he left. He did not want to come up short with Abdul-Hakim.

He then drove back to Freeport to get a better feel for the small city. It was small, and he smiled as he passed a sign that said "Where Fun Happens." With only a little over twelve thousand people, it primarily depended on Dow Chemical and other technical companies, most with connections to oil industry needs, some tourism, and fishing for economic stability. He looked at the schools, city hall, and some of the residences, realizing that he was looking at small-town America. After spending a small amount of time looking around, he headed back to the Towne Place Suites and a quiet evening of thinking and some prayer.

Sunday—January 9
Freeport, Texas

The next morning, after his prayers, Ramiz headed back out to the marina. This time he paid more attention to the road access and what problems they might encounter in gaining access and leaving quickly. The parking lot was easy enough, since it was unguarded and open to access anytime. The highway was just a normal county road, again with no restrictions that he could see, although it dead-ended a little further on at the gulf. He saw no problems with the roads or access. He pulled into the parking lot and parked the car. He decided to look at the slips and the access capabilities of the marina itself. Walking out on the piers, he noticed that there were no restrictions to the marina other than the usual signage for "No Wakes." Water access was wide open. He hadn't thought about the possibility of using a boat to get in or get out. He would have to think that one over. It was a good possibility.

As he was walking along, he nodded at several people who were working on their boats or leisurely sitting enjoying the morning sun and air. He said nothing, but made the assumption that there were people living there on a full-time basis. At the end of the last pier, there was construction underway with a full concrete crew building forms for a pour in a few days. He stood there and watched for a few minutes before turning around and heading back to the car. Part of the way back, he ran into Ryan walking out to the construction site.

"Hello there. Back for another look?" Ryan stuck out his hand in greeting.

Ramiz shook Ryan's hand but was slightly taken aback by the chance encounter. He recovered enough to respond, "Yes. Yesterday I didn't come out onto the piers to see more of the facility. So I decided to take a look this morning. I hope you don't mind."

"No. That's fine. Do you have any more questions?"

"No. In fact, I was just heading back to the car. I have a flight to catch in a few hours and need to get going. But thank you for your help. I'll be in touch." And with that, he headed back to the parking lot, started the car, and left.

Ryan thought it was a bit abrupt, but maybe that was just the way he was. It seemed a bit peculiar, though. He turned and headed out to the construction crew on the pier.

An hour later, Ryan headed back to the marina office. He busied himself with some paperwork and receipt filing for an hour before heading out to get some lunch. He stepped to the door.

Betty said, "Ryan, that fellow who was in here yesterday?"

Ryan stopped with the door half open. "Yes?"

"He was here again an hour or so ago. He walked out onto the piers and looked around. Didn't come in here, though."

"Yes. I know. We talked very briefly out on the pier."

"I don't trust him. He seemed to be probing with some of his questions yesterday. Just didn't seem to be very up front. If you decide to do business with him, be careful. I can't explain it, but he just doesn't seem to be right." She cocked her head a little to the side and said, "Do you know what I mean?"

He looked back at her, then out the door, then back again. He said, "I'm not sure. I have my doubts too. But it may be just his personality. We'll probably never see him again, so I wouldn't worry about it. Okay?"

She nodded. "Sure. You're probably right. Enjoy your lunch and I'll see you in an hour or so."

He smiled back at her, turned, and left the office for the parking lot. As he walked out, he thought, *Well, I guess I'm not the only one a little cautious about Ramiz. An odd duck!*

Ryan headed to the Dolphin Restaurant just down the road and had a fish sandwich, onion rings, and a Coke for lunch. Sitting there looking back down the long fishing pier toward the shore, he thought about the modifications he was making to the marina. It was the first part of a two-phase upgrade. The rest would be done in the summer after he figured out more details. It would bring the marina up to the standards of the rest in the area, and in some instances above the standards. He was looking forward to the finish of this phase of the construction work so he could get back to day-to-day management.

His mind turned to the conversation with Ramiz. While he had been explaining the various policies and marina amenities, Ramiz had looked around a bit and seemed to be a bit distant, like he wasn't really interested. Then his follow-up visit had been hurried and short. Strange.

Ramiz headed out of the parking lot and turned toward the hotel. He had met Ryan, taken a measure of him, and found him to be quite competent. It may be a bit of a challenge to get to him effectively. It would take some thought. He went back to the hotel, packed his few things, got a bottle of water, checked out, and headed for the airport in Houston. He couldn't think of anything he had missed.

Two days later he was back at the center on Socotra. He developed a report of what he had found and made a few suggestions for the next step. He made an appointment to talk with Abdul-Hakim. Two hours later, they were in discussion.

"Well, Ramiz, what did you find out?" asked Abdul-Hakim, setting the unread report aside.

"I was able to find several people involved in the planning. But one stood out among the rest. Obviously there were a lot of people involved in plotting the strike. One person was instrumental and he wasn't an active duty military guy. He is a retired Navy SEAL and has a place on the Texas coast. His name is Ryan McKenzie."

"Is he still involved with planning against us?"

"I don't know that. I went to his place in Texas and talked with him for a few minutes. We didn't talk about his involvement, because I didn't want him to know why I was really there."

"I see. So we really don't know what his current involvement might be?"

"No. But he was heavily involved in the destruction of the stronghold. If the Americans find out where the center is, he'll probably be involved again. At least, that would be my guess."

Abdul-Hakim looked out the window at the sky and blue Indian Ocean. He thought a moment and then said, "Except for outright revenge, I don't see any reason right now to do anything about this Ryan. What's done is done. But I think we need to know more about him and how he is tied in to the U.S. administration. Were you able to find out how he is involved?"

"Yes. He and the president are friends from several years ago. They were involved in some research work on underwater submersibles. When our people tried to destroy Ryan and his boat, because he had seen one of our submersibles in the Gulf of Mexico, they didn't succeed. The president heard about it during one of his routine briefings and brought McKenzie into the action."

"So he's kind of working the situation as a specialist for the president directly?"

"Yes. That about sums it up," responded Ramiz.

In dismissal, Abdul-Hakim said, "I see. Okay. Thanks for the information. If I need anything else, I'll contact you."

Ramiz bowed his head in respect, turned, and left the room.

Abdul-Hakim thought for several minutes, running the information through his mind. *So, we unwittingly brought McKenzie into the act. Must have been Malik doing it, because he was in charge of the Gulf of Mexico operations then. Then he was captured and apparently killed, since his body was returned to us through the Iranian authorities. But was McKenzie involved in that too?* He continued to muse over the information, but got nowhere.

He would think about their next step for the next several days. They had time. He was in no hurry.

Chapter Ten
Oil Ministry Visits

Wednesday—January 19
Riyadh, Saudi Arabia

The small six-passenger private jet approached King Khalid International Airport north of Riyadh, landed, and proceeded to the general aviation terminal. It was met by a limousine, and three passengers departed the airport on the modern highway to the city center.

As they drove, the ayatollah, Khatib, and Ramiz viewed the evidence of wealth and prosperity in the Saudi capital. While the local population obviously benefited from the oil wealth, the outlying population elsewhere in the Saudi kingdom was not as fortunate. It was the king and his various ministers who controlled the oil and the production facilities. They were the problem. The oil shipments to the west, and the massive production and consumption these shipments represented, needed to be drastically reduced.

The ayatollah had decided to visit with the oil ministry in Saudi, and other oil-producing countries, to convince them of the folly they were engaged in. The oil needed to last for centuries, not decades. And the prolific evidence of waste in the construction of the large western-style cities in the oil-rich Middle Eastern countries just added insult to injury. It was his intent to convince them to cut down the production of the oil and reduce their exports drastically. He had asked Khatib to arrange a meeting with the oil minister in Saudi and Iraq. Ramiz, because of his western education, yet fervor for the movement, was along as an observer. This was the first of the two to be visited.

After spending the evening and night in Riyadh, they drove to the minister of petroleum and mineral resources headquarters for their appointment with Ali Naimi, the current oil minister. They were escorted into the building and provided with temporary visitor's badges, then on to a moderate-size conference room. Water and some fruit were available on the table. After several minutes, Ali Naimi, along with two other ministry personnel, came into the room and greeted them.

63

After the usual pleasantries and greetings, they all sat down as Ali Naimi began, "I welcome you to our city. I trust your journey was a pleasant one and your evening enjoyable. And, I might add, I hope your trials and difficulties with the U.S. government have come to an end."

The ayatollah responded, "Yes, the journey was quite pleasant, as was the evening. It will remain to be seen what the future holds for my dealings with the U.S. I thank you for your comments and concern." He stopped for a moment and then continued, "But I am not here to discuss the U.S. and my difficulties with their government."

It seemed fairly abrupt, and Naimi nodded just slightly and motioned with his hands for the ayatollah to continue.

"I came to ask you to reduce your production of oil and cease shipping the oil to the west. We"—he looked around the room at everyone—"need to recognize that oil will not last forever. Our children's children should benefit from this Allah-given resource, but that will not be the case if we continue to use it so rapidly and unwisely."

Naimi's eyes showed shock and dismay. "I have certainly heard of this primary focus in your movement, but we simply cannot abide by your wishes. The requirements, and that is a kind word, that you presented to the UN last year are simply too unreasonable in today's international world."

"Why not? The west is playing us for fools and taking advantage of our natural resources for their own ends. They consume all of theirs and import ours to sustain their unsustainable appetite for energy. It cannot continue this way."

"The interconnected economies we enjoy with the west have many mutual benefits. Our population is benefiting in many ways. Free health care, good roads, schools that are excellent. We cannot cut that short. And we are investing in other processes and resources so that when the oil begins to diminish, we can continue with the lifestyle all of us, including our general population, enjoy. I see no merit in your suggestion. We simply cannot do it, nor should we." And, looking sharply at the ayatollah, he continued, "And your attempts to coerce the world into complying with your demands will not work. We will not permit it." He said it with distinct emphasis.

The ayatollah sat forward on the edge of the chair and held out his hands. "But you must. We cannot continue to allow the west and its ever-growing energy requirements to suck us dry."

"As I just explained, we are providing for the future. There will be no sudden return to the poor ways of our ancestors when our oil resource is in decline." Ali Naimi then stood, looked at the ayatollah and then over to Khatib and Ramiz, and said, "This interview is over. Your demands and requirements are totally unrealistic in today's world and we will not support you. I wish you well personally, but you will fail in your quest." He bowed slightly and then left the room, followed by his assistants.

Naimi, as he was walking down the hallway, turned to one of his assistants and said with noticeable firmness, "Contact Aramco and have them increase their security at the wells, refineries, and docks. I don't trust this ayatollah, and he very well might get back at us. His fervor is evident, but his methods of achieving his goals through threats won't stand." The assistant nodded and departed the room to accomplish the assignment.

Two days later, there was a significant increase in the patrols and armed guards monitoring and patrolling the various oil production and storage facilities. It was obvious that the ayatollah's visit had had an effect on the Saudis, but it wasn't what the ayatollah wanted. He had succeeded in putting the Saudis on alert to possible sabotage, and, given his background and their knowledge of his methods, it was a wise precaution for the Saudis to take.

Monday—January 24
Baghdad, Iraq

The same small Cessna jet landed at Baghdad in Iraq a few days later. And the same process was repeated, and with the same result. The Iraqi oil minister was immobile and refused to even consider the ideas. Iraq needed the cash infusion from the sale of the oil to the west and wasn't about to reduce the flow.

He understood where the ayatollah was coming from but had no sympathy for it. As they were sitting in the well-appointed conference room, he said, "We have to live in the present. Not the past and not the future. But right now. Your ideas, if implemented, would throw us back two centuries and our people would suffer greatly. Their health care and other benefits would have to be drastically reduced, and overall the standard of living would go down. The simple answer to your inquiry is no." He then abruptly stood and left the room.

The ayatollah turned to Khatib and Ramiz and said, "I think we have just wasted our time. These people are so westernized that they have no understanding of what our people want and need."

Khatib agreed, saying, "They obviously are just looking at the present, not the future. What do you proposed we do now?"

"Since we are in their meeting room and there may be some surveillance here, let's go back to the airplane and we can discuss it further there."

Khatib bowed slightly in understanding, turned, and motioned to one of the staffers accompanying them to contact the pilots and get the aircraft ready. They departed the Iraqi oil minister's facilities and were immediately driven back to the airport.

Once settled on the aircraft, the ayatollah continued, "Obviously a straight discussion and appeal for the future is futile. We need to sit down and come up with a plan to convince them that our course is right. I think a course denying them the use of their port facilities might work well."

Both Ramiz and Khatib nodded in agreement.

Ramiz said, "I'll look into it and see what we might be able to come up with."

As they flew back to Socotra, Ramiz began to plot how they might impact the Saudi port facilities. Using the extensive capabilities of the internet, he was able to access a fairly detailed map of the Ras Tanura port complex and its outlying facilities. The facilities were quite extensive and covered several square miles of area. It would be quite a challenge to attack and destroy a reasonable amount of the facilities. Coordinating with Khatib, he decided it would be best to wait until they got back to Socotra to begin the actual planning activities. The mission would be quite large and would require significant resources to accomplish.

Tuesday—January 26
Socotra Island Operations Center

In his office/quarters, Ramiz looked at the information he had on the Saudi oil terminal complex at Ras Tanura. It was quite extensive, with significant oil storage facilities and the capability to load multiple crude carriers at the same time. And since it was on the water, there were definitely ways to get to it via the Persian Gulf. He looked at overhead photos, available on the internet, of the complex. It was on a peninsula, which surprised him due to its vulnerabilities, and located just north of Bahrain and Qatar. There was road access in addition to water access. It was undoubtedly guarded, but Ramiz was not worried about that possibility. Guards, and their procedures and methods, were easy to overcome with the right plans and actions.

He sat back and thought for several minutes. He recognized that taking out the entire complex was probably not possible with the few resources they currently had. But there could be some serious damage to parts of the facility. And while it would not shut down the export of oil from Saudi, it would impact them, and, hopefully, wake them up to the foolishness of dealing with the west.

He looked again at the photos and began to formulate a plan. After a few hours of additional work and research, he had laid out an idea. He set the information down in his laptop and set up a timeline. To get all the resources together, and trained, for his plan would take another couple of months. And that was dependent on resources being made available. He wasn't sure that was possible because of the efforts at reconstituting the New Persia movement. But he also knew that it was the ayatollah's call, and he would do what the ayatollah directed.

He decided to let his planning activities sit for a while. Perhaps, by putting them down and letting his unconscious mind work on it, additional considerations would occur to him and he could revisit the plans in a few days. Then he would run the planning by Khatib, get his thoughts, and take it to the ayatollah for his consideration.

He smiled to himself. It was a good plan, and one that would get the world's attention. The New Persia movement would be back, and back in force.

Two days later, Ramiz had not come up with any additional ideas. He was anxious to get moving with the plans, and approached Khatib.

He said to Khatib, "I have defined plans for denying the Saudis the use of their Ras Tanura terminal facilities if not totally, then at least with a significant reduction. I would like to explain the plans to you and then see what the ayatollah thinks."

Khatib looked back at Ramiz and said, "Okay. Let's go over them."

After reviewing the plans, Khatib looked at Ramiz with a great deal of respect and said, "I think you have come up with some ingenious ideas and they will certainly cause an uproar for the Saudis. The loss of over forty large storage tanks and several dock locations in the terminal will certainly give them reason to reconsider their position. Perhaps to the point that they may curtail their exports to the west. Let's see what the ayatollah wants to do."

The next morning, Khatib and Ramiz met with the ayatollah. Pleased with the planning, he said, "You have done a fine job of planning this mission. Let me have a copy of the plans so I can further consider them. Given our current situation regarding our reconstitution efforts, I will have to consider the resources needed. It is a good plan; I know that. I just don't know whether we can implement it right away."

Ramiz immediately gave the ayatollah a copy of the plans. Both he and Khatib understood the concerns. After slightly more discussion, they both departed the ayatollah's office, pleased with the result.

Chapter Eleven
Suspicions to the President

Wednesday—January 26
Washington, D.C.

Ryan was puzzled. He knew the B-52 strike had wiped out the stronghold and destroyed a good deal of the ayatollah's capability. But the ayatollah, one of the main targets of the raid, may have survived the attack. He was convinced, given the discovery of the zip line, and the satellite images of a meeting on site the next day, that several senior members of the ayatollah's staff had survived. And there was a good chance the ayatollah had also. After reviewing his thoughts with Dave and Jasper, and they concurred with his conclusions, he decided to see if he could brief the president on his concerns.

Ryan, working through Maria and Jackie Conover, made an appointment to see the president and, with Dave and Jasper, flew to Washington. That evening he met with Jackie and they spent the night together. In the morning all four of them were driven to the White House by the Secret Service and escorted into the waiting area of the Oval Office.

Maria welcomed him with a smile and offer of coffee, which he politely refused, saying he had already passed his caffeine quota for the day. She smiled and understood his meaning. However, it was business hours and nothing else other than water and soft drinks were available. After a few minutes of waiting, Ryan, Dave, and Jasper were escorted into the Oval Office for the meeting with the president.

The president came striding into the Oval Office from his morning staff meeting. They shook hands all around and settled into the comfortable chairs in front of the president's desk. Jack Harrison was also there, along with Admiral Watkins.

The president began, "Ryan, I want to thank you, again, for all the help you, Dave, and Jasper provided in resolving the New Persia thing. It was quite an effort and it worked out quite well."

Ryan responded, "Thank you for the kind words, sir. We appreciate that." He stopped for a moment and gave the president and Jack an apprehensive look.

The president picked up on it and said, "What's the matter? You looked troubled about something."

Ryan looked off for a moment and then finally said what was on his mind. "The reason we requested to see you ... is quite troubling. Despite our meeting last month, and all the good, and bad, comments on the raid, bluntly put, I don't think we got the ayatollah or several members of his staff." He looked at the president, Jack, and the admiral with their look of surprise. Then he continued, "I think we did a lot of damage to his movement and probably took out many of his key support people, but I think we missed him. I believe we will see more of their activities in the near future after they have a chance to recover and develop replacement capabilities."

The president had put his hand up as a signal to stop. Then he said, "Wait a minute. We blew that stronghold to hell and back. Lieutenant Rider, the SEAL team leader, said they saw the ayatollah just before the B-52 flew over. What do you mean we missed him? It sure looked convincing to me!" He hesitated a moment and then said, "Why do you feel he got away?"

Ryan looked at the floor for a moment then back at the president and said, "Because there are several things I have seen, and a report I have read, that leads me to think this way."

The president nodded and indicated that Ryan should continue.

"Sir. I know a lot went into this effort to eliminate the stronghold and finish off the ayatollah. I know this may be a shock to you, but hear me out."

Ryan hesitated a moment, and the president, again with some impatience, motioned for him to continue.

Ryan continued, "Number one was the discovery, by the SEALs, that there was a zip line from the stronghold down to the power plant. One of the SEALs, in his report, said that he had seen moonlight glinting off the power cables a few minutes before the B-52 hit. I think he was seeing the zip line being used as an escape from the stronghold and the glinting was not on the power lines but rather the flexing of the zip line as people were moving down it.

"Number two was the high-speed run made by a large yacht back toward the Iranian coast. When I was on the bridge of the *Kennedy*, one of the crewmen mentioned to me that the very large yacht I had seen the previous day had reversed course and was up on foils moving at a very high rate of speed. That yacht looked exactly like the one we captured in the Gulf of Mexico last year owned by New Persia. I think it was heading back to the coast to pick up senior survivors of the raid. Possibly including the ayatollah. And finally, I checked some of the surveillance video from the satellite taken the next day of the stronghold. A high-ranking visitor from Tehran came in on a helicopter and conversed with an individual that, if he wasn't the ayatollah, was his twin brother. We don't know what they were talking about, or who the visitor was, but he was important. We're still trying to identify him. And finally, the next day several trucks departed the remains of the stronghold with luggage and a fair number of people. I think it was the ayatollah and some of his staff. I don't know where they were going."

The president leaned back in his chair and teepeed his fingers in front of him in thought. He looked intensely at Ryan and, after a few moments, said, "Ryan, you make a good case." He continued to teepee his hands in thought, dropped his hands to the armrest, and then continued, "But it's all circumstantial. He might not have been on that zip line. It might have been someone else the visitor was talking to, and the high-speed yacht might very well have been recalled by survivors just to help out. I'd be very surprised, assuming the yacht does belong to them, if it wasn't heading back in a hurry to help out."

"Yes, sir. That is all possible. But I think it would be prudent to keep our ears open and see if there are any rumors out there that would confirm it one way or another. I'd surely not like to see him turn up at some future date and surprise us."

"Okay." And with a little bit of frustration in his voice, the president continued, "That does make sense. But I don't want to be very overt about this. Unless we determine otherwise, it was a successful mission and he's dead. I'm quite sure there were some survivors in his staff, and that might have been what you've found."

Ryan nodded in agreement.

The president then turned to Jack and said, "Jack, contact Kenton Marshall over at State and see if they can quietly pulse the Iranians to see if there is any information on this. And get with Mark at CIA and see if they have any information. Just in case. I don't want to brush Ryan aside if there is any element of truth to his suspicions."

Jack nodded and made a note.

Ryan then said, "Thank you, sir. Actually, I hope I'm wrong, but I think it would be best to check it out completely."

The president looked very seriously at Ryan, Dave, and Jasper and said, "For the life of me, I hope you are all wrong. But it would be a mistake to not check it out. It should be a simple thing to do." Then he glanced at Ryan's leg and asked, "How's the leg? All healed up now? A .45 bullet in the leg can really do some damage."

Ryan glanced down and rubbed his right thigh. "Yes, sir. It gives me some pain every once in a while and probably always will. But I'll live with it."

The president nodded and smiled. "Okay. As soon as I hear back on this issue, I'll give you a call. Thanks for coming over."

Ryan took the hint. He, Dave, and Jasper shook hands with the president, Jack, and the admiral, and left the Oval Office. While they'd accomplished what they had come for, Ryan wasn't happy over the attitudes. But at least they were going to check out their suspicions.

After Ryan and friends left, the president turned to Jack and the admiral. He said, "I think this is all bullshit." He shook his head in dismay. "We knocked the hell out of that piece of Iranian desert."

Jack looked back and shrugged. The admiral just nodded.

Jack said, "Yes. I agree with you. But we can't afford to be too careful. We have to check it out. Oh, and another thing. Remember Jasper's suggestion about the trucks? Well, Mark passed on to me that they did see some trucks, enhanced the recordings, but couldn't see much. They were covered in what appeared to be fiberglass covers and did look like supply trucks. We just can't tell."

The president just nodded in return. He was deep in thought.

They would just have to wait and see.

Chapter Twelve
Staff Results

Thursday—February 10
Washington, D.C.

It was two weeks later and both Kenton and Mark asked to see the president. Jack Harrison made arrangements through Jackie to schedule a short meeting for late that afternoon. As he was scheduling the meeting, Harrison was on the phone with Mark, and asked, "What's this about?"

Mark replied, "We have some information on the New Persia thing you folks asked about a little while ago. Both Kenton and I need to talk with you and the president privately. Can't talk about it over the phone."

Jack didn't like the sound of it, and just said, "Okay. We'll see you at four this afternoon in the Oval Office."

Mark agreed and hung up.

At 4:00 p.m. they all met in the Oval Office. The president, Jack, Admiral Watkins, Milt Swanson, the VP, Kenton, and Mark sat down in the easy chairs. The president looked quizzically at Mark and said, "Okay, Mark. Your show. What's going on?"

Mark looked at Kenton, who nodded slightly and then back to the president. He said, "Bluntly put, the ayatollah survived and is rebuilding. We don't know where he is yet, but he and several members of his senior staff made it out and are getting—"

The president quickly stood up, turned around, and looked at both of them incredulously. In a raised voice and with arms spread wide, he said, "He couldn't have! We saw that place totally destroyed! How could ..."

Kenton, looking quickly at Jack, who had also reacted with a surprised movement, grabbing the arms in his chair, interrupted, saying, "I've got the same basic information through our channels in Iran. While it is not common knowledge, several of the Iranian internal government ministers have confirmed that he made it out. They don't know where he is, but the interior minister talked with him in the middle of all the rubble of the stronghold the day following the

73

strike." He hesitated, then said with emphasis, "He's alive and trying to rebuild. He's even talked with the Iraqis and the Saudis about cutting off the oil exports to the west. He was rebuffed in both cases."

Both the president, who sat back down, and Jack were stunned speechless, literally. They didn't know what to say. Both just stared at Mark and Kenton for several moments. The admiral sat quietly in his chair, watching the exchange in amazement, slowly shaking his head. From all the previous information and satellite coverage of the strike, it didn't seem possible.

Jack stood up, walked over to a window, looked out at a dull and wintery day for a moment, then turned back with his hands spread slightly in front of him and said, "Are we sure of the sources of this information? This isn't just some ploy on the part of some of the Iranians to shame us? There were elements in the Iranian government who favored what he was doing. They could be putting out false info hoping to put egg on our face." He looked at Mark and then at Kenton.

Mark said, "No. Some of our resources are from the street and not internal to the government." He made a gesture with his hands outstretched to his sides and said, with some emphasis, "He made it out. We can't ignore it."

Kenton added, "You can doubt it all you want. But we have heard it from three different sources now. The Iranian interior minister talked with him face to face the day after the strike at the destroyed stronghold, the Iranian UN Ambassador has also said he made it out, and one of their economic advisors said the same thing. I don't think it's a ploy."

Jack threw up his hands in frustration. "I don't see how he could have done it." He stopped what he was saying as a light dawned. Then he looked at every one as a group and said, "Ryan's comments during the brief the other day. Is it possible Ryan was right? We know there was a zip line and they got out that way?"

Mark said, "Don't know. But that sure could have been it. And, I might add, he lost about seven hundred people that night, but still has something over fifteen hundred remaining who were not in the stronghold. Still a respectable number."

The president, recovering from his shock, said, "Okay. Given these sources and comments, we have to assume the worst and that he made it out. I hate that idea and find it very difficult to believe, but prudence would dictate we assume the worst. How he did it is really irrelevant.

"I accept that he apparently got away after our B-52 strike in southeastern Iran last November. Lord help us. Several independent sources in the Middle East have confirmed it. So the question now is, where is he and what do we do about it?"

Mark Alison, the CIA chief, said, "We don't know where he is. We are monitoring all the communications traffic in the Mideast to see if we can spot any activity he might be starting. So far, we have come up with zip. Nothing. It appears like he isn't using any of his own communications links. He must be using normal commercial comm to do whatever he's doing."

"Can't we monitor that traffic through our satellite surveillance?" asked Milt Swanson.

Mark responded, "We are working on that, but keep in mind that roughly ninety percent of all commercial traffic doesn't go over satellite links; it goes by undersea fiber cable. And that is very difficult to intercept and monitor. Especially if it is encrypted, which most of it is in today's business environment."

Milt looked back in surprise. "I thought most of the international comm traffic went by satellite these days."

Mark just shook his head and said, "No. Actually it doesn't. Cable has a greater capacity and is more secure and reliable."

The president then interrupted, "Okay. We don't know where this guy is. We missed him and he's out there somewhere probably planning some nasty surprises for us. Back to the original question. What do we do about it?" He looked at his staff members, and none had a comment to make. The president stood up, went over to the coffee pot and poured himself a short cup, took a taste, frowned, and put it back down. He walked back to his seat, all eyes following him as he moved about.

He sat down again, looked at the table, then looked up, saying to Kenton, "Can we get any intelligence from any of our 'friends' in the Mideast? Someone out there has to know something. This guy can't just disappear without some help from someone. We need to find out who and how."

Kenton responded, "We can try again. But when we inquired about his escape, it made the sources suspicious and they were very reluctant to talk. But maybe there's someone else out there that we haven't queried that we could tap. I'll have to look into it further and get back with you. But I wouldn't hold up much hope."

The president looked back, thought a moment, and then said, "How about a roundabout inquiry through the Brits or Germans? Questions from them may not cause as much concern as they would coming directly from us."

Kenton thought a moment and responded, "I'll talk to my guys and we'll come up with something. Let me work it for a few days and get back to you when we have something."

The president looked back at Kenton and nodded. "Okay. Let me know when you have something."

He stopped for a moment and then continued, "We need to keep this very quiet for now. I think we need to get a very small and select group of people together and figure out what, if anything, we need, or can, do. Jack, set up a meeting here in a couple of days. It will give us some time to think about it." He nodded at Mark and Kenton and said, "Keep this under wraps for now. Plan on attending the meeting." He looked back at Jack and said, "Let's have Ryan back, and get Newt, Jerry, Mike, and Abe involved. No others for now."

Jack made a couple of notes and nodded. He took a deep breath and blew it out through puffed-out cheeks as he contemplated the meaning of what they had just heard.

The ramifications could be huge.

Chapter Thirteen
Trimaran

Monday—February 14
Socotra Island Operations Center

The very large trimaran, a three-hulled ship, finishing a training exercise, moved quickly across the Arabian Sea en route to the new base of operations for the New Persia movement. An experimental design, it was over seventy-five meters in length and had a beam of fifteen meters. The two masts could be laid down horizontally on the deck so the twin-turbine engines would be more efficient when used for exclusive power. Its main mast was nearly fifty meters high, and, its foremast slightly shorter, it carried a huge amount of sail. Enough that men could not handle it. Electronics and mechanical/electrical winches and pulleys were used to raise and lower the masts and sails. Using the turbines, the trimaran could make better than fifty knots. A swift machine, and one with many of the comforts of a yacht, it replaced one of the mission yachts, *Persian Wind,* that New Persia had been using. *Persian Wind*, being recalled by the Chinese owners, was to be converted by the Chinese Navy into one of their own high-speed littoral interceptors.

Kadar was pleased to have been selected to captain the new vessel. It took several months for him and his crew to train on the trimaran and learn its various mission capabilities. There were significant changes from *Persian Wind,* and it was quite a learning process for both he and his twenty-four-man crew. The new trimaran was named *Persian Desert*, with the title written in Arabic and English on the stern. The name came from the attempts by New Persia to better the environment while improving the lives of the Arabic people.

However, the mission Kadar was commanding with *Persian Desert* had not changed from *Persian Wind*. He was delayed, due to the stronghold strike nearly three months earlier, in getting into the northern Pacific, but it was just a delay, not a cancelation. Once his training was complete, in another few weeks, and they could get resupplied and linked up with some of the critical mission-required equipment, they would set off to the east and into the northern Pacific to complete the previously interrupted mission. He was looking forward to it.

It had been a pleasant day in the Arabian Sea. They had left the center two days earlier to conduct exercises and continue with the training provided by their Chinese instructors. It had not been easy, and some of the lessons required repeating multiple times for his crew to become proficient at handling the new ship. It was different. And with some mission-required ship configuration changes, there were new characteristics to learn and be aware of. But they were getting there, and he was pleased at the progress.

As they pulled into the harbor under turbine power, Kadar lined up with his assigned pier and slowly approached the docking area. He had a joystick instead of a standard wheel, and the sensitivities of the electronic control were something they were still getting used to. Normally a helmsman would be doing this docking maneuver as Kadar gave directions, but Kadar was enough of a perfectionist to want to be able to master this task himself. Through these exercises, both he and the helmsman would become very good at guiding the trimaran both in the harbor and at sea. They slightly nudged the pier and mooring lines were thrown and received. The ship was made fast to the pier and various connections for electrical and water were established. A small portable gangway was put in place, and Kadar, along with some of the crew, disembarked to a training facility at dockside for a debriefing of the past couple of days and a brief discussion of the next mission.

Thursday—February 25
Socotra Island Operations Center

Every Thursday morning the ayatollah conducted a staff meeting of all his primary advisors. He depended on Khatib to set up the meeting each week and to assure that the current status of each of their projects was available for discussion. They met in the main conference room of the operations center.

The ayatollah entered the fully occupied room and took his seat at the head of the conference table. All had arisen on his appearance, and he motioned for them to sit down so the meeting could begin.

The ayatollah said, "We have received word from the stronghold that many of the new recruits are being trained and we have recovered our strength. It has now been three months since the infidels struck, and we are back. It won't be long before the world will know that." He looked around at his advisors as he spoke, noting the nodding of the heads. He also noted that there was a significant difference in attitudes over the past three months ... from despair and discouragement to pride and straight-backed postures. They were truly ready from a spirit perspective. After some more preparation activities, the world would know that they were, again, a force for Allah's mission.

He turned to Ghanim and asked, "What is the status of our two ongoing missions—the British action and the crew training of the *Persian Desert* for the mission to Alaskan waters?"

Ghanim replied, "We continue to monitor the American administration's flight schedules, but they have no plans, thus far, to fly in to Heathrow. We will continue to watch that, since it can change quickly. As far as the progress of training on the *Persian Desert*, it is moving along quite well. We anticipate meeting schedule, and the ship should depart on March 11."

The ayatollah nodded and then said, "Good. Good. It sounds like we are on track, and I am pleased." He then turned to Marin, who had recently arrived at the center, and said, "It sounds like the people are doing well at the stronghold. What is your assessment?"

Marin, the logistics planner who had taken over the management of the stronghold after the strike, responded, "Sir. We are doing quite well. Over eight hundred new recruits have arrived and our training program for them is progressing very well. We have also been able to improve our facilities to better train. I anticipate some of the recruits to be ready in another month, should we need them."

The ayatollah sat back in his chair and looked at his people. He smiled and enjoyed the thought of being able to continue his movement. He sat back forward in his chair again, then continued the meeting, getting the status of finances, facilities, communications, and future plans from each minister. It was a fairly complete package, and they were making good progress.

New Persia might just be back ... the world just didn't know it yet!

Chapter Fourteen
Ryan Summoned to Washington

Friday—February 18
Ryan's Marina, Freeport, Texas

It had been about a week since he had left Washington, and Ryan was monitoring the construction crew as they were preparing to pour some new concrete into forms around the pier. He was upgrading, in stages, all of the walkways and piers in the marina. As one section was completed he moved on to another section, and hoped to have all the work done in about eight months. To do this he had to move his regular customers in a kind of musical chairs, so they all had berths while the work was being done.

He was watching a concrete pumper moving its boom around as the crew was distributing the concrete throughout the forms. The concrete delivery truck was off to the side dumping the concrete into the hopper on the pumper truck. It was a satisfying moment for him, because he had been planning these upgrades for several months now. The crew then spread the concrete out over the rebar, using a sonic probe to assure that there were no holes or gaps in the fresh concrete, ran a float over it to initially smooth the surface, and began the tedious task of smoothing and doing an initial finish on the surface. He marveled at the almost artistic manner as these concrete finishers performed their work. Smoothing and finishing, with just the right touch, to ensure a level, good-looking product.

As he was watching, he heard a call from the marina office and looked up in that direction. Juan was calling to him with a motion saying that he had a phone call. He waved at him indicating that he didn't want to take it right now. Juan shook his head emphatically and waved at him again. Ryan shook his head in disgust and headed up to the office. Damn interruptions! What could it be now? Hopefully it wasn't the building department with some new requirement that would translate into another delay. There had been a couple of those, and they not only cost him time, but money also.

He hurried to the office and looked questioningly at Juan. Juan mouthed back at him, "It's the president calling!"

Ryan stopped for a moment and then took the phone.

Ryan answered, "Hello."

A female voice came on the line, "Hello, Ryan. It's Maria Aragon, President Martinez's secretary. It's good to hear your voice. How are you?"

Ryan responded, "I'm fine, Maria. I hope all is going well for you too. What can I do for you?"

"Yes. All is well, thank you. Please stand by for the president." There was a slight click on the line.

"Ryan! How are you doing?" asked the president.

"I'm fine, sir. We're just in the process of pouring some concrete and enjoying the upgrade process."

"Good. Good," he said with some obvious detachment. "Well, Ryan. I guess I owe you an apology."

"How's that, sir?"

"Well, remember our discussion last month regarding the possibility of a mission failure? I'm sorry, but on this open line I can't get too specific."

Ryan was guarded but said, "Yes, sir. I remember. Has something changed?"

"Yes it has. It seems you were apparently right in your assessment. And I'd like you to come back to Washington for another meeting to discuss that change. Can you support us?"

"Certainly, sir. Do you want Dave and Jasper along also?"

"Yes. They might be able to lend some help."

"I'll check with both of them. When did you want us there?"

The president responded, "It's Friday and my schedule is completely booked for Monday and Tuesday. Can you make it on Wednesday? We'll send an aircraft, as before."

"I know I can make that, but let me check with Dave and Jasper. I can let Maria know, if that would be okay with you."

"That works for me. Again, we'll have some information for you on the aircraft, and I'll look forward to seeing you on Wednesday." He hesitated then said, "And Ryan ..." and hesitated again.

"Yes, sir?"

"I really appreciate your help on this." Ryan could hear the tension in the president's voice.

81

Ryan only hesitated for a second and said, "No problem, sir. Glad to help."

"Good. See you next week." And he hung up.

Ryan slowly put the phone handset back in its charger and stood there for a minute trying to collect his thoughts. He had obviously been right. The ayatollah had escaped and was probably rebuilding somewhere. Here we go again!

He called both Dave and Jasper and had to leave a message with both of them.

Then he headed back down to the concrete pour to monitor what they were doing, if he could keep his mind on it.

So, his suspicions had been correct. It was a disturbing thought. The ayatollah would not give up easily, and since he had been hit hard in the strike on his stronghold, he would probably be out for blood. It was not a comfortable thought. What would happen next?

Ryan reached the pier where the concrete pour was just finishing. He continued to watch the concrete finishing for several minutes and then headed back up to the office. Perhaps Dave and Jasper had replied to his calls.

Tuesday—February 22
En route to Washington

The weather forecast was for some storms, which meant some choppy and rough skies. Ryan looked out the oversized Gulfstream windows at the scudding clouds rapidly going by. Ryan was on board the U.S. Air Force Gulfstream V C-37 VIP aircraft with Dave and Jasper when the subject of New Persia came up ... as expected. There was a large amount of discussion over how the senior leaders had escaped. Ryan thought he had it figured out from his previous thinking and investigation. But they couldn't quite figure it all out at this point, and there was a lot of speculation.

As they were discussing some of their impressions, a young Air Force staff sergeant approached them from the rear of the aircraft, hanging on to the seats as he made his way forward. He confirmed who they were and, after checking their identifications, handed each of them a small envelope with top-secret markings. Ryan looked at it and nodded. This must have been what the president had been referring to last week when he called. They were identical envelopes. Ryan, Dave, and Jasper opened theirs and read on CIA letterhead:

Top Secret—Briefing Note

Through the State Department and the Central Intelligence Agency, we have been able to confirm that the Ayatollah Abdul Sarhardi, the leader of the New Persian movement, survived the attack of last November 18 on his stronghold in southeastern Iran. Several of his senior staff also survived. Multiple sources within the Mideast sphere of influence have stated that he has been active in trying to get Middle East oil exports to the western nations reduced or eliminated.

We are trying to ascertain their current whereabouts but have, thus far, been unsuccessful. Efforts are continuing in this regard and we anticipate some progress shortly.

Through national means, we have also determined that the surface areas of the stronghold are still being used as an apparent base of training activities. There has been a significant increase in activities there and a noticeable increase in the population. Several buildings have been erected and appear to be training and support facilities.

As more information becomes available, we will provide updates.

At the bottom of the single sheet of paper was a handwritten note:

Ryan, Dave and Jasper.

This is the information I was referring to last week in my conversation with Ryan. Looking forward to seeing and talking with you all tomorrow.

And it was finished with the initials "AM" from President Martinez.

Jasper looked up from his copy and said, "Well, I guess that clears some of this up. I wonder if they've had any luck finding this guy?"

Ryan responded, "Don't know. But I'll bet they have a full-court press on right now to do just that."

Dave nodded and commented, "Sure hope so. He's dangerous and needs to be put away. But I wonder what the president has in mind for us. We haven't a clue as to where the ayatollah might be, and I don't see what we can do to help."

Ryan and Jasper just nodded in agreement.

Jasper, changing the subject, said, "I was thinking about this the other day, and I'm wondering why we are doing all this chasing and work trying to capture what amounts to pirates and thieves."

Dave looked him and said, "Okay. What conclusion did you come to? Any bright thoughts?"

"Yep. I don't know anything about them, but somewhere out there I've heard of an outfit called Interpol. They're supposed to be some form of international police organization. Wouldn't they be the right guys to chase this thing down?"

Ryan shrugged. "I've heard the name but don't know anything about them. Sounds like, if you're right, they might be the right ones to pursue this."

Dave looked at them both, rolled his eyes to the ceiling, and started to chuckle. "I don't believe it. You're both quite right. You guys have no idea of what you're talking about."

Ryan looked over at him and said, "Okay. Help us out here. What do you know about them and why wouldn't they be the right ones to chase this?"

Dave looked back and said, "Interpol is not really a true police force. Yes, they do a lot of police work, but it is primarily coordinating-type work and not chasing down criminals. They are headquartered in France and have offices in several other countries. But their primary focus is passing on information on safety, terrorism, environmental crime, war crimes, drugs, piracy, and a bunch of other areas of criminal activity. Yes, they may have information that could help us out, but they don't go after the criminals as such. That's up to the individual countries that support it."

Ryan said, "Well, it might help to see if they have any info on where the ayatollah and his friends might have gone."

Dave responded, "Yes. It wouldn't hurt. But just remember they don't go after people—however, they might be able to help pinpoint the ayatollah's location."

Ryan responded, "Well, we need to keep that in mind. The next time we have the opportunity, perhaps we could bring it up with President Martinez. He might be able to do something with it."

Chapter Fifteen
Congressional Notification

Saturday—February 19
Washington, D.C.

"I've asked you both to come over for some news that isn't good. Sorry about the weekend call, but I think it's necessary." The president looked at Texas Senator Jim McIlroy and New Jersey House Speaker Representative Marty Gibbons. They both looked quizzically at him. He continued, "As you know, we put a lot of effort into eliminating New Persia and its leader Ayatollah Sarhardi. However, several days ago we got word that the ayatollah survived the raid and may be rebuilding his movement."

Both men were stunned. Jim sat back for a moment, covered his eyes with his hands, and then looked back at the president. "But we saw that complex absolutely destroyed!" he exclaimed. "How could he possibly have survived all that dirt and rock just flying all over the place? It would have been crushing. He couldn't have survived that!"

"Yeah. Well, that's what I thought too. But we have had information from several sources now that say otherwise. Somehow, he got out of it, along with several of his minions. We got a lot of his people and destroyed the actual stronghold ... but we missed him. And at this point we don't know where he is."

Marty Gibbons, always the practical one, looked out the window, got up from his chair, leaned on the back, stared at the floor, and said, "Well, if he got out and is rebuilding, what is our next move?" He looked up again, at the president, and said, "He has to be stopped." He thought for just a moment, nodded, and repeated, "He needs to be found and stopped."

The president looked back and said, "Agree. I don't know yet what our next move will be. I wanted to make sure you knew what was going on before it becomes common knowledge. I've directed some of my people to see if they can locate him and his organization. All we know is that he took a ship and headed south out of Iran after the stronghold hit. On top of that, if this gets out, I'm afraid we may have a real press debacle on our hands."

They both nodded in understanding. Senator McIlroy then said, "I think we need to anticipate this and make it public before we are forced to. I think that way we appear to be out in front of it."

Gibbons was noncommittal, pursing his lips and folding his arms in front of his chest, as he looked over to the president. He looked at the floor for a minute then back to the president and finally said, "Given the circumstances, it's a no-win situation for us."

The president said, "Let me think about it. My first reaction is to keep it under wraps, but perhaps you're right, Jim. I need to think on it some more." With that, he got up and the two congressmen left the room.

He turned and looked out the window. He knew Jim McIlroy was right in suggesting they talk to the press. Come clean about the failure. But he was quite uncomfortable doing that. There were too many unknowns about it, and the press would not be reluctant to ask probing questions that he had no answers for right now. And if he wanted to keep it quiet until they could locate the ayatollah, as Kenton had said, the last thing to do would be to notify the press.

It was a real puzzle. And not a pleasant one.

Chapter Sixteen
Presidential Discussions

Wednesday—February 23
Washington, D.C.

The president strode into the Oval Office from his morning briefing sessions. Ryan, Dave, Jasper, General Newt Foley, Jerry Ocasio, head of Homeland Security, Kenton Marshall, Mike Detirro, Mark Alison, Vice President Milt Swanson, General Abe Fairchild, the Air Force chief of staff, and Vice Admiral Watkins were all present, and rose as he came in. He motioned for them all to be seated and got himself a cup of coffee before taking his seat at the head of the table. He studied his coffee for a moment as the rest of the people in the room maintained a respectful silence. Then he began, "I think all of you now know why we are here. We now know that the ayatollah and several key members of his senior staff made it out of the attack alive. They not only made it out alive, none of them were seriously injured, and they are, as we speak, rebuilding the New Persia organization. We don't know for sure how they did it, but that is actually irrelevant. They are not finished." He stopped for a moment and looked around at the assembled group. He pondered for a minute then said, "You know, this guy is really turning into a relentless target. We thought we had him and now we know we missed. And now we have to go after him again. Just relentless ... and very frustrating."

He turned to Mark and asked, "Has there been any more information other than what you had last week?"

"Not really, sir. We do know that word is getting out amongst the more fringe elements in the Arab world, and he is getting a lot of recruits to his cause. It seems a lot of them want to join his efforts at taming the 'Eagle.' That's us, of course."

"I see. So our attack may have had the opposite effect as far as some members of the Arab world are concerned."

"Yes, sir."

He paused and then turned to Kenton. "Does that agree with what you are hearing?"

Kenton responded, "Yes, sir. The information coming through the embassy channels reflects the same matter. While they may have lost several hundred people in the raid, they will probably more than make up for that loss."

The president nodded, took a deep breath, and let it out slowly. "And I suppose we will be the target of his wrath," he said, almost rhetorically. Heads around the room nodded in agreement. Then he added to the room at large, "Do we know where he is at this point, and any more info on what he is actually doing?"

Mark looked at Kenton and around the room then said, "No, sir. Not yet. We are trying to find that out. We do know that he headed south out of the old stronghold and was picked up in the northern Arabian Sea by one of his working yachts. Where they went is anybody's guess. They haven't advertised where they are or where they may be going. We just don't know at this point. And, just for your information, the area around the old stronghold is where all the new recruits are gathering. There's been some reconstruction, though not underground, around the stronghold, with some of it training practice areas. Someone in that area is orchestrating their arrival and training, but we don't know who as yet. There just isn't much detailed information out there. But we're keeping an eye on it."

President Martinez said, "We were monitoring the stronghold for several days after the strike. Did that include any of the areas where he might have boarded a ship? I'm wondering if we have any way of tracking where he went."

Mike offered, "I'll have to check on that. We were concentrated on the stronghold, but it's possible some of the camera coverage covered the Gulf of Oman ports near him. I just don't know yet. I'll look into it and get back to you."

The president nodded. "Let me know as soon as you can. We need to know where he went."

"Yes, sir."

The president turned to Mike and Kenton. "Do either of you have any suggestions on locating the ayatollah?"

Mike looked at Kenton then back to the president. "We can see if there are any increases in message traffic on the satellites from that general area. If there are, maybe we can pinpoint a possible location."

The president said, "Do it."

Mike looked over at General Abe Fairchild. Abe responded, "We'll see what the folks at Schriever AFB in

Colorado can do for us. They have the satellite coverage in that area and might be able to help."

Kenton commented, "I don't think we should be trying to get information from our ground sources, at least not yet."

The president turned to him and asked, "Why do you say that, Kenton?"

"Because at this point they may not be aware that we know they made it out. And if we start a major effort on locating them, they will go further underground and be very difficult to locate. I think we need to do this one step at a time and see if we can ferret it out on our own."

Milt added, "Since we have already questioned the Iranians, that cat may already be out of the bag."

"Yes, it might be. But our continuing to question about their exact location would be a real red flag to the ayatollah. I think we should lay low and get what we can on our own through satellites, and possibly from some really good friends like the Brits. Then, if we have to, we can always start asking telling questions."

The president said, "I think you have a point, Kenton." Then to the group, he said, "Let's keep it quiet for a little while and see what we can find out through our own resources. We can always open a can of worms later."

Ryan spoke up: "Sir, could Interpol help out? They may have some info sources on this, since they track international criminals."

The president thought a moment and turned to Mark. "While I doubt they can help much, quietly check it out."

Mark nodded, took a note, and looked back up.

Jasper spoke up: "Sir, Has there been any more information on those missiles that were fired at the B-52s?"

The president turned to Mark and raised his eyebrows in question.

Mark looked back and then over to Jasper. "Yes. We have put on a significant effort to find out what those were. We now know they were Chinese state-of-the-art short-range missiles. By short range, I mean we think they have a range of ten to fifteen miles. They were truck mounted, so they're very mobile, and, again we think, use a form of camera technology for guidance, combined with infrared technology for terminal guidance. In other words, they locate the target with the camera, thus no radiation occurs, and once the missile is in close enough, switch over to heat seekers. That's how they got the bombers. They came in from above and picked up the engine turbine exhaust. We never saw them coming." He looked over at General Foley and General Fairchild before continuing, "We've passed this information on to the engineers at Boeing and the Oklahoma City Logistics Complex. They are wrestling with how to defeat the missiles as we speak. Hopefully, they will come up with something soon. But they are working on it. Unfortunately, it may take some time to develop a counter."

The president said, "Okay. Keep me informed of what they come up with. Obviously we need some form of defense or countermeasure."

Mark nodded in response.

The president, in thought, then looked around the room. He caught Ryan's eye and asked, "Anything to add?"

Ryan said, "Yes, sir. Just a thought. It's been a couple of months now since the raid, and the activity at the stronghold seems to have picked up. At least that's my understanding."

The president nodded in agreement.

Ryan continued, "I follow the direction you just gave to Mike a few minutes ago and would add that the stronghold must be communicating periodically with the ayatollah, if for nothing else to keep him informed of their progress and maybe some form of training information or status. So, if they're communicating, perhaps we can track down how they are doing that and figure out his location from that information."

"Good point," said the president. He turned to Mark and Mike and asked if there had been any action to check that out.

Mike shrugged his shoulders and shook his head.

Mark then responded, "Yes. We know that they are using couriers, but we don't know how often or where they are sending the information. It's a very old method of communicating, but since the ayatollah knows we are trying to find him, he's not using what we would call 'normal' modern communications. And they send out multiple runners each time they do it, so we don't know which runner is carrying the mail. Smart. We're working it, but not with much success so far."

The president and Mike both just nodded. Ryan shook his head and grimaced at that information.

The president then turned to each individual in the room, pointed at them and said, "Any further suggestions or thoughts?" Each person, including Ryan and friends, had nothing to contribute. "Okay. We'll meet again in a few weeks and see where we are. In the meantime, it should go without saying that this is very sensitive. Keep it to yourselves. I don't want a massive press disclosure with all the trappings that involves."

People in the room nodded, and a few chuckled slightly.

Chapter Seventeen
Transit To/In Alaska

Friday—March 11
Socotra Island Operations Center

While it took slightly longer to complete than originally anticipated, three weeks later all training had been accomplished. Kadar and his mission crew were ready to go. Supplies had been loaded, the communications center on the trimaran was fully operational, resupply points had been established further to the east in China, and the mini-submarine was mission-ready and on board. Final mission briefings had been accomplished the previous evening, and a final meal provided in the dining facility for the mission crew members. All was ready. It was early morning. Several of the leaders, including Khatib and Abdul-Hakim, and ministers in the New Persia movement had come down to the dock to wish them farewell. Kadar took his place on the bridge, the engines were idling, and the folding masts were upright with sails furled.

Through radio contact with the dock personnel, the mooring lines were released, and Kadar directed the helmsman to back away from the pier. The engines churned the deep blue harbor water and the *Persian Desert* began to move slowly back away from the dock. The helmsman, using the joystick, turned the ship around ninety degrees so the bow was headed out to sea. He then placed the engines in forward and slowly eased out of the harbor and, after a few minutes, came around to an initial course. They would clear landfall using the engines before setting the sails for the long cruise to the northern Pacific Ocean and their mission location.

Relieved, they were off ... finally.

Saturday—March 12
Arabian Sea, Northern Indian Ocean

The trimaran *Persian Desert* was eastbound in the Arabian Sea and headed for the northern Pacific Ocean. Her course would take her across the Arabian Sea, around the southern tip of India, past Sri Lanka, across the Bay of Bengal, through the Strait of Malacca, then up past Singapore and into the South China Sea. She would find temporary berthing in Hong Kong for a few days as she resupplied for the rest of the journey north and east. From Hong Kong she would head east through the Philippine Sea and then northeast past Japan and into the mission area past the Aleutian Islands and just off the southern coast of Alaska.

There she would be the force striking the Americans back for the stronghold destruction.

Payback! To Kadar, it was so sweet.

Wednesday—March 17
Washington, D.C.

Erin Muega worked her way out to the podium. At thirty years old, she maintained herself quite well through biking to work and hiking through parts of the Great Smoky Mountains on weekends. As the president's press secretary, she held a press conference every Wednesday morning precisely at 9:00 a.m. A graduate of Kent State University's television and radio program, she had assisted with the press coverage during the president's successful candidacy and then stayed on to support the president.

She went through the president's schedule and answered several questions on the president's position on pending legislation. Nothing out of the ordinary. Then, during the question-and-answer portion of the briefing, she was hit with the question. Tom Jordan, of ABC News, said, "There have been rumors that the New Persia ayatollah survived the bombing last November and is rebuilding his organization. Can you comment on that, and, if it is true, what is the administration doing about it?"

Wham! Out of the blue. Not even a hint this would be asked. They had not discussed this during their press preparation sessions. She was aware of the worldwide hunt for the ayatollah but was not ready to comment just yet.

She looked down at the podium for a moment and then back to Tom. She said, "Yes, we are aware that he survived, but have no knowledge of what he might be doing. As soon as we have some information, we will update you on our planned actions." Tom just nodded.

Then she pointed to another reporter. "Well, what are we doing to catch him? Is the military involved again, and if so, what are they doing?"

She responded, "No. The military is not involved. We are pursuing some leads through the State Department but have no further information at this time." The reporter made a quick note and raised his hand again, but she did not respond to his non-verbal request for a follow-up question.

She quickly looked around and then left the stage. Sweat was beginning to show on her brow. She really didn't like to get caught like that with no administration-cleared response.

In the papers the next day, and on the evening news broadcasts, mention was made of the comments, and several editorials were written criticizing the Martinez administration for hiding their actions. The president and Jack, when told of the incident, agreed that they would let it die down and not make further comments until they had something positive to say.

Thursday—March 18
Washington, D.C.

Mark sent a note over to Maria for the president. As a follow-up to the tasking to see if Interpol could help, Mark had contacted them in Lyon, France, where their headquarters was located. They could only provide the same information the CIA already had. They could not assist with locating the ayatollah.

Thursday—April 21
Bay of Alaska

It took slightly under six weeks for *Persian Desert* to travel the distance, including the stopover in Hong Kong, but they had made it without any serious incident. There had been a few shake-out issues with one of the engines, but that had been resolved in Hong Kong and they arrived as scheduled. Once on station, they were over 150 degrees of travel around the globe, nearly on the other side of the world, from the operations center. Kadar, using an encrypted satellite link, communicated back to the operations center that they were on station and would be starting the mission activities within the next twenty-four hours. He received an acknowledgement with congratulations on making it to the area on schedule. Operations was pleased at the progress they were making.

Monday—April 25
Pipeline North of Valdez, Alaska

Bob Abernathy was slowly cruising in his pipeline patrol truck along the dirt road that paralleled this part of the eight-hundred-mile-long Alaskan pipeline. He was looking for trouble spots or any problems that might require repair. He was approximately forty miles north of Valdez, the southern terminus of the pipeline, and enjoying the pleasant spring morning. Spring was well on its way; however, the air was still crisp and cool. He could really marvel at what nature did in this part of the world, with the dramatic seasonal changes, wildlife, and natural geography that was nearly overwhelming. In his opinion he had the perfect job working the line ... sometimes by helicopter, but more often by pipeline service truck, since he could see more and could more quickly determine if a problem was present. Also, with the truck's kit of frequently needed parts, he could immediately work a problem, but by helicopter he had to find a place to land and make a determination. By truck, he was right there, and it didn't hurt that he enjoyed the solitude of the truck and nature.

Bob was a big man, standing just over six feet and weighing in at 220 pounds. He had a high forehead, close-cropped brown hair usually hidden by a well-worn Alyeska Oil Company ball cap, and weathered face due to the frigid Alaskan air, hidden behind a full beard. He had deep blue eyes, both with crow's-feet, protected from the arctic sun with sunglasses. A modern-day Paul Bunyan. His nearly ten years in the U.S. Army with helicopter operations and maintenance prepared him well for this chosen work on the pipeline. The rigors of working on the pipeline had hardened him, but his mannerisms were gentlemanly and he was polite almost to a fault.

He headed south at a leisurely pace, taking his time and looking the pipeline over as he went. He wasn't in a particular hurry, and wanted to make sure his inspection was reasonably complete. He periodically stopped and walked over to one of the pipeline support stanchions and looked it over with a practiced eye. Each of the stanchions supported sixty feet of the pipeline. The pipeline could not exist without them, and their construction, as part of the pipeline, was extraordinary. Satisfied that all was fine, he went back to his truck and continued his way south.

Bob radioed his location back to control and continued on his way. Many people would have thought of this type of work as boring, but having been raised in Alaska, Bob appreciated the environment and the opportunity to do this type of work. Outdoors and working with such an important part of the American economy. Tough to beat!

Bob's thoughts were interrupted by a call on his radio. Control was calling for assistance with a nearby part of the pipeline.

"Rover One here. Go ahead, control," he said, using his call sign.

"Bob, we need you to head over to mile marker 38 and make a repair. Some vandals have shot part of the pipeline and we need the damage inspected and possibly repaired."

"Roger. Will head over there right now." Damned vandals, thought Bob. But it was a common occurrence, and he frequently had to do these repairs. He never could make sense of why they did it. And wayward hunters sometimes took shots at the line too. Boredom, he supposed.

Bob got to the assigned section and found the damaged line. Fortunately, the damage was minor, since the pipeline was so strong. Normal rifle bullets couldn't do much damage to it, but every once in a while they had to shut a section of line down when a high-powered slug penetrated it. Then they had a little more complicated repair process to follow. Bob made minor surface repairs to the line, called in to control, and headed back into town and home. It was now late afternoon, and he planned to continue the inspection tomorrow.

Wednesday—April 27
Bay of Alaska

On the foreign-registered trimaran, sitting idle about twenty miles off the coast in the Bay of Alaska, three divers were preparing to depart via the mini-sub. Due to a compressor problem, they had been delayed for several days. Kadar somewhat anxiously watched as his men prepared for their distant mission on American soil. He wanted to get moving, and the delay had put him in a bad mood. They would take a mini-sub in to the distant, mysterious, and forbidding shore at night, and disembark after hiding the sub.

The western nations had to be taught that the future required restraint in the use of oil and to not use it so wastefully and frivolously. If the world's children were to see the benefits of oil, the oil must be saved and not be squandered, as the western nations were doing. It would also demonstrate to the world that the New Persia movement had not been destroyed and was still capable of worldwide actions. The world would learn, and, especially in this particular case, the U.S. would learn.

Standing just off the coastline of Alaska in international waters, they began their preparations. The mini-sub crew was well prepared for the mission, and reviews were conducted to make sure there were no last-minute problems or concerns. The mini-sub crew, headed by Junayd and seconded by Abdul, along with an explosives expert, Jabbar, were anxious to get started. They had trained long and hard and wanted to get moving with the real mission. After the final briefing, and a blessing from Kadar, they headed down to the center bay, where the mini-sub was suspended from the main deck of the trimaran. The mini-sub was actually the middle "pontoon" of the trimaran. When it was released into the water, the trimaran became a two-hulled catamaran. The effect was to camouflage the mini underneath the catamaran, thus hiding the submarine capabilities of the ship. When attached to the ship, it rode as the third hull and assisted with the support of the whole assembly.

Junayd and his two fellow saboteurs waited until nightfall then went below to the waiting mini-sub. To an outside observer, they were on a wealthy individual's trimaran, anchored with a party underway on board. One would not suspect that within the hull of the trimaran was the mini-sub and its cargo of destruction, about to depart undetected on a historical mission against the American oil industry.

Weaving their way through the various umbilical cords and cables, they entered the mini-sub via a hatch in the top. After settling in at the crew stations, they began their final systems checks and assured, both themselves and the monitoring crew on board the catamaran, that the mission was a go. This particular mini-sub was an upgraded version from the one previously assigned to them. It could carry up to six additional personnel and function as an underwater commando transfer vessel. While it did not have the depth capability of the previous model—it could only go down to five hundred feet—it did have the capability of working in the close-in waters of the shore and harbors.

Coordinating with the trimaran onboard operations center, Junayd prepared for the release of the mini-sub into the still-frigid Bay of Alaska waters. He was both anxious and excited.

Nerves were on edge, and it would be good to get underway.

Chapter Eighteen
Explosive Setting

Wednesday—April 27
Bay of Alaska

After making a few final checks of the mini-sub's systems, and making sure, through buddy checks, their spring clothing and gear was on and set up properly, they proceeded to check the lightweight explosives and timing gear. They had to get thirty-five miles overland, and back, and did not want to have a problem with the explosives when they reached their target. All was ready, and the training they had undergone over the past year was about to pay off in a—hopefully—successful mission accomplishment.

For this total mission to succeed, they were to take out the pipeline at three locations, in a simultaneous timed explosion. Multiple locations would complicate the pipeline repair process. Two of the locations were overwater pipe bridges, and the supports at each end of the bridge would be destroyed. The third location, the one they were targeting for tonight, was located just north of the southern terminus at Valdez, Alaska. They would be setting explosives on the forty-eight-inch pipeline that would destroy several hundred feet of pipe, along with the support stanchions.

Junayd, working for Kadar—and, of course, Allah—was leading the sabotage effort. A man of twenty-eight, he had been trained in the southeastern deserts of Iran and had excelled in explosive setting and placement. His knowledge of the engineering of bridge and pipeline support structures was thorough, and his practical experience in blowing up simulated pipelines in training impressed his peers and superiors. That was why he was the lead on this particular mission.

At precisely 8:00 p.m. local time, Junayd, seated in the pilot's console/position, powered up the mini-sub as his companions took their positions. He maintained communications with the launch team within the trimaran and did final checks of the sub's power and position indicators. All was ready. It was very dark and cold in the Alaskan spring. They had come a long way for this moment and trained for

99

many months for this specific mission. This was the culmination of months of planning and training, and he was anxious to get underway.

The launch team, in coordination with Junayd, released the sub from its retaining harness and umbilical. Junayd then initiated the dive routine, quietly blowing air from the tank vents, and slowly disappeared into the cold, inky darkness of the water. He sank a full thirty feet into the dark water before he began forward motion using the main thruster, thus avoiding any possible contact with the pontoons of the *Persian Desert*. From his depth, and looking out into the dark, frigid waters of the Bay of Alaska, he felt a combination of exaltation and dread ... exalted over the mission he was on and the honor of leading it ... and dread over the possibility of being discovered and the shame that would accompany that discovery. He was determined ... they would not fail.

Utilizing the inertial navigation guidance system, he came about on a course to take them in to their preselected landing point. They would land just south and east of the community of Valdez, where they would hide the mini and begin their trip to the target area of the pipeline.

They hoped to reach their target section of the pipeline by 11:00 p.m. local, set the explosives and the timers within two hours, and get back to the mini-sub by 2:30 a.m. It would still be dark at that time and they could get back to the *Persian Desert*. A completely clandestine, undetected mission. It would remain undetected until two months later, when the explosives all detonated together, causing a massive oil spill and damage that would take many months to repair. The pipeline, over its entire length, held over nine million barrels of oil, and the damage would cause a significant amount of it to not just spill, but, since it would be under significant pressure, to spray out over the nearby countryside. An environmental disaster of huge impact and importance.

Junayd dropped the mini-sub to just above the bottom and slowly, following the inertial guidance system and forward-looking sonar, moved in toward the shore. This would minimize a possible collision with other ships that might be in the area. He also had passive sonar that would tell him of any approaching ship traffic so he could avoid them. He certainly did not want to have the mission cut short by an underwater collision.

After an hour of smooth running, and tracking his progress with the inertial systems, he avoided several ships that sat at anchor and shifted his attention to the shoreline. After surfacing very slowly to minimize any water noise, through a viewport he got a good bearing on the shoreline, spotting several landmarks he had studied as part of the mission preparation. As part of the mission package, previous "visitors/tourists" to this area had identified several landmarks that he could use. They had been right on, and he knew exactly where he was and where he needed to be. Checking the sub's chronometer, a highly accurate clock updated constantly from a satellite, along with his navigation system, he was pleased to see that they were right on course and schedule.

Junayd located the small covered pier that had been arranged for them, and pulled in under the cover. Still floating in small patches of ice, he opened the cockpit, and Abdul and Jabbar jumped to the pier and made fast the mooring lines. The plain, beat-up, six-passenger pick-up truck was parked nearby with the keys under the front floor mat. Moving silently while Junayd secured the mini-sub, they loaded up their packs into the truck and checked their side arms. They did a quick check of their electronic map on the phone, made sure the initialized point matched their location, and started the truck. Junayd joined them and they quietly moved out.

They had a course laid out in the phone and simply had to follow it. The phone application even had hazards that they needed to avoid identified for them. In the dark they were able to make very good time skirting around the terminal complex, and headed north on Highway 4. To a casual observer, their dark truck added to the darkness of the night, making them nearly invisible. You would have to know they were there to be able to see them.

They made good time, with very little traffic to slow them down. After an hour they had made their target location thirty-five miles north of the terminus. It was dark, it was cold, they were in a foreign country, and they all were quite nervous as they moved along. With the explosive packages left behind, the return trip would not be, in their minds, as difficult. While they had all trained for this mission in the winter in the Himalayas, it was, somehow, not the same, and they were all anxious to complete it and get back to the safety of the *Persian Desert*.

Junayd pulled off the road and took a small side road used for pipeline inspections and maintenance. He reached a small clearing where maintenance vehicles parked. No one was there. He parked under the trees and shut down the truck. They got out, removed their supplies, and began their work.

Junayd, moving closer to the actual pipeline, took a close look at one of the support stanchions. It was exactly as he had seen in the training camp and would not be difficult to destroy. It supported the forty-eight-inch pipeline and was designed to allow for lateral movement as temperatures changed. He took two of their explosive packages, set the lithium battery timer to go off exactly in two months at 10:00 p.m. local time, and strapped one to each leg of the support using plastic electrical ties. He then took a can of spray paint and sprayed several spots on the legs and on the package. When he was finished, it looked like someone had done some temporary corrosion control work, and the package had blended quite well to the support structure.

Moving down the line of support structures, they set explosives at four more of them, for a total of five. At sixty feet between normal supports, this would take out over three hundred feet of pipeline. A significant breach of the pipeline, and one that would take a while to repair. In the meantime, the pipeline would not be functional. Oil from the north would not be flowing, and just the news of the stoppage would cause major impacts at the gas stations and fuel depots of the Americans.

Having completed their task, they turned to the next effort: the return to their mini-sub without being detected. After cleaning up some of the packing materials they had used, and saving the paint cans, they repacked for the trek back to the mini. They had made good time and were still on schedule. Checking the phone map again, Junayd gathered Abdul and Jabbar, made sure there were no materials left to indicate that they had been there, and drove off. It was 1:00 a.m. and they should, barring any problems in the darkness, arrive back at the sub by 2:30 a.m. ... right on schedule.

The drive back was as uneventful as the one outbound. They had no interference from the very light traffic and, once again, skirted around the terminus facility. As he drove, Junayd mused to himself about how the Americans were so trusting and had not protected such a valuable resource. The mission had gone off without a single problem.

They located the pier as they had left it, parked the truck, transferred the packing material trash to the mini, and, after Junayd had powered up the mini-sub, Abdul and Jabbar disconnected the mooring lines and they reversed out. Junayd was ecstatic. They were a bit early. The mission had gone off without a hitch and they were on their way back with absolutely no problems. And the Americans were none the wiser!

Thanks be to Allah!

He backed out of the mooring point, turned around, and, once the water was deep enough, started the dive sequence again. The water was fairly shallow, so he stayed near the surface and navigated out. Anyone seeing them moving in the water, although unlikely at this early morning hour, would mistake them for some form of large marine life. Once he had reached deeper water, he took the sub down to the bottom and followed the bottom out on his preplanned course. Since the *Persian Desert* wasn't expecting them until a little later in the morning, Junayd piloted the sub out near the rendezvous point and settled it on the bottom to wait. He and his two men sat quietly as they reflected on a night's work well done. Each had his own feelings of satisfaction. They still had to place the explosives at the other two locations on the pipeline bridge some three hundred miles north of here, and that would take another week of effort in the near future, but a major task was completed tonight.

They waited until 4:00 a.m. and moved slowly to the nearby rendezvous point inside U.S. waters. They sent out a prearranged low-powered signal and were pleased to get a response almost immediately. The *Persian Desert* lowered four sensors into the water, and Junayd was able to line up on them and slowly bring the mini-sub into alignment with the trimaran's middle support structure, where the launch crew, reversing what they had done earlier, attached the lifting harness to the sub. The sub was then lifted up to the attachments for the middle pontoon and the mission was complete. A jubilant but tired Junayd departed the sub for a well-earned rest on board the *Persian Desert*. Abdul and Jabbar began assisting the maintenance crew with their resupply and recharging chores.

Junayd, relaxed and feeling very satisfied, headed up to the small conference room, where he met with Kadar. Junayd gave Kadar an informal briefing on the success of the effort, answered a few questions on placement and final location of the explosives, and received congratulations for a well carried out mission. He then retired to his small cabin for some rest.

Kadar put together a brief description of the mission and sent an encrypted satellite message off to the operations center at Socotra. He then directed his crew to head further out to sea for preparations on Phase II of the mission. He didn't want to remain in U.S. waters while he did more detailed planning for Phase II.

In spite of available funding, Kadar had one odd quirk in his planning activities. He intensely disliked computers, and thus his planning activities were documented in various paper formats. He felt it was much easier to see the whole picture of the mission when laid out in paper, and easier to find, and fix, planning shortfalls. Once he had his plans completed, he had them converted to a computer, but only because the operations center insisted on it, and because it was the only way to rapidly send the plans to the operations center for their approval.

After sending the message to the operations center, Kadar, watching the water pass as the ship proceeded on course in the cool evening air, stepped out on the center support structure and watched the sails billowing slightly in the soft breeze. They were using the sails to conserve the turbine fuel, and the sail efficiency was truly amazing. He looked off in the distance, looking at the lights along the Alaskan shore, and thought of the peacefulness of the evening. Thinking back, he realized how fortunate he was to be there, supporting the mission and Allah's desires.

He spent several minutes reflecting on his life so far. Born and raised in the southeastern Iranian deserts, his poor parents had taken him to the southern shores of Iran as part of their wanderings to find work, and he had become entranced with the endless waters of the Gulf of Oman. After finishing his basic schooling, he left home and, following his life's desires for the sea, enlisted in the Iranian Navy and became proficient in navigation and small ship handling. Impressed, his superiors continued to send him to more complex courses, and he became a real technical asset on the bridge of moderate-sized vessels.

After his enlistment was over, he departed the Iranian Navy and signed on with a Panamanian-registered cargo ship, spending seven years sailing the world's oceans and gaining his chief mate's license. He was highly respected for his work on the deck and bridge, and gained an excellent reputation. In his wanderings in his seventh year at sea, he discovered the New Persia movement through a concerned crewman. He, too, felt that there was too much waste in the world, and thought that many times their movement of cargo was just a waste of energy to satisfy some rich country's luxuries. Completely unnecessary.

Contacting the New Persia movement was actually not easy, as he soon found out. They were suspicious of someone at his level of experience and expertise, and it took several meetings with the assistant, Khatib, and their security director, Abdul-Hakim, to convince them that he was sincerely interested in contributing to the movement's mission. But convince them he did, and he joined their efforts. He had proven to be a very valuable addition to their core personnel.

And now, he was at the shores of Alaska, performing a key part in their mission goals. The ayatollah and Allah would be pleased. He thought for a few more minutes, then went back inside to the warmth of his cabin/office.

Kadar retired for several hours of rest as the *Persian Desert* moved out of Prince William Sound past Montague Island and into international waters in the Bay of Alaska.

The sabotage had been set and only required execution.

Chapter Nineteen
Pipeline Target

Friday—April 29
Valdez, Alaska

Bob got up early, as usual, and fixed a helping of eggs, ham, hash browns, and toast, and the usual strong black coffee. He always fixed a large breakfast, since it really got him starting out the day right. Several administrative chores in the office had interrupted his inspection schedule and he would be continuing his routine inspection of the pipeline today. He hoped to finish up his assigned sections by the end of the day. After completing breakfast, cleaning the kitchen, and getting himself a last cup of coffee and a thermos, he headed out to his truck, replenished his supplies from last week's repairs, checked in by radio with control, and headed out to the pipeline.

It was a cool morning; the sun was bright and the air was clear. Bob arrived at the pipeline at the point where he had finished up last Monday and did a quick check of his repair work. Satisfied that all was okay with the repairs, he notified control that he was beginning his route south again. Control gave him a "roger" and he was on his way. He couldn't see all the stanchions from the road and periodically stopped to check a series of them. At sixty feet between stanchions, there were over eighty of them for every mile, and it took some time. With their records of the stanchion inspection visits, they made sure they got to each one at least once annually. More frequently if they had problems or maintenance records indicated some special requirement.

Bob had lunch and pulled back onto the road to continue his inspections. So far, he had been lucky and the thirty-five stanchions he had looked at were all fine. Some minor corrosion that he took care of was the only repair needed. It was getting late in the afternoon as he pulled over into a small maintenance parking area for the next series of stanchions, and parked his truck. He notified control of his location and walked back to the first stanchion. Walking up to the concrete and steel structure, he noticed a bit of unauthorized spray paint on the legs, looked at his records for the stanchion, and noticed that there had been no repairs to the stanchion in several years. There shouldn't have been any spray paint unless vandals were at it again. But vandals wouldn't have just sprayed a few spots—they would have done a more "thorough" spray job.

He looked closer at the area and his brain couldn't believe what his eyes were telling him. Spray-painted wires, a boxlike thing a little bigger than a large matchbox, and some strange-looking lumps attached to the stanchions were obvious on closer inspection. He hesitated only a moment, as he registered what he thought he was seeing. He hesitated, looked again and stared for several more moments.

It was a ... bomb! Here in his section!

He backed away slowly and turned completely around, looking for anybody that might set it off while he was standing there. He didn't see anybody at all. Nobody in the trees and no one up or down the pipeline. At least that he could see. He continued to look around fearfully, but didn't see anyone as he ran back to the truck. By the time he reached it, he was breathless and breathing hard to catch up, even though it was just a hundred yards or so. It was a combination of fast running and serious emotional upset.

He took a few moments to calm down and catch his breath. Nothing had happened so far. Maybe he was just lucky. He nervously keyed the mike, called control, and said, "Control, we have an emergency. I'm at my first afternoon stanchion and I think there is a bomb attached to the support structure, repeat ... a bomb."

Dead silence from control. Finally: "Bob, did you say a bomb?" And then some hesitancy. "Come on now. You have a rough night last night?" All pretenses of call signs were gone. This was really serious.

Bob responded with some fear in his voice, "No, I'm not kidding. Get somebody out here to help. I have no idea what I'm dealing with and I'm not going anywhere near that stanchion. It's wired, and if it does go off, it'll be a real mess."

Control came back quickly with, "Ahh. Roger. We're contacting authorities now. Agree with you. Stay away from it but stand by for more traffic as we get a response going. And Bob ..." The dispatcher hesitated, and Bob could hear unintelligible conversations in the background on the still-keyed mike at control, then the dispatcher said, "Can you check the stanchions near this one to see if we have more than one?"

"Yeah. Sure. But I'm going to use my field glasses. This has me pretty nervous. But I'll look and get back to you."

"Thanks Bob. Stand by. We'll be getting a response team out to you from the company and the state as soon as we can."

Bob double-clicked his mike in response and dug though his stuff to find his field binoculars. He wasn't about to walk up to another stanchion until he was sure it was safe. None of them!

He found his field glasses and moved around a bush blocking his view of the next stanchion. He focused the field glasses on the base of the stanchion and slowly looked over the supports. He almost missed it. Again, he spotted some mismatched spray paint and, while from his distance could not make out much else, assumed that he had found another one. He couldn't believe his eyes. One minute his life was a calm business of inspection and maintenance and the next he had a possible national incident on his hands. "Man, what the shit!"

He made his way around the second stanchion and approached, from a reasonable distance, the third stanchion up the line. He was relieved to see that there didn't appear to be anything amiss at that one. But he wasn't going to get any closer to make sure. He moved back to the original stanchion and headed to the next one south of it. Again, to his dismay, he spotted the spray paint. He'd seen enough. Back at the truck, he radioed control.

"Control, Bob," he said with a still-shaky voice.

"Go ahead, Bob."

"Control, we have at least two more. Three total. And I'm not looking further. It looks like one to the north and one to the south. Where's that help?"

Control responded, "Okay, Bob. Thanks. Sounds like we have someone out there trying to cause us some real serious harm. Alaska Highway Patrol is on the way and we have an Army bomb disposal unit alerted at Fort Wainwright. They will be en route soon, after they get higher headquarters approval, but are a good six to seven hours away. Just stay away from the stanchions and wait there for help. We are also notifying the governor's office to see if they can help out. We may need National Guard support before this is all over."

"Thanks. I'll back off and stay put. I'd suggest we shut down the flow in this section. If that thing blows, we don't want more spillage than necessary."

"Okay. Good point. But the brass will have to make that decision. It is a huge cost to do that. We'll get back to you soon."

Bob, feeling a little more in control and relieved that help was on the way, backed his truck further out of the parking lot to put more space between himself and the bombs. Without knowing how they might be triggered, he didn't want to take any more chances. He had, unknowingly, approached them and not set them off, but wasn't about to take any more risks than necessary. And approaching darkness didn't help.

After thinking about it some more, Bob called in to control again. "Control, Bob."

An immediate response, not the usual delay: "Bob, control. Go ahead."

"It's getting dark out here now and there doesn't appear to be anyone around. Should I just stay put and wait or should I bail out of the area?"

"Stay put but back off a bit from the bomb locations. We don't want the area deserted. You will be able to guide the help, when it arrives, to the bomb locations so they aren't stumbling around in the dark."

"Roger that. Any idea when some help will get here?"

"Alaska State Patrol should be there any minute. The closest patrol was fifty miles away when we called. It's only been about an hour since you called it in and they are responding."

"Okay. Thanks. I've backed away and will stand by."

Bob heard a double click on the radio indicating they had heard him and agreed.

He looked around at the darkening area as night fell. It was quiet and he was finishing up the last of his thermos of coffee. What a day! And he was getting pretty tired with all the excitement and the tension that had happened. As he was thinking about the situation, he saw two state highway patrol cruisers rapidly approaching with full lights flashing. Looked like a parade. They turned off the main highway and pulled up next to him. He breathed a sigh of relief.

At least some of the cavalry had arrived.

Friday—April 29
Bay of Alaska

The trimaran was stationary in the water twenty miles off the southern coast of Alaska. Kadar was feeling quite satisfied with the progress of their mission on Wednesday. He had completed the first briefing to the ayatollah at the Socotra operations center and thought it had gone quite well. They had succeeded in getting the bombs in place and were now planning the next emplacement further up the pipeline. He was looking at a map of the pipeline and planning the tentative route in for the bomb placement when he was interrupted in his thoughts. The radio operator, responsible for monitoring the pipeline radio frequencies, came in and gave him the bad news. A maintenance inspector had found three of the bombs and there was a significant reaction going on right now to respond to the discovery. According to the radio, they were shutting down operations in that sector to minimize damage should the bombs go off.

Kadar was incredulous. They had just placed the bombs two days before and they had already been discovered! That meant the Americans were alerted to a threat and they would be checking the entire pipeline, plus increasing security at key points. And the Americans would be hunting for the people who had placed the bombs on the pipeline.

They would have to re-plan the whole operation and try to work around the increased security. It would be a lot tougher going than he had expected. And he had to notify the operations center of this situation, which he was very hesitant to do. The ayatollah would not be pleased. Before sending such a message, he had to come up with a plan to overcome this setback so there would be some mitigation to the situation.

Kadar looked at a map of the pipeline again and realized that, with over eight hundred miles to secure, there had to be some vulnerabilities, and he had to find them for Phase II of the mission. The Americans simply could not guard, literally, the whole pipeline. There had to be places where he could accomplish his mission. And accomplish it well. He had to find a way, and find it before he sent the message out to the operations center. In spite of the discovery by the Americans, he was determined to succeed, and wanted to send a message to the operations center with positive comments. Failure was not an option.

Much later that night, and after hours of study and effort by his whole team of experts, he thought he had a way out. A way to cripple the pipeline and put it out of action for perhaps weeks, if not months. It was risky, but the explosives necessary were with him, and with his plan, placing them would not be obvious to an inspection team. Hundreds of feet of pipeline could be taken out with just a few strokes. If it worked.

He was confident it would work and asked each of his team to be critical. He didn't want another failure. His team, after working out some more of the details, could not think of any failure models for the plan. They had reduced the risks down to almost nothing. Kadar sent them back to their quarters as he thought about it some more. It was a good plan.

Kadar then composed a message to the operations center explaining how the Americans had discovered the explosives on the stanchions and were now alerted to a threat. He didn't know if the Americans knew what the threat was, but they were now vigilant. He then outlined his plan for cutting the pipeline and taking it out of service for several months. He asked for approval. After reviewing the message several times, he sent it off.

Kadar went out into the quite cool ocean night and relaxed on the center structure of the trimaran. He liked this part of the ship, especially at night, because he could think in private and gather his thoughts of the day's activities. The coolness of the Bay of Alaska waters and night air was always refreshing, and it cleared his head. He did not anticipate any problem with acceptance of his plan, since it was so well thought out. And the ayatollah had a lot of faith in his capabilities.

The finding of the explosives by the Americans had just been a stroke of bad luck for his mission. There was no way he could have anticipated the situation. But these things did happen, and it was perhaps a fortunate event for them, because now they had an improved plan that might prove even more effective than the earlier plan. At least he hoped so. Smiling ruefully and shaking his head at the dynamic change of events over the day, he headed below to rest. Perhaps Allah was working in some strange way that he didn't understand. He hoped so.

The next morning, he heard from the operations center and was to proceed as he had suggested. They were disappointed in his "lack of progress" (interesting way of putting it!) but needed the pipeline put out of action. Proceed

111

at once and set an explosion to occur in two months. That would give New Persia time to warn the west of "dire consequences for not following the demands" of their group.

Kadar was not happy over the obvious implications that he had failed, but knew he had to succeed in the long run and that he needed to get moving to finalize his plan of action against the pipeline. He spent several hours reviewing, again, every aspect of entry, bomb placement and locations, and exit in his paper plans.

Kadar directed his communications technician to continuously monitor the American bomb response process. He had an idea … and wanted to know what the Americans were doing.

Finally satisfied that he had covered every aspect of the mission, he began to relax.

He called each of his team together and spelled out the details of the mission to take place within the next week. It would take several days to accomplish the mission once they started, and they needed to study the plan and make adjustments due to the increased security. They also now had to meet the mandate from the operations center to destroy the pipeline in two months.

They had their work cut out for them.

Chapter Twenty
Alaskan Blow-up

Friday—April 29
Alaska Pipeline

Bob was discussing the situation with Mark Blackwell, the Alaskan state trooper who had been detailed to support the removal of the bombs. Mark had arrived with several other troopers an hour after Bob had called the problem in, and cordoned off the area for several hundred yards around the known bombs. Even though darkness slowed them down, Bob and Mark carefully checked several more of the stanchions and came up with a final total of five stanchions that had suspicious wires and "packages" attached to their support structures. Five bombs! And they didn't know when they might go off or what might set them off. Control was notified, and Mark modified the cordon to include the total number of bombs and increased the distance. They stayed well back and waited for further directions. The U.S. Army was en route with a bomb disposal team. They were several hours away, and Bob, after consulting with control, agreed to stay with Mark and keep anyone away from the area.

It was getting late, and Bob and Mark were both getting hungry. Mark called over the junior patrolman in his group and convinced him to make a chow run. Bob felt a little embarrassed about it, but recognized the same basic process from his service days. They provided the patrolman with some additional personal funds and an order for food and an oversized coffee request. He took off, reminding them before he went that it would be a little while before he could get back. Bob and Mark both nodded and waved to him to get him moving on his mission of mercy.

An hour and a half later, the patrolman returned and they ate with gusto even though the food had become tepid. Fortunately, the coffee was still pretty hot.

One other "problem" occurred as they were discussing the situation. The media descended on them almost en masse. The major television stations out of Anchorage had sent in reporters. Since they all monitored the state police radio bands, they were aware of the highway patrol response to the bomb site. KTUU, KTBY, KTVA, and KYUR all had people and crews on site before the bomb squad from Fort Wainwright arrived. The patrol had to keep them back a good distance for their own safety. The various reporters were trying to get interviews with anyone they could find who looked remotely like they knew what was going on. It was a circus ... and not very pleasant. But they had no option but to put up with it. Part of the American way.

Bob, with Mark's agreement, went back to his truck, lay on the seat, and got a little bit of sleep. He was awoken by the sound of heavy trucks and other vehicles as the U.S. Army explosive disposal team arrived.

Saturday—April 30
Alaska Pipeline

Seven hours after receiving Pentagon approval, the U.S. Army explosive ordnance disposal team from Fort Wainwright, just outside of Fairbanks, arrived on site just after midnight, Saturday morning, and took over.

Much to Bob and Mark's relief!

They further expanded the cordoned-off area and set up a perimeter watch to make sure no one inadvertently entered the area. They also verified, through their command channels, that the pipeline had been shut down by the Alyeska Pipeline Service Company to minimize damage should the bombs go off. With them were two medic units, with three personnel in each unit should something unfortunate occur. Not wanting to take a chance in the darkness, they set up a watch for the rest of the night.

Later that morning, after sunrise, the bomb disposal team activated a small portable robot with manipulating arms and a stereoscopic camera. Developed several years earlier during and after the Mideast conflicts, these robots had saved many lives and were now in routine use in terrorist bomb situations. After looking the situation over from a respectable distance, the team remotely guided the robot toward the first stanchion with a bomb attached. Nothing happened. Kadar's group had set the bombs to go off in another two months, and the bombs were just sitting there ... biding their time.

Nothing happened as the robot approached the bomb. Nothing was really expected to happen. The team knew that Bob had inadvertently approached it and had not set off any action, so they assumed they could do the same. And the probability that it would go off just as they came up to it was pretty slim.

Through the robot's cameras they looked it over, without touching it, and recorded multiple images of it from different viewpoints. The images were transmitted back to a control point they had set up at the perimeter. At the control point, the disposal squad leader looked over the images and directed his team to return the robot to the control point. He wanted to get everyone's opinion before proceeding further. He now had an idea of what they were dealing with, and wanted confirmation from his team before they proceeded to disarm and remove the bomb. He was confident they could remove it but wanted to make very sure before taking action.

Bob maintained contact periodically with Alyeska control to make sure they were aware of what was happening. The control facility was, in turn, keeping the senior Alyeska Pipeline Service Company personnel informed of the progress. In addition, the Alyeska maintenance disaster team of technicians and engineers arrived with several large trucks with supplies and equipment should a major repair be required. For Bob, it was quite nerve-racking to sit on the side and wait for others to take action.

The EOD team, including the Alyeska maintenance team lead, reviewed the video images. After an explanation of how to proceed, the disposal squad leader radioed his brigade headquarters and requested permission to proceed. After some discussion and a review of the video in the headquarters, brigade agreed with the plan and the squad leader was directed to coordinate with Alyeska and go ahead.

Kadar and his team had made one fatal assumption in their planning for this bomb placement. They had assumed that the bombs would not be found and therefore did not set up any type of contingency for automatically setting them off if they were disturbed. They did have a manual provision, but not an automatic one. That was the factor that gave the bomb disposal squad leader so much confidence. He had seen from the video that the bombs were very simplistic devices and that they could be safely handled once they disabled the timers. But there was a catch. One that would prove costly. The manual backup.

The team members again directed the robot to approach the first bomb. It had been attached to the support structure with some simple plastic straps and a bit of heavy tape. The robot removed the tape with its manipulating arms and then removed the straps. Nothing happened. The robot then removed the plastic explosives and the timing unit from the stanchion and disconnected the unit from the detonators in the plastic. Nothing apparently happened, and they all breathed a sigh of relief.

They were wrong.

When the straps had been removed, a miniature transmitter under the plastic sent a signal into the air for anyone to receive. But it was Kadar and his men who were tuned to the frequency and received the disconnect signal. While there was no automatic detonation capability if the bombs were disturbed, they had preserved the capability to manually trigger the bombs if they needed to. Kadar and his men heard the signal, and Kadar, implementing his idea, directed his men to activate the contingency plan for the other bombs. After a few minutes, they sent a destruct signal to each of the other four bombs.

The U.S. Army team members were moving the robot back to the entry control point with the bomb materials in a safety casing when the world around them went crazy. At each of the other four stanchions, receivers on the devices picked up the destruct signal from Kadar's men, and, as designed, the circuitry activated the destruct mechanism. The bombs blew up. It was like a mortar attack. They totally destroyed the stanchions and the attached pipeline. Crude oil still in the pipeline went everywhere, and the immediate area was drenched in the messy black/brown crude. The internal pressure in the pipeline, thanks to the shutdown of the pipeline, was near zero, but there was *some* pressure, and this dissipated quickly as the oil sprayed over the nearby countryside. Pieces of pipeline and concrete from the stanchions acted like shrapnel, cutting through the air, taking out small trees and two men walking back to the control point. They were killed instantly in the explosive force. Two more of the disposal team members were slightly injured from the multiple concussions as the bombs went off. Several members were drenched in the crude as it sprayed out everywhere.

Bob and Mark were stunned. They were back at their vehicles when the bombs blew up. They involuntarily ducked as the miscellaneous debris items came flying. Parts of the stanchions, the pipeline, and the surrounding land were blown into the air, and several hundred barrels of crude oil sprayed out. Both were concerned that the team had met their fate and that they would need to get more medical help out there.

After a few moments, they determined that the medic teams were on it and treating the injured. The squad leader, fortunately, had set up the entry control point far enough away that no one at the control point was seriously hurt ... though a few eardrums were still ringing, and those soaked in the crude had to be processed by a decontamination team. A medivac helicopter was called in to remove the two dead soldiers and injured. Quite a mess.

A quick meeting at the control point with the team members, and the partially destroyed robot that had removed the bomb, revealed the small transmitter and what had probably happened. The squad leader was very angry about not noticing the transmitter before they began the disarming sequence—however, it had been well concealed. All four of the other bombs had gone off, and the initial assumption was that the local transmitter had caused it. And there had been a short timer sequence initiated when the straps were removed. No one even thought of the real sequence—that Kadar and his men had manually set off the other bombs—thus no one thought to search the land and ocean nearby for someone who might have set off the bombs. Kadar and his team were invisible and inadvertently successful.

The pipeline in this section had been disabled and the Americans were scrambling to get it fixed. A tough job. Monitoring the radio traffic, Kadar had verified the successful explosions on the pipeline. He had partially redeemed himself. He nodded to himself in satisfaction. Now he had to finish his tasking. He had to implement Phase II.

The disposal squad leader immediately contacted the brigade headquarters with a situation report. The headquarters had been monitoring the events through the telemetry from the robot, but could not see what happened to the rest of the pipeline when the explosives blew up. They forwarded the sitrep from the squad leader to U.S. Army headquarters in the

Pentagon. Due to the unusual nature of the event and the criticality of the pipeline, President Martinez was quickly briefed on the situation.

The Alyeska Pipeline Service Company, through their central control, which Bob had been working with, began an immediate repair and cleanup by the personnel and supplies out of Valdez, and also notified the EPA of the event. The personnel, repair equipment, and some supplies were on standby at the site in case a pipeline breach occurred. Given that over three hundred feet of pipeline were destroyed, they would have to reroute, slightly, a temporary pipeline with repairs until they could make a complete and final repair. A process that would take several weeks. But the temporary rerouting, using large high-pressure hoses and pieces of pipe, would only take a few days to accomplish.

Significantly less than what the New Persia Socotra operations center desired.

Saturday—April 30
Washington, D.C.

The president was in a Saturday meeting with his financial advisors when Jack Harrison was summoned out of the room. Admiral Watkins, who had been briefed by the Pentagon Situation Room, briefed Jack on the Alaska pipeline situation. Jack then returned to the financial meeting and whispered, in the president's ear, the news of the bomb damage and fatalities. The president sat up straight and whispered back to get as much info as possible, and they would discuss it after the meeting was over. Jack left and passed on the tasking to Admiral Watkins.

The president just shook his head silently and continued the meeting for another half-hour.

After the meeting, Admiral Watkins and Jack sat down with the president. The president turned to the admiral and said, "We were briefed this morning on the situation when they found the bombs. So what happened and where do we stand right now?"

Admiral Watkins gave him a quick rundown of the situation since the morning brief, and finished, "Unfortunately, two men were killed and several injured in the explosions. However, they are already making some repairs to the break in the pipeline and cleaning up the mess. Fortunately, the pipeline had been shut down and the damage to the environment is pretty minimal."

"Who did this? Do we know?" the president asked with a disgusted look. "Anyone take credit for it yet?"

The admiral responded, "No, sir. Not yet, but we have both Army and Air Force analysts working on it. They are looking at the area and what was within radio range of the explosives. Something set them off. Hopefully they will have some results in the next few days."

"I see. And I take it the pipeline is being inspected to make sure there are no more of these out there?"

"Yes, sir. Alyeska is conducting a complete physical look at the whole pipeline as we speak. The Alaska National Guard is helping in that effort."

"Okay. Keep me informed. I'll be interested in finding out who did this."

The president turned to Jack and said, "Draft a letter to the families of the men killed and injured. I want them to know that I, and the United States, care."

Jack nodded with a tightened jaw.

The meeting broke up. Admiral Watkins got on the phone to the Pentagon. He wanted updates every four hours, or if there were any more events, immediately.

Chapter Twenty-One
Overwater Bomb Placement

Sunday—May 1
Bay of Alaska

Kadar, realizing the pipeline had been crippled with the earlier attack, and after the message exchange with Socotra, made the decision to immediately begin the placement of bombs to take out portions of the pipeline that were supported by bridgeworks over waterways. This was Phase II of his planning. He just had to hurry it up a bit. After all, the operations center wanted the capability to blow up the bridgeworks in two months. He did not have a lot of time, and weather could always be a factor. He felt that he needed to act now.

He called Junayd and his small team of raiders together, along with his support staff, spelled out the detailed plans for them, and told them to be prepared to launch the following night. While in the *Persian Desert* conference room, he contacted his clandestine support at Valdez and asked for the truck to be fueled and ready to go by tomorrow evening. The bombs were to be assembled and loaded on the mini-sub, and the raiding team was to prepare for up to five days in the springtime Alaskan wilderness.

The same process they used the last time would be used to launch and recover them. Only the timing would be different. Since it was spring, darkness was retreating. They would depart the *Persian Desert* at 8:00 p.m. for Valdez, get the truck, transfer the bombs and their necessary equipment, and head north for close to three hundred miles, where their target was located. The target was a five-hundred-foot span of pipeline across open water and swampland. It was partially frozen and the ground was very dangerous at this time of year.

Monday—May 2
Bay of Alaska

The three-man raider team spent the next morning and early afternoon preparing for their mission into Alaska. The support staff made sure the mini-sub was equipped and fueled for the trip. The bombs were assembled and loaded on the mini-sub. The team loaded their gear, food and water supplies, and cool-weather camouflaged sleeping gear. Fortunately, they would be able to haul this gear in the truck and not have to carry it across the half-frozen tundra. In the late afternoon they rested, for the evening's effort would be significant.

As before, they gathered themselves at the mini just minutes before departure. They loaded themselves in and Junayd took over the controls. All was ready. The trimaran had quietly moved within a few miles of the coast, and the launch, as it was the last time, was successful. They were on their way. They found the same berth, moored the mini in the dark, transferred the materials to the truck, and were on their way north ... again. Only this time they had nearly three hundred miles to go. A credit card, with its associated codes, had been left in the truck for when they needed gas or other supplies. Droning northward over the road, they made reasonable time, and, as before, no one paid them any attention. Which was interesting to Junayd. Their earlier attack should have caused significant security increases. Where were the roadblocks and checkpoints with armed men? That was what he would expect to see in the Middle East. He thought about it. Perhaps the remoteness was the cause of the lack of apparent concern. Whatever the cause, he was glad for it.

The target was in the middle of nowhere. While the main road had been maintained, the distance back to the bridgework stations was close to half a mile, and they were going to have to hike back in over the unbroken tundra. Apparently this part of the pipeline was maintained using watercraft, since there was no trail or road that they could find back to the bridgeworks. The tundra was treacherous because the half-frozen water was never a sure thing. A person could break through and get soaked in the freezing water at any moment, and, while you wouldn't drown, you could die of hypothermia very quickly. They parked the truck on the side of the road out of sight as best they could, loaded up their small daypacks with the explosives, some water, and a few snack-type meals, and headed out. It was now 4:00 a.m., still very dark, and no one was around.

They were following a combination of compass readings and GPS signals. They were also treading very slowly across the tundra and some small forest clumps. None of them wanted to break through the muck. After a couple of detours caused by very unstable conditions, they emerged from a tree line, and finally reached the pipeline and turned north. They reached the first of the bridgeworks and could see in the distance some of the open water this pipeline bridge crossed. Taking the pipeline out in the spring, with the uncertain weather, would cause a major disruption in the pipeline deliveries. Because of the uncertain weather, it would be months before the Americans could get repairs done. Allah be praised!

They approached the bridgeworks and studied them for a minute. It looked like a normal, though narrow, bridge, and it just carried the single main forty-eight-inch pipeline with a maintenance and inspection catwalk alongside the pipe. At the support stanchion, there were some stairs, blocked with a locked gate that provided access to the catwalk. The locked gate gave way quickly and they moved up to the catwalk. The stanchion was significantly larger, since it supported the lengthy bridgework and would take larger charges to bring it down. But they had anticipated the stronger stanchion and were prepared for it.

Looking to the north, following the pipeline glowing in the moonlight, Junayd noticed a very bright light in the sky moving rapidly in their direction. He quickly realized that some form of airborne patrol was coming down the pipeline and scanning the line for anything unusual. He turned and hurriedly directed his men to get back down off the catwalk and under the pipeline. As they were rapidly doing this, they began to hear a thumping sound. It was a helicopter patrolling the pipeline and coming their way. They were able to get off the catwalk and hide under the pipeline as the ancient UH-1 U.S. Army National Guard helicopter went flashing by. At about one hundred knots of speed, it would take a pretty obvious problem to be noticed. Junayd shook his head as he realized this patrol would probably miss almost anything except a serious breach in the pipeline. They peered out from under the pipeline and watched as the helicopter, not straying from its course, disappeared to the south. They had not been seen. Their tracks, visible in the snow and muck leading into the tree line, were not seen by the patrolling helicopter. They could all calm down now and get back to their tasks.

They got back on the catwalk and, looking at the support structure, were analyzing how best to destroy it. It was a reinforced bridge structure with the crisscross steel beams on the side and a similar floor supporting the pipeline itself. He didn't know the terminology, but understood the strength of that structure. He decided to place the bombs at the juncture of the structure with the four oversized concrete stanchions and to blow all four of the structures at once. Combined with blowing the other end of the bridgework, which they would set tomorrow night, that would drop the entire five-hundred-foot section of pipeline out of alignment. That would fracture it, since it was not self-supporting, causing a huge oil spill into the water below. Convinced he was right, they set the charges, placing double charges on all of the points to make sure the bridge would fall. Looking out from the catwalk to the tundra, he had a moment of wistfulness realizing that in a couple of months this area would be an environmental disaster area. It was sad, but necessary.

Then he remembered. Today was May the 2nd. Two months would be July 4th. How fitting, and praise Allah! He was smiling slightly as they finished placing the charges, making sure they were not visible from the sky above, adding a little spray paint to help conceal the charges, and got off the catwalk. They put the gate back into position, made the lock appear okay, and began slogging back to their truck. It had been an interesting and educational night.

They would now find a hidden area, park the truck, and spend the rest of the daytime resting and sleeping. One of them was always on guard, even though they were off the beaten path. It was still spring, and someone might be able to pick up their tracks, if they were interested. There were several flights by helicopters, both commercial and military during the day, as patrols were obviously looking for problem areas. But nothing came of it. They spent a quiet day, had some warmed-up food, some heavy Arabian coffee, and spent most of the day sleeping.

That night, again beginning around 7:00 p.m. and in darkness, they headed out in the truck for the other side of the waterway so they could access the other end of the bridgeworks. They did not run into the problems of soft ground and were able to hike back in to the support stanchions with no difficulty. It was a duplicate of the other end. They placed the charges on the stanchions and the bridgeworks as they had the previous night. They again avoided a helicopter patrol. It all went well, and they were back at the truck within a few hours.

Both sets of bombs were set to go off simultaneously two months from now.

Now Junayd had a decision to make. It was quite late, and if they hit the highway heading south, they might be spotted by the highway patrol and pulled over as being suspicious. Especially since the bombs had been discovered further south. The authorities would be a bit jumpy. But if he waited until early morning, they would be less suspicious appearing because they could be just a group of roughnecks heading to work. They had plenty of time, because they had up to five days to complete the mission. They had done it in about two and a half days. And with no problems. He thought about it for a few minutes and decided to stay put in the hidden truck for several hours. Then they would head south, gas up wherever they could, and keep going back to Valdez.

It was close to 11:00 a.m. when they decided to leave their hidden spot. It was broad daylight for that time of the year, and they felt confident that they could get back without interference. With a spotter on the road to make sure nobody was coming, they pulled out of their covered hiding place, picked up the spotter, and headed south at a reasonable speed. They didn't want to attract any attention to themselves. And they didn't.

They were able to gas up about a hundred miles south, got a couple of soft drinks, and continued on to Valdez, arriving close to 8:00 p.m. They located the berth, transferred some of their supplies, parked the truck, fired up the mini-sub, and pretty much, in the darkness, repeated what they had done during the previous mission. It was a successful mission even with the increased security measures, such as they were, applied by the infidels. The security increases had proven very ineffective. Just a foolish waste of manpower.

After the team arrived back on the *Persian Desert*, Junayd gave Kadar an informal debrief of what they had done, the close call of the first helicopter patrol, and the final placement of the explosives. It had been a very successful mission. Kadar was quite pleased with the results. He developed a message to the operations center telling them of the success and that they could warn the west as they desired.

They had succeeded in temporarily crippling the pipeline with the manual triggering of the first set of bombs. In two months, the pipeline would really be down, and down for the count. Out for probably several months. They had done a wonderful job.

Allah, and the ayatollah, would be pleased.

Chapter Twenty-Two
American Petroleum Institute

Monday—May 9
Mobile, Alabama

The American Petroleum Institute (API) planned a meeting at their headquarters in Mobile, Alabama for the week of May 9th. This group was a lobbying organization for the oil industry within Texas, Louisiana, Alabama, and Mississippi, along with other areas, and had made significant contributions to the various senators and congressmen from their respective districts. It was a powerful organization in that part of the country.

Each of the congressional representatives had been invited to this meeting and none had turned the invitations down. They knew that to do so would be to risk future contributions to their campaigns and the potential for not succeeding in the next election. And any politician will tell you that they simply cannot afford to risk non-election. After all, a politician who is not in office has a significant problem with influence and cannot impose his will upon others. And, on top of it all, there are the perks!

Senator Jim McIlroy was walking down the hall of the API building to attend the meeting. He was accompanied by Senator Bob Jackson of Louisiana and Senator Charles Sebastian of Mississippi. They were not in a good mood. They had been briefed a few months earlier that the strike on the stronghold in Iran had not succeeded in killing the ayatollah, the mastermind behind the New Persia movement. On top of that, speculation was rampant in Congress that the New Persia group was responsible for the recent Alaskan pipeline bombing. Congressmen directly associated with the oil industry were in a grim mood.

The three senators headed into the conference room and were met by the rest of the congressional delegation from each of the affected states, along with the API leadership. In addition, several of the more senior congressional staffers were there to bolster their interests and to provide more expertise should it be required. The inevitable side conversations were being conducted with few, if any, reasonable conclusions drawn. The ayatollah had escaped; they knew that. And the Alaskan pipeline bombing was being blamed, at least in private conversations, on the New Persia group. They were immersed in speculation but had no real facts. However, they were enjoying the coffee and pastries that were a fixture in these types of meetings. As a result of the conversations, there was a general consensus, within the congressional delegation, that the oil lobby folks needed to come up with a briefing and explain what was happening, from their perspective, and explain what they wanted from the congressional delegation.

Jack Findley, a portly man of almost three hundred pounds with nearly pure white, close-cut hair, the head of the API, spoke above the voices in the room and asked all to take their seats so the meeting could get underway. After people had found their seats and settled in for a moment, he thanked the various members of the delegation for being present and explained the agenda. He introduced Mr. Patrick Nelson, who would begin the activities with an overview of the situation as the API viewed it. After the short presentation there would follow a general discussion of what course of action might be followed, and then a short recess to conduct private conversations. This would be followed with a reconvening and further refinement of what might be done about the situation.

He then concluded, "Gentlemen. We have a situation within our industry that is giving us a great deal of concern. Concern for our country and concern for our economy. And we see no action being taken by our government in Washington to correct the problem. That situation is, in a nutshell, a rogue group in the Middle East trying to blackmail this country, and the rest of the western world, into submitting to their ridiculous demands. The strike we conducted several months ago apparently failed to achieve all of its goals, and they may be ready, again, to begin their blackmailing activities. As I outlined a moment ago, Pat will give a presentation, we will have some discussion and time to organize, then we need a plan of action to get the administration to confront this terrorist group with additional decisive actions. When this day is done, we need to have an action plan to quash this terrorist group." He looked around and said, "Pat, your presentation, please."

127

Senator McIlroy interrupted at this point and said, "Hold up a minute. I want to point out that the government is, in fact, taking action. It just isn't obvious at this point, but action is being taken. After thirty-three years in the Senate, I can assure you that there are times when things must be done quietly and without fanfare. I want to hear your presentation and assist in developing an advisory for the administration, but I don't want to get into an environment of threats or coercion. We need a cohesive face from this group, not a bunch of vigilantes working on their own agenda." With that, he motioned with his hands for Pat to start the presentation.

Jack, nodding at Pat, sat back and thought for a few minutes as the presentation was started. He didn't care for this attitude on the part of Senator McIlroy, and some of Jack's fire had been dampened. The senator, with his long service in the government, would be very difficult to manipulate in the way they required, in spite of the implied threats to his campaign coffers. But they needed to get this menace finally stopped, and they needed to satisfy their oil-producing members, or, from a personal standpoint, he might be out of his lucrative position.

Pat went through his presentation, outlining the reasons for the strike in Iran that was supposed to finish off the New Persia movement, showing some of the video from the strike. He then provided some history regarding the production wells that had been affected by New Persia, and even had some photos of the Gulf of Mexico underwater mission Ryan and Dave had nearly died on. He also had some grainy underwater photos taken of the New Persia mini-sub. Those pictures were new to several in the congressional group, as they had not been in on the briefing given by the president on the current situation. Pat also went through some of the protective security measures they had taken, to include many camera installations at suspected wells. Until the New Persia-installed diversion valves could be removed from the affected wells, they weren't taking chances. He explained how the monitoring was still being accomplished, and that, while they had not seen a sub since the one that had been captured, they were still on the lookout for any future menace that might show up. It had happened once and it might happen again. But it pointed out the need to be prepared to disrupt the New Persia activities, and they needed to figure out how to do that.

After his presentation was finished, Pat turned the meeting back over to Jack.

Jack looked around the room, taking in the powerful congressional delegation that was present, along with various congressional staff people, many of whom were many nearly as powerful as the congressmen. He cleared his throat and began to speak. "All of you have benefited from a very cordial relationship with us in the past. Believe me, we want to continue that relationship, and are asking for your help in this matter. At this point we do not know what else the ayatollah may do. He may strike back at us directly or he may do something clandestine. But whatever he decides to do, we need to be prepared to deal with it. The main purpose of this meeting is to make sure you are all aware of the potential threat and that you have our backing in countering whatever happens. After all, it is all of our jobs and way of life on the line, not to mention the economy of the U.S."

Senator McIlroy just nodded, acknowledging the comments. He looked at his colleagues for affirmation, receiving a series of nods.

Jack then went through a list of actions that API had put together. They were:

1. *Locate the whereabouts of the ayatollah and his team*
2. *Capture the ayatollah and leading team members … they are considered international criminals*
3. *Continue to remove the diversion valves from affected wells*
4. *Use U.S. Navy divers to help with the diversion valve removal effort*
5. *Increase the patrols of the Alaskan pipeline*
6. *Begin security patrols of the Keystone pipeline*
7. *Increase company security on land-based wells*
8. *Alert/increase petroleum reserve security*

Jack went through each one of the suggested actions and said there may be others as the meeting progressed, but that this was a starting point for people to consider. As he went through the list, there were a few questions asked, but, for the most part, the list was pretty self-explanatory. He finished up the discussion and they broke off for the day to confer and caucus.

The more senior staffers got their heads together in the hallway and, along with the senators and congressmen, split up into several working groups and set an agenda for the rest of the day. In all cases, email and the telephones were used to connect with various contacts in Washington to try to determine what was really going on. They needed information on the current administration actions, and they needed it yesterday.

In the process of trying to find out what the administration was doing regarding this situation, several of the senior staffers well known to Jack Harrison tried to reach him. He ignored the calls until he realized there were quite a few from senior congressional aides. Taking a call from Bob Jackson's chief of staff, he concurred that multiple actions were underway. He was informed of the meeting and he requested any results be forwarded to him. He would then discuss the results with the president and get back to the senior congressional leadership.

Several other experienced staffers began calling their contacts in various administration offices. Through this process they were able to find out several of the actions underway and discovered that some of them duplicated what the API had come up with. The administration was, in fact, taking several quiet actions to solve the problem. The petroleum reserve security had been beefed up and several of the petroleum companies had increased their security patrols. The Air National Guard in Alaska was assisting with increased patrols of the pipeline. And, most important, there was a significant effort by several different agencies to locate the ayatollah. Once located, it was up to the president to decide a course of action.

However, not all the actions suggested in the API briefings were being accomplished, and the consensus was that the suggestions, as already compiled, should go over to the White House. That would also satisfy Jack Harrison's request for the results of the meeting.

The bottom-line impression gained from the information available to the various staffers was that the situation was serious and the administration was taking some action, but not really enough.

After conferring with members of the administration, and finding out most of the actions that were underway, the congressional panels met late in the afternoon at the API headquarters facility. They worked into the early evening, modifying the list of suggested actions for the administration to take in confronting the New Persia problem. There was general agreement to send the list API had developed without deleting any items. An additional item was added recommending that each of the oil industry companies increase their checks of the various pumping stations, transfer points, and storage facilities to make sure nothing was missed. With over fifty thousand miles of pipeline in the U.S. it would be a daunting task, but one that needed to be done to ensure security.

The next day, they all met again, finalized the letter to the administration under API letterhead, and Jack Findley forwarded it over to Jack Harrison for consideration and discussion with the president.

Their inputs would be considered.

Chapter Twenty-Three
Presidential Staff Follow-up

Wednesday—May 11
Washington, D.C.

The president called Mark Allison and asked him to come over to discuss some possibilities with the New Persia movement problem. In his early forties, and with a U.S. Army intelligence background, Mark was a moderate five foot ten and 180 pounds, with a military-style short haircut and firm, square jaw. Mark was a sharp, analytical person and had been instrumental in several past instances of resolving sticky issues. He had been a member of the president's election campaign council and was now in charge of the CIA. If anyone could help, he would be it.

Mark showed up and was shown into the Oval Office by Maria. He casually helped himself to a cup of coffee that was always available, shook hands with the president, and sat down across from the president's desk. He took a sip of the coffee and looked over at the president with a questioning look.

The president looked back and said, "Mark. We need to find out where the ayatollah and his gang have gone. We need to get in front of this, try to anticipate what they may be up to, and head it off. Outside of the group-grope we had last month, do you have any ideas?"

Mark studied his coffee for a moment and then replied, "There are a couple of possibilities that I can think of right off the bat." He hesitated for a moment, gathering his thoughts, then said, "The ayatollah was apparently picked up from a harbor in the Gulf of Oman. He was transported somewhere and is holed up. He is licking his wounds and getting prepared for some form of comeback. At least that's what we think at this point. He is too determined an individual to just go away."

The president thoughtfully put his left hand on his chin and nodded.

Mark continued, "We don't know where he went, and the yacht we think he took is worldwide capable. We did look at the wide-range satellite view but could see nothing indicating his departure or course. He could be anywhere. But, and this is a questionable assumption, he would probably stay in that part of the world. His support base and religious base is there. It wouldn't make any sense for him to go to, say, Australia or New Zealand. He wouldn't be welcome there, and the governments would not be friendly to his movement. So, assuming he stayed in the general area of the Middle East, where would he likely be?"

The president, sitting back in his chair said with a rueful smile, "That's my question."

Mark nodded and continued, "I think we need to continue to monitor the communications links in the Middle East for traffic that he might originate. It isn't easy, but there are some routine lines of traffic that we see all the time on the satellites. Mike Detirro referred to that traffic during the meeting. I think we can look at the overall traffic flow and see if we can spot any significant changes over the past few months. If so, maybe we can pinpoint a location. It will be very time-consuming and hard to do, but it is possible. And we've noticed a drop-off in apparent courier traffic. We think they are using comm links again. Our guess is that they've discovered that couriers are just too unwieldy and slow."

The president again put his hand on his chin and thoughtfully nodded. "If we limit our monitoring to the Middle East, the chore becomes much easier. What about State keeping an ear to the ground on possible locations?"

"We're already doing that in both the CIA and at State. When this first came up a few days ago, Kenton and I got together and decided it would be a good idea to see what we could find out in the rumor realm. Unfortunately, so far there hasn't been much activity. But it is still early and something may develop. I can't believe an organization of two to three thousand people can be totally quiet for very long. People talk. Something will give."

The president said, "Okay. I agree. Can you arrange to get the satellite monitoring in place?"

"Already underway. After the meeting the other day, I got with Mike and we coordinated on it. I authorized the slight change in satellite coverage to be able to monitor that entire area. It will take a few days to establish what is actually normal in those areas where we weren't monitoring, and then we can look at abnormal traffic." He hesitated for a moment then continued, "I'm also getting a couple of analysts to look at the area and see where he might have gone. The end result, though, may very well have to be a wait on our part, until he makes some form of move and reveals his location." He raised both hands in minor frustration as he said, "Until then, we may not be able to get ahead of this."

The president looked at Mark for just a moment then looked away. "I can't disagree with what you have said, but I'm afraid the first we may know of his activities will be when he strikes someplace else. The pipeline could be an opening shot, with more to follow." He looked directly at Mark and continued, "And that someplace will be American, because of a retaliation for the B-52 strike. How do we protect from that?"

Mark looked back and said, "I don't know. Hopefully, he will give away his location first. However, he is focused on our, and the world's, oil supplies and trading networks. His attempts to reduce the overall oil use, and especially the exports from the Middle East, may be a hint for our security emphasis. I think the Alaskan pipeline incident is part of his planning to hurt and reduce our oil usage. We need to beef up our patrols on all our pipelines and get the oil companies to do the same on their facilities."

The president, contemplatively looking at the floor, said, "Yes. Hopefully." Then he looked over at Mark and said, "Thanks for the help and your thoughts. I think they are quite good." He stood. "And we need to keep our ears to the ground and see if we can ferret out this menace."

With that, they shook hands again and the president escorted Mark to the door.

Jack Harrison walked into the Oval Office. The president said, "Ahh. Jack. I asked you to come in. We need to increase our oil systems security and get the big companies to do the same. Any suggestions?"

Jack sat down and thought for a few moments. "The Alaskan Air National Guard, at Governor Mantis's direction, started patrols about two weeks ago. So that's already underway. I think we can task the Army and Air Force to increase the patrols over the Alaskan and Keystone pipelines. But I would suggest that both pipeline companies be asked to do a thorough inspection, meaning every foot, of their pipelines. They may find something not visible from the air. Then we can go from there."

"Sounds good to me. Work with Mike in Defense and get with API to see if they can help."

Jack pursed his lips, pondered that comment for a moment, smiled slightly, and said, "Well, sir. Funny you should mention that. API is meeting right now down in Mobile, and, from some of my sources in the congressional staff, coming up with some suggestions for handling the New Persia situation."

The president tilted back in his chair, put his hands behind his head, and smiled slightly. "What do you mean? What kind of suggestions?"

"Actually, I think we have most of them covered, but I thought I'd wait until they send them over in a few days and see what they come up with. They might have something new we could agree with. If that happens, we could go along with it and make them feel more comfortable that they contributed. It's a Republican group, and we could play the cooperation card on them. Kind of a bipartisan effort. Since they are doing this, and we are already taking most of the actions, it would be tough for them to attack us on their own suggestions."

The president smiled. "Okay. Let's get the Army moving over the Keystone and wait to see what the API group comes up with. Could be interesting."

Jack nodded and smiled as he departed the office.

The next morning the letter from API arrived in Jack Harrison's email box. Jack looked the letter over, noted the twenty or so signatures, and slowly shook his head. With the exception of two of the API items, they were already either doing the task or, in the case of finding the ayatollah, working on it. Use of U.S. Navy divers for commercial work was not viable and might not be legal, and they would go ahead and implement the suggestion to check, through the industry, the rest of the system-level pipelines. Otherwise, they were already performing the rest of the API suggestions.

Jack took the letter in to the president and briefed him. The president then agreed that Jack would write a short note back to the API basically stating that all the actions had been considered and appropriate actions were underway. And that would, hopefully, end that correspondence trail.

API had wasted two days of the congressional delegation's time. But given the quasi-party atmosphere of the meeting, perhaps the delegates didn't realize that.

Chapter Twenty-Four
Trimaran Capture

Monday—May 16
Bay of Alaska

Quietly cruising slowly in an erratic circular pattern a few miles off the southern coast of Alaska, just south of Valdez and in international waters, the large foreign-registered trimaran was monitoring radio traffic from the damaged portion of the Alaskan pipeline. A little over two weeks earlier they had succeeded in destroying a portion of the pipe just north of Valdez, and were monitoring the ongoing repair activities. As part of their overall program to disrupt the U.S. oil supply, they had finished setting the explosives three hundred miles north of Valdez over a section of over-water and swampland pipeline. The explosives were set to go off in two months—coincidentally, on the 4th of July. This would cause a significant and severe disruption in the pipeline and carry on with the ayatollah's mission and goals.

Kadar and his crew had been requested by the operations center to remain on station monitoring the Americans while the New Persia managers determined the next world contact. They could possibly be tasked to perform additional missions on the west coast of America. Refineries and port facilities in California were a possible target.

Friday—May 20
Washington, D.C.

Tasking had been received from the White House down through military and Treasury Department channels. The trimaran's activities were now being watched by U.S. Coast Guard and U.S. Air Force monitoring capabilities. After analyzing the events leading up to the pipeline destruction near Valdez, Alaskan state and U.S. military analysts concluded that the placement of the bombs and the signal necessary to set them off had to have come from a source relatively close to the pipeline. The bombs had limited transmission capabilities. They could only signal that they had been disturbed. They had

136

no self-destruct command capability. Therefore, the command to self-destruct had to originate elsewhere, which set the analysts off on a hunt for that source.

A fifty-mile radius circle had been drawn on a map around the site, and intense analysis done on this area. Satellite surveillance photos, taken by the U.S. Air Force immediately after the damage occurred, revealed several ships in the Bay of Alaska within that fifty-mile circle. All of the ships were eliminated from consideration by analysts—except this one expensive, elaborate, and very large trimaran. The trimaran was not outwardly elaborate, but from the antenna array on its masts and other locations, and apparent communications capabilities, it was obviously technologically elaborate. Signal analysis was performed by the U.S. Air Force and the messages coming from and going to the trimaran were from the Middle East. The specific location in the Middle East could not be determined. But with that intelligence information, the U.S. Coast Guard station in Anchorage prepared to take action.

Planning information was sent to U.S. Coast Guard headquarters in Washington for approval of the proposed actions. Since the trimaran was outside the twelve-mile territorial limits, coordination with the Department of State was initiated and the White House was also informed.

Discussions were held with President Martinez and, with Ryan and his team present, the final resolution was to go ahead with the stop-and-board plan. Ryan was able to give them some of the details from his time capturing the Gulf of Mexico yacht. Jasper was flying to Anchorage to observe the mission as the president's representative and, in no small part, because of his interest in seeing this New Persia group stopped. He was well acquainted with the planning process. He would accompany the boarding team to observe, firsthand, what these terrorists were like. Coordination through the State Department was also accomplished in notifying the Canadian government of what was about to happen. The potential for a run to a Canadian port had to be considered. Thus Canada was brought in on the planning.

After all had concurred, the president sent his approval for the proposed action, and final plans were initiated in Anchorage aboard the Coast Guard cutter *Jefferson Davis*. This cutter, 325 feet long, and carrying an impressive weapon arsenal, was state of the art. Capable of nearly thirty-five knots, it could outrun and outgun most legal civilian ships of its size. They also were aware of the hydrofoils on the Gulf of Mexico yacht, and made preparations to counter any potential high-speed move by the trimaran.

Saturday—May 21
Bay of Alaska

Jasper arrived in Anchorage and was fitted out by the local Coast Guard in a matching boarding party outfit. The dark blue/green overalls, with a weapons belt containing a Glock 9mm pistol, and lightweight combat boots, blended in with the Coast Guard boarding personnel. After being fitted out, he joined the rest of the team on board the *Jefferson Davis*. Fully armed and prepared for action, the cutter headed out to the trimaran's constantly changing position. As they approached the trimaran, the *Jefferson Davis* commander, Lieutenant Commander Caleb Billings, called CB by his peers in the Coast Guard, realized just how big a ship it was. He estimated it at well over two hundred feet overall length, with very sophisticated electronics. The antenna array was very impressive. The gray of its hulls blended well with the water, and, judging from the bow wake, it was moving briskly through the water.

The trimaran's bridge crew noticed the approaching cutter, but since they had seen these cutters before, they were not concerned, and ignored it. Approaching the unsuspecting trimaran, the cutter hailed them over the radio and also over the loud hailer from the cutter's bridge. Kadar, concentrating on another review of the plan for exploding the over-water pipeline devices, was startled by the calls from the cutter. Realizing that they were caught on the high seas, Kadar protested the cutter's actions over the radio and got a repeat demand to heave to and prepare for boarding. Noticing the cutter's obvious combat capability, he saw no option other than trying to outrun it. He notified the engine rooms to stand by for a maximum effort from the turbines.

As he considered this option, two U.S. Air Force F-22 fighters flew low past him on his port side, climbed up to several thousand feet, and began to circle around for another pass. It was an obvious, and effective, show of force. There was no way he would be able to outrun those fighters. He directed his bridge crew to send a message to the cutter agreeing to be boarded, and directed another message be sent immediately to the operations center telling them what was happening. The engine rooms were then directed to stand down. He began to destroy his planning documentation.

Commander Billings, in concert with the boarding party leader, Ensign Conroy Michaels, radioed back to Anchorage their exact position and that they were boarding the trimaran. From Anchorage they received a short and simple "roger."

The trimaran slowed to a halt and lowered a boarding ladder. The heavily armed twelve-man boarding party, led by Michaels and including Jasper, approached and tied up to the impressive sailing vessel. They scrambled up the ladder, leaving two members aboard the boarding boats. The trimaran was boarded without incident. After some initial verbal resistance, the party split into three groups. One three-man group plus Ensign Michaels headed for the bridge, while the second and third groups went into each of the trimaran's hulls below decks. Jasper went to the bridge with Ensign Michaels, since that was where he expected to find any documents regarding terrorist actions.

As Ensign Michaels approached the yacht's bridge with three of his heavily armed seamen, Kadar stopped his destruction of the plans, stepped out, and stopped the ensign with a hand to the ensign's chest. "How dare you board my boat?" he said with a raising voice. "We are in international waters and you have no right to do this. We are doing no harm and you are violating international treaties through your actions." He glared at the young ensign. Ensign Michaels directed his men, and Jasper, past Kadar to finish searching the bridge, and turned to Kadar.

He slapped Kadar's hand away from his chest. At six foot and two hundred pounds, he was eye to eye with Kadar, and heavier. Glaring right back, he said, "We have direction from our authorities to board your boat. We suspect you are involved in the recent pipeline sabotage and intend to find out if it's a valid suspicion. I would appreciate your full cooperation, but if I don't get it, will still complete our mission and search this boat completely. Am I clear ... *sir*?"

Kadar grimly nodded in acquiescence. There wasn't much choice.

A voice crackled over the ensign's headset. "Sir. Seaman Yauch, Team One. We've found some interesting documents here on the bridge. One of the crew was destroying them, but I think we got a good part of them. You might want to take a look-see."

"Roger. I'll be there in a minute," replied Michaels. He turned to Kadar and said, "Why would your crew be destroying documents if you are, as you say, just an innocent boat here in the gulf? Something's not right, and I intend to find out what."

On the bridge, Jasper and the team had found Kadar's schemes and parts of his plans for more damage to the pipeline. They had interrupted his attempts to shred the plan documents, as it had only been about ten minutes since they first hailed the sailing vessel, and saved a lot of the paperwork. Included was a map of the explosive locations and the radio frequencies for detonation. Jasper was astounded at the detailed plans. What he had found just confirmed to him that this outfit needed to be stopped, and soon.

Ensign Michaels sent copies of the plans back to the *Jefferson Davis* by courier. After reviewing the plan documents, and realizing the significance they contained, Commander Billings sent a message to Anchorage headquarters giving the location of the over-water explosives that had been placed on the Alaska pipeline.

While reviewing some of the documents, Ensign Michael's headset crackled again. "Sir, Team Two. This boat sure isn't what it appears. We've found a mini-sub as the middle pontoon of the trimaran. I think you need to have a look. It's quite interesting."

Upon hearing this, Jasper turned around and took off running. He headed down through a passageway for the middle pontoon of the trimaran. His pulse was really up and the adrenalin was running. He might actually be able to see, for real, one of these operational mini-subs at sea.

While Jasper headed out for the middle pontoon, Ensign Michaels responded, "Roger Two. I'll be down in a few minutes. Make sure you secure the whole area and get all personnel rounded up and in a central location. I'll be back to you shortly." He received a double click in response and changed channels.

"Checker, Invader. Do you copy?"

From the cutter: "Invader, Checker, status?"

"Checker, need ten more personnel to assist with security. Also send analysts for communications setup. We've struck pay dirt and need to see how rich the mother lode is."

Michaels was referring to the communications center capabilities.

"Roger, Invader. Backup team en route in five."

Ensign Michaels then left the bridge and proceeded, with Kadar, down to the center of the trimaran. Coming through the passageway hatch, Ensign Michaels was stunned at the sight. The sophisticated mini-sub, support equipment, cranes, sensors, and other pieces of underwater support gear were a sight to behold. He joined Jasper standing in a combination of awe and admiration. This operation was so well thought out, and financed, that it really drove home how dangerous these people were.

Recovering from his surprise, Michaels keyed his microphone and said, "Team Two, what's your exact location and status?"

Team Two lead responded, "To your left. We're in a small planning room with fifteen detainees. All's secure." Michaels noted that Team Two lead did not use the term *prisoner*.

Michaels quickly located them, provided some instructions, and told his team that backup was on the way. Then he told Team Two lead, "Once backup arrives, I want you to search every inch of this boat. We may have some bad guys hiding out somewhere. Got it?"

Team Two lead Kelly Marcus gave him a thumbs-up and turned back to his chores with the detainees. A minute or two later, Kelly Marcus' head snapped around at a sound they all recognized. They heard a short burst of automatic weapons fire from down below in the left pontoon.

Michaels then keyed his mike again. "Team Three, team lead. Status?"

Team Three came back with, "Stand by. Got some trouble."

A short time later there was a single shot heard and then feet running rapidly down a passageway. Team Three came back with, "Team lead, Team Three. Left pontoon secured. One bad guy splashed. One guard wounded. Request immediate medic assistance."

"Roger. Medic on the way." And the ensign motioned for the medic to move out fast. He was already running for the pontoon.

A moment later, across the net came, "Team lead, Team Three. Pontoons secure and personnel being handed over to Team Two for holding. Medic treating wounded seaman.

Outboard pontoons are engine rooms and living quarters. Engines are interesting. Very powerful turbines. Left pontoon turbine was damaged in the gunfire. It's out of commission. This vessel is not what it seems. Over."

"Roger, Team Three. Hold positions."

Again a double click was heard over the net.

Michaels then turned to Kadar, who was furious over this boarding and searching situation. Michaels said, "I don't know what is going on here, but we have some people on the way who can figure it out. This certainly is not a pleasure boat. Armed people on board, and now we have to deal with casualties. We are placing you and your vessel under arrest and will be taking you to Anchorage for further investigation. I don't want any more resistance, and will deal with it severely if it occurs." And with further emphasis, he continued, "Do I make myself clear? Absolutely clear?"

Kadar just glared back at the young ensign. He didn't respond to the question.

The backup team arrived and were given a short situational briefing. The communications analyst went below to the control center and began taking notes on a notebook computer. Within a short period he was amazed at the sophistication, specifically the satellite communication burst capabilities.

Ensign Michaels, accompanied by Jasper and the wounded seaman, then proceeded back to the cutter and gave Commander Billings a short brief on what the team had found. A follow-up message was sent to Anchorage with news that they were impounding the boat, arresting the crew, and escorting it back to Anchorage for further investigation.

Under armed guard, the boat's crew was then ordered to proceed to Anchorage followed by the cutter. While en route, the cutter sent a flash message back to Washington Coast Guard headquarters outlining what had been discovered and where they were going. They also requested further instructions.

When word reached the president, through Admiral Watkins, he was ecstatic. He sent word back of congratulations to Jasper and the team, and, in a more somber tone, asked the State Department to prepare for some additional international protests.

Jasper continued with the Coast Guard cutter as it made its way back to Anchorage. He reviewed many of the captured documents so he would be better prepared to deal with these idiots. When he arrived, he spent the night and took a Gulfstream V C-37 back to Washington the next morning. He wanted to get with Ryan and the president as soon as possible and see what the next steps might be.

He was not disappointed.

Sunday—May 22
Alaska

As a result of the finds, the Coast Guard station notified the Alaskan State Patrol and the Army reserves with the bomb location information. The explosives were found and carefully disarmed.

The pipeline, for now, was safe.

Chapter Twenty-Five
Ayatollah Direction

Sunday—May 22
Socotra Island Operations Center

At the New Persia operations center, the ayatollah was furious over the combination of the capture of the yacht *Persian Dawn* in the Gulf of Mexico, which occurred last year, and the Bay of Alaska *Persian Desert* capture. He quickly resolved that he would teach the U.S. and the other western powers not to challenge his New Persia goals.

The ayatollah, sensitive to the costs and manpower losses of these boat captures, asked his operations and logistics lead to meet with him. Ghanin and Marin came in after a few minutes and they sat down to talk.

As the ayatollah sat down, Ghanin said, "Sir, before we begin, we have had word that the American Homeland Secretary Jerry Ocasio will be flying to Heathrow on June 6 for a meeting with the British prime minister. Can I assume that you would like us to activate the cell and see to it that he does not make it to the meeting?"

The ayatollah sat back in his chair, and his eyes nearly gleamed. A prime individual in the U.S. administration was coming into his crosshairs. And how fitting that it would be the man responsible for security, and the capture of his vessels, would be that target.

He turned to Ghanin, smiled, and said, "At last. And how fitting a target! By all means, notify our man in that area and have him perform his mission. It will be a great day and an appropriate response to the American's actions in Alaska. We are not to be trifled with. They must meet our demands or there will be more problems."

Ghanin nodded and bowed slightly at the table. He would do as directed.

The ayatollah then continued, "On with the main purpose of this meeting. Ghanin, as you know, we have now lost two of our ships to the American infidels. Is there any way we could recover them?"

Ghanin, internally, felt surprised at this question. He responded, "I don't know of any way to do that. The boats are under armed military guard by the Americans in their own port facilities. To do that would require total surprise and a fairly sizable force of commandos at each location."

Marin commented, "I doubt that we could succeed with a recovery of the vessels. I agree it would be quite a coup to do that, but the difficulties would be very great, and we would possibly lose many men in the attempt."

The ayatollah thought about that for a minute, then turned to Ghanin and said, "The Americans would not be expecting such a daring attempt. I want you to see what might be done and how many men it might take."

Ghanin responded, "I will do the planning. It will be done."

Marin then spoke up again: "If you are going to plan to do it, I would suggest you only plan on the trimaran in Alaska. The yacht in the Gulf of Mexico has been severely damaged and would be of little use to us without a major overhaul, and the Chinese don't want it back. Both the forward hull and the left hydrofoils were nearly destroyed by the American fighter's missile. It would be very difficult to sail it halfway around the world without it sinking. Internationally, the Chinese claim to know nothing about it, even though they built it." He paused for a moment. "And it would cost many millions for the repair, and probably over a year to get it done. It's just not worth it."

The ayatollah thought about that for just a second and said, "You are very right. That yacht is too damaged to be of use anytime soon." Turning to Ghanin, he said, "Plan out a recovery for just the trimaran in Alaskan waters. We probably have a better chance up there anyway. It's quite remote, and we may be able to get it into Russian waters before the Americans can react. And I want to get Kadar and his crew back. He's too valuable to us to allow him to sit in an American jail. "

Ghanin responded, "Yes, sir."

Ghanin and Marin then left the ayatollah to his thoughts.

Ghanin began planning for the recovery of the *Persian Desert*. He also needed to find out where Kadar and crew were being held by the Americans and figure out a way to rescue him. It would be quite a tasking. He was sure the trimaran was being held in Anchorage, since that was where they understood the primary Coast Guard station was located. And the news that he had read, and it had been covered fairly extensively on the internet, said that was where the Coast Guard had taken the vessel after it had been captured. It was possible that Kadar was also being held in federal facilities there in Anchorage.

Back in his small office in the operations center, he began to think of the requirements to get the ship back. He would need travel and logistics support, in addition to probable security forces of some sort. And they would need to have some form of weapons should the Americans interfere, which they undoubtedly would, in the recovery of the *Persian Desert*.

After Ghanin and Marin left, the ayatollah sat for several minutes pondering what was going on and how to best handle it. He called Khatib in. "Khatib, please send Abdul-Hakim in to talk to me. And I want you here also."

Khatib simply bowed and left the room.

A few minutes later, Khatib and Abdul-Hakim were in the ayatollah's office/study.

The ayatollah said, "We have been rebuilding for several months now and it is time to put more pressure on the U.S. They have succeeded in capturing two of our vessels now and stopped our activities in Alaska. Last year they stopped our activities in the Gulf of Mexico. All this was done with no real consequences for their actions. However, we now have the British action underway, so there will be some consequences for them so far." Looking at Abdul-Hakim, he continued, "You sent Ramiz to the States. Did he come back with any information that might be useful to us?"

Abdul-Hakim responded, "Yes, sir. He was able to track down, and actually talked to, the man who was main coordinator for the attack on the stronghold. He also found out that the man—his name is Ryan McKenzie—lives in Texas and is romantically involved with the primary scheduler for the president. Her name is Jackie Conover. Ramiz was able to get this information from a contact in Washington."

"So we know who he is and where he lives?"

"Yes, sir."

The ayatollah thought for a moment and then said, "We need to make our case in a more personal manner. The president needs to realize that we mean business. And to bring it home to him personally." He looked at Abdul-Hakim and said, "I think you need to take several actions that may result in concerns for the president." He then proceeded to lay out a series of actions he wanted Abdul-Hakim to accomplish.

Abdul-Hakim listened intently, as did Khatib. Both were surprised at the tasking, but agreeable to the actions requested. And none of the actions would interfere with their efforts at rebuilding.

After some additional discussion and clarifications, Abdul-Hakim and Khatib left the room. As they were proceeding down the hall, Abdul-Hakim was smiling. They finally had the permission to take the fight to the Eagle. Khatib, moving quickly to keep up with Abdul-Hakim, cautioned him to make sure the ayatollah's desires were met. Abdul-Hakim suddenly stopped and said, "I will keep you informed as we proceed. And ... I will succeed. Allah be praised at this direction!"

Abdul-Hakim then turned and went to his own quarters, where he had a conversation with Ramiz and set his plans into action. He had a lot to do between finding out the status of the trimaran and her crew and implementing the ayatollah's other directions.

Ghanin called Marin, Abdul-Hakim, and several others with expertise in American ways. He also included Ramiz because of his background with the Americans. They met later that afternoon, and Ghanin laid out the tasking from the ayatollah. The reaction was interesting. To a person, they were all questioning the wisdom of attempting the mission. To grab their ship out of American waters, which would be heavily guarded by American forces, break Kadar out of the American jail in Anchorage, if that was where he was being held, and get all of it into Russian waters was one tall order.

But directions were directions. Abdul-Hakim said, "The ayatollah, earlier today, tasked me to determine Kadar's status. That syncs up with his direction to you, Ghanin. My first thought is we don't have any assets in Anchorage, but we do have two people in Valdez. We could send them to Anchorage and check the situation out. They could verify if *Persian Desert* is still there and find out if Kadar and crew are being held there."

Ghanim nodded. "We do need to verify that before we do any serious planning effort. Otherwise, we could be wasting our time."

Ramiz looked thoughtful. He said, "I would guess that Kadar and the rest are being held in the Alaskan Correctional Complex in Anchorage. They are probably being held for the FBI until they can get their evidence and various bits and pieces together and then charged by the U.S. Justice Department." He thought again for a minute as the others digested the information. "If they are still up there, it will not be easy to get them out. The facility is well built and well protected and fairly new. I think"—he looked at Abdul-Hakim briefly then back to Ghanin—"I agree with Abdul-Hakim, and we should have our two people in Valdez go up there and look around a bit. Nothing suspicious; just look around."

Monday—May 23
Valdez/Anchorage, Alaska

Mahmud received direction to head up to Anchorage to see what he could find out about the *Persian Desert* and her crew. Were they there and, if so, where were they located? He and his partner, Haroun, supporting the New Persia movement as a side to earn more money, took the day off their normal oil systems maintenance positions and made the drive of slightly more than three hundred miles up to the Anchorage area to see what they could find.

It wasn't hard. The *Persian Desert* was tied up at the Coast Guard station and in plain sight from the fence perimeter. They noted that it had two armed guards around it and there were several people milling around its main deck. Some were looking at the antenna systems on the lowered main mast. It was obvious that they were studying the ship thoroughly.

Mahmud and Haroun then went to a small coffee shop to discuss what to do next. How would they determine where the crew was, and, more specifically, where Kadar was? After several minutes of discussion, they hatched a plan. Simple.

They went out to the Anchorage Correctional Complex and observed the structure closely. It was well built, surrounded by fencing, and clearly would be difficult to assault. They walked in to the main visitor's office and asked to see Kadar. Bold. The police administrator behind the bulletproof glass looked at them questioningly.

Mahmud said, "We are here to see Kadar. He is my cousin and I want to see if I can help him in some way." Haroun listened quietly but attentively.

The administrator looked at a computer, nodded, and said, "Sorry. But you'll have to see him during our regular visiting hours. The visiting hours closed an hour ago. You'll have to come back tomorrow."

Mahmud nodded and looked down as if disappointed. Then he looked up at the administrator and just plain asked, "Is the rest of his crew here also?"

The now suspicious administrator said, "I can't tell you that. We aren't allowed to tell who is here unless you are an attorney. And then you would have to work through the system to get access."

Mahmud looked disappointed and said, "Okay. Thanks for the help." The administrator just nodded in response and turned back into the secure room. Mahmud and Haroun then left the facility.

They made the drive back to Valdez and, using an encrypted satellite phone in their small home, sent an email to the operations center telling Abdul-Hakim and Khatib what they had found. They also commented on the strong security at both the Coast Guard station and the correctional facility. Getting the ship and the crew rescued would not be an easy task.

However, they had found the ship and Kadar. And probably the rest of the crew. Their immediate mission was a success.

Chapter Twenty-Six
Possible Ayatollah Location

Wednesday—May 25
Washington, D.C.

Mark Allison and Mike Detirro met with the president Wednesday afternoon. The CIA had what they thought might be a lead on the location of the ayatollah, and the president and defense secretary were quite interested.

They entered the small office off to the side of the Oval Office where the president liked to conduct his more personal conversations. They settled in the comfortable couches, with water in a pitcher in front of them on a coffee table.

"Well, Mark," started the president. He looked at Mike and said, "Have you got something that we can act on?" then looked back at Mark.

"We think so," responded Mark. "After doing a lot of signals analysis, there seems to be activity from the New Persia group coming from a small city in Oman called Salalah. It's on the coast and is a major shipping port for Oman. The signals, we think, are coming from and going to the New Persia group, and are coming from that city."

"How do you know they are from, or to, the ayatollah?"

"We have a partial identifier for the ayatollah. With every signal he has sent out in the past, he has finished the message with the phrase 'Praise be to Allah.' By eliminating traffic that does not have this phrase in it, we have been able to narrow the traffic down significantly. Then, after we broke his encryption, we were able to intercept several routine messages being sent to the old stronghold. And there were several messages to and from that sailing ship in the Bay of Alaska we caught a few days ago."

The president raised his eyebrows in surprise. "That would appear to be pretty obvious proof of who is sending the messages."

"Yes, sir. That's what we thought. We started following that particular source, put our satellite on it, and discovered Salalah. The problem we found was that we didn't initially see any antenna that could be used for communications through a satellite. We put our satellite on constant watch over the city and discovered a hidden antenna. A roof of one of the warehouses near the port facilities rolled back, revealing an antenna, and then covered it over after the transmissions were complete. Quite ingenious. If we hadn't had the satellite on a 'stare' program, we wouldn't have seen it."

The president responded, "So we think we have found the antenna he is using. Is there any sign of a compound or other headquarters in this city?"

"No, sir. We have put the cameras on various areas of the city and have not been able to find any sign of a compound or other activity he might be conducting." Mark hesitated a moment and then said, "However, the city is full of buildings and personal compounds, and he could have scattered functions there and we couldn't tell. As a significant port, there are a lot of warehouses and he could be using one or more of them. The only way to really be sure would be to get some people in there and look around."

"Got it. Good progress. What's the next step for you?"

"We'll continue to monitor the traffic and see if he reveals where he really is. Also, we may pick up on some of his future planning and get a heads-up on what he may be up to."

"Sounds good. I'll have to think about your suggestion for someone to check it out. Do you have any personnel in the area that could help us?"

"No, sir. We have some people up the coast in Muscat, the Omani capital. I could have them go down there and look the area over. We'd have to come up with some form of cover story, but that shouldn't be too hard."

Mike Detirro then added, "Since it is a significant port for Oman, it would have refueling and resupply capabilities our ships might use. We could always say we were looking into specific capabilities should we need to use them."

The president was in thought as he listened to Mark. He looked back at Mike and Mark and said, "Okay. Let's do that and see what comes up."

Wednesday—June 1
Washington, D.C.

A week later, Mike and Mark came back to the president with a status report.

Mark started: "We sent a couple of our people down to Salalah under a cover of looking at both their resupply and refueling capabilities at a fishing research terminal they have there. After looking around and asking a few cautious questions of the locals, they came up with zip regarding the ayatollah. No one has heard of any organization like New Persia. They did get a good look at the building that houses the antenna, but it was completely locked up and was just a normal-looking warehouse. Nothing unusual about it. There were power cables running into it, but they couldn't see any communications cables or lines going into the building other than normal telephone lines."

"Any people visible or around?"

Mike added, "Not really. Just the normal warehouse truck traffic, some bicycles, and a few pedestrians. Nothing unusual. The port facilities people were very interested in servicing some of our ships. So, to maintain some degree of credibility, we will have a couple of our ships visit Salalah."

The president looked at Mike, chewed on his lower lip a bit while nodding, and turned to Mark. "So, if there is a compound, it's either well hidden in Salalah or isn't there at all?"

"Afraid so. Our analysts now think the antenna complex may be just a transfer point for information and comm traffic. We think the ayatollah and his group are located somewhere else. Where, we don't know yet."

"If it's just basically a transmitter site, how do they get the signals to the antenna?"

"There are three possibilities that we have come up with. One would be to have a microwave system for line-of-sight transmission. The second would be for them to have buried cable going into the building. The third would be a satellite ground hop where the signal came from one satellite to this station and was then sent up to another satellite. I think we can discount that one. We didn't see any sign of microwave, so we think they have some form of ground cable support. Haven't figured out the details of that yet."

"Okay. Keep at it. If they installed cable, someone in the western world probably installed it. If not, then someone had to have made the cable and sold it to them. There could be some record of that somewhere and shipping it to Oman."

"Yes. That is a possibility. One other possibility that just occurred to me would be an undersea cable. The warehouse is in the port area, and, if they are not in Oman, they could be anywhere using undersea fiber-optic cables. Have to look at that."

"Hmmm. Yes, that could be the case. Chase it down and see what you can find. We'll talk again in a week or so."

Mark and Mike took the comment as it was intended and stood, shook hands with the president, and left.

Chapter Twenty-Seven
Marina Upgrades

Friday—June 3
Ryan's Marina, Freeport, Texas

For some time now Ryan had been planning further upgrades to his marina, both because he wanted it to look good and because the change would make him more competitive. He knew the dock improvements would be especially appreciated by the full-time residents.

He had also planned, and had installed, an upgrade to several parts of his security system. The first installation had only involved the marina office and his small apartment above the office. He had been discussing several upgrades with Jackson Alarms to put security equipment out in the dock areas.

Earlier upgrades to the water, electrical, and waste systems were partially complete. Combined with the concrete work, it would be almost a total rebuild, but the end result would be quite functional and state-of-art modern.

The various inspections by the city, county, and state, and in one case federal inspectors, kept him busy. The federal check was to make sure he hadn't violated any laws regarding modifications for his access to the Brazos River.

But through it all, he continued sailing on the gulf and enjoying his waterborne hours. And he continued to worry and wonder about the whereabouts of the ayatollah and what he might be planning. He had done all that he could do by giving the president his concerns. Hopefully, they would locate the ayatollah soon and capture him.

Getting bids from various contractors and sorting out plans with the various building authorities at city, county, and state level kept Ryan quite busy for several weeks. But most was sorted out now, and further work was underway. More electrical, plumbing, and concrete work was scheduled. The marina residents had been notified of the work schedules. Jasper and Dave visited periodically, and they enjoyed both lunch and watching the progress of the upgrades.

Ryan decided to call Admiral Watkins and see if he could get an update on how things were going. And it would be good to have Jasper and Dave present during the call too. He called Maria on her private line and said, "Maria, Ryan here. How are you doing?"

Maria, with the usual delighted tone to her voice, said, "We're just doing fine, Ryan. I take it all is well with you also."

"Yes. Things are going along as planned. And thanks for asking. Maria, the reason I called is to see if I could call Admiral Watkins and get an update on the current status of New Persia."

"Let me check and see. Hold on a minute." And she left the phone on hold. A minute later she was back and said, "He said he will forward you a point paper on the current status. The president was just recently briefed and he will send you that same information. That sound okay to you?"

"Sounds good. I would assume that if I have some questions I could contact him?" he asked.

"Yep. I'm sure that would be fine."

"Thanks, Maria. Talk to you later." And he hung up the phone. Apparently the admiral didn't want to take the time to actually discuss the situation until he had a chance to come up to speed.

That would work.

Two days later, FedEx delivered a small envelope to the marina. The return address was 1600 Pennsylvania Ave.

Ryan opened the package and found an internal package wrapped in brown paper and stamped "Confidential—To Be Opened by Addressee Only." Since it was addressed to him, Ryan opened it and found a short briefing/point paper on White House stationary. It said,

New Persia Actions Status

The current status of actions regarding New Persia are as follows:

A. *The trimaran vessel seized in the Bay of Alaska continues to be analyzed by experts from several different government, military, and contractor organizations. It is a very advanced ship in terms of technology, and a point paper will be developed in a few months after the full systems are completely analyzed. And that includes the mini-submarine that is part of the package.*

B.   *The captain and crew of the trimaran continue to be held in Anchorage for the time being until the Justice Department can make several determinations regarding their disposition.*

C.   *The whereabouts of the New Persia leadership continues to be a mystery. However, we have been able to trace some of their communications activities to the Omani city of Salalah. Further work is being done to locate the actual source of the communications. We know Salalah is not the center of action. It appears to be a transfer point.*

D.   *The Chinese government continues to deny any knowledge of the trimaran or its systems (even though nearly all of the ship is of Chinese origin).*

E.   *Due to the extreme possibilities of further attacks, we have increased our patrols of pipelines throughout the system, and various storage facilities across the country have increased their security significantly.*

F.

Attached to the briefing paper was a short handwritten note. It read,

Ryan,

Hope this finds you in good health. Here is the basic information you were asking for. I hope it is satisfactory. If you have further questions, please don't hesitate to call.

And it was signed by Admiral Watkins.

Ryan read through the status brief again quickly and sat down to think.

They really weren't making a whole lot of progress.

Chapter Twenty-Eight
Attack on Homeland Secretary's Aircraft

Monday—June 6
Airborne Over the North Atlantic

Jerry Ocasio was winging his way across the Atlantic heading for a meeting with the British prime minister and discussions of several issues, including the problem of the oil embargo that had been attempted by the New Persia terrorist group. The air was smooth at their cruise altitude, and the ride had been quite comfortable since they left Washington several hours earlier.

The Air Force pilot of the C-32, USAF Lieutenant Colonel Rick Stanley, had been briefed on the unauthorized modification to the electronic countermeasures (ECM) system that had been corrected by the Oklahoma City Air Logistics Complex team. While he had been briefed on the problem, he was extremely wary. The ECM system was the primary warning system telling them if they were being tracked by a missile radar system either before or after launch.

As they were en route, Rick gave the ECM situation some thought, brought the system up from its normal standby mode, put the system through a self-test, which resulted in no apparent faults, and then left the system in the "on" position. Since they were flying at a normal commercial altitude, he didn't feel there was any real danger, but decided to play it safe. The ECM system would stay on alert now regardless of their situation. As a reminder, he also, as part of the self-test, did a test alarm to make sure he and the copilot knew what it sounded like and they could react quickly if there was an alarm. The attempts on the defense secretary last year, and the discovery of unauthorized modifications eight months ago that essentially disabled the ECM made him very cautious. As a former fighter pilot with several hundred combat missions under his belt in the Middle East no-fly zone several years earlier, he didn't want to take any chances.

As they approached Heathrow outside of London, both pilots were alert to the possible alarm on the ECM. It is a tense environment in the cockpit of a modern aircraft as it approaches a busy airport, with the necessity to remain very alert to traffic and directions from radar approach control and the tower. And that's without the potential for getting shot down.

They were descending from their cruise altitude to get to their assigned altitude of ten thousand feet for a vectored approach to Heathrow's runway 27R. All was normal as they reached the assigned altitude. But tension was high. The controllers at London were giving the aircraft priority attention because of the Homeland Security secretary's presence. They, too, were aware of what happened to the defense secretary ... after all, it had been all over the news several months ago. In the tower, as a matter of routine, video cameras were monitored as the aircraft approached so there would be a good recording if something happened.

Patrick "Paddy" McFarland, responding to the tasking and aircraft arrival information he had received from the operations center of the New Persia movement, was in position just to the east of the approach to Heathrow. He was parked in an old, rundown, and empty residential area consisting of old-style brick homes with urban decay clearly showing. The area had been cleared of people and eventually would be cleared for airport expansion work.

Paddy was a small man, grizzled in appearance from hard work in the Irish potato fields, and had a fierce temper. When his mind was made up, there was no turning back. He seldom listened to any reasonable argument, preferring to already "know better." He was a hard man. He had been incensed by the constant escalation of energy use by the west and was known to hold very strong—actually, some said they were extreme—views on the subject. It was just part of the wholesale greed and corruption, supported by oil money of the big corporations, in both the British and American governments. And it didn't help his mood that a significant oil spill had occurred just off the coast of Ireland, where he was born and raised, and done serious damage to the local waters and landfall areas. He agreed with the views he read in the newspapers, several months before, of the so-called New Persia group, and was determined to support their cause. Even though he was not a Muslim, he was now part of their clandestine organization and had been trained in the use of the new Chinese-built advanced rocket-propelled missiles and how to down the American aircraft. His training at the remains of the stronghold had been very thorough.

He waited in his false plumber's truck and listened to the airline traffic on his modified radio. The vehicle had clearly seen better days, with peeling paint, scratches, small dents, and an idling engine smoking like an old coal-burning stove. But he was ready. He heard the large blue and white twin-jet aircraft approaching from behind him and turned to look.

It was here.

The U.S. Air Force C-32 was on final approach and coming in on the centerline of the runway. The engine and flight instruments were all good and the aircraft was flying true to its course. All was normal. The passengers were belted in and secure. The winds were reasonably calm and it would be a smooth landing.

The aircraft, with the landing gear down, flew directly over Paddy. He quickly took careful aim at the right engine of the C-32 and the camera locked on to the image. He hesitated a few moments until his nervous shaking calmed down. The plane continued its descending path through the slightly humid air. He finally fired the first ARPM from a hatch in the roof of his truck. He was partially hidden by the ladders and pipes on the top. He was using a state-of-art Chinese-made ARPM that used camera guidance technology and a smokeless solid rocket fuel. The rocket burst from the launcher and reached hyper-velocity speeds en route to the C-32, and took dead aim at the right engine.

As Paddy reached down to get the second ARPM, he heard police sirens wailing with their distinct high/low sound. He hesitated for a moment and decided to get out of there right away. Maybe someone had seen him and called it in. He quickly closed the hatch, got into the driver's seat, and slowly moved out of the area. He didn't want to attract attention to himself by speeding away. Slow and easy did it. There would always be another day.

The active ECM radar immediately picked up the incoming missile and the alarm went off.

Both pilots reacted immediately. The copilot pushed the throttles all the way forward to maximum, rapidly bringing the engines up to full thrust, and radioed the tower that they were breaking off the landing. Rick Stanley's old fighter instincts took over and he banked hard to the left and pulled on the elevators to make the turn even sharper. The aircraft's left wing nearly hit the ground as the bank angle went severe. The nearly eighty-two thousand pounds of thrust, over forty tons of push, from the twin Pratt and Whitney 2040 engines, combined with the light fuel load remaining from the trans-oceanic flight, accelerated the aircraft at a phenomenal rate ... nearly as strong as some afterburner-equipped aircraft.

The aircraft continued in a radical left turn and pitched up as the pilot took advantage of the huge thrust from the engines and sought to evade the possible rocket. Dispensers automatically deployed large quantities of chaff to confuse the guidance of the approaching rocket. The dispensers had little effect on the camera guidance system, which ignored the metallic chaff. He then banked the aircraft hard to the right and continued the climb. If the rocket was close enough so its guidance couldn't react in time, and his maneuver was violent enough, he hoped the rocket would miss. He wasn't even sure there was a rocket out there, but he was taking no chances. The ECM alarm going off just as they were on final approach, combined with the earlier news about the defense secretary's plane, convinced him that they were under attack.

The ARPM bore down on the right engine as the camera and software ignored the chaff. The camera tried to follow the rapidly moving engine pod as the aircraft violently rolled and climbed to the left and then hard over to the right. ARPM camera signals to the small missile steering fins kept calling for sharper turns, but the small fins were deflected to their limits. It wasn't enough to keep up with the extreme banking and acceleration of the C-32 wing. The wing velocities and intercept angles were just too great for the missile guidance and control system. Fortunately.

The copilot, knuckles white on the twin throttles, glanced out the right side of the aircraft and was startled as he saw a small object flash past the wing at a very high rate of speed and then disappear. He started sweating realizing how close they had come. The missile had missed! If they hadn't reacted as quickly as they did, they would all be dead. He began to shake and reached over to touch Rick's shoulder, indicating where he had seen the missile. The copilot couldn't talk. His throat was locked up. The fear and reaction were obvious to Rick. He had seen it in wartime over the gulf. Rick also began to breathe again. He understood what the copilot was reacting to. Leveling the plane off, he reduced the throttles and radioed Heathrow tower for another vectored approach. The tower had seen the gyration he had put the aircraft through, and asked if everyone was okay and did he need assistance? He radioed back that they were okay, that something had just missed their right wing, and apologized for the disruption to the traffic. Heathrow came right back with a new vector to place them in a landing approach again.

Rick then got on the intercom and told the passengers what had happened and hoped everyone was okay. Jerry returned the call with a handset in the seat of the aircraft and thanked him for the evasive maneuver. He told him that, fortunately, everyone was belted in and okay—a few bruises from the restraints, but okay.

They were able to land with no further incident. But then, on the ground, there was a real welcoming committee. Not only the usual government greeting for the secretary, but police and security personnel were all over the aircraft parking area, with cordons and armed escorts every few feet. The greeting party did not know what had happened, but had seen the aircraft do the violent banking turns and thought for sure they were going to crash. Relief was apparent as the greetings were conducted.

The police found the missile a couple of kilometers away, having impacted a closed repair garage. The garage was destroyed and the neighborhood shaken up, but no one was hurt. They cordoned off the area and British Air Force personnel were dispatched to the scene. Missile fragments and debris were collected for analysis. The police dispatched several patrol cars to the neighborhood where they suspected the missile was fired from, but found nothing.

Paddy wasn't there.

He continued slowly for just a few minutes to get out of the immediate area, parked the stolen truck, and got in a Ford Fiesta he had previously positioned for this purpose. Taking off, he set off a small explosive that set the truck on fire. He didn't want any evidence left behind, and burning the truck would take care of that. A few minutes after, the rocket fuel ignited on the second ARPM and the warhead exploded, obliterating the truck. Nothing was left of it.

He drove off north through Harlington up to the M-4 and then west, disappearing quietly into the English countryside.

Even before they got off the airplane, Lieutenant Colonel Stanley had contacted both the 89th Airlift Wing Command Post at Andrews AFB and the Pentagon Situation Room, and gave them a quick overview of what had happened. In both command centers, the personnel were thunderstruck.

Another attempted downing; another major near miss!

Chapter Twenty-Nine
Anchorage Planning

Tuesday—June 7
Valdez, Alaska

A message was sent from the Socotra operations center to Mahmud and Haroun in Valdez, tasking them to go to Anchorage. Now that they knew the ship and crew were there, the mission was to determine how they might be able to free Kadar and the crew. They also were tasked to figure out how New Persia might recover the *Persian Desert*.

Both men were a bit nervous over the assignment. Taking on the U.S. federal government would not be a small undertaking, and they were not sure how to proceed. But they were just gathering information as best they could.

They drove up Alaska Highway 4 to Alaska 1, turned west toward Anchorage, arriving a little over six hours later, and proceeded to the U.S. Coast Guard station to see if the trimaran was still berthed at the station dock. It took just a few moments and they could see the large ship tied up. There was activity on the deck as various technicians were busy analyzing the ship's capabilities. They could also see that most of the communications and navigation antennas were disassembled and lying on the dock. The bridge area of the trimaran was in apparent disarray, as many of the components were disconnected and, in some cases, missing entirely. The reverse-engineering process was obviously well underway. They concluded that there was no way to try and move the ship. With some hull damage and at least one engine out of commission from the capture effort, combined with the apparent disassembly on the deck and dock, the ship just couldn't be moved.

They took digital photos, with a telephoto lens, of the action on the dock and the main deck of the ship. They recognized that there was no way to spirit, or capture in some other form, the ship and move it. They needed proof to send to Socotra for their information. It also backed up their decision.

After discussing it briefly, they decided to go to the Anchorage Correctional Complex detention facility where

Kadar and the rest of the crew were being held. The facility was relatively new, and looked it. Probably no more than fifteen years or so. From their previous visit they knew here was a guarded lobby and the rest of the facility was inside locked and guarded doors. Getting someone out of there would be a major effort.

Again, very quietly, they took pictures of the facility for later transmission to Socotra. While the prison was not a major fortress, it still would be difficult to get anyone being held there out. The heavy walls, some concertina wire, and armed personnel were all very real deterrents. Looking at the facility in the daylight, Mahmud realized that the best way to get their people out would be when they were being transferred to another facility. But when would that happen and how would they approach it? Frontal attack or something more devious? It would take considerable planning to pull this one off.

But that wasn't why they were there. They were to just gather information and leave the rest of it up to the people and planners at Socotra.

They finished up their observing at the Alaskan Correctional holding facility, went back to the Coast Guard facility, and made sure they hadn't forgotten anything. They determined that there wasn't anything further they could accomplish, so they hit the road heading back east and south to Valdez.

After getting back home in Valdez, they took the information they had gathered, built a short report, and sent it off to the operations center in Socotra. They also sent their recommendations with the package, including the digital photos, and included their opinion that the ship could not be recovered.

The operations center in Socotra received the information and passed it on to Khatib and Abdul-Hakim. Both were highly disappointed. Abdul-Hakim called Ramiz in for assistance. Ramiz sat and thought about the situation, and, since he had a good understanding of American ways, understood what was going on. The Americans, of course, were reverse-engineering the ship to better understand its capabilities. They should have anticipated it. Khatib was not happy about the situation. He had expected that they would be able to get the ship back intact. Obviously, he was wrong.

They got together in the main conference room and discussed what the next step should be.

Ramiz started, "Well, I guess we should have anticipated this. It is what the Americans could be expected to act on. They want to know as much about the ship as possible, since it is so unique and built by the Chinese. I'm sure the U.S. Navy brass want as much information as possible, given the growth in the Chinese Navy over these past few years."

Khatib nodded and added, "Yes. I guess you're right. But I had hoped to get it back. There just doesn't appear to be any way to do that, though." He stopped for a moment and then said, "How about towing it out of there? If we could get some type of vessel in there, tie a line to it, and tow it out, would that work?"

Ramiz said with some mirth in his eyes, "No, I don't think so. Even if you got in and attached a line to it, the Americans would overtake you in a short time and stop it. Towing a ship of that size would not be a rapid move. You'd never even get out of Cooks Inlet there in Anchorage. It could be towed, but not fast, and certainly not fast enough to get into Russian waters before they caught up. So, no. Not really a possibility."

Khatib nodded again and just looked out the window. After a little bit, he said, "Okay. Sounds like that one is out. What do you think about getting Kadar and the crew out?"

"Now that will take a little thought. It sounds like they are pretty well locked up, and it will take a bit to get them released. But I do have an idea on how we might be able to do it. It won't be easy, and there is certainly some risk of someone getting hurt or killed, but I think it will work. Here's what I have in mind." Ramiz then proceeded to tell Khatib and Abdul-Hakim what his plan was. It was audacious and would be quite difficult to pull off, and it would be fairly expensive, but he thought they could do it.

Khatib, after listening to what Ramiz was suggesting, sat back for a moment in thought. They needed to get Kadar and crew back. But this plan was very fraught with possible disaster. They continued to discuss it and try to figure out how to implement it without creating too much risk for the crew. It would be hard, but Ramiz finally convinced Abdul-Hakim and Khatib that it could be done. More details needed to be worked, though.

165

Mahmud didn't like the tasking he was now asked to perform. He had returned to the correctional facility and was standing near the front entrance looking for the plaque. Stepping over to the door, he found what he was looking for. The dedication plaque for the facility was firmly attached to the front entrance wall. Looking over the plaque, he found near the bottom the information he needed. There, in slightly smaller brass lettering was: *This facility was designed by the architectural firm of Davis, Johansen, and Marcus of Anchorage, Alaska.*

Mahmud and Haroun then did the simple thing and looked up the firm on the internet using the library computer. They found the address in downtown Anchorage, drove to it, and were a bit surprised. They expected a fairly large firm located on an upper floor of some significant building. Instead, they found the firm occupying what had obviously been a former filling station, completely converted to the architectural firm's specifications. But the basic building resembled a converted gas station. It was small, and after some minor checking, Mahmud and Haroun found out that the firm specialized in jail and correctional facility designs. They had designed most of the current modern jails in Alaska. The three principals and a secretary were it. They cased the place and found no sign of alarms.

That night, two shadowy figures approached the Davis, Johansen, and Marcus architectural building, quiet and stealthy. They looked over the building again and found no sign of any type of alarm system. Then they thought, *Why would an architectural firm need alarms anyway?* If they weren't in the business with classified information, it wouldn't be needed. And they wouldn't be keeping large quantities of money on hand, like a bank. And for clients who wanted to keep their designs a secret, there were always locking filing cabinets. Mahmud and Haroun eased around the back of the building. They were able to gain access through a back door just using a credit card for a sliding release.

Once inside, they went to the secretary's desk, looked for some form of indexing method, and found one that listed all their work and projections for future work. Looking through the materials, they went back several years and found the reference for the local facility. Bingo! The reference was to a set of hard copies, since this was before the computer age really took hold, kept in a filing box, which they located in a storage area in the back of the building. Entering the file storage area, they were busy looking for the proper box.

A light flashed outside and they froze. They had not turned on any lights and were working with flashlights, which they extinguished immediately. Looking carefully around the door to the room, they could see the outside front and a parked and idling local police cruiser. He was doing a routine check of the facility and had used his spotlight to view the building. They stayed out of sight and he went away after a few minutes. Nerve-racking ... and close.

They found the box they were looking for, took out the schematics, and spread them on a worktable in the room. They then began to photograph the schematics and notes until they had them all done. After close to an hour, they were finally finished, put the box back where it had been, and very quietly left the building. Having worn latex gloves for the entire episode, there was no trace of them being there.

It took another six hours of travel to get back to Valdez. They made a short report of their findings and action, added the digital photos of the schematics, and sent the material to Socotra.

A week later, and after several more exchanges with Mahmud, and a repeat trip to Anchorage to get even more additional information, they had worked out a detailed plan. Ramiz had gone over the schematics very carefully and satisfied himself that several vulnerabilities existed that they could exploit. It was obvious that whoever had designed the complex had not thought through the possibility of a major assault. It would be difficult but they would try. And it would take several weeks to pull all aspects of it together and get the required skilled men trained. They also needed to smuggle in, to southern Alaska, weapons and other supplies to accomplish their strike. It would be several months before that could also be coordinated and accomplished.

The information and planning details were briefed to the ayatollah. He was pleased at the progress and urged them on. Recovering the crew would be quite an accomplishment against the infidels.

Chapter Thirty
Socotra Identified

Wednesday—June 8
White House—Washington, D.C.

A week later, the president, Mark, and Mike met again in the small presidential office.

The president said, "After this week's attack on Jerry's airplane at Heathrow, we really need to get this guy. They used the same type of Chinese missile used on the SecDef last year. Thank God the pilot was so good. Well, how is it going? Any progress?"

Mark said, "Yes, sir. Some progress. As we thought, there are no microwave activities involving that building. But the building was just built several months ago and we were able to get plans from the local government. There is a high-speed fiber-optic cable leading to the building through a communications pipeline under the port facilities. According to the plans, it comes in from an undersea transmission cable. The puzzling thing about this is that the government documents indicate the presence of an undersea cable, but there is no reference to a cable terminating in Salalah in the international registry. It may be there, but it isn't on the official international records."

The president's eyebrows went up with this news. "So, it's possible that the New Persia group put in an undersea cable to somewhere and did not register it?"

"Exactly. We don't know when or how they did it. We haven't been able to find any record of an installation so far."

"What do you suggest, then?"

"Well, the plans indicate an undersea cable terminus. I think we need to get some equipment in there and see if we can find it. We think it is in the same building as the antenna but aren't sure. If we can locate it, we may be able to determine where the other end is located. And that would tell us where the signals are coming from."

"Sounds reasonable. How long would that take and how would you go about it? It's not a country totally friendly to us."

"Agreed. I think we need to set up some form of artificial excuse, ship some tracking equipment under disguise, and send some people in to that area. Maybe establish some form of shipping company with some communication equipment to do business in Oman. Salalah advertises for additional business opportunities on their website and we might be able to take advantage of that. I'm figuring on it taking at least a month to get it moving."

"Okay. Let's try it and see what you can find out. Keep me informed and we'll see what happens."

Wednesday—June 22
White House—Washington, D.C.

Two weeks later, Mark and Mike met with the president again.

Mark started off: "We did some analysis of the area comparing satellite photos from a year ago to the current. The building that houses the antenna wasn't there a year ago. It is near the ocean and has some access to the harbor on the northern side. The key here is that it is near the ocean, only one hundred yards or so. And between the building and the ocean, there is evidence of a construction trench that was dug and then filled in. We think it may be the location of the undersea cable."

The president looked at Mark and smiled. "Looks like we need to trace that possible cable and see where it goes." Mike nodded and agreed with a smile on his face. He finally saw some action for DOD coming his way.

Mark, smiling back, said, "Yes, sir. I think a quiet search of the ocean bottom to locate the cable and follow it would be quite appropriate."

Mike said, "By the way, we have received some interesting news on that trimaran we captured in Alaska a few weeks ago. It, too, was built by the Chinese, just as the yacht was their design and build. They claim it isn't theirs, but half the equipment on board is their manufacture and the engineering of it follows some of their practices for placement of various capabilities and equipment. And the mini-sub, disguised as the third pontoon, is quite capable of actions around the Bay of Alaska. We were, from some documents found in the bridge, able to trace where they had come ashore, and located a truck they had used. So that pretty well wraps up the threat from them on the Alaskan pipeline, at least for now. And, of course, the explosives have been dealt with. Interestingly, they were set to go off on July 4th. But I would continue the patrols and checks we have been performing. They could always try again."

The president looked back at Mike and said, "Well, thanks for the info. It's a damn good thing we caught them. Talk about a mess if those bombs had gone off."

Mike and Mark both just looked back and agreed.

The president stood up; Mark and Mike left.

Thursday—June 23
Northern Arabian Sea

The nuclear submarine *SSN North Carolina* was on routine patrol in the northern Indian Ocean when an ops message was received directing them to the port of Salalah in Oman, with more traffic to follow. They diverted to the northwest and arrived off the coast of Oman two days later.

Additional messages directed them to locate and follow an undisclosed undersea cable from Salalah to an unknown destination. Cruising at a depth of 150 feet to avoid any tanker traffic above them, they cruised back and forth well outside the port of Salalah, trying to locate the undersea cable. Sensors on board the *North Carolina* would be able to pick up the electrical impulses in the undersea cable, especially where a repeater was located.

After several passes over the suspected area, they picked up some faint signals, then used the photonics system on the bow and located the cable running across the ocean floor. They came around to a course paralleling the cable and followed it to the south from Salalah. They were able to follow it for several miles when the cable dropped into an underwater trench several thousand feet deep. The signal was lost at that time.

Assuming that the cable was laid in a roughly straight line, they continued on course across the trench until the sea floor started to rise. Again, they had to do a zigzag pattern, but finally located the cable again after a full day's work. They were now in the far western Arabian Sea, proceeding generally south. After slowly following the cable for another two days, the sea floor began to rise again to a relatively shallow depth of just over two hundred feet. They were just off the coast of a small island called Socotra. After putting divers into the water, since they did not want to surface, they confirmed that the cable ran to the island and was buried several hundred yards from the beach leading in to the beach. They had found the other terminus.

Where it went on the island, they didn't know. But the undersea cable did go to Socotra.

Tuesday—June 28
Washington, D.C.

The next morning, which was bright and warm in the early summer, Mark and Mike were in the waiting area of the Oval Office. They got some coffee from the Keurig and sat down. There had been some interesting developments in the hunt for New Persia.

The president came out and they shook hands. They went into the Oval Office and took seats next to each other on the couch. The president looked expectantly at Mark, and, with raised eyebrows, asked, "Well, what have you found out? Do we have a location for the ayatollah and his bunch?"

Mark looked back, nodded emphatically, and said, "Possibly. We have been watching the message and voice traffic in the northern Arabian Sea area, anticipating that he may not have gone too far. Moving his entire group of people would have been too difficult for any major distance."

Mike Detirro cleared his throat to get their attention, and gave them a rundown on what the *North Carolina* had found. "They were able to locate the cable and tracked it to an island called Socotra in the Arabian Sea in the northern Indian Ocean. It's located just off the east coast of Africa and belongs to Yemen."

"So the thought would be that the ayatollah and his gang would be on this island?"

Mike said, "That's what it looks like. But I think we need to get some folks in there to make sure. The island is quite unusual in that it has some strange plants. But the local populace is primarily engaged in fishing and small animal farming. Goats and the like. Otherwise there's nothing of interest from our perspective there."

The president got a puzzled look on his face. Mark picked up on it and said, "Socotra is an archipelago off the east coast of Africa. It is a small group of islands, belongs to Yemen, and has a total population of around fifty thousand. Mostly fishermen and sheepherders. It's ancient. Some of the pirates in that area have used it for a fuel and supply stop recently, but not much anymore. It's been populated since back in history, but of no real consequence now."

The president nodded and asked, "So we are seeing unusual traffic from this island group? It's not something Yemen is doing there that would cause the traffic increase?"

"Not that we can tell from our intercepts of the Salalah terminal. Some of the information is logistical in nature and the rest is dealing with personnel matters. Since some of the traffic is going to and coming from the old stronghold location, we are assuming it is New Persia again. So it appears that New Persia has a center of some sort on the main island ... also called Socotra."

The president sat back on the couch and thought about what he had just been told. Another center, and in a relatively unfriendly Muslim country. Reconstituting for more action against the west, and, no doubt, especially toward the U.S. It all fit.

"Do we have any idea of what this center might look like or how capable it might be?"

Mark responded, "Not yet. We've only just discovered it. We haven't had a chance to focus in on the actual location and try to narrow down on them. As Mike said, Socotra is an odd island with many strange species of plants. It is quite barren and economically backward. They have some tourist activity but not much, and what there is mostly eco-tourist ... people interested in the ecology of the area. As far as capabilities are concerned, at this point I would think there isn't much there. Of course, we think New Persia still has some ships capable of worldwide operations. But we don't know that for sure yet. We've got two of their ships and don't know how many may be left. It's only speculation on my part."

"Okay, Mike, Mark. I appreciate you taking the time to brief me. I have the staff meeting to attend to. I'll think this over and get back to you in a few days."

They looked back and nodded. Mark said, "Okay. We'll continue to monitor it as best we can. I'll also put some analysts on it. Maybe there's been some construction increases or changes in their normal imports. We'll see what we can find out."

The president nodded, gave them a thumbs-up, and they left the Oval Office.

Chapter Thirty-One
Found—Socotra Operations Center

Thursday—June 30
Washington, D.C.

Two days later, they again asked to see the president. Maria arranged it and they met late that afternoon.

The president said, "Well, you two. You're back pretty soon. What have you got?"

"It wasn't too hard. Our analysts looked at some of the shipping records to Socotra, both for sea and air. For about a year before we hit the stronghold, and with a strong uptick since we hit it. The island has had a significant increase in construction materials. And that includes electronic transmission and satellite transmission equipment. Something they have never had before. And, as far as we can tell, there are no commercial upgrades going on over there. Informal information from Sana'a, the Yemen capital, indicates the government isn't doing anything unusual there. It has to be the New Persia center."

The president raised his eyebrows. "So you don't think it's some commercial interest moving in there?"

"No. There's simply no market for anything there. It's an island of impoverished fishermen and sheepherders. Nothing any commercial interest would look to. And it is a bit off the beaten path for tourism. They have tried to increase the tourism but haven't had much luck. Nothing big that would interest commercial guys."

The president looked thoughtful. "Can we focus the satellite image capability on the island to get a better idea of what they are doing?"

"Already being done. We should have some pictures within the next few days. I've asked the folks over at NSA to get whatever they can find and forward it to us. We'll be looking hard for any unusual capability."

"Good. Keep me informed. I want to keep on top of this. If they are up to what I think they are, by that I mean another strike on us, we need to nip it in the bud. The attacks on Alaska and Jerry could just be opening shots ... so to speak."

Friday—July 8
Washington, D.C.

A week later, they again asked for some time on the president's schedule. They came over that afternoon and sat down to talk. Mark had a sheaf of paper with him, and he brought out several other papers as they sat in front of a cocktail table.

"Sir. We have pictures of what we believe to be the new center of operations for New Persia." He spread out a series of papers in front of them that were photographs taken from a very high altitude. They looked directly down on the complex of buildings that Mark was calling a center.

Mark continued, "The complex that we have here was not here a couple of years ago. As part of the overall mapping of the world that has been going on for many years from space, we can compare these photos with some from the past. This complex did not exist two years ago. And it coincides with the sudden increase in imports to Socotra."

The president looked at the photographs. He pointed at the antenna dishes visible to the side of one of the larger buildings. "I take it that is a series of communications antennas."

"Yes, sir, it is. No place else on the island has that kind of technology or capability. It is the only site like it on any of the four Socotran Islands. It may not be operational, since they are still using the Salalah terminal. We don't know for sure."

"And this large building, it's the main operations center for the movement?"

"That's our impression. There are several buildings on the outskirts of the area that appear to be dormitories or apartments for a reasonably large number of people. There are also some smaller outbuildings that seem to be warehouses, a power plant, and vehicle storage and maintenance facilities." Mark stopped for a moment as the president leaned over the photos in concentration.

The president pointed to the west of the complex. "Is this a harbor?"

"Yes, sir. They have a man-made harbor capable of handling fairly large vessels. That pier, and the buildings near it, could easily handle a three-hundred-foot ship. The yacht we captured last year in the Gulf of Mexico could easily have berthed there. So could the trimaran we captured in Alaska." He pointed at several images as he said, "There's currently another trimaran there, along with some patrol boats and another yacht like we captured in the gulf last year."

The president sat back. "I see. So we are looking at a facility that has nothing to do with the native population, wasn't there a couple of years ago, and contains an unknown number of people. Are we sure this is something the ayatollah has done? After all, the Yemenis could be doing this for some reason."

"That's a good synopsis. As far as your last comment. No, sir. We aren't sure who is behind it. We think it is the ayatollah due to the message traffic we have been monitoring. But we are not a hundred percent sure. Ninety-five percent sure, yes. There are just an awful lot of pointers saying this is it."

"Okay. We aren't absolutely sure. So what would you suggest we do next? We can't hit a complex based on what you have found out so far."

Mark said, "I agree. What my people and I feel needs to be done is to put a 'tourist' in there and see what he, or she, can find out. After all, Socotra is a mecca for environmental groups and individuals due to its unique plant life."

"Interesting thought. Any ideas on who we could send in?"

"Someone with a bit of a scientific mind, yet also able to look at the complex from a military view. They need to be able to assess the complex and try to determine if it is, in fact, the ayatollah's group. I'd suggest Ryan and Dave and maybe one other person."

The president raised his eyebrow over the suggestion. "Ryan and Dave?"

"Sure. Ryan has the skills to determine the military potential, and Dave is smart enough to act as a plant and environmental expert. They need to be convincing enough to make the locals think they are legit. I think they could pull it off. And they already know the problem with the ayatollah. No need to bring them up to speed."

The president thought for a few moments, then leaned over the photos again. He shuffled through a couple of them and then stacked them neatly. He said, "I think you are right about putting someone in there to nose around. But whether it should be Ryan and Dave, I'm not sure."

"Well, think about it. I think they would do a good job. We could get them up to speed fairly quickly and turn them loose. Obviously, your call."

The president turned to Mike Detirro and asked, "What do you think? Should we put someone in there and nose around a bit?"

Mike looked at Mark and back to the president as he said, "Yes, sir. I agree with Mark. Sure, we could argue whether it should be Ryan and Dave, or someone else. But the logic of sending them in is tough to beat. They are up to speed, they are civilians, and are not known to the New Persia folks. If I sent one or two of my guys in, there's a good chance they would be spotted, and we don't want that to happen, especially if it turns out that we are right and that this is the new center of operations for them."

"Okay. I'll think about it. Ryan and Dave have helped out already and I'm sure they would be more than willing to help now. But I also don't want to compromise them again. Ryan is limping on that leg from the .45 bullet he took because of these folks. And they were both almost killed in the Gulf of Mexico fiasco."

Mark and Mike both nodded. Mike said solemnly, "Yeah. That's all true, and that's also the reason they could do a good job of it."

The president grinned at the comment and said, "I'll think about it. See you guys later." He shook hands with Mike and Mark. "Thanks for the info. Good work and I'll be in touch."

Tuesday—July 12
Washington, D.C.

The president was in the Oval Office and was pondering the information Mark Allison had provided to him last Friday. He looked at copies of the photos on his desk. It just made sense to get someone in there and look at the situation firsthand. And he couldn't think of anyone better suited to that task than Ryan McKenzie.

He reached over, touched the intercom button, and said, "Maria, see if Ryan and his guys could get on the phone with me tomorrow. I'd like to discuss their thoughts on the New Persia thing. Maybe they can come up with something we haven't thought of."

He hesitated a moment then added, "And ask Jackie to come here for a few minutes. I need to talk with her."

She placed a call to Jackie Conover to see what changes could be made in the schedule to accommodate a phone call. They agreed that he could be available for thirty minutes around 11:30 a.m. Then Jackie went in to see the president.

Maria placed a direct call to Ryan's Texas number. Ryan answered after the first ring.

"Hello. Ryan's Marina. May I help you?"

"Morning, Ryan. It's Maria. How are you doing?"

She could hear the pleased tone in his voice as he said, "I'm doing well. How are you?"

She said, "Fine. I have a request for you from the president."

"What's that?"

"Can you be available for a telephone conference with him at 11:30 a.m. tomorrow? That's Washington time. He'd like to talk with you and your guys at that time."

"Sure. What's the subject?"

She smiled to herself as she said, "Guess. It's New Persia again."

He thought for a moment, wondering what had happened now. But he responded, "Sure. I'll get Dave and Jasper here in the morning and wait for your call. Say hi to Jackie for me." And smiled into the phone.

She said, "Will do. When are you coming back here to see her again? She's really missing you fella."

"Not sure yet, but it's going to have to be soon. I miss her too much."

"Okay. Ryan, you have a good day and we'll talk again tomorrow. Bye for now."

They hung up, and Ryan was left wondering what had happened that the president wanted to talk with them again. Hopefully nothing serious. It had been pretty quiet since Jasper had returned after capturing the trimaran in Alaska in late May. He turned back to his desk and picked up several invoices for some electrical work he was having done. He looked at the invoices, but his mind kept going back to tomorrow's call. What was going on now?

Wednesday—July 13
Ryan's Marina, Freeport, Texas

Ryan, Dave and Jasper were all in Ryan's office waiting for the call to come in from the president. Maria appeared through the Skype program on the large monitor.

Maria, with a smile in her voice on seeing the three of them, said, "Ryan. Stand by for the president."

A few moments later, the president appeared on their screen. "Ryan. It's good of you, Dave, and Jasper to meet with me on such short notice."

"Yes, sir. What can we do for you? We are all quite curious about this call."

"I can't talk the details over this connection, but we have some changes in information on New Persia and I need to meet with you. When can all of you come back to Washington?"

"I've got some final electrical work right now. But I think I can get away in a few days. Let me figure it out and get back to you." Ryan turned to Dave and Jasper and asked, "Do you have anything that would stop you from going to Washington next week?" Both shook their heads. "Let me get back to you on a specific time."

The president said softly, "Fine. I'll look forward to hearing from you. We could aim to meet late next week if you can. Oh, by the way, I assume you already know Jackie's coming down for a few days later today."

"Yes. We're spending a few days together here. Thanks for the call and I'll get back with Maria on the specifics." They could see the president reach for the mouse as he smiled and said, "Goodbye. Enjoy the weekend."

And the connection broke.

Ryan looked at Dave and Jasper and said, "Pretty brief and noncommittal. I wonder what's up now?"

Both just shrugged. Dave said, "Well, I guess we'll find out later next week. My guess is that they need help in specifically locating the ayatollah."

Jasper added, "I think there may be some sneaky work that needs to be done and he wants us to do it. Just a hunch." He smiled.

Chapter Thirty-Two
Attempted Kidnapping

Wednesday—July 13
Washington, D.C. and Freeport, Texas

Jackie came out of the White House and went to her parking spot in the garage. It was Wednesday afternoon and she had been given a week off. She intended to enjoy them with Ryan at the marina, and headed out to her apartment to gather a few belongings before going to Reagan National for her flight. After arriving at her apartment, she packed a few items that she would need in an overnight bag, checked the security settings on her alarm system, set the alarm, and headed for the elevator.

As she got on the elevator, her phone rang and she answered Ryan's call. He confirmed her flight into Houston and told her he was really looking forward to her visit. She smiled at the thought, said she was looking forward to seeing him again, and said goodbye. Slipping her phone back in her bag, she went into a bit of a dreamlike trance as she descended the fifteen floors to the parking garage in the basement of the building. She wondered where it was all going to end up. She loved Ryan, but she loved the Washington scene too, and they weren't exactly compatible.

She stepped out of the elevator and walked over to her Volvo C70 convertible, got in, and turned the key. She looked around, making sure it was clear, and backed out. Soon she was on her way to National and her flight. She parked, took the shuttle in to the departure area, check in at the kiosk, checked a bag, went through security, stopped at a bar for a martini, and sat down to relax a bit. It had been a long day and she was looking forward to a few days' rest at the marina. She was anxious to see the changes Ryan had made.

They called her flight and she boarded, first to Atlanta and then a transfer to another plane for Hobby Airport in Houston. There she would get a rental car and head for Freeport and the marina. It was a bit of a process, but necessary in today's traveling environment.

Ramiz watched as she went through security. He followed her down to the gate area, got a book, and watched as she boarded the plane for Atlanta. He threw his commuter ticket, which had got him past security, into the trash and went back into the terminal. He went up to the Delta service counter and asked for flight information from Atlanta to Houston later that day. The service representative readily gave him several flights. He said thank you and returned to his rental car. There was a flight to Houston forty-five minutes after she reached Atlanta, and he assumed she would be on that one. He then called his contacts in Houston and passed on the flight information.

They had received their tasking two days before and had to hurry to be ready. Their quarry, Jackie Conover, would be flying to Houston, and she was to be detained and held. These instructions had come directly from Abdul-Hakim and were not to be taken lightly. Ramiz flew to Washington to observe from that end, and the other three members of the team flew to Houston. The Houston team rented a nondescript white Ford cargo van, got a hotel room near the airport, and waited for her arrival. A picture of her had accompanied the directions and they were sure they could identify her.

Wednesday—July 13
Houston, Texas

Four hours later, Jackie got off the plane at Hobby Airport, went through the older-style round terminal complex, and headed for the car rental agencies. She was greeted by the agent, took the keys to the car, and headed out to the parking area where the car awaited.

Jackie proceeded out to the parking lot and approached a modern-looking small, four-passenger, two-door Tesla. She had seen a few of these on the road before but not driven one. Called a Current, it was all electric and capable of going close to one hundred miles per hour and over 250 miles on a charge. It could be recharged from any fifty-amp outlet and carried adapter cords for both standard charging stations and plugging into a fifty-amp home stove receptacle. Normally, when away from the car lot, she could locate a Tesla-installed charging station from information provided in the glove box. In her case, however, she would be able to recharge the vehicle from Ryan's marina fifty-amp connections. Cool.

She did a quick walk-around to make sure there wasn't any damage, threw her checked bag in to the rear seat, got in, and started up the car. Whisper-quiet as she drove out of the lot, she could feel the power and capabilities the little car had. With the torque of the electric motors (two of them), the pick-up was quite noticeable, and she enjoyed the cabin comforts of the stylish interior. All the bells and whistles! And disturbingly silent.

She headed out of the parking area, located the highway she was looking for, and began the drive south.

She didn't get far, however, before trouble arrived.

Leaving the airport parking area, Jackie was spotted by the three men—Mahdi, Nidal, and Rafi—and they followed her out of the airport. The information from Ramiz had been accurate and they were prepared. They followed at a reasonable distance, not wanting to alarm her until they were ready to implement the capture.

Out of the airport, she took Airport Road to Telephone Road, made a left, and a few miles further made a right on Texas 35 toward Highway 288. She turned on her signal to approach the left turn for highway 288. This was it. She was still slow enough to be easy to stop. Mahdi, the driver, pulled up next to her and began to ease over to the right.

As she began pulling onto Highway 288, a white Ford Econoline van pulled up next to her on the left and began to ease over in her direction. She was forced to the right and onto the shoulder of the road. She blew her horn but it did no good. She had to slow down; the white van slowed down with her. She eventually had to stop entirely. Looking over at the van, she was in a near-panic and quickly verified the doors were locked.

Mahdi was quite satisfied with the action so far. She had stopped, and he gave Nidal and Rafi the go-ahead to grab her. They quickly moved to the back of the van, drew their guns, opened the rear door, and hopped out. Nidal headed around to the right side of her car, and Rafi stood outside on the left and just behind her, waiting for Nidal to get in position. Nidal got to the right side, quickly tried the door, and found it locked. He yelled at her to open the door, but she had ducked down and didn't move. He fired at the window.

As she stopped, two men hopped out of the rear door on the van with guns drawn. One of the men yelled something at her but she couldn't understand him. His gun was understanding enough. She ducked down, expecting to be shot, but the shot that rang out only shattered the right-hand window. An arm reached in to unlock the door. Realizing her danger, Jackie quickly put the car in reverse and, as the arm came in, she gunned the car backward, throwing the arm, with the man attached, down the side then out in front of the car. The left rear window then exploded as Rafi shot it out, but she didn't hesitate to keep going backward. She quickly did a maneuver in reverse around the van and back out on the highway. She screeched to a stop and put it in forward, with her foot pressing through to the floor. The little Current took off like a scared rabbit with maximum electrical torque as she headed on down the road looking for any possible help. One man had been left on the roadside, the other had climbed back into the van, and they were in hot pursuit of the Current.

Mahdi looked on in amazement as she suddenly backed up, throwing Nidal to the dirt in front of her. Rafi jumped back to avoid being hit by her as she gunned the little electric. He fired his weapon as she went by, breaking out the rear left window. Mahdi watched her go by up the entrance ramp as fast as she could move, eyes concentrating on the ramp. Rafi threw himself into the van and began crawling forward as Mahdi hit the gas and began to chase the Current. They couldn't let her get away. Failure was not an option. Rafi finally crawled into the passenger's seat and rolled down the window. Mahdi continued to gain on the Current as they raced down the highway. The weather was clear and visibility very good.

The more powerful van pulled up next to her, and Rafi, in the front seat, with the window rolled down, took careless aim at her and fired. Just as she hit the brakes hard. The bullet shattered her door window but did not hit her. She screamed as the glass bits sprayed across her. She floored it again, and the little car jumped ahead. Her heart was beating hard as she tried to think. She was running on instinct. What could she do? Her gun was in her bag in the back seat, and she couldn't drive and still get it. She had to get it and return fire. The wind was whipping in through the shattered windows, and it and noise of both vehicles was deafening. The highway seemed to be flying by, with the centerline just a blur. A brief thought entered her mind as she tried to think of what to do next. Whoever said that time slows down in these kinds of incidents had it all wrong. If anything, time seemed to her to speed up. Things were happening fast!

An exit to an overpass appeared ahead as they were racing down the highway nearly side by side. She maneuvered into the left side of the right lane as the van came up on her left again, its engine racing hard. Mahdi saw the exit too, and tried to force her over into it. She hit the right front fender of the van hard. Mahdi suddenly realized he was going to hit the guardrail on the ramp, and hit it head-on at speed. He suddenly cut to the left and missed the guardrail, but also missed the exit. He fought for control as he bounced down the hillside of the ramp, and succeeded in getting stopped well past the exit on the shoulder of the road.

While he was fighting for control, Jackie hit the brakes, then hit the "gas," turned slightly to the right, and raced up the exit ramp. Mahdi cursed as he was taken by surprise and missed the exit. He had to back up against the traffic.

She reached the top of the ramp, stopped, released her seatbelt, quickly stretched and reached back, grabbed her bag, threw it into the glass-covered passenger seat, unzipped a pocket, and accelerated again.

She shot forward into the on-ramp and headed down toward the highway as the van reached the intersection at the top of the exit. He had to stop for traffic, and then she saw in the rearview mirror his wheels smoking as he tried to catch up with her. Driving with one hand and glancing from the road to her bag, she searched in her bag and finally found the 9mm Glock. She aimed the car briefly, let go of the steering wheel, and quickly worked the slide on the Glock, then back on the steering wheel. She was ready. She took a deep breath and exhaled. She took another deep breath and exhaled again. Who the hell were these people? Her Marine training finally kicked in. This would be close. She had to time it right.

Mahdi pulled up behind her and nudged her rear bumper. Then he backed off and moved into the left lane. Mahdi motioned for Jackie to stop on the right, to move over.

She could see in the outside rearview mirror, as the man in the front seat, slightly behind her, began to extend his hand with a pistol in it. A mistake.

Timing, timing, timing.

She softly, but quickly, hit the brakes, backing up several feet until the van was slightly ahead of the Current. Rafi, in the right seat, was startled as he went past her on the left, and his eyes went wide as he briefly saw the weapon in her hand. He yelled something unintelligible. With her right hand crossed in front of her, she fired three shots as fast as she could pull the trigger. The bullets rocketed out of the muzzle and crossed the short space between the two vehicles. It was only a few feet. Two of the bullets slammed into the side of Rafi's head, killing him instantly. The third bullet went through the windshield, making a star-shaped hole in front of Mahdi.

Mahdi immediately slowed down as Rafi slumped forward, hitting the dashboard, dead. Mahdi cursed loudly and pulled to the right and off the highway as their quarry drove on down the highway. He tore off his shirt and wiped the windshield quickly to remove the blood and gore that had sprayed out on it. He did this a couple of times until he could see again. He pulled a blood-covered Rafi down out of the seat onto the floor of the van, got back in the driver's seat, looked back at traffic, and pulled onto the road, doing a u-turn. As he headed back to pick up Nidal, he wondered how such a simple grab could have gone so badly. They had not anticipated the reception that had occurred. Abdul-Hakim and Ramiz would not be happy over this turn of events!

He pounded the steering wheel with his closed fists and let out a stream of curses in Arabic.

Chapter Thirty-Three
Investigation

Wednesday—July 13
East Texas Highways

Jackie continued on down the road several hundred yards and then pulled over until she was able to breathe again. Looking back at the van, she saw it make a sudden u-turn right across the grassy median and head in the opposite direction. She kept the gun in her hand and put a fresh magazine in it just in case she needed the extra rounds. She gathered her wits, called 911, and explained what had happened. The dispatcher wanted to know her location, and said they had already had several calls on the situation from other motorists, and a Texas State Highway Patrol cruiser was on the way.

Jackie waited for several minutes at the side of the road, watching carefully in case the van came back, and finally heard a siren faintly in the distance. After a few more minutes, two Texas troopers with flashing lights blazing pulled up behind her. She stood on the road shoulder on the driver's side of the car, placed her gun on her car seat, and waited as they cautiously, with guns drawn and aimed at her, approached. She told them that there was no danger and that her gun was on the front seat. One holstered his weapon and the other pointed hers at the ground as they cautiously checked the area around her car. Finally, they approached her and asked her what was going on.

She related what had happened, motioned to her car and its damaged windows, and said she had no idea why they were after her or why they shot at her. The troopers checked her carry permit, with raised eyebrows, since it was from the FBI and had a White House endorsement. She described the attacking van to them, but they were a bit noncommittal and said there were thousands of those vans on the road. Without the license number, they couldn't do anything about it. They filled out a report on their cruiser computer, had her electronically sign it, printed a copy for her, and let her go. The report went into the Texas Highway Patrol files and was considered un-investigable, since there was so little to go on and there were no witnesses. Another dead end.

Jackie, shaken up but otherwise okay, called ahead to Ryan. He was surprised to hear from her and asked where she was. She related what had happened and he told her, with a great deal of concern in his voice, to stay put. He was dumbfounded. She was only about forty-five minutes away. He would come and get her right away.

Mahdi drove back to the on-ramp where they had left Nidal, found him sitting next to the road looking dejected, picked him up, and headed back to their hotel. Nidal looked at the dead Rafi on the floor of the van and realized how close he had come to being a dead man. He looked out the window and unconsciously shuddered at the thought. He got away with just a sore arm and some abrasions from the road, but his friend had died. They arrived back at the hotel, carried Rafi into the room, set him in the bathtub, and went back to the sleeping area to think what their next move should be.

The evening had definitely not gone according to their plan.

About forty minutes later, Ryan arrived from the marina along with Juan, and after discussing the situation for a while, they got in the cars and headed for the marina. Juan drove the damaged Current, and they would have to see about the insurance claim in the morning. Unbelievable.

Jackie sat quietly for the first few miles and then started to break down. It had been a very traumatic event. Looking out the window, tears started to roll down her cheeks. She shook her head in amazement. First the attack, and then the lack of any apparent concern on the part of the Texas Highway Patrol. She looked out the window at the dark passing scenery. She glanced over at Ryan, who was concentrating on the road and deep in his own thoughts. She took a deep breath and then suddenly hit downward on the front dashboard with her fist. "Damn it!" she screamed.

Ryan quickly looked over at her.

She looked back at him and continued, "What in the hell is going on? Why did they attack me that way and what did they really expect to get from me? I'm sure I killed one of them. Why?"

Ryan looked back at the road and said softly, "I have no idea. Could you recognize them if you saw them again?"

"I doubt it. Maybe. Who knows? The guy I think I killed? I might be able to identify him given he was so close to me."

"We'll have to check it out tomorrow," Ryan said as they pulled in to the marina.

When they got out at Ryan's, Jackie went upstairs, put her bag in the bedroom, and took a long shower. She put on white shorts and a dark blue tank top, along with rhinestone decorated flip-flops, and joined Ryan on the outside deck. She looked lovely, and he gave her a long kiss. He had fixed her a strong drink, which she took with a smile. She took a long swallow of the Beefeater martini and tried to relax. She was still pretty tense over the attack.

It had been a very trying experience, and she was still a bit hyper from it. Ryan fixed himself a drink and they sat together on the lounge chairs overlooking the marina. Jackie related the whole incident again for Ryan, from getting off the airplane to his showing up on the highway. He looked at her and just shook his head in wonder. It was a miracle that she hadn't been injured, or worse. Under that pressure, she had really done well.

But she was there and safe despite the experience. He refreshed the drinks and, since it was still too early for bed, set out some shrimp and cocktail sauce he had prepared as a snack. He turned on some music, a bit of Neil Diamond, and they settled in for several moments of no conversation, enjoying the music and snack.

The night air was humid and warm. The martinis were cold and good. They finally began to relax. He pushed the lounge chairs together so they were touching each other and they held hands while sitting, silently thinking.

He said, "I'm so thankful that you are here and safe. You mean so much to me that I couldn't handle it if you were hurt, or worse."

She looked back at him and smiled. "I'm finally beginning to settle down after all this. Thank you for the comment. I love you, and perhaps we can find out what this is all about. But we won't do that until tomorrow. For now, let's just enjoy the moment and the evening." He nodded and squeezed her hand, and she squeezed back. They finished their drinks and went upstairs to bed.

She went into the bathroom and came out a few minutes later with a lacy, sexy outfit in a bright red color. Combined with her petite frame, nearly flawless complexion, brunette pixie-cut hair, and really well-proportioned breasts with raised nipples outlined in her lacy bra, she was a real beauty to behold. He had taken off his clothes and was sitting, partially covered, in the bed. He looked up and smiled broadly. She said with a come-hither smile, "Well, we can't let a little thing like attempted kidnapping spoil the evening, now can we?" He shook his head and she came over to him. He put his hands around her and pulled her toward him. His head went into her chest and she put both arms around his head, holding him tightly. He moved his hands up and undid her bra, and it fell to the floor, along with the rest of her outfit. He reached around, moved his head away, and felt her left breast fill his hand. He softly pinched her nipple and she arched her back slightly, moaning at the sensation. Both of them were over the top with emotion. They kissed deeply with tongues, ravishing each other's mouths. They stayed that way for several minutes, stroking each other, before he rolled over on top of her and was inside her almost immediately. Her arms, around his back, tightened in a hard embrace. After several moments, he rolled them both over so she was on top, and she continued the action with a passion he just loved. They climaxed together, and, after several minutes, she slid down off him.

She cuddled up very close to him, and he could feel some slight shivering. He held her for a long time, kissing her softly until she finally dropped off to sleep. He was awake for better than an hour more as he thought through what might be, could be, couldn't be happening. Why would someone try to kill Jackie?

After an hour of thinking, Mahdi decided they needed to get rid of Rafi, clean up the room, and leave as soon as possible. They went to a local Walmart, got some supplies, including a bolt cutter, and returned to the room. They stripped Rafi of all clothing and his personal effects.

Mahdi then pulled out the bolt cutters and stood there for a moment looking at his dead friend. He quietly sighed, reached over, grabbed Rafi's left hand, and told Nidal to hold the hand. Nidal looked at him but did as he requested. He held the hand as Mahdi cut off the thumb at the first knuckle, then moved to the next finger and did the same thing. Blood dripped slightly from the wounds. He finished with both hands and had the ends of all ten digits in a bag sitting on the floor. He went over to the bathroom and, a few at a time, flushed the digits down the toilet. Nidal, knowing the necessity of what they were doing, was still deeply disturbed at the sacrilege to Rafi's body. He shuddered at the thought.

They put Rafi in two large garbage bags fastened by duct tape and put him back out in the van. They cleaned up the room with Clorox wipes, including the bathtub, and left. They headed out a back country road they picked out at random well south of Houston, found a small swale in the road, and put the bag with Rafi into the culvert running under the road. No one observed their odd behavior. It was not seen or reported to anyone.

Then they headed northeast back toward Houston. After a couple of hours of circuitous traveling, just wandering around, they arrived at Hobby Airport. They parked the beaten-up Econoline van in the long-term parking lot, wiped it down with Clorox wipes, and went in to the ticketing area. They booked a late night flight for New York leaving in three hours and found a small restaurant.

After a meatless meal—rice, a salad, and tea—they went through security then to the gate, and waited. Mahdi called Ramiz and hesitatingly told him what had happened. Ramiz was quite surprised at the failure, asked several questions, and determined to fix the problem himself in the near future. It was obvious that they had really underestimated the woman. Two hours later, they boarded their aircraft and left the Houston area. The flight to New York was uneventful, and two days later they were in Socotra reporting their failure to Abdul-Hakim.

Ramiz had already notified Abdul-Hakim of the failure, so he wasn't surprised at the news. But he grilled Mahdi and Nidal with little let-up for better than thirty minutes. He just couldn't understand how three of his better people could fail at capturing a woman, any woman, regardless of her background. And to have left Rafi behind in the care of the infidels was even worse. His desecrated body would not rest, and they must regain it so they could see to his proper burial in true Muslim tradition.

Abdul-Hakim gave the fate of Rafi some thought. There were Muslims in the United States that were sympathetic to the New Persia movement, and, given the circumstances, could probably be asked to conduct a proper burial for Rafi if requested. He would have to look into it, but he didn't want to leave a trail back to New Persia. It might be a bit touchy.

Thoroughly embarrassed and shamed, both Mahdi and Nidal were then dismissed and assigned to debrief the combat training personnel on their failure. At least their experience could be used to train others in what not to do. The general consensus was that they should not have tried to pull Jackie over, but rather wait until she stopped somewhere and then snatch her. It would have been much cleaner, and they probably wouldn't have run into any form of interference. They were given some remedial training and assigned to the security pools patrolling the operations center perimeter and manning the guard stations.

Thursday—July 14
Ryan's Marina, Freeport, Texas

The next morning Ryan decided to make a phone call back to Washington to notify the president of the attack on Jackie. While there did not appear to be any connection to the administration, he needed to make sure and, if there was some form of connection to alert them of the incident.

Maria answered after the first ring. "Hello, Ryan. It's always a pleasure to hear from you. What can I do for you?"

"Maria, I need to talk with the president very briefly, and you can listen in."

"Why? What's this about?"

"There was an incident last night and Jackie was attacked. I think I need to let you and the president know about it in case there might be other attacks."

Immediately concerned, she said, "Just a minute. I'll put you through and listen in."

A moment later, the president came on. "What! What do you mean she was attacked? Is she okay? By who?"

"She's okay, but shaken up. Her car was totaled between collisions and shots fired. But she is okay."

"Shots fired? You mean someone actually shot at her?"

"Yes, sir. Several times. She was finally able to get her gun and return the fire. She thinks she got one of them, and they backed off in a hurry. The Texas Highway State Patrol took a report but didn't think they could do much. There weren't any witnesses and she didn't get the license number of the van. Probably a dead end there."

"But she's okay?"

"Yes, sir. She's here with me now. I thought you might like to know about it in case there may be other attempts on other people. I don't know whether this is something personal or if it has to do with the government. But I wanted to make sure you were aware of it."

"Man, McKenzie. You sure know how to stir up a hornets' nest, don't you? Well, at least she's safe for now. I'd suggest you get some kind of security in there so if they try again, you aren't totally caught off guard."

"Yes, sir. I have that already installed here. But I'm concerned there may be other attacks on your administration people. Quite frankly, this may be tied to the New Persia group. They may be out for some form of revenge."

"Good point. You say the troopers couldn't do much? Was that just their first go and they quit or are they looking further?"

"I think the report went into the archives and is forgotten. No. I don't think there will be any more from it."

"Hmmm," said the president. Then quietly, "We'll see."

The president concluded, "Ryan, take good care of her and watch your back. If this is New Persia, we could have some real problems."

"Yes, sir. Will do. We'll talk later." But Ryan was talking to a dead line. The president had already hung up.

Abdul-Hakim looked out at the smooth, calm tropical waters and felt the warm on-shore breeze filter through his open office window. Regret. It was a strong emotion, and he really felt it for Rafi. Unknown and buried in a foreign country. But then, every country and every war or serious skirmish resulted in these types of deaths and burials. Some much worse than others. He put his hands on the windowsill. There was simply no way to recover Rafi from the infidels' land. He had to accept that ... and if they tried, it would lead back to New Persia and they could not risk that. For the good of the New Persia movement, Rafi would have to remain where he was, a martyr in the struggle.

Chapter Thirty-Four
Investigation Follow-up

Thursday—July 14
Washington, D.C.

Maria came into the Oval Office and shook her head. She was obviously scared. Her eyes were pinched and her jaw was quite tight. She said, "We can't just let it drop …"

The president gruffly interrupted her. "We aren't going to let it drop. Get me Governor Overton on the phone. His Texas guys are way too light on this one. There has to be something they can do to find out who did this."

She nodded, stepped out of the office, and returned to her desk. A few minutes later she came over the intercom: "He's not in Austin right now. They're tracking him down and will call back as soon as they can."

"Okay. Thanks. Let me know the minute he's on the phone."

An hour later, Maria buzzed him and he picked up the phone.

"Mr. President, this is Jim Overton. What's going on? My staff said to get a hold of you immediately, and they emphasized *immediately*."

"Jim. I need your help ASAP." And he related what he knew of the incident, including that the troopers were shuffling off on the investigation.

The governor responded, "I don't know anything about this. It was one of your staff that was attacked?"

"Yes. Jackie is my primary scheduler taking care of my day-to-day activities. She's sharp and a real asset. Can you look into this and get some action going? I want to know who did this and why. There has to be some evidence somewhere. And there's the potential that someone out there is targeting my administration."

"I'll look into it immediately and get back to you as soon as I can. Sorry about this, but these things do happen."

"Yeah. I know. Let me know what you find out. And thanks." With that, the president broke the connection.

Thursday—July 14
San Antonio, Texas

Governor James Overton was concerned. This could blow up into a major political mess if he didn't respond quickly and get some information to the president soon. He called his chief of staff, Johnny Lewey, over. He gave him a quick rundown of what happened. Lewey's very bushy eyebrows went up as he heard the story, and from the president, no less.

After listening for a few minutes, he said, "It sounds like we need to get Commander Garrison on the line and see what we can break loose. They should have done a forensics check of her car, and we can check the cameras that are on the overpasses for that road and time. We put a lot of money into those cameras; maybe they will help this time."

The governor responded, "Good thoughts. Go ahead and get it moving and keep me informed."

Johnny nodded, made a note to himself, and headed out of the room to find a quiet spot to make a phone call.

Friday—July 15
East Texas Country

At close to the same time that Mahdi was briefing Abdul-Hakim, Jack Warner, a rancher in the Lake Jackson area of Texas, was idly driving down the access road to his home. He had been in town getting some fencing supplies. He came to the swale in the road, noticed a large garbage bag blocking the drain, and stopped. He didn't want the rain, during the next heavy fall, to get blocked and flood part of his fields. He climbed down into the ditch and grabbed the bag. He pulled hard on it, since it was heavy and, he thought, stuck in the culvert. Part of the bag separated. He stared at the break in the plastic. What the ... !

He stared totally dumbfounded. It was a dead body!

He stood there for a minute. Then thinking returned and he backed off, shaking his head in dismay, turned around, and headed back to his truck. He drove the half-mile to his home and called the Wharton County sheriff. He reported what he had found and they dispatched a deputy. He met the deputy at the swale, pointed out what he had found, and sat back to see what would happen. It took a while, but a lot happened.

Several more deputies showed up, including the sheriff himself, and the county coroner made his appearance an hour later.

Jack was interviewed by both the sheriff's deputies and the Wharton County coroner. He didn't have much to add to what he had told them over the phone. The coroner eventually removed the body and took it back to the county morgue for an autopsy. A John Doe. And an apparent foreign one, at that. With two 9mm bullet holes in the head, and all his fingertips missing, he didn't die of natural causes, and whoever did this did not want him identified.

The coroner filed the usual paperwork with the state, and initial arrangements were made to bury the body as a John Doe at county expense. With no papers on the naked body and no DNA record in any of the criminal or service databases, there was no real option. His body was placed in the coolers until final cemetery arrangements could be made, which usually took a week or so.

Friday—July 15
Ryan's Marina, Freeport, Texas

Ryan and Jackie were out on the pier working on one of the water taps when Betty called them on the radio. "The Texas Highway Patrol is here, and he wants to talk with you, Jackie."

They looked at each other. Ryan shrugged and Jackie glanced up toward the marina office. Ryan said, "Go ahead. I'll finish up here and join you in a few minutes."

She nodded and headed up to the office. When she got there, a trooper was waiting, clipboard and camera in hand. "I'm Trooper Wilson. I've got a copy of the report that was submitted on the incident this past Wednesday. We've been directed to look into the matter in more detail and see if we can identify who was after you. While I've got the report and have read it, would you please explain what happened?"

Jackie and the trooper sat down at one of the outside tables with an umbrella, and she went through the details from when she was on the on-ramp to when the attackers left her. She left nothing out, including her thought that she had hit one of them as she returned fire. The trooper looked up at her with a questioning look. She elaborated that the one in the passenger seat had slumped forward after she fired and as they backed off.

He asked, "So you were able to return fire even at those speeds?"

"Yes. I didn't feel I had any choice. They had fired at me several times and we weren't in any position to talk."

"And you weren't able to get the license number?"

"No. I was too busy trying to get out of there."

"So. It was a late-model Ford Econoline. Three men in it initially. One left behind as you sped away, and one possibly killed on the road."

"That about sums it up."

"Hmmm. Can I see the car you were driving?"

"Sure. It's in the parking lot. We haven't returned it yet. Something we were going to do later today."

With that comment, they got up from the table and went out to the parking lot. Ryan joined them there, since he had finished on the pier. Ryan introduced himself and the trooper shook hands with him.

Trooper Wilson carefully looked the car over and noted the damaged left front fender and the blown-out glass on both sides. He took photos of each of the damaged areas, along with photos of the front seat with all the glass on it. He took samples of the glass, putting several pieces in an evidence bag, and then looked over the interior very closely. Down on the floor of the passenger side, he spotted a hole in the heater vent. Digging into the hole slightly, he removed a bullet. It was misshapen and only partial. He put it in an evidence bag. Looking at the exterior of the car, he took samples of the white paint that had scraped off the van when the collision occurred. He was pretty thorough, and said nothing as he went about his chores. He backed away from the car and looked at it from several directions, taking photos all the time. He made several notes. Finally it looked like he was finished. He came back to where Ryan and Jackie were standing.

He said, "Both the front windshield and the rear window are still intact." Then he made a questioning motion with his hand.

Jackie replied, "Yes. They never hit those for some reason. I have no idea why. When he pulled up behind me and bumped the rear, he backed off and came up on my left. It really had me spooked. Since they had already fired at me, I didn't take any chances and fired back. That seemed to take the wind out of their sails and they stopped."

196

The trooper nodded in thought. "I see," he said. "Is it possible they were just trying to get you to stop?"

"Yes. I've thought of that. When they initially stopped me on the ramp, they hopped out of the van with guns. What would you have thought? I'll tell you. I thought I'd better get out of there! And when the gun went off on the right side and again on the left, with the windows exploding, I had no question about it."

"Yeah. I suppose that would be my reaction too." He thought for a moment more then said, "I'll be sending in an enhanced report, and we'll see if the lab can come up with anything on these samples I've taken. We'll also be checking the local hospitals for any gunshot wound reported in the past day or so. Due to the attention this thing has, I'll personally get back to you with any results. Should take a few days at the most, since this has some very high-level attention."

Ryan interrupted, "How high are we talking about?" He was suspicious that the president had done something behind the scenes.

Trooper Wilson responded, "I don't really know, but the governor's interested, so naturally, we're interested too."

"I see," said Ryan. The connection in his mind was immediate, and he internally smiled to himself.

With that, the trooper asked that they keep the Current until he got back to them, and then he left. Ryan and Jackie were left in the parking lot looking forlornly at the damaged Current. Ryan said, "Well, it looks like we're stuck with the Current for a while. I'll call the rental place and let them know what happened. I'm not sure how the insurance and all will play out on this. We'll just have to wait and see."

Jackie just silently nodded and shivered internally. She didn't like having the Current around to remind her of the harrowing experience she had gone through.

Sunday—July 17
Ryan's Marina, Freeport, Texas

Two days later, Trooper Wilson stopped by with some information for them. There had been progress made but it appeared to still be a dead end. He said, "We ran tests on the glass and the shard of bullet. The glass did have gunpowder burns embedded in it, so there was definitely gunfire involved." He looked at Jackie, who had looked very frustrated at the

197

implication, and said, "I know. I know. But we have to verify everything we can on an incident like this. We also could determine, best guess, that the shard was from a .45-caliber bullet. Not a small weapon! So both pieces of evidence I got from the car backs up your story."

"And ..." said Jackie, her arms crossed in front of her, looking up at the trooper with an irritated look on her face.

"And we pulled down the digital recordings from the overpass cameras on that road at that approximate time. We found you, running like hell, with a white van either on your tail or at your side, depending on the camera view."

"Holy mackerel. You're kidding. You have it on film?" she exclaimed, leaning slightly forward with her hands on her hips.

"Yes we do. And we got the license plate of the van. We traced it back to the rental agency and they said it was still checked out to a Mr. Carol Simpson. When we did a check on his name and address, both were bogus. Until we find that van, we're dead in the water. We do have an all-points out on it, but it may take a while, especially if they parked it somewhere."

Trooper Wilson said, "We track reported unusual deaths in the state. When a coroner has a John Doe, we are notified to see if there might be some means of identifying the individual. We have one now and think it may be related to this incident. He was killed by two shots to the head. And they were 9mm. We want to check your gun and see if the ballistics match. I'd like to take your gun today so we can run the tests and either confirm it or not. The coroner also noticed that there was automobile glass in small quantities in the hair. The glass was analyzed and had gunshot residue on it. It would appear that he was either shot through a car window, or was very close to a window when the bullets hit him."

Jackie looked at the trooper and said, "Sure, you can take the gun, but could I see the man? I might be able to identify him. While it was pretty hectic in those moments, I did see him and he was only a few feet away from me."

"I think that can be arranged. He's at the Wharton County coroner's office. It's west of here, about a two-hour drive. I'll set it up and give you a call. We'll try to get it done today or tomorrow. And perhaps we can get the ballistics done and your gun back to you."

Jackie nodded and looked at Ryan, who had been silent the whole time. He said, "Sure. I can drive you over there anytime it can be set up. It might help solve this mystery if we can identify him."

Both Jackie and Ryan nodded in understanding. They were still at risk and didn't know by how much. Tension was there and getting stronger. After a few moments, Ryan escorted the trooper out to the parking lot, shook hands, and they were left to their own thoughts.

While Jackie had her eight years of Marine MP training to help, she still felt scared. There were too many loose ends. And she felt she was one of them. And there were still two men out there somewhere who'd tried to capture or kill her. Where were they now?

Ryan came back to the office. He looked at the obvious stress on Jackie's face and said, "Let's head on down to the Dolphin and get some dinner. I could use a break and a stiff one. You look like you could too."

She nodded. They locked up the office and walked the short distance hand in hand down to the pier where the Dolphin restaurant was located. They walked in, found a seat in the informal place, and ordered drinks. It had been a long and tension-filled day.

Governor Overton received a report that day on the progress of the investigation. Since he and the president were reasonably close, he sent a note via email to Maria explaining what they had found and what the next steps would be. He received a reply two hours later basically thanking him and letting him know they waited for the next update.

The next day, after receiving a call from Trooper Wilson, Ryan drove Jackie over to the Wharton County coroner's office. The coroner had made a ballistics match on her pistol and the bullets recovered from the head of Rafi. After viewing the body, Jackie positively identified him as one of her assailants. But they still didn't know who Rafi was or where he came from. The eventual finding of the van did not help any, because it had been wiped down and there was no evidence to tie it to a real person, other than some blood samples from a vent that matched their John Doe. Rafi was then buried in a local cemetery at county expense.

Nothing else could be done. A dead end ... especially for Rafi.

Chapter Thirty-Five
Silent Attack

Tuesday—July 19
Freeport, Texas

Ramiz drove his rental car down from Houston, where he had flown in a few hours before to continue with the efforts directed by Abdul-Hakim. He was still upset and irritated at the failure to capture Jackie the previous week, and the loss of Rafi. He simply couldn't understand why such a simple grab could go so wrong.

The evening air was humid and warm as they headed south on Highway 288. He had been met by Kamal and Ishaq, who had arrived a few days before. Both spoke excellent English and understood the American culture quite well. It was well past midnight when they pulled into a marina just north of Surfside, Texas, several miles from Ryan's marina. They were on a deadly mission for the ayatollah and the New Persia cause.

Kamal and Ishaq had spent the last two days looking for a good high-speed powerboat they could steal, and had finally located what they were looking for in the marina north of Freeport, Texas. It was a 2016 twenty-foot Stingray with open cabin and a 260-horsepower engine. Through the internet they were able to get some technical data on it and figured out how to hot-wire it for their use.

After the drive south, they arrived at the marina where the powerboat was moored. Arriving in the dark of the early morning, they parked a half-mile away from the marina and walked back to it. They scaled a fence surrounding the marina and made their way out to the pier undisturbed. It was quite dark, and everything was quiet as Kamal pulled the cover off the boat and crawled under the instrument panel. With a very small LED flashlight, and a couple of small jumper cables, he was able to power up the panel. He checked it for fuel, found it full, and, touching two wires together, started the inboard engine. It started quickly and settled into a low rumble through the twin exhausts. After throwing off the mooring lines, with the engine at idle, they eased the powerboat out of its slip and into the marina harbor access, leaving the running lights off. They were just a faint apparition in the watery darkness.

As they eased out of the marina, they kept a close eye on the other boats in case someone awoke or raised an alarm ... but nothing happened and all was quiet. They quietly cleared the breakwater, powered up, and headed out into the Gulf of Mexico. They calculated that they only had about a twenty-minute run, maybe less, to Ryan's marina on the other side of the Brazos River.

Ramiz lit up a cigarette, and the flare from his lighter revealed a Middle Eastern man of about thirty. Now with a full beard and a mellow look about him that masked his determination, Ramiz had been here before, and would now complete his mission for Abdul-Hakim and the ayatollah. His accomplices were two of the better and more knowledgeable men that Abdul-Hakim had in his group.

After twenty minutes, they came to the mouth of the Brazos River and turned into it looking for the entrance to Ryan's marina. Shortly after turning upriver, they spotted the entrance and the dimmed lights of the marina on the west shore. Ramiz was familiar with it from his previous scouting trip six months earlier. Ramiz slowed to idle to minimize noise and his wake, and eased the powerboat into the marina access. All was quiet. Nothing appeared to be moving. The boats in the various slips were either not occupied or the people aboard were sleeping. They could see, on one of the larger boats, the glow of a large TV through closed curtains. People were either up late or had fallen asleep watching.

They quietly eased into an empty slip, looped the mooring lines over the small bollards, and tied the lines off. Ramiz, reaching under the instrument panel for a wire, shut down the engine. Then he rearranged the wire so they could get started quickly when they were finished with their mission.

They silently made sure they had their weapons and knives, took a brief swallow of water, checked the time—it was 2:30 a.m.—and stepped off the boat onto the pier. All was quiet. Their mission was nearly half over and they had succeeded in getting into the Eagle's nest. Soon the Eagle would be dead and they could return to their business supporting the ayatollah's vision.

The recently installed alarm system was persistent. Ryan was struggling to recognize, in his half-foggy brain in the middle of the night, what that racket was. Jackie, also awakened by the noise, reached over and lightly touched his arm. His head cleared immediately. He knew it was a cautionary touch. Something had set off their marina alarms. They waited for just a few moments and then both got out of bed, slipped on robes, grabbed their pistols from the nightstands, and moved over to the desk with the security system laptop. The computer was out of sleep mode and active. It was set on the security system, and they could see the flashing frame of the marina entrance camera and sensor. Something had entered the marina via the water.

Ryan, with a few taps on the keyboard and manipulating the mouse, scanned between the two cameras looking for something that wasn't right. There was a boat in a slip that hadn't been there earlier. He focused a night-vision camera, mounted on one of the slip light poles near the boat, and did not recognize the boat at all. It was a complete stranger to him. No one appeared to be in the boat, so whoever had arrived had already gotten out and was wandering around. Something wasn't right, not at this time of the night.

He moved the camera around, seeing nothing, and switched to another camera. Again, nothing.

They were off the side pier and on one of the two main piers, slowly progressing toward the marina office building. They hesitated for a moment. There had been a noise. They moved more slowly and heard the slight noise again. Ishaq looked around and spotted what he was looking for. A camera on one of the light poles was scanning—he could hear the slight sound of its drive motor. He froze. The camera happened to be looking away at the moment, but it was slowly scanning back toward them. It stopped and started several times. The lens moved slightly in and out, focusing on something. That meant someone was awake and controlling it. It wasn't on an automatic scan. Someone was looking for them. He reached over and touched Kamal and then Ramiz. With his head, he motioned to the camera and indicated they needed to take cover before the camera came around further. Ramiz looked surprised. There had been no cameras when he had been there before.

But reality was reality … deal with it.

They located an area behind a berthed boat that was in line with the scanning camera. Moving quickly, they got behind it and ducked down below the boat's railing.

Ryan was scanning each of the piers with the two cameras he had available. Several times he thought he saw something, but then realized it wasn't anything abnormal. Jackie was staring at the screen willing it to show something they could act on. Nothing. But the strange boat was still there. It hadn't moved. Very quiet.

The phone rang. Jackson Alarm Systems. Ryan told them what was going on and that he would like the police notified. They moved on it while he was still on the phone. The police were on their way.

Watching the camera through the boat rails, Ramiz knew this particular mission would not work; it was gone. No way they could continue. He would have to retreat. Their element of surprise was obviously blown. He watched as the camera slowly panned. He sat back and tried to think. What next? Kamal and Ishaq did the same.

Ramiz watched the camera move around past them and motioned to Kamal and Ishaq, and they headed back to the boat, watching for any other motion on the piers. They got back to the boat, started it, and began to back out.

Ryan watched with the second camera as three men bolted from behind one of the berthed sailboats to the strange powerboat. He couldn't see their faces in the dark, but they were all good size and obviously up to something. He walked over to the kitchen wall and hit the main light switches for that part of the pier.

Suddenly the pier was bathed in bright lights. Ramiz glanced up at the bright lights, then back to the instrument panel. He gunned the motor and sped away out the marina entrance and on into the river. Never looking back, he raced downriver and into the gulf, Kamal and Ishaq hanging on. Frustration outlined on his face. He would have to re-plan the whole thing.

Ryan watched as the boat raced out of the marina and headed downriver. He quietly thanked Jackie for suggesting the installation of the alarm system several months back. She nodded back and put her Glock away.

The police showed up shortly after and watched the replay on the laptop. But there was nothing they could do. The boat had gotten away and they couldn't make out the registration number.

Jackson Alarms dispatched a technician immediately. After about thirty minutes, he arrived. He brought special enhancing equipment with him, hooked it up to the laptop, and went through a series of digital tests. After the technician worked for several minutes, both Ryan and Jackie were amazed. When Ryan had turned on the main lights, the pier had been illuminated. They were able to identify the boat with its registration. They reported it to the now-departed police, but it had been reported stolen an hour before.

They had also caught the image of the men. Looking at the enhanced image, Ryan was only partially surprised. He recognized it from several months earlier. He had met the apparent leader of these intruders. He was looking at the face of Ramiz. He didn't recognize the other two.

But who was Ramiz, really? Why was he after them?

Chapter Thirty-Six
Shootout

Tuesday—July 19
Ryan's Marina, Freeport, Texas

After the technician was closing up his equipment, Ryan began thinking again. He sat down and made himself a cup of coffee. Jackie refused one with a shake of her head. He was getting very wary of what was happening. First Jackie had escaped either a kidnapping attempt or outright killing effort, and second, within just a few days, an apparent attempt on his life.

Jackie came over and sat down at the kitchen table with him. She could see the worry on his face and knew what he was thinking. She took his hand on the tabletop and said, "This certainly isn't a coincidence after the attempt on me the other day. Someone is really after us, and in a very serious manner."

He looked back at her. "Yes. But who, and why?"

She shrugged. "Good question." She thought a moment then said, "You saw that face a few minutes ago on the computer enhancement. Obviously you recognized him. Who is he?"

"His name is Ramiz, and he visited here a few weeks ago. Looking for a possible berth for his boat. Betty and I both had doubts about him. Although now I think he may have just been scouting out the place. I don't know anything about him, since he didn't leave a card or contact."

"So we don't have any way to track him down?"

"Not that I can think of right now."

"What kind of a name is Ramiz? Maybe we can think that over and come to some conclusion. It might be that nasty word 'profiling,' but it also might help us."

"I think it's Arabic or Middle Eastern."

Her eyes lit up a bit. "Don't you see it?"

He looked back at her, puzzled.

"The ayatollah! He's behind this. We have pulled his tail and he is striking back at the people who worked the details. Us."

He shook his head slightly as she continued.

"He can't get directly to the president and his staff, but he has found out about you and me supporting this whole thing, and is striking back at us as a way to warn the president."

"That's a stretch."

"Maybe so. But it fits what's going on."

He sat for a moment and realized that she had a point. Sharp woman! Then he looked over at her and said, "Okay. Let's assume you're right. Any suggestions on what to do about it? They failed tonight, so I think we can anticipate that they will try again. But we don't know how or when. That thought is nerve-racking."

Again, she shrugged. Then she grabbed his hand again and said, "Let's get back to bed. I've got a few more days here after talking with Maria earlier. We can worry about it more in the morning. Nothing's going to happen yet tonight."

She was wrong.

Ramiz and his two assistants beached the boat further up the coast from where they stole it and walked back down to their parked vehicle. Ramiz was furious. Such a simple task, and they had failed again! Why was it that each of his efforts was failing? Why?

They got back in the rental car and drove off into the darkness. It was now a little past 4:00 a.m. and they had not completed their mission. So far it was a failure, and he couldn't tolerate that. A determined look came over his face. Ryan and his girlfriend would not be expecting anything else to happen tonight ... so it would be the ideal time to strike at them and take them out. They would kill Ryan and try to kidnap Jackie Conover. If Jackie was killed in the process, so what? It would serve as even more of a warning to the president that the New Persia effort was not to be fooled with. A strike now would work.

Daylight would begin in another hour. They had to move fast. He explained what he had in mind to Kamal and Ishaq. They readily agreed, and they drove down to Ryan's marina.

Driving past the parking lot, they turned around at the dead end on the county road, pulled over onto the berm of the road, and parked. They were right across the parking lot and could see the entrance to Ryan's apartment above the marina office. There was just a small sliver of light in the sky to the east, as the morning was just starting. It wouldn't take more than ten or fifteen minutes and the stronghold would be partially revenged. They had to move, and move fast, to accomplish their mission and get out of there.

They quietly got out of the car and, running in a crouch with guns drawn, crossed the parking lot to the front entrance to the apartment. Ishaq quietly opened the screen door, bent down, and looked at the front door lock. It was substantial and he couldn't pick it quickly. They moved around to the side of the marina and found the back door on the lower level much easier to pick. After just a few moments, they were inside the marina office. The alarms went off but they ignored them. They would be finished and gone in the next few minutes. The police couldn't react that fast. Quickly moving through the back of the office, they climbed the stairs that led to Ryan's apartment. Ishaq tried the door and found it locked. Kamal was right behind him on the stairs, and Ramiz was at the bottom waiting for them to get through the door.

The phone rang.

The damn intruder alarm had gone off again. Only this time it was the parking lot and marina door. Jackie and Ryan struggled out of bed again and looked at the computer. Nothing on the parking lot monitor. Ryan quickly played, at high speed, the last two minutes of recording and saw three men crossing the parking lot. He watched as they checked his front door and then disappeared into the marina office. Then real-time coverage resumed. A view into the main part of the marina office showed one man at the base of their stairs. Gun drawn and ready. Ryan went over to the closet and got his twelve-gauge shotgun, made sure it was loaded, and went back to the desk. Jackie had her pistol out and was looking at the stair door. He glanced at the clock. It was 4:35 a.m.

The phone rang again.

Automatic weapon shots were fired through the door from the stairs. The door rattled loudly and the frame splintered as the door was suddenly kicked in. Jackie, crouching low and off to one side, fired several shots directly into the door opening, and Ryan fired the shotgun, with an earsplitting explosive sound in the small rooms, in the same direction. Twice. Ishaq caught the first shots directly in the chest and head. The nine number ten shot pellets from the shotgun blasts tore his chest and face apart, and there was blood splattered all over the stairwell. He was dead before he hit the top of the stairs and tumbled to the bottom. Kamal was hit in the right arm and took some of the second shotgun blast in the head and neck. He collapsed, was knocked over by Ishaq on the stairs, and followed Ishaq tumbling to the bottom, unconscious. A twelve-gauge shotgun can do a tremendous amount of damage to a human at short range, and it certainly did this time. Shredded and very bloodied tissue resulted from the blast. Ramiz, shocked at seeing the carnage from the foot of the stairs, bolted out of the office and ran across the parking lot. All of it recorded in the alarm system.

The phone was still ringing. Ryan answered it. Jackson Alarms. Police were on their way ... again.

Ramiz, not in a panic but close to it, tore out of the marina building, crossed to the car, quickly started it, and threw some small gravel as he headed north toward town. He couldn't get the image of the two men torn apart by the shotgun out of his mind. He got about a half-mile down the road, glanced in his mirrors, realized he wasn't being followed, and slowed down. He pulled over to the side of the road as three police cruisers went flying past him with all lights and sirens going. He certainly knew where they were going! He watched the rearview mirror as they disappeared over a small hill. He sighed slightly and then hit the soft top of the dashboard with his open hand in frustration. His teeth were gritted together and he was just plain mad. They had failed again, and this time he was in the middle of it. And he had lost two of his best men in the attempt. While there wasn't any way to trace the identities of Ishaq or Kamal, since they weren't in anybody's database, it was still a loss to the New Persia movement. A loss he could not sustain. At least this time they would get a proper burial, since they both carried Muslim identification ... just nothing to tie them to New Persia.

He drove another several miles to get outside any roadblocks that might be put up, and pulled over again to think. While he didn't believe in luck, this fellow McKenzie just seemed to be very difficult to get to. They had tried multiple times now and each time failed. The failures would not sit well with Abdul-Hakim or, especially, the ayatollah. He could not go back without some form of additional plan to take out Ryan and, better yet, his whole crew. But he would have to improve his planning so that it was a foolproof action. He had his work cut out for himself.

It was now getting very light outside as the morning sun came up over the horizon, and he pulled out on to Highway 288 heading north. He decided to go back to Houston and then on to Socotra. He had lost several men in these attempts and could not afford to lose more. Plans needed to be made, and with all the expertise they could muster from the operations center assets.

Several minutes later, the police arrived in force at Ryan's marina. Shots had been fired and police emotions were very high, since they didn't know what they might face. Three squad cars arrived, and all the officers had their riot guns in their hands as they cautiously approached the marina office and apartment complex. Over the phone Ryan told the dispatcher that he was going out to meet them and for them to put their guns down. All the action was over and there was no danger. A few moments later, Ryan could hear the dispatcher talking on the radio, and the officers backed off a bit. Ryan then put his shotgun down and went out to meet them. The sergeant, a man by the name of Channel Gibson, walked to meet Ryan as the other two officers went into the marina office. He shook hands with Ryan and said, "You sure do lead a lively life, don't you, Ryan?"

"Yeah. But I think I could do without this kind of thing."

The sergeant was interrupted by a radio call from the officers that were in the building. "Hey, Sarge. You'd better get in here. We have a dead body, shot up pretty badly, and the other one is close to expiring. Need the coroner and the medic guys. Oh ... my partner needs a barf bag too."

Gibson, grimacing, keyed his shoulder mike and said, "Roger." He changed frequency as he started to walk toward the marina office, and told the dispatcher to get the coroner and a medic unit on the way. As he was walking, Ryan told him what had happened and that one person had gotten away.

After several hours, and retelling the tale several times, Ryan and Jackie were told they were okay for now. The bullet holes through the outside of the door and the shotgun blast through the door from the inside pretty well told the tale. Combined with the recorded surveillance tapes, it wasn't hard to see what had happened. The coroner removed Ishaq's body and the medics arrived to tend to Kamal. He was taken to the local hospital but expired on the way. He was dead on arrival.

The police worked up their report, and Ryan and Jackie were asked to come down to the police station to give a statement. They did that and then returned to the marina. It had been a long night and they were quite tired.

Ryan sat at the kitchen table thoroughly exhausted. Jackie sat across the table from him sipping on some ice water. He looked around at the partially devastated apartment with the blown-in door and shattered doorframe. It was quite a mess, and the blood down the steps was not very pleasant either. He would have to get someone in first thing later in the morning to clean it up. Yuck.

"Well," he said. "That was quite a night. They tried twice and both times failed. Thank heavens for that alarm system you convinced me to put in. It really saved the day for us."

She looked at him and said, "Yes. But I sure was wrong earlier after the first attempt. These guys are really something. Talk about being determined! What's next?"

"I don't know. But since a couple of them were killed, and there were only three to begin with, maybe they'll back off for a few days. We're going up to Washington tomorrow, so we should have some break from this. I hope so, anyway."

"Yes, but it is really something to think that we may have to live looking over our shoulders until this outfit is finally put away for good. I don't like the thought of that, and we could be facing some real problems in the near future."

He looked at her and couldn't disagree. He shook his head and said, "All the more reason to get them and put them where they belong. We'll have to see what the president has in mind day after tomorrow."

She just nodded. But he could see the worry on her face. It could be hell.

Juan was called in, and he and Ryan made some emergency repairs to the apartment. Jackie waited until mid-morning and then called Maria in the president's office. She told Maria what had happened. They were due to fly up to Washington the next day at the president's request. Jackie told Maria that she would be on the Gulfstream V C-37 aircraft and back to work the following day.

With nothing resolved in these situations, it was very upsetting and nerve-racking.

Chapter Thirty-Seven
New Tasking

Thursday—July 21
Washington, D.C.

It was a beautiful summer day. Tourists were all over Washington, D.C., and ground transportation was hard to come by. Traffic was quite a mess. Ryan, Jackie, Dave, and Jasper had flown up that morning on the C-37 aircraft and were due to meet with President Martinez at 2:30 p.m. in the Oval Office. Transport was not a problem for them however, since the black suburbans picked them up at Andrews and took them directly to the White House.

After going through security, they were escorted into the Oval Office and sat down in the couch area. The president wasn't there. After a few moments, he came striding in, with Jack Harrison slightly behind him, and apologized for his tardiness.

The president walked up to Ryan and Jackie and put his arms around their shoulders. He said, "Maria told me what happened very early yesterday morning. That had to be quite frightening, and I'm certainly glad to hear that you both are okay." He looked at both of them and continued, "It just re-emphasizes the need to get these people and put them where they belong ... either in jail or in the ground."

They all sat down and the president began, "Well, I'm sure you're wondering what this is all about."

They all just nodded.

He continued, "I'll get right to the point. I need three of you—Ryan, Dave, and Jackie—to go to the island of Socotra and ferret out what you can about what we think is the new headquarters of the New Persia movement. And we are going to have one of our people out of Sana'a join you. His name is Corey Gaskins."

Jasper looked over at Ryan and did a little fist pump. He had been right.

Ryan looked back with a questioning look and asked, "Where's Socotra and what's there?"

The president gave them a quick rundown on what had been happening and how the CIA and Defense Department had tracked the signals to that island.

"So, the CIA feels you would be the best to get in there and find out what's there, and perhaps what they are planning."

Jasper asked, "And you don't want me to go along?"

"No. I think we need to keep you sort of in reserve in case we need to send in a second mission."

Jasper, looking a bit disappointed, just nodded.

Ryan asked, "Why Jackie?" Jackie looked at him with arrows and darts. She thought it was a good idea, since the president had suggested it to her earlier, and she could keep up with Ryan and keep him out of trouble.

The president responded, "Because, in the guise of plant experts, she would make the exercise more realistic. And she has the background to help you guys stay out of trouble." He said with a knowing smile.

"Okay. So we go in as experts to see if plants they have could be of some use in our southwest. Is that what I'm understanding?"

"Yes. In the process of studying all those strange plants, you should be able to get in close to what we think is their center of operations and check it out. You may not be able to actually get into it, but between seeing it and talking to the locals, you may be able to get some good feel for what it is. And … maybe we're wrong. It may be something totally different from what we think. But that's up to you to figure out."

"Okay. When did you want us to leave?"

"You probably need to make some arrangements, so I would think early next week, and even expedited, it will take that long to get Yemeni visas."

Ryan looked around at everyone, got nods from them, and said, "Sounds good. I guess I'd better brush up on my plant biology."

The president just smiled.

Ryan then said, "As you know, someone appeared to be trying to kill Jackie and me."

The president looked very serious and said, "Yes. I heard."

Ryan then gave him a quick rundown of what had happened. He finished, "So, if the ayatollah is behind these attacks, we want him put away permanently. It's gotten personal for us."

"I can certainly understand that. As you prepare, be very careful and please keep me informed of your progress. Use Admiral Watkins as a point of contact."

The president then stood and shook hands all around, and they left the Oval Office.

Plans needed to be made.

They went to the Ritz, where they were staying, had a drink in the lounge, and agreed to meet in Ryan's room in an hour. They had a lot of planning to do and not much time to do it.

Jackie had joined them at the hotel, and was very pleased with the outcome of the meeting with the president. She had excitedly accepted the idea and the combination of this type of mission, and to be able to do it with Ryan was right up her Marine background alley. She loved it.

After they had a chance to refresh themselves and get some food, they met in Ryan's room for some strategizing. Once they figured out where Socotra was located from an internet query, they were able to get flights and hotel reservations set up. They had to process actual requests for visas, but coordinating that through the State Department, considering the presidential interest, was relatively simple.

It would be an exciting trip.

Ramiz arrived at the small airport in Hadibu and immediately was picked up by one of the security patrols from the operations center. He had already called ahead and told Abdul-Hakim what had happened, so there would be no surprises for the defense chief. Abdul-Hakim was livid about it, but calmed down after a few moments. It was what it was, and he couldn't do anything about what had already transpired. He agreed to a meeting to see what the next steps should be.

After getting his things together and resettling in his quarters, Ramiz met with Abdul-Hakim. He was surprised to see Khatib and the ayatollah present also. There was obviously a lot of concern over the recent events, and they wanted to hear, firsthand, what had happened. Then they would figure out a future course to pursue.

Ramiz, with a certain amount of nervous energy in his body, related the events that had occurred. He covered both the attempted kidnapping of Jackie and double attack on Ryan's marina in detail, including the very unsatisfactory ending and loss of three men. Khatib just looked at him. The ayatollah, deep in thought, said, "We seem to be missing something here. I have no doubt that the attempts so far have been well planned and well intentioned. But they have not worked, and all they have done is caused the loss of our men and put this McKenzie person on alert—and probably, President Martinez." He paused for a moment and then continued, "While I directed these efforts, perhaps I should rethink that direction."

Khatib looked at the floor and then out a window. He wasn't sure where the ayatollah was going with his line of thought. He said, "With all due respect, sir, I don't think the direction was wrong. The execution of our plans was faulty and we need to continue with our efforts. In other words, we need to regroup, re-plan, and get it accomplished."

The ayatollah looked at Khatib and smiled slightly. He nodded. Then he looked over at Abdul-Hakim and Ramiz and said, "What is your opinion? Should we continue?"

Abdul-Hakim looked briefly at Ramiz and then back to the ayatollah. "I think we can succeed. We seem to have run into some difficulties with our attempts so far. But McKenzie is a man and can be done away with. I think another attempt is in order, and perhaps, Allah willing, we will succeed."

"Very well," said the ayatollah. "We will make one more try at it."

He looked at Abdul-Hakim and Ramiz and added with a very serious look, "Don't fail this time."

Chapter Thirty-Eight
Socotra Visit

Friday—July 29
Socotra Island Operations Center

The new operations center was above ground with a well-spread-out facility. It was built on a small rise on the western exposure of the island of Socotra, which was located in the middle of the Arabian Sea. A part of Yemen, this island group was made up of four islands off the northeastern coast, or horn, of Africa. The center was built with security barricades that did not offend the eye. The idea was to make the center as unremarkable as possible ... hiding in plain sight. It had a full complement of communications equipment through the undersea cable to the Salalah satellite terminal. The communications would be upgraded in the near future with a local satellite terminal in the complex, given the renewed importance of the center now that the stronghold had been destroyed. The total complex, a real boon to the local economy, could house close to a thousand people in apartments and individual units. It was only about a mile from the sea and overlooked the small harbor and marina that had been built to handle the New Persia ships.

The actual island of Socotra, inhabited by fishermen and families for many centuries, is quite unique. Since it is quite remote, there are many species of plants and some animals that developed in isolation that are found nowhere else in the world. It ranked only behind the Galapagos and Hawaii regarding unique species. It was due to this remoteness, and a friendly government to their cause, that New Persia chose to locate the alternate center in Socotra.

Ryan, Jackie, and Dave flew in to Hadibu, the only major city/town on Socotra with a population a little over eight thousand. They were met by Corey Gaskins, a U.S. State Department representative for Yemen, got a taxi, and were taken to the Taj Socotra Hotel.

The hotel was in the main part of town and constructed of concrete block, like so many other structures. Some parts of it had a coat of stucco on it, and it was a slight off-white in color. The entrance was a few steps up off the street. The lobby had a bar, but it only served water and soft drinks. The registration desk was small but adequate. The interior matched the exterior in that it was also stuccoed.

The rooms were Spartan. With worn rugs and doorways with transoms, the overall affect was one of age. The doors were painted white and had old-fashioned regular key locks. The walls, some with little critters attached and moving around a bit, were painted a pale green and in some need of refreshing. Each room did have a private bath, two twin beds, and a cooler for soft drinks. A hard-back chair was in the corner, and a table with a light was between the twin beds. Another small writing table held the telephone and some hotel information packets. The windows were covered with a semi-transparent gauze-like material that permitted the breezes to flow. The bathrooms were dirty and not stocked. Ryan and group had been forewarned ... bring your own toiletries. The overall effect reminded them of something from a B-movie out of the late 40s or early '50s.

It had been a moderate-length flight from Sana'a, the Yemeni capital, and they were not too tired. They met in the bar, had a few Cokes, and got a rundown on the local customs from Corey, who had flown in from Sana'a the previous day. Corey stood just under six foot and had both a military bearing and somewhat muscular, burly build. At slightly over two hundred pounds they realized He would be a real asset in a serious disagreement.

After the discussion, which took about an hour, they accompanied Corey on a short tour of the small city. In the process they were able to arrange for a vehicle for the next day. As was the custom in Socotra, the vehicle came with a driver, Karim, who spoke only pidgin English, but well enough to get by. Plus, Ryan, Jackie, and Dave had been around a bit and could get their point or question across via sign language and gestures. And Corey spoke Arabic quite well, another benefit of having him along. They weren't worried about language problems.

They had devised a cover story for their presence on the island, since their real purpose was not to be revealed. They were on a botanical survey with the U.S. Interior Department looking at unique species of plants for consideration in the

American southwest. As such, they had the bush clothing and materials expected of people going cross-country. After looking over maps of the island, they worked with Karim until he understood where they wished to go. They arranged for him to pick them up at 7:00 a.m. the next morning in front of the hotel. He nodded and headed off, happy with the rental and probable generous tip from the American scientists.

Saturday—July 30
Socotra Island

The following morning, with clear skies and the temperature already approaching eighty degrees, they met at the front of the hotel and loaded up into the four-wheel-drive Land Rover that had seen much better days. With the four of them, some equipment, and Karim, it was a bit of a squeeze, but they managed. They headed west past the airport and on toward Ghubbah, turning south just before reaching it. They were headed inland toward Kafshifo, and made several stops as they viewed and admired much of the unique plant life near the road. They spent part of the morning in Kafshifo and, through Karim acting as an interpreter with Corey's help, asked some of the locals what life was like in the remote area. After several minutes of conversation, and back and forth with questions, they understood the nomadic type of existence from goat herding and subsistence farming.

One aspect that popped out, which drew their attention, was a comment that they'd had a recent economic boom when some construction work was performed down the road several miles from the town.

A large residential and business structure had been built behind some earthen berms and large fences. A harbor had been developed that would take a fairly good-sized ship. Several hundred construction workers had come to the area and built it over close to a year. Some of the local men had been hired as part of the construction crew. A road connected the harbor to the complex inside the fence line and also to the highway they were on. It was a bit of a mystery who was behind it, but the work for them was good and there was some ongoing support work. It was a lot better than goat herding.

Ryan looked at his friends and raised his eyebrows when he heard the information. It confirmed what they had been told from analysts reviewing satellite imagery. This might be the new stronghold or center for the New Persia operations. He feigned no interest, but internally he felt they were getting somewhere. They needed to see what they could while they were in the area. That was the real reason they were there in the first place.

After more conversation, they departed and headed further down toward the south, keeping alert for any sight they might have of the complex. As they came over a rise in the terrain, off to the left and behind another small hill, they saw a roofline of a fairly significant-sized building. There was a paved road that came out from the hills and intersected with their highway. The fencing was high, and there was a manned guard shack standing perhaps fifty yards back from the intersection. They directed Karim to pull over and, while very obviously looking at a map, looked at the building as best they could without appearing to be too interested. Then they asked Karim to move on down the road toward the south coast of the island. In the process of driving further, part of the land opened up and they could see a new road off to the left, and a man-made harbor with two moderate-sized piers in the distance. Moored at one of the piers was a yacht very familiar to Ryan and Dave. It appeared to be a duplicate of the yacht they had captured in the Gulf of Mexico last year. Moored at the other pier was a very large trimaran. Three patrol boats were also tied up. There was no activity on either pier. All appeared quiet. The harbor had a small breakwater and the piers were large enough for a good-sized vessel. Some small buildings appeared to be storage or maintenance facilities on the land end of the piers. Concrete walkways and access roads were connected to the piers so vehicles could service or load cargo on the vessels.

Looking back up the hill, they were surprised to see two commercial-sized ten-meter communications antennas near the larger building, aimed almost straight up to apparently intercept signals from geo-stationary satellites. Part of the way down the hill from the communications complex was a series of apartment buildings and units. Obviously, the apartments were for use by the workers at the complex. All of the complex was surrounded by high fencing, though not topped with concertina wire, so it didn't quite appear threatening. Here and there along the perimeter, berms had also been constructed. Quite an impressive layout. And one that had been well planned over a period of time. It was pretty well hidden, had its own power and water supply, and was remote enough to not draw any worldly attention. Ryan was impressed. They had thought it through. It would be interesting to see what they had in the large building that was obviously the center of their operations.

They directed Karim to continue on down to the coast at the town of Mahfirhin, where they could refuel. They stopped and, while Karim was refueling, stepped away from the vehicle. They made a deal of stretching and pumping their legs, and glanced at each other knowingly. They had found the operations center. They were sure of it. The yacht, tied up at the pier and very familiar to Ryan, was the real clincher.

To maintain their cover, they asked Karim where they might see more of the unique species of plants and pointed at some pictures they had of the dragon's blood tree. He nodded vigorously and pointed further down the road to the left. They nodded in understanding and motioned for him to drive them there. After twenty minutes of rest and a soft drink each, they headed off to the west along the coastline. Thirty minutes later they were staring at a very strange-looking tree. One of the unique species on the island, the thing looked like an overgrown umbrella. The dragon's blood tree was found nowhere else on earth, and they were impressed with it. They spent several minutes with the tree, not touching it, but measuring and studying it as if they were academics, taking notes and conversing amongst themselves. Corey was smiling and enjoying the show, since he was aware of the real purpose of the visit. They needed to maintain their cover.

They repeated this activity for several other species of plants, and Karim was able to help them "study." After close to two hours of this, they asked the driver to take them back to the hotel, the way they had come, so they could begin writing a report on their findings. He readily agreed and they began the trip back.

As they climbed the hill coming out of Mahfirhin, Ryan, with a gyro-stabilized miniature camera in his lap in the open-air back seat, began digitally filming parts of the complex on the right, taking special note of the harbor and the communications complex. He also noted that there was very little activity to be seen. Only two individuals were out walking around or moving, and one of them was a guard on foot patrol. Corey suddenly asked Karim to stop, and he complied quickly, looking puzzled. Corey then hopped out of the front seat and went over to a plant he hadn't seen before, and motioned Dave and Jackie to come over and join him. They joined him and Corey explained, while enthusiastically gesturing at the plant, that he was creating a diversion so Ryan could get some decent film without the bouncing Land Rover causing problems. Even with the gyro-stabilized camera, the ride was probably too rough. Dave grinned and pointed at the root area of the plant and nodded vigorously, going along with the ruse. Jackie stood back, glanced out to sea, and watched the show. Ryan kept filming from the low side of the Land Rover. He was able to pan the entire hillside, and got the harbor and the communications area. Corey and Dave then came back to the vehicle, got back in, and continued a discussion of the plants' construction while Karim, shaking his head and smiling as if he understood, started back up again. Ryan put the digital camera back in his vest pocket. They went past the guard shack, and Jasper got a shot of it with his tablet while looking like he was trying to see something in the bright light. They could see a uniformed armed guard watching them from just outside the shack.

Due to the condition of the roads—not good—it took a few hours to drive back to the hotel. It was early evening when they returned, and they made arrangements with Karim to pick them up the next day at the same time. They wanted to go down the southern coast again.

Including Corey, who had proven to be very valuable to their efforts, they all convened in Ryan and Jackie's room, where they enjoyed a couple of mixed drinks courtesy of Corey's foresight. Yemen was an Arab country and liquor wasn't available in any of the markets.

After a good, long discussion over what they had seen that day, and a good look at the digital film on their laptop, Ryan developed a very short report, attached the digital film to it, and sent them via secure satellite to Admiral Watkins and a copy to his own home computer. It had been a good day.

Saturday—July 30
Socotra Island Operations Center

It had been a very quiet several months since the departure of the *Persian Desert* to Alaskan waters, and the various staff members and ministers were busy developing programs from the new operations complex. The operations staff was still recovering from the failure and capture of Kadar and the *Persian Desert* two months before. The weather on the islands, while hot, was also pleasant, with frequent breezes. The remoteness of the site had the benefit of not providing distractions, so work could proceed at a rapid pace.

Inside the operations complex was a series of control locations for the logistics, maintenance, security, personnel, and operations of the movement. Each of the control centers reported in to a central operations center located in the middle of the building in a secure area. That central operations center was modern and underground, for greater security.

The security control location had multiple daytime monitoring capabilities, both auditory and visual, throughout the compound, to include all the entrances, the harbor area, and the apartment complex. Anyone approaching the complex would be seen and heard. If an individual approached who was not recognized, they would be challenged and checked out. In most instances, so far, people approaching were either curious or non-threatening, or they worked with one of the contractors building or modifying the complex. Nighttime sensors were still being installed and would be operational in a few weeks. Guards at all the entrances, along with roving patrols, were in place to assure nighttime coverage.

Humam was at the monitoring station watching the multiple screens when he noticed a beat-up Land Rover on the main road pull over near the main gate and stop. It didn't look like anything serious, but he did notice it, primarily because there wasn't any other activity to draw his attention. Everything was quiet. He watched and panned the camera in for a closer look. It looked like a small group of eco-tourists looking hard at a map and gesturing to their driver. Several times they glanced in the direction of the guard shack, but didn't appear to make any note of it. After a few moments, they drove off down the road. Humam made a note in his log and continued monitoring the ever-changing screens for any other activity.

Several hours later, Fawzi was on duty and monitoring the security screens for any activity. He noted a Land Rover slowly moving up the road. It stopped and two men and a woman got out of the vehicle, gesturing at something on the ground just beyond the edge of the road. After a few moments they got back in the vehicle and headed on up the road and beyond the camera's view. Because they had stopped, he made a note of the incident in the log and continued his monitoring activity.

Each day, as part of his normal routine in the new quarters, Abdul-Hakim reviewed the daily activity logs maintained by the shift monitors. Normally they were very brief and contained nothing of serious note. This evening, however, he noticed that on two occasions a Land Rover had stopped on the outside of the perimeter of the complex. He read the computerized log again and pulled up the digital film that constantly recorded activities on the perimeter. He viewed both incidents and quickly realized that the vehicle was the same vehicle. From appearances, and the timing of the vehicle sighting, it looked like it was going toward the southern beach areas and then later returning. It might be very innocent, but it also might not be so innocent. He stopped the film in both instances with the vehicle in view, then enhanced the image with new software. The image was clear and he could see the four people in the vehicle, plus the driver, who was obviously Socotran. He made note of the vehicle registration.

It was too late for further action. He would have to look into it tomorrow. As with many things these days, Abdul-Hakim was very suspicious.

Chapter Thirty-Nine
Identified

Sunday—July 31
Socotra Island Operations Center

Abdul-Hakim, with his recent experience with the Americans after the bombing of the stronghold, and the failure of Ramiz's mission, was suspicious. After thinking about it overnight, he became more worried. The strangers' presence came so soon after the failures in Texas. It couldn't be just a coincidence. He had convinced himself these were not European eco-visitors. What were they doing here and why had they really stopped on the road? He picked up the phone on his desk, called the Socotran Transportation Office, and asked for the identity of the vehicle owner. He was given the name, Karim Abdul-Nasser, and his local address. He was a local equivalent of a taxi driver and lived in Hadibu.

Abdul-Hakim thought about it for several moments and decided it would be better safe than sorry. He called in one of his more physical assistants.

"Akram. Go to this address and speak with this man. He took several tourists around parts of the island yesterday and I'd like to know who they are, where they are from, and what are they doing here. No need to get difficult, but please impress on Karim that we are serious and need the information. Oh ... be pleasant about it. I'm sure he will agree. If we have some form of difficulty, we will handle it later. All that understood?"

Akram nodded briskly once and simply said, "Sir." He departed the operations center immediately, without any other help along, since he did not want to appear intimidating during his visit.

Raised in the city of Aden in Yemen, Akram was well versed in various tactics for getting information. Strong and direct, he could be personally intimidating. Akram found the address with no difficulty. It was in a run-down section of the Socotran capital, the home of many of the poor people barely able to make a living off the sea or relatively rare visitor. The Land Rover was parked nearby. He parked the aging Toyota

223

Corolla he had driven, to avoid notice, and approached the small door. He knocked softly and the door was opened by a middle-aged Arab-looking person of very slight build. They exchanged a short greeting, and Akram got right to the point of his visit. He asked if the man was the driver of the Land Rover, and the response was yes. Where had he picked up his fare yesterday, the European-looking group? He had picked them up at the Taj Socotra and had taken them around the island. They were actually Americans looking at the local plants for possible use in their own country. He may have them again tomorrow but wasn't sure yet. He didn't know how long they might stay. Yes, he could let Akram know, for a price, the next time he was hired to take them and where they went.

With that information, Akram thanked the driver and left with no further delay.

Karim couldn't believe his luck! He was hired to take the Americans around the island and getting paid for it. He was now also getting paid to report where they went and what they did. Double pay for the same basic effort! Praise Allah for these blessings!

Plants!

Somehow, even in Akram's mind, that really didn't ring true. It sounded like a cover of some sort. If they were really interested in the local plants, there would have been someone from the Yemen Interior Ministry with them. But there was no one like that that he knew of. But it wasn't his problem. He had just been asked to find out who they were and what they were doing. He had accomplished his mission and would report back to Abdul-Hakim with the information. He glanced at the Land Rover and did not notice anything unusual about it. An older model that had seen its better days. He started the Toyota, backed into a small turnaround, and headed back to the complex.

He turned off the main road, and the gate in front of him opened up without him having to stop. They were on the ball and watching. He parked the Toyota in its assigned spot in the garage and headed inside for a meeting with Abdul-Hakim.

"Well, Akram," began Abdul-Hakim, "that was quick. It only took you a few hours and you're back already?"

"Sir. It wasn't hard, and Karim, the driver, was quite cooperative. He didn't seem to have anything to hide."

"Fine. So what did you find out?"

"They are Americans here supposedly to look at our local plants for use in their country. They arrived two days ago and he didn't know when they might be leaving. He took them around the island a bit yesterday and they may go out again tomorrow, but he doesn't know for sure. They're staying at the Taj for now."

Abdul-Hakim looked at Akram and said, with no expression in his voice, "Plants?"

"Sir. Sounds strange to me also. There isn't any sign of the Interior Ministry in this, and I don't think that is what they are really doing. But I don't know what it might be."

"I agree with you. Keep an eye on this for me and let me know what you find out. And get some pictures of them. I want to know who, and what, we are dealing with."

"Sir, Karim agreed to let me know if he gets them again."

"Good. Perhaps a few more days will reveal their real purpose." He waved his hand in dismissal, and Akram left the room.

Abdul-Hakim then turned, picked up his telephone, and called Ramiz in. A few moments later, Ramiz knocked on his office door.

"Come in, Ramiz. I want you to be here tomorrow when Akram brings back photos of some visitors to the island. I am suspicious of them and want to know if you might recognize them."

"Certainly. What time will he return?"

"I'll call you. Just be ready."

Ramiz bowed slightly and, with that, left the office.

Monday-August 1
Socotra Island

The next day Akram met with Karim, gave him a camera, and told him to get some pictures of the Americans. And to make it appear as if he were just taking some general pictures of the countryside. Karim lowered his head in acknowledgement, took the camera, looked it over carefully so he was sure he knew how to work it, and went to pick up the Americans.

Later that evening, Karim met with Akram again and returned the camera. Akram stood there and reviewed the digital images. There were a few images of scenery, but most had some or all of the Americans in the scene. He noticed that a woman was in several of the pictures. He had not anticipated that, and asked Karim who she was.

Karim replied, "Her name is Jackie Conover and she is with the Americans. I don't know her background because they have never discussed it in my presence. But I gather that she is well connected in the American government. She and the fellow Ryan are apparently a couple, since they are staying together in the hotel."

Akram raised his eyebrows at this statement. He would have to keep this matter in his mind as things began to unfold. He looked at the other pictures, studied the men in them, and came to no other conclusions. They could have been there on a biological hunt; it was possible. But it just didn't feel right, especially without any representative from the Yemeni government with them. He knew the Yemeni government was very careful about visitors, and especially eco-tourists. He was quite suspicious. He thanked Karim, gave him a payment of one thousand rials, took the camera, and left.

He went back to his apartment in the center, threw the camera on the bed, and sat down to think. He could come up with only one reason for them to be here. They were spying. They were spying on the operations center and the movement. That was the only thing that made sense. He decided to take his suspicions to Abdul-Hakim and see what he might think of it. He was the boss and needed to be aware of any concerns Akram might have. It was not only part of his job, but it might be critical to the future of the center.

He went down the hall to the office where he thought Abdul-Hakim might be. He wasn't there. He took a blank piece of paper off the desk, wrote a note, and left it on the desk.

Two hours later, Abdul-Hakim came back to his office for a few minutes before going on to his quarters. It had been a long afternoon, and there were many details on several of the missions that needed to be sorted out. Not the least being the snooping Americans. He passed by his desk, noticed the note, picked it up, and quickly read it. He went to the intercom, called Akram's room, and asked him to come to the office immediately.

Akram came in to the office carrying hard copies of the photos that had been taken that day by Karim.

"Tell me what you found out today," stated Abdul-Hakim.

Akram responded, "They were on the far side of the island along the southern coast looking at various plants and some of the rock formations over there. That's where Karim took these pictures." He spread out the pictures on a small conference table in Abdul-Hakim's office.

Abdul-Hakim immediately spotted the woman in the pictures, pointed at her, and said, "Who's that? I didn't realize they had a woman with them."

Akram said, "Her name is Jackie Conover and is apparently involved with this Ryan McKenzie." As he said it, he pointed Ryan out in one of the pictures. "He's the apparent leader of the group and is the one directing their actions."

Abdul-Hakim pursed his lips and nodded in understanding. He thought, *That might complicate matters. Hadn't planned on a woman in the mix.* He looked at each of the photos in detail. His mind was in a quandary. Where had he heard the name McKenzie before? It was there. It was in his mind but he couldn't quite remember it.

Abdul-Hakim called Ramiz and requested he join them in his office. After several minutes, Ramiz came into the office with a puzzled look on his face. Abdul-Hakim showed Ramiz the photographs. Ramiz took them in his hand, noticed the background, and looked at the people, and his eyes widened slightly. He said with surprise, "They're here. They've come to us. Why?"

Abdul-Hakim said, "Apparently. Who are they?"

Ramiz said, "This is Ryan McKenzie, the guy from Texas, and the woman is Jackie Conover, the president's primary scheduler. I don't know the other two men."

Abdul-Hakim was startled. That was where he had heard the name! So this was the Ryan McKenzie that Ramiz had talked with and failed to kill. He mused for a moment. "Now what are the chances that the same man Ramiz had met and talked with would show up here? The man who had organized the strike on the stronghold." He smiled slightly. Slim to none.

He noticed that, in the background of several of them, he could see some parts of the center beyond some of the perimeter fencing. They were at the sandy beach, but within sight of the center. If they were spies, they were in a good spot to see a lot of the center. It they weren't spies, the coincidence was quite striking.

Ramiz was quiet. But his thoughts weren't. Their missed target had come to them. He inwardly smiled at their good fortune. It would be quite easy now for him to complete his earlier task and do away with Mr. McKenzie.

Abdul-Hakim studied the photos some more.

Chapter Forty
Watched

Monday—August 1
Socotra Island Operations Center

Abdul-Hakim, after hearing the brief from Akram on who the visitors really were—Americans, not British or some other European nationality—grew even more concerned. Ramiz had just confirmed it. The new operations center location was supposed to be kept secret for as long as possible, and it had only been a few months since the ayatollah and his staff had arrived. And this McKenzie guy was here already! They had been able to get another mission underway, the one into Alaskan waters, but only through extreme efforts by the New Persia staff and support people. Now there was a strong possibility that they had been discovered already. While not paranoid about the situation, he wanted to be very cautious.

He spent several hours, going into the very late evening in his office/study, thinking about what might be occurring. If these people were, in fact, some form of spying mission, that meant the Americans were aware of their location. If they were legitimate, and just doing some investigation of the plants and he was overreacting, it could also be seen as a reason to investigate his actions by the Americans. He again looked at the digital video of the two instances where the Land Rover had stopped outside their gate, and saw nothing new. Yes, there were some casual glances in the direction of the center, but no long stares or pointed fingers or any sign of specific notice being taken. Yet he was uncomfortable. His instincts told him he was looking at trouble. The Americans' reason for being there were just not credible in his mind. Yes, the plants on Socotra were very unusual, but ... but ... but ... It just didn't seem right!

The swarthy-looking, nearly six-foot Akram knocked on Abdul-Hakim's door, startling him out of his thoughts. He stepped into the room and said, "Sir. It appears to me that we need to get some more information on these Americans. I don't buy their excuse for being on the island and think they may be here for another reason."

Abdul-Hakim nodded in agreement but said nothing.

Akram continued, "I think I should look around a little more and see what I can find out. Would you agree to that?"

Abdul-Hakim thought for a moment and said, "Yes. I agree with your assessment but don't know quite what you could do. What do you have in mind?"

Akram explained what he had in mind and that it might take a few days to get it accomplished. It would involve a few other people he knew on the island. It would also possibly cost a few rials. There would be no violence involved, but there would be some surveillance needed.

After some more discussion, Abdul-Hakim authorized Akram to go ahead and implement his plan. Akram nodded and quietly retreated from the room. He now had a mission to accomplish and was back on track supporting the ayatollah's goals. He smiled slightly at the thought and headed out to the motor pool to get his Toyota. He liked these small, surreptitious work details and knew they were quite valuable to Abdul-Hakim. This one would be interesting to see what he could uncover. The devious Americans were not here to look at plants. They were here for another reason, and he intended to find out what that reason was.

Tuesday—August 2
Socotra Island

Very early the next morning, Akram drove out of the motor pool, was let out the driveway gate, turned right at the road, and headed in to Hadibu. He had some friends there that he needed to enlist in his efforts, and they could use the coin he could now provide. Even temporary work was welcome in this economy.

Once he got out on the main road past the airport, he entered the outskirts of Hadibu, which weren't much. A few stone cabins/hutches were alongside the road, with just some small subsistence farming, and maybe a goat or two, barely able to keep the families alive. Yes, his work efforts would be welcomed by his old friends. Since the arrival of the New Persia movement on their lands, work had been provided to several hundred people and their families. They were quite grateful for the new income and had no interest in the reasons the New Persia movement existed. They just supported as required. It benefited them all.

He reached his destination and pulled into a small dirt courtyard surrounded on three sides by the rock-built homes. If there was one thing in abundance on this island, it was rock, and the local people used it to make all kinds of shelters, fences, roads, paths, and anything else they could think of. In some places it reminded him of the pictures he had seen of Ireland and the stone fences and homes there. Except here, nothing was green. Just more rock and some desert-type plants. He didn't like it here surrounded by water. He wanted to go back to his mountains and deserts in Yemen. But the ayatollah's message overrode his personal desires, and he served as required.

He stepped out of the Toyota and moved toward the front door of the house on the left. As he approached, the door opened and Boulos greeted him. "Allah be praised. Do you have some more work for me today?"

Akram stepped into the house, looked briefly around the small, sparely decorated living room, and responded with a nod. "Yes, Boulos. I have a small chore for you to perform. It will take some time, but you will be rewarded for your effort."

"Anything, sire," Boulos said with significant respect.

"I want you to—beginning immediately after I leave—go to the Taj and watch for several Americans. If they leave, you are to follow them without them knowing it. Stay with them for the entire day. In the evening I will return and you will tell me what they did. Can you do this for me?"

"Yes, sire. It will be done."

"Good. Until later, then." And Akram departed the house.

Boulos stood there for a minute, not believing his luck. He was almost destitute, and this would mean he could get some fish and vegetables and feed his family for several days or even a week for just one day's effort. Allah was looking kindly on him. He spoke briefly to his wife and hurried out to the Taj to begin his watch. When he arrived, he found a spot across the road in the shade of an old vehicle and sat down. He pulled his thatched hat down over his head and pretended to be dozing in the sun. It might be a long day—or his quarry could show up in the next minute. He didn't know. He waited.

In the late afternoon, Corey, Ryan, Jackie, and Dave came out of the hotel with Karim and headed to the well-used Land Rover parked near the hotel entrance. They were going

231

out to the southern beaches to spend the night and review the plant life in that area. Camping was a major attraction on the island, and was used by many tourists to both cut costs and spend time in the unique environment. Ryan and Dave wanted to continue with the ruse, and Corey willingly went along with it. Jackie went along with it but felt they should be more overt and just approach the compound with questions. But she was overruled. They would head back on the same highway and direction they had taken the previous day, but stay on the southern side of the island for a more extended period. They hoped they could better observe any activity in the complex from that viewpoint. They might also see some activity in the harbor.

Boulos, picking up on their departure, since they were the only Americans staying at the hotel, followed them out to the beaches in his beat-up Subaru. He just followed without being obtrusive. It wasn't hard, since the other traffic was also mostly well-used vehicles. He pulled over near the location where they were setting up camp. After watching for a few minutes, it occurred to him that Akram would want to know about this, since they weren't staying in the hotel that night. He thought about it for a minute and decided to head back to the hotel and a meeting with Akram.

He got to the hotel as the sun was setting and waited outside the main entrance. Akram, unannounced, got in the passenger seat. He said, "So where are they and what have they been doing?"

Boulos said, "They didn't leave until late this afternoon. They have set up a camp on the beach on the southern side of the island. They are not here. I don't know what they are doing, but that's where they are."

Akram nodded. "And they didn't go anywhere else today?" he asked.

"No. I was at the hotel since this morning when you asked me to begin the watch. They never left the hotel until late this afternoon, when they drove over to the beach."

Akram handed Boulos two thousand rials for his efforts that day. Boulos thanked Akram and began to leave. Akram stopped him. "I want you to go back to the beach and watch them for the night. I will meet you here tomorrow morning and receive your report."

Boulos responded, "Yes, sire. I will do as you command."

232

Akram got out of the vehicle and Boulos started up, went home briefly, and then headed down the road toward the back country and the southern beach area. He was smiling, and thankful to Allah.

Chapter Forty-One
Discovery Confirmed

Tuesday—August 2
Southern Beaches—Socotra Island

It was late evening and the night air, while cooler than the day, was still quite warm and humid. Akram headed back in to the town and went to the Taj. He walked into the lobby and up to the desk. Behind the desk was an attractive young lady of about twenty-two years. She looked up as he came to the desk, smiled, and asked if she could help him. He made his request and she stopped smiling. His posture and demeanor was sending her a no-nonsense message. From her, with no resistance, he obtained the room number and a key to Ryan's room. He also got one for Dave and Corey's rooms. There were no questions, just a demand and acquiescence. She just did as he requested and went back to her work, nervous but composed. She quickly knew where he was from and wanted no problems with this man. Nothing else transpired.

Akram went up to the rooms, found Ryan's, knocked to make sure no one was in there, opened the door, and looked around. Checking the closet, he found an empty, well-worn suitcase and nothing else, other than some clothing that was obviously for use in the outback. Both a man's clothing and a woman's clothing. On the table lay a small tablet with a power cord attached to an adapter and then to the wall outlet. He turned the tablet on, and in just a few minutes was in. He was no stranger to computers. He checked the mailbox sent items and discovered the photos and a commentary on the center.

It was what he was looking for. Proof of what they were really up to. Yes!

They were here spying. Plants had nothing to do with it.

He shut down the tablet, checked the other rooms, and found nothing of consequence. He didn't really expect to. He had found what he was looking for. Tomorrow he would notify Abdul-Hakim and the ayatollah of his discovery. They would have to determine a course of action. He was sure it would not be a pleasant result for the Americans.

That night, Ryan, Jackie, Dave, and Corey were all on the lookout for any activity at the center or in the harbor. With the assistance of Karim as their guide, they had made camp on the beach, as was the custom in Socotra for many of the visitors to the island. In fact, it was the normal course of action for the outdoor-minded tourists that traveled that far to see the sights. But the rest of the tourists were more interested in the local plant life than Ryan and crew.

They wanted to move on down the beach in the early evening and check out the harbor and the interesting, and unconventional, trimaran tied up there. They also wanted a close-up look at the yacht. But Karim presented a problem. They didn't know if he could be trusted, and assumed he could not. Since he was local, they had to assume he had some connection to the center. With the employment situation, everyone on the island had to be suspect. So, they wondered, how did they get closer so they could complete their task?

It was very pleasant, though still quite warm, with a slight breeze in the air. The group sat by a campfire on the beach several hundred yards from the entrance to the harbor area. The harbor was fenced on all sides, except, of course, the sea. A boat could easily slip in, but they had no access to a boat. And Karim might create a problem if they tried to get one. The sea was probably not a viable solution at this point. The main problem was getting rid of Karim for a few hours so they could scale the fence and take a close look. He was their guide, but also an obstacle to their mission. He was there for the evening and showed no signs of wanting to leave.

They stared at the fire for some time. Dave and Ryan got up several times and moved away from the fire to look out to sea. It was a beautiful evening, and they needed to get in to the harbor while they still could. Murmured conversation between them resulted in nothing. No ideas came up. Frustrating. So close.

A diversion would be necessary, and they would have to, somehow, get Karim out of the area so they could do a proper scoping out of the harbor and the ships in it. Ryan was stumped. As was Dave. Corey couldn't come up with anything either. They played with the fire and, adding some dry brushwood to it, felt the frustration building, as they were so close to completing their mission.

As they were standing there, just a few steps away from the fire, Jackie came over and sidled up to Ryan. She had a

235

strange look on her face and he wondered what she was up to. Not embarrassed, but not altogether confident either. Just sort of unsure of herself. He hadn't seen her that way before. He looked at her questioningly. She tugged on his shirtsleeve and pulled him away a little farther. She told him what she had on her mind. He looked slightly startled at first, and he quickly recovered, hoping it hadn't been noticed by Karim. He started to nod in understanding. It might just work. He said a few words to her, and she returned to the fire.

A few minutes later, she went over to the tent and went inside. After a short time she came out, looked at Ryan, and headed over to Karim. She approached Karim while Ryan tried to ignore what was going on. "Karim, I need to go back to the hotel for a few minutes. Will you drive me back there?"

"Now?" he asked. "It's early evening and we can't go back there. It will take at least three hours to make the round trip. And I wouldn't want to leave your friends here alone."

"Karim. I really need to get back to the hotel."

"Why? Can't we wait until morning?"

"No, Karim. I need to go right now. My friends will be just fine until we get back."

"But why?"

She looked at him, then down at the sand and back to him, then hesitatingly said, "Karim, are you married?"

"Yes."

"Then perhaps, if you think about it, you'll know why I need to go back to the hotel for a few things. And why I need to do that now, not in the morning."

Karim thought for a moment or two and then nodded in understanding. "Ahh. I think I understand. A woman thing?"

Jackie didn't answer, but blinked once and nodded.

"I see," said Karim. "Let me see if there is any problem with Mr. Ryan. If not, we can leave right away."

Karim then went over to Ryan and said, "Sir, Ms. Conover has a problem and we need to make a quick trip back to the hotel. It will take about three hours to make the round trip. Will that be okay with you? I'll get back as soon as I can."

Ryan looked at the ground for a moment, not wanting to react too quickly, and then slowly nodded. "Yes, that will be all right Karim. But please drive carefully. It is nighttime and I don't want you to have an accident. I'm sure we will be fine right here tending the fire and enjoying the beach and water."

Karim looked relieved, and went over to Jackie. "It's okay with him. Let's leave right away so we can return soon."

Jackie just nodded, went to the tent, and gathered a small bag. She walked over to Ryan, gave him a kiss on the cheek, a knowing look in her eyes, and then walked over to the Land Rover with Karim, and they departed.

Chapter Forty-Two
Spying and Captured

Tuesday—August 2
Socotra Island

Ryan stood there and watched as they left. He looked at his watch. They had, on the outside, three hours to get into the harbor, look around, and get back. They needed to move. He walked over to the fire where Corey and Dave were sitting. Neither had moved as they watched the charade develop. Both just sat there with bemused expressions on their faces as the Land Rover disappeared down the road. Women! But it had worked. Karim was occupied for the next several hours.

They built up the fire and checked around for any other people that might be in the area. There were none that they noticed. Corey said, "I'd suggest that I stay here and tend the fire. I wouldn't know what I was looking for if I went with you. And I can keep a lookout in case someone shows up. You two can go do the stealth thing."

Ryan nodded, and Dave said, "Okay. I think that makes sense. We'll get back as soon as we can. It's only about three hundred yards down to the harbor fence. Once inside, it shouldn't take too long to check it out. We should be back in plenty of time."

Corey just nodded and made a shooing motion for them to leave. Ryan gave him a thumbs-up and grabbed a small flashlight and a mini-camera, and he and Dave headed out in the darkness toward the fence line. After they were out of sight in the darkness, Corey turned back to the fire and added a few more branches and small logs to it to keep it burning brightly. It was going to be a long couple of hours. He sat down on a blanket and looked around. Nothing to see. He could hear the gentle lapping of the surf at the dark ocean edge. The warm night sky was fairly well lit, with a huge display of brilliant stars. It was quite peaceful.

Ryan and Dave ran most of the way to the fence. It was a chain link fence about eight feet high, and this section was topped with concertina wire. No way over it. They looked both ways and saw no break in it, except where the rocky harbor breakwater entered the ocean water. The fence stopped just beyond the water's edge. They trotted down to the edge of the water and looked it over. The fence went into the water about five feet and stopped. They looked at each other and quickly entered the ocean. They walked/swam around the end of the fencing to the other side on the breakwater. They were in. Ryan looked at his watch. It had taken them nearly twenty minutes to get this far. They climbed up the rocky breakwater and headed into the harbor.

They saw the two piers and suddenly stopped. Just as they looked at the piers, two guards appeared from one of the service buildings next to one pier. They froze and slowly moved down on the rocks. They had no weapons. In the dark they looked like two large boulders, if they were noticed at all. The guards, talking slowly and moving just as slowly, walked down the pier away from them and passed out of sight around one of the patrol boats.

Ryan and Dave headed for the large yacht, since it was closest to them, and did a quick check. Nobody on board. Dave, hiding behind a small maintenance shed, maintained a watch as Ryan boarded. He quietly climbed the familiar passageway, using his flashlight just a little to avoid tripping, to the cockpit, and looked over the instruments. They were identical to the ones on the boat they had captured in the Gulf of Mexico the previous year.

Knowing they were time-limited, he quickly rejoined Dave on the pier. Moving on to the patrol boats, they did the same thing. Nothing surprising there. There was no one around except for the guards, and they were roving. They had to be careful.

Ryan told Dave to hang loose for a minute and then went over to the end of the largest patrol boat. He looked at the Bushmaster rifle mounted to the floor. A 25mm monster, twice the size of a .50-caliber. It could do a lot of damage. Why was it here? There was nothing to use it against. He looked around, found what he was looking for, and made a modification to the gun. He was satisfied with his work and joined up with Dave again.

They quietly worked their way over to the trimaran, noted the name *Persian Quest* on the stern in both Arabic and English, and boarded it. Dave was amazed at the size of it. He did a quick scan of the centered interior cockpit area inside a spacious cabin, then moved down into the center of the boat. It was obvious that the sails had to be operated by electric and hydraulic assists.

As he moved down into the center of the trimaran itself, he came across a startling discovery. The center was actually a mini-submarine; the mini was similar to what they had captured in the gulf. Not the same, but similar. This "trimaran" was really a catamaran with a fake third hull. As he looked at it, he shook his head in amazement. The launch and retrieval equipment was mounted in the bottom of the center section of the trimaran. It matched the information he had seen on the trimaran captured in Alaska. What a concept! They took multiple pictures of various operational areas of the ship. They could be useful in future engineering analyses.

Leaving the trimaran, they quickly headed over to the service building on the end of the pier. The doors were locked and there were no windows. Couldn't see a thing. They returned to the service building the guards had come out of. That door was unlocked. They went inside and found themselves inside a large warehouse.

Glancing at each other, they both realized that inside was row after row of weapons stored in boxes on pallets. They looked closer and found small arms, RPGs, ARPMs, automatic weapons, and several different types of land mines. There was enough material for a small army. They looked at each other again, recognizing what they were looking at, then back to the boxes. They'd seen enough. They took several more pictures and quietly made their way back to the door. They carefully opened the door and crept out. They retraced their steps and headed back to the ocean, around the end of the fencing, and down the beach. It had taken them nearly an hour and a half, but they had found out what they wanted to know. This center was an armed camp ready to do battle.

Corey was still tending the fire and looking very bored when they returned. They gave him a quick rundown of what they had found. He nodded thoughtfully and said, "I think we have found what we were looking for. It's time for us to get out of here."

Ryan nodded. He said, "The next flight out of here is day after tomorrow. I think we should be on it. In the meantime, we need to continue with our little game about the plants. Dave, you have any thoughts after what we saw over there?"

Dave responded, "I think we saw enough to convince the president that we've found the new center for New Persia operations. And that trimaran. That is quite a boat. I'll bet it is a duplicate of the one we captured in Alaska. We could learn some real lessons from it. I'll bet we see it on the high seas before long, and it won't be very friendly."

Another hour passed, and they were all getting very tired. Ryan wanted to wait up for Jackie to return, since it shouldn't be much longer. Corey and Dave decided to go to bed, and turned in to their sleeping bags and tents. Ryan continued to tend the fire in the comfortable seashore darkness.

Finally, Ryan saw headlights coming down the road. Karim and Jackie drove up to the campsite. Karim turned off the Land Rover and headed for his tent. Jackie joined Ryan at the fire. Karim came back out of the tent, turned, headed down the beach to the water's edge, took care of some personal business, and returned to his tent. He nodded at Ryan and zipped the flap.

Jackie looked at Ryan, and he returned the look. She understood, and they turned in for the evening.

Boulos, who had trailed them from the hotel, watched Ryan and Dave circle the fencing into the harbor and then saw them return after a while. In a small, dark inflatable kayak, he observed from a couple of hundred meters out in the ocean waters as they all bedded down for the night. He worked his way several hundred meters down the dark beach until it was safe to come out of the water, and worked his way through the small dunes to his vehicle. He turned in for the night determined to be up at first light to continue his watch. He knew Akram would be very pleased with what he had to report.

Wednesday—August 3
Socotra Island

The following morning they broke camp, unaware of Boulos's presence nearby, and Karim drove them further down the coast for some more time looking at plants and marveling at the environment. They kept this up for several hours, and then asked Karim to head back to town. They showed him some of the pictures they had taken of the plant life, and he was impressed with the technology. Instant and very detailed images.

They arrived back at the Taj late that afternoon, paid Karim, and headed back to their rooms. As soon as they got in, they all noticed that the rooms had been searched. Whoever had done it was not worried about being caught. While not destroyed, their things had been moved around a bit. Nothing appeared to be missing, so it wasn't just theft. It worried Ryan, though. It was obvious that nothing was safe in this environment. He checked his laptop, but found nothing apparently wrong with it. But he was still concerned.

Boulos followed Ryan and the group back in to town, then, after watching the group enter the hotel, reported to Akram. His report on Ryan's activities brought a smile of accomplishment to Akram. His impressions and thoughts were right! He paid Boulos a bonus of ten thousand rials and quickly departed for the operations center. It was a win-win for New Persia. Boulos was ecstatic about his windfall, and Akram was excited over what he had to report.

They were all standing in Ryan and Jackie's room discussing what had happened when there was a stomping sound outside the room. Heavy footfalls, but not in any cadence. Then a strong knock on the door and the door swung open without invite. Five large men were standing in the hall and doorway ... none looked friendly.

The obvious leader, as he looked at all of them, said in broken English, "Come with us. Our security manager wishes to speak with you. Do not resist or you will be hurt."

Ryan shrugged. Ryan, Corey, Dave, and Jackie all left the room with their escorts. The last escort picked up Ryan's laptop and, closing the door, they proceeded downstairs to two waiting vehicles and were driven off to the complex. Going through the gate, they were driven up to an entrance to the main building. All four of them were paying very close attention to the details of the road and where they were going. They climbed out of the vehicles and followed the big guy into the building. The other four men followed them. They were escorted down a hall and turned right, and a little further on were pushed into a room. The door was slammed shut and they heard the lock being set.

A few minutes later, Abdul-Hakim entered the room. He sat down in a steel chair, feet flat on the floor, and said, "Mr. McKenzie, my name is Abdul-Hakim and I am the defense minister for this complex. You and your companions have been spying on us, and I want to know why."

Ryan looked back at him and said, "Defense minister for what? I don't know what you are talking about. We are here looking at plants for possible use in our American southwest. We haven't been spying on anyone."

Abdul-Hakim absorbed Ryan's comments, sat there for a few seconds, then quickly stood up and said, "Silence. You are lying. I shall return shortly." Then he left the room.

Chapter Forty-Three
Interrogation

Wednesday—August 3
Socotra Island Operations Center

Khatib interrupted the ayatollah. "Sir. We have an issue that we believe needs your attention."

The ayatollah looked up from his reading and asked, "What is that, Khatib?"

"Abdul-Hakim has four people being held in his office area awaiting an audience with you."

The ayatollah, standing up, looked puzzled. "Who are these people and what does he expect?"

"They are Americans, and Abdul-Hakim believes they are spying on us. He is requesting that you interview them and determine what you think should be done."

The ayatollah thought for a few moments then said, "Let me talk with Abdul-Hakim first. Then I will determine if I want to be involved in this issue, and ask Ramiz to be present too."

"Yes, sir."

A few minutes later, Abdul-Hakim knocked and then entered the ayatollah's office apartment. Ramiz followed him in.

The ayatollah looked at him expectantly. He silently motioned to Abdul-Hakim to explain.

"Sir. I have taken the liberty of detaining four visitors to the island. They are all American and tell the story that they are here to look at the plants. The idea being that they would look at the plants in this dry environment to see if they could be transplanted to the American southwest. However, after quietly watching them for a couple of days, and doing some background checks of our own, I don't think that is why they are really here."

The ayatollah looked at him questioningly. He sat down and made a motion with his hands to continue.

"They have been looking around the outside of the center, ostensibly looking at plants. But they have been pretty much all around the perimeter in their looking. They also took several pictures that had the center in the background. There also is no Interior Ministry representative with them. If they were really here as they claim, someone from the Yemeni government should be accompanying them in an official capacity." He hesitated a moment and then continued with more detail of their activities, including the previous evening's invasion of the harbor. He added some additional information he had from his contacts in the United States.

At the end of his comments, the ayatollah again raised his eyebrows in surprise. "So, what do you propose?"

"Sir. From the photos I have seen of this group, they are being led by Ryan McKenzie." The ayatollah's brow furrowed and he looked over at Ramiz. Ramiz continued, "Yes, sir, the same. They have come to us for some reason. It appears to me that you might wish to talk with them.

Abdul-Hakim said, "I have them in a holding room and would like you to talk with them. I think you may be able to make more sense of this."

"All right. Bring them here."

Ramiz left and returned to his quarters, since he did not want Ryan to know he was in Socotra, or let Ryan know he was tied to New Persia.

Abdul-Hakim hurried from the room and walked rapidly down to the room where his "guests" were being held. Opening the door, he motioned for Ryan, Jackie, Corey, and Dave to follow him to the ayatollah's office. The five "guards" followed at a discreet distance … but they were there.

The ayatollah, speaking very good English, welcomed the group. He said, "Welcome to our compound. I am Ayatollah Sarhardi. May I inquire as to why you have visited this island?"

Ryan responded, "We are here to look at some of the local plant life to determine if some of the species could be transplanted to our American southwest."

"Why would you want to do that?"

"We are looking for plants that do not require much moisture so we can replant some of the barren areas. The winds are blowing some of the soil, poor as it is, away, and we need to stop it."

The ayatollah looked hard at Ryan and the others in the group and finally said, "I don't think so. You were seen last night going into and looking over our harbor area. You have sent off messages to someone in the States with pictures of our complex attached. I agree with Abdul-Hakim and think you are spying on us." He paused, looking hard and angry, then

245

continued, "We have already taken a hit from you Americans at our former stronghold, and I think you are doing work to prepare for another strike. We have tried to keep our location secret, but it is obvious from your presence that we failed."

Ryan was taken aback by this small tirade, and surprised by its accuracy. He said, "Whoa, whoa. Wait a minute. I don't know what you are talking about. We are here on a peaceful effort regarding plant life."

The ayatollah looked at Ryan for a moment, then said very softly but with extreme menace, "Silence. You test my intelligence with your blathering. I do not wish to waste my time with you and your kind. You are here, and a danger to my movement, and I cannot let you continue with your activities." With a quick look to Abdul-Hakim, he rudely dismissed them. They were then escorted by the guard force back to their holding room.

After the guards left with Ryan and the group, Abdul-Hakim stayed in the ayatollah's office/quarters area. He had been told by Khatib a few minutes before to remain, and had no idea why.

He met with Khatib. "You asked me to meet with the ayatollah. May I ask why he wishes to see me?"

Khatib looked back at Abdul-Hakim and simply said, "No." Then he added, "He will see you now."

This response really made Abdul-Hakim nervous and uncharacteristically unsure of himself. He proceeded through the door and back into the ayatollah's office. The ayatollah was working at his desk and looked up as Abdul-Hakim came in. He looked serious and even a bit severe.

Without getting up from his desk, and without asking Abdul-Hakim to sit, he immediately began.

"Abdul-Hakim, you are my defense minister, and yet we find ourselves on an island in the middle of the ocean and chased away from our now-destroyed stronghold in the deserts of Iran. And now we have these infidels spying on us in our own home. I want to know how it is that you have failed us so."

Abdul-Hakim began to sweat, and was quite nervous over this uncharacteristic query by the ayatollah. He began to speak, but the ayatollah held up his hand, silencing him immediately.

"I'm not finished. We lost several hundred men and women in the raid that you failed to protect us from. And that was in spite of the fact that you had modern weapons and tracking systems. You failed, and it has cost us an enormous amount of personnel, time, operations, and money." He stopped for a moment then continued, "And now we have these Americans in our midst. Four spies who know where we are and have told their superiors where we are located. A lot of work has been accomplished to hide our location, and that whole effort is now compromised."

Khatib was in the room, and watched Abdul-Hakim closely as he was being raked over the coals. His eyes were focused on Abdul-Hakim and took in every movement and emotion as the ayatollah spoke. It was obvious that Abdul-Hakim was very nervous.

The ayatollah continued, with a menace in his normally calm voice, "What would you suggest I do about this? You have been one of my most trusted advisors now for several years. Have you been deceiving me with our so-called invincibility? Is there any way we can avoid detection in the future and continue with our work? How can we proceed if we are constantly looking over our shoulder for the enemy forces that are trying so hard to locate and destroy us?" He hesitated then added, "I want you to think about what I have just said and leave me alone. Do not respond to these questions at this time. I want to emphasize to you the criticality of your position and the need to assure our safety. You need to reassess what you are doing and make sure you are using all your resources to make us secure and safe. I don't want to have to replace you, and you know what I really mean by that, but, if these incidents continue, I will have no choice. Am I clear?"

Abdul-Hakim, thoroughly chastised and still sweating profusely, glanced at Khatib then back to the ayatollah and responded, "Yes, sir. I understand."

The ayatollah then waved his hand in dismissal.

Abdul-Hakim bowed slightly, turned, and hurried out of the room.

Ryan, Jackie, Dave, and Corey were all escorted back to Abdul-Hakim's office. Abdul-Hakim followed a short time later. The "escorts" were standing by in the room, and it was plain to see that they were not free to go.

Abdul-Hakim came in to the office, obviously shaken and very nervous, and announced, "You are all under house arrest. We are going to hold you here until the ayatollah has determined a course of action. You have interfered in our business and, as he said, cannot continue with your spying activities."

Ryan looked at him, shook his head rapidly from side to side, and said, "Just a minute. You can't do that. We are here on a peaceful effort and are no danger to whatever it is you are doing. We're leaving." And with that, Ryan headed for the door. Abdul-Hakim motioned at the escorts, and the door was immediately blocked and Ryan was threatened by two of the guards. Ryan turned around, facing Abdul-Hakim, hands clenched in fists and ready to fight. Corey was on his feet and spring-loaded also.

Abdul-Hakim said, "I don't think you understand. You are under arrest and we will hold you for the time being. Do not resist or harm may be done to you. You have no choice."

Ryan stopped. He looked at Jackie, Dave, and Corey. They shook their heads slightly and acknowledged that this wasn't the time for resistance. Ryan slowly looked back at Abdul-Hakim. The escorts moved around behind them, and they were all herded out of the office into the hallway, then back into the room they had previously been in. The door was closed behind them and they heard the lock being set.

Jackie sat down on one of the chairs and looked around. Not much to see. Just a plain, windowless room with a table and a few chairs. The ceiling was painted an off-white, with fluorescent fixtures. The walls were painted in a faint blue. Very boring. A cheap conference room from the looks of it. The only way out was the door where they'd come in, and it was firmly locked. Corey and Dave sat down on two of the uncomfortable metal chairs. Ryan paced around for a minute and then stopped.

"Well," Ryan said. "Obviously they have been watching us and ..." He hesitated for a moment as Corey shook his head somewhat vigorously, raised his eyebrows, and looked at Ryan with wide open eyes. Ryan caught it and continued, "... are completely off base. Why would they think we are spying? Those photos are just of some of the plants here. There's nothing to them."

Corey added, "I don't understand it either. But, given the circumstances, I think we have no option but to wait and see what happens." While he was talking, Corey got up and began to look around the room. He didn't have to go far. He went over to the light switch at the entrance door and flicked it a couple of times, finally leaving it on. Jackie got up, stretched her arms out, and walked around also. Then she sat down again in the same chair. Corey went over to the near corner of the room next to the door and motioned to everyone that there was a camera in the switch.

Dave caught on immediately. He pursed his lips and put his hands over the lower part of his face. He looked at Ryan. Then he turned his head slightly and looked at Jackie and Corey. He was thinking. He was a small person, balding and lightweight. His solid-frame glasses and a comb-over hairstyle gave him an owlish look. But he was a brilliant engineer and underwater submarine expert. He looked at the ceiling and then back down at the table.

"Okay, Dave. What's on your mind?" asked Ryan. "I can tell the old brain is just whirring away."

"I'm thinking. I think we may have really screwed up here. I had no idea this complex of buildings was so sensitive. I thought it was some kind of school, or possibly a retreat. Perhaps we stayed too close to Hadibu and should have moved further out on the island to do our investigations. You know, thinking about our actions over the past couple of days, I can sort of understand why they might think we were spying."

Ryan, Jackie, and Corey could tell Dave was talking to whoever was listening in. His position was in line with the camera and he could be seen by whoever was monitoring it. It was an excellent performance. Quite convincing.

An hour later, they were visited by Abdul-Hakim.

"The ayatollah has decided. In spite of your claims to innocence, and I might add"—he stopped and smiled—"your performance while in this room, one of you will take a message back to your president and the rest of you will remain here as our guests. We are sure that your president knows of your mission here and you should have no problem getting the message to him."

He looked at Jackie and said, "You will take the message to him."

Ryan interrupted, "Why doesn't the ayatollah just send the message to the president through diplomatic channels? Release us and let us go about our business. We will leave you alone and you leave us alone."

Abdul-Hakim looked at Ryan and the other two men. He said angrily, "We are convinced that you are spying on us. I will brook no interference with our plans. As the defense minister for the New Persia movement, I have a responsibility to make sure we are secure. You have attempted to breach that security and will be held until we decide otherwise. Is all that clear?"

Ryan, Dave, and Corey all nodded. Jackie nodded also, then said, "Why me? Why not one of the men?"

"Because, Ms. Conover, as the president's primary scheduler, he will not only listen to you, but he will be convinced that we are serious and not to be trifled with. Your friends here will be held to make sure the president understands our requirements."

Jackie, Ryan, Dave, and Corey were all stunned. New Persia knew who she was and what her role was in the administration. That meant they probably knew of the rest of their backgrounds and were not fooled by the charade.

Ryan just looked at the floor, hands on his hips, and shook his head back and forth slowly. He took in a deep breath and exhaled.

Damn it!

Chapter Forty-Four
Messenger

Wednesday—August 3
Socotra Island Operations Center

The next few hours were spent in uncertainty for the group. They were kept in the conference room and provided with some food and water. Nothing else. As Abdul-Hakim left them, he told them to knock on the door if they needed anything, and a guard would help as required.

Dave looked surreptitiously at the door to see if there was any weakness. The hinges were on the outside. Then he remembered that the door had swung into the hallway, not into the room. The doorknob just released the door. The deadbolt was on the corridor side, with a smooth plate on the room side. There was no way to pick the locks. It was solid.

Wednesday—August 3
Washington, D.C.

The president called Maria into his office. "Maria, Ryan and his group of explorers didn't contact us last night, as they usually do. Have you heard anything from them?"

"No, sir, I haven't. Let me check a few of the folks here and see if they have, and I'll get back to you shortly."

The president nodded and she left the office.

A few minutes later, she came back and said, "Negative. Nobody's heard from them. The last we got was the pictures of the center two days ago. I wonder if something has happened."

"I'm wondering the same thing. Send a note back to Ryan, something innocuous, and see if he responds. Maybe something about anticipating his return and findings of the plant life there. Let me know the results."

Maria nodded and left to send the message. She drafted a question as the president had suggested, closed it with her name, and pushed "send." The message flew off into the ether-world of the internet, and remained still and alone on the server. There was no operating laptop for it to connect to. Ryan's inbox just got bigger ... by one more message.

He couldn't answer it.

Thursday—August 4
Socotra Island Operations Center

They spent the night and part of the next day in isolation, except for escorted visits to the restrooms. In the early afternoon of the second day, Abdul-Hakim came in and handed Jackie a sealed envelope. He said, "You are going to be released in a few minutes. You are to take this message, intact, to the president. It is for his eyes only and you are not to open it or try to read it. Do you understand?"

Jackie took the envelope. "Yes. I understand." She looked over at Ryan. Tears welled up, but she fought them down. She didn't want to leave the group, especially under these circumstances. She was well aware that she might not see them again. She looked back at Abdul-Hakim.

Abdul-Hakim stood back away from her and said, "You are free to leave now. Yousef"—he nodded toward a nondescript person standing by the guard at the door—"will guide you out of the building and take you to your hotel. Flight arrangements have already been made for you. Yousef will accompany you to the airport and watch as you go through security. You leave in three hours."

Jackie nodded, went over to Ryan, looked at him, and demurely kissed him on the cheek. As she did, she slipped something into his front pocket. He felt it but didn't react to it. She backed away, shook hands with Dave and Corey, giving each a brief hug, and turned to Abdul-Hakim, and he motioned for her to follow Yousef with the envelope in her hand. She went to the door, took a quick glance back, and headed down the corridor, following Yousef. Her mind in a turmoil. And fear in her heart.

Yousef took her outside, where an old vehicle of nondescript condition was waiting. He motioned for her to take the front passenger seat and she climbed in. He climbed into the driver's side, and she could smell days of dust and sweat on him. He drove her to the hotel, where she packed her few things, again noticing that some had been scattered around the room as the room had been searched. It hadn't been tossed, but it had been searched.

She looked for Ryan's computer to send a quick message to Maria, but remembered that one of the guards had taken it to the operations center. She couldn't call for help or even advise them what was going on. She called down to the desk for a vehicle to take her to the airport. She was told that a vehicle with Yousef was still waiting. She didn't check out, since she and Ryan were staying together. Then going back downstairs and, taking the waiting vehicle, with Yousef driving, she left for the airport.

The airport was only a couple of miles away, and they made the trip with no problems. Yousef assisted her with her luggage and watched as she got her ticket and went through a very cursory security process. There were no customs for outbound passengers. Her mind was a whirlwind of concern and anxiety. She had the message that was so important to the New Persia movement, but she was leaving behind her friends and lover and might never see them again. It was getting late as the plane arrived and taxied to the terminal. She had to make a decision, and make it quickly.

After Jackie left, Abdul-Hakim turned to the men and said, "We do not have a proper holding facility for you here. This room is secure, and we will be using it until I can arrange for another secure area. Keep in mind that we have an armed guard just outside the door." He looked hard at each of them and then said very emphatically, "Escape is not possible, and if you try you will be shot." And with that harsh comment, he left.

Ryan reached in his pocket. What had Jackie slipped in there? He was startled when he realized it was her lipstick. Now what could he do with that? There must be something unique about it, and he would have to figure it out. He couldn't pull it out of his pocket because of the surveillance camera. He manipulated it. Smooth case all the way around. Nothing unusual. Must be something inside. He would have to wait until later, when he could pull it out and figure out what she had done. He was intrigued.

Jackie, sitting in the passenger waiting area, thought and thought. Back and forth, back and forth. Her mind in constant turmoil. Fretting and very worried. She knew that if she got on that airplane, there would be no turning back.

She waited as the older Boeing 737 pulled up to the gate and the stairs were rolled up to the door. She had been a

Marine for eight years and had never left a buddy in trouble. Why was she doing it now? But Ryan and the president would want her to get the message to the president ... then they could take action. But she was here ... now. And she was about to leave. It didn't make sense. Her training kicked in. She picked up her bag and went to the ladies' room. She looked at herself in the mirror and saw the strain and concern reflected back. She couldn't leave. She had to go back and get them. By the time she got the message through to the president, they might be dead. Probably would be. She couldn't handle that. The self-recrimination and blame that would happen. No. She had to go back and get them out of there. Decision time. Her brow furrowed and her jaw tightened. No questions, just resolve. Action time. She wasn't leaving without them.

But how? How could she get in there and get them out? She had to think. Had to think up a plan and carry it out quickly. After all, part of her training had emphasized that, when captured, you had to escape as soon as possible. That was when the most successful escapes occurred, because you weren't usually in a secure area and guards were less attentive. But they were in a secure area and there was an attentive guard, so it would be much harder to get to them and get out again. How?

She began to formulate a plan. She sat down on a stall seat in the filthy restroom and thought it through. It might work. And if it didn't? They would probably all die. But there was a good chance they would die anyway. Really ... nothing to lose. She sat upright. Being a woman would help for something like this in this backward country. The plan should work.

She grabbed her bag and headed out of the ladies' room. She looked back where Yousef had been, but he wasn't there. Apparently he had left after she went through security. She crossed the small waiting area and headed for the slight ramp up toward the customs personnel. She was in with the rest of the passengers that had just arrived. Customs was very cursory. He questioned why she was returning so soon. She said there was a missing part of her report and she would have to spend a day redoing it. The customs agent just shrugged and stamped her passport again. She was through. Now what?

She made it through the throng of vendors and transportation people, picked a taxi at random, and was dropped off at the Raj. She went inside and up to their room on the second floor. It was still as she had left it. She went through all of their things again, looking for anything she might use to help rescue the men. In addition to a daypack, they had a fair amount of camping gear, including two nine-inch bladed knives. She took those, along with spray can of bug repellent, two small LED flashlights, several feet of cording, and a package of long matches. She also found a watch cap and some gloves, which she put in the daypack. No guns. They wouldn't have gotten them through security when they had arrived, and they might have given away their real mission. She reviewed the items. Not much, but it would have to do.

She went back downstairs and approached the desk. She asked if they had a business center, and was directed to a single table with a computer on it. She powered up the computer, was connected via satellite to the internet, and sent off a quick message telling Maria about the situation, and that Ryan, Dave, and Corey were all prisoners. Then she logged off.

It was getting dark. She went down to the street level. She knew the route back to the complex, since they had just come from there. She estimated it was about three to four miles to the gate. She got one of the drivers' attention, and he wanted to know where she wanted to go. She told him an intersection that was about half the distance. At least she wouldn't have to carry her stuff so far. The driver was a little confused, but did as she asked and left her at the intersection. She started hiking up the road with her daypack. Since she normally ran several miles every morning, the hike was not a strain for her. She crested the hill and saw the gate a short distance down the road. Now completely dark outside, it was lit up with lights aimed down the entrance driveway. She would have to get past the guard and into the complex.

In the darkness, she crept up to the fencing, followed it to the entrance driveway, and stood just out of sight.

Chapter Forty-Five
Jackie's Action

Thursday—August 4
Washington, D.C.

Maria had powered up her computer when she got in the office in the early morning. A habit she performed every working day both out of habit and necessity. Once the system was up and running, she immediately went to her email to see if there was anything of note, again, as usual. This morning it was not usual. She looked in disbelief and reread the message twice. She sat down and read it again. All three of the men were captives, in that foreign country so far away on the other side of the world. The president wasn't in yet, and wouldn't be down from his upstairs quarters for another hour. She couldn't wait. He had to know. She dialed his private cell phone. It rang.

The president answered with a simple "Hello." He didn't want to divulge his identity in case someone had dialed it in error.

Maria said, "Sir. I've just received an email from Jackie. They're all captive and being held in the compound."

"What? That can't be. How'd that happen?"

"I don't know, sir. I just got in and found the email and thought you would want to know right away."

Somewhat absently, he responded quietly, "Yes, of course. Thank you, Maria. I'll be down shortly." And he cut the connection.

Maria went back and read it again. Nothing came to her. They were captives, and the Washington group could do nothing about it right now. She wondered what had happened and how they got into that predicament. And how had Jackie been able to send the email?

Thursday—August 4
Socotra Island

She removed her daypack, removed her jacket, took off her dark watch cap, opened the top two buttons of her shirt and shook out her hair. *All men are pretty much alike,* she thought as she prepared to approach the gate. She took some of the cord and wrapped it around her waist, and put the small can of bug spray in her back pocket. She took two deep breaths, exhaled, and stepped into the light of the entranceway. The guard was caught by surprise, and had a startled look on his face that slowly turned into a smile as he watched her come closer. He came out of the guard shack, unclipped the restraining strap on his holstered .45, and stepped toward her. She saw the slight motion as he unstrapped the .45 and realized that this might not be the easiest takedown she had ever done. He was being quite cautious. He stopped about ten feet from her and raised his hand, indicating that she should stop also.

She didn't stop. He looked at her again as she continued to step slowly toward him. She smiled at him. He looked puzzled. No words had been exchanged. He looked at her from her head down to her feet and back up again, hesitating at her breasts before looking at her eyes again. She tossed her head to move her hair a bit. He followed the motion with his eyes. He wasn't sure what to make of this situation. He looked at her again, and she stopped about three feet in front of him. He was much taller than she, and considerably heavier. She looked over his shoulder and smiled even broader. He took the oldest bait in the world and glanced over his shoulder at what she was looking at. In that split second, she had the can of bug spray out, and as he quickly turned back to her, she gave him a face full of it. Right in the eyes, mouth, and nose. He froze ... then screamed. His hands flew to his eyes. Burning, stinging, blinding, immobilizing. The spray did its job. She took a step forward and kicked upward with her boot, with the grace and force of a football place kicker, squarely into his crotch. His hands shot quickly down from his face as he turned and dropped in excruciating agony. He was out for the count; not unconscious, but completely disabled and moaning in pain. She struggled as she dragged him back into the guard shack on the floor and quickly tied him with the cord. She took his socks and his belt, gagged him, and used the belt to hold the gag in place. He was still moaning with his eyes tightly closed when she got the gag into place.

She quickly stepped outside and recovered her jacket and the daypack. She stepped back into the shack, removed his .45, and extracted the magazine. It was full. She rammed it back home, set the safety, and put it on the shack counter. She looked around for a minute and found another full magazine. She put that in her daypack. She put on the jacket and the daypack, then reached for the .45. Putting it into the jacket pocket, she put her watch cap back on and headed into the complex.

It was only a short distance, a few hundred yards, to the main complex building where the men were being held. Since she had left the building, she was already familiar with the doors and the corridor arrangement. She quietly tried the door and found it unlocked. How convenient and careless of security! Looking around, she saw several lights still on in the building. People must still be working, and that was why the doors were still open. After removing one of the knives from the daypack and putting it in her boot, she set the pack on the ground behind the door. Quietly she opened the door and slipped inside. The corridor was well lit, and that made her quite uncomfortable. Fortunately, no one was in the corridor, and she was able to move down to the first intersection with no trouble. She carefully looked around the corner. The guard was sitting just outside the door looking at the floor. He was half-asleep with boredom, but was still awake. She backed up for a moment, thinking. Would it work twice? And if he screamed, help would arrive very quickly.

She got the .45 out, took off her watch cap, and tousled her hair. She took a deep breath and marched squarely around the corner at a rapid pace, not running, but rapid. The guard was studying his hands and didn't see her right away. He heard something and glanced up just as she reached him. He was startled and tried to get up from the chair. She knocked the chair out from under him, his arms went up in reaction to the fall, and she hit him with the .45 in an upward karate chop with all she had right in the voice box. He fell, making a strangling sound, and reached for his strapped and holstered .45. She stepped down hard on his instep, crunching a bone, and sprayed him with the bug spray. His hands went to his face, which was contorted in agony. He was trying to scream, but only made a strangling sound due to a crushed voice box. She reached over quickly and flipped the deadbolt on the lock. She opened the door to three incredulous men. Ryan quickly saw what the situation was, and they dragged the guard into the room and shut the door. Dave quickly ran over to the "hidden" camera at the light switch and covered it with his body.

Ryan looked at her with total shock on his face. Then he looked at the guard and how she had managed to incapacitate him. Dave and Corey were reacting in much the same way. She quickly told them what she had done and that they needed to get out *now*. They nodded. Corey quietly opened the door, then ducked back in quickly as someone went walking by in the corridor. Then, after a few moments, he opened it again and looked out. It was clear.

Never delay in that kind of situation. They took the guard's .45, smashed the light switch with the hidden camera, and rapidly left the room, locking it again so the guard couldn't get out and raise an alarm. They ran down the corridor, turned to the left, and went out the door. Jackie picked up her daypack as they left, and they headed back across the unlit grass to the road just before the entrance shack. It continued down to the harbor inside the fence line of the complex.

They took no chances, and headed straight down the interior complex road, staying off the pavement, leading to the harbor. After several minutes of running, and once they reached the harbor, Ryan called a halt to the run. They looked over the harbor and back on the path. All appeared to be quiet so far. He sat down on the dirt next to the road and motioned them all to do the same.

"What are you doing?" he whispered to Jackie. "I thought you were on your way back to the States by now."

She looked at him and said, "I never left buddies behind. I figured I might get out, but you three were very questionable—your survival, that is. So I decided to get you out and then we'd figure out what to do." She added, "And I don't want to lose you, either. The decision was not hard to make."

Ryan eased up a bit. He looked at the harbor again then back at all three of them. He said, "I don't think we can fly out of here. The distance is just too far, and the small planes they have here won't reach any place we would want to go, even if we could get to the airport."

Dave said, "I agree with that, but nearly all these boats"—he motioned at the harbor—"haven't the range either. And that big trimaran would take a crew of ... well, a lot more than we can handle. The other boats are primarily close-in patrol boats. They couldn't get us very far either, at least not without refueling somewhere. The one exception is the yacht, and it's pretty good-sized." He hesitated, then added, "If it has fuel."

"There's no place for refueling except possibly Somalia, and I don't think we would be very welcome there," said Corey.

They were all looking around as they talked. It was a bit nerve-racking to be sitting there and having very few or no options. There had to be an answer, but it sure wasn't apparent at this point. But they were committed. If they were caught, they would either be killed outright or things would be made much worse for them.

Ryan said, "I don't think we have much of an option. We need to take one of those boats or the yacht, load as much fuel on it as we can, and beat feet. And we need to do it now. I haven't heard any racket yet, but they are going to wake up soon and we need to be somewhere else."

They looked at each other, then back at Ryan, and simply nodded. The yacht that was tied up at the pier was big, and would normally require a regular crew to handle it. It was just like the one that had been captured in the Gulf of Mexico the previous year. Ryan was familiar with it because he had helped capture it. They quickly looked over the three patrol boats in the distance and determined that they were too small and couldn't possibly be used. The only other vessel was the trimaran, and it was too complex for them to handle.

Ryan didn't see much choice. It was either try the yacht or go for the patrol boats. He made his decision. The yacht. After all, most of the crew on a yacht were for service and comfort of the passengers. Four of them might be able to operate it, especially with the computer controls on board.

"Dave, do you think you can operate the engines on that thing?"

"Probably, but I'll have to look," Dave responded.

"Anybody disagree with us taking her out? I don't see any other option at this point."

As a group, they all agreed.

Chapter Forty-Six
Ocean Escape

Thursday—August 4
Socotra Island Operations Center

Aban, supervising the evening guards assigned to watch the prisoners, had just finished reworking next week's schedule. As part of his normal evening routine, he came around the corner of the hallway and stopped short. The chair was there outside the door, but there was no guard on duty. Where was Haytham? He was supposed to be watching the door and the prisoners. Aban's radio squawked. Control had lost the signal from the prisoners' room camera. Aban became very animated and concerned. He ran up to the door and looked at it. No damage. He looked through a small peephole and saw Haytham sitting on the floor with his head in his hands. Aban quickly unbolted and opened the door and looked in. No one else was in the room except Haytham! The prisoners were gone!

He yelled at Haytham, "What have you done? Where are the Americans?" Haytham just looked up at Aban with very red and irritated eyes from the bug spray. Aban shook his head in disgust and, turning quickly, left the room, running down the hall to the outside doorway. Nothing there either. No sign of the prisoners. Aban quickly radioed back to the central control that the prisoners had escaped.

Muwaffaq, supervising the control room, set off the alarm in Abdul-Hakim's room. Abdul-Hakim came running into the control center a few moments later. Muwaffaq explained what had happened. Abdul-Hakim couldn't believe it. How had they managed to escape? It only took him a minute or so of thought to realize that they had to have had help. The woman! He knew he shouldn't have trusted her. But arguing with the ayatollah wasn't advisable either.

Thursday—August 4
Socotra Island Harbor

Since the harbor was inside the perimeter fence of the complex, there were no guards specifically assigned to the piers. There was a roving patrol for the harbor area, as Dave and Ryan had already discovered, and the basic perimeter was guarded. The security had been considered adequate by Abdul-Hakim.

Ryan started to move out onto the pier where the yacht *Persian Destiny* was tied up. Corey, Dave, and Jackie were a few steps behind him, looking around closely at the harbor complex. Ryan had a .45 in his hand just in case there were some crew about. He reached the boarding ramp to the yacht and was both startled and surprised when he heard a shout. Looking back and further down the pier past his friends, he saw two guards running fast toward them with weapons drawn. He didn't understand what they had shouted, but he sure understood their intent.

Jackie quickly stepped out from behind Corey with her .45 also drawn and ran up to Ryan. She quickly said, "I've got the left, you take the right." Ryan rapidly turned sideways and raised his weapon on the guard on the right. He took careful aim. The two guards stopped when they realized they were facing weapons. Both raised their weapons to fire. Ryan fired first, taking out the guard on the right. The guard on the left beat Jackie to it and fired. Ryan shifted slightly and fired again, taking out the guard on the left. Both guards were now a heap on the dock. He realized that Jackie had dropped. She wasn't moving on the dock. Corey came running up to help.

They turned Jackie over and saw blood pouring out of a wound on the right side of her head. She was unconscious. Ryan, extremely concerned, tore off the sleeve of her shirt and wrapped it around her head, compressing the wound. The bleeding slowed to just a trickle.

There was a two-way radio on the ground where the guards lay, and someone was yelling on it. Corey said, "They're trying to reach these two. I'm sure there will be a lot of help in a few minutes. We'd better get going and move out now!" Ryan picked up Jackie and, leaving the guards, they ran for the yacht.

Ryan, carrying an unconscious Jackie, quickly boarded the yacht. As he boarded, a crewman arrived at the rail and fired at him. The bullet grazed the boarding ramp rail, burning a trail across Ryan's arm. He dropped his .45 but held on to Jackie and heard a small explosion next to his head. The crewman dropped to the deck as Corey's .45 tore through him. Ryan picked up his .45, looked over at Corey, and shook his head with a concerned look. He went up to the bridge with Jackie and gently set her down on the deck of the bridge while Dave headed for the engine room. Corey stayed on the pier as a lookout. After a few moments of waiting, Corey took off, looking for more crewmen on board. He didn't find any more.

After several moments of fumbling around, Ryan was able to make out some of the controls, and he was quite familiar with the navigation equipment. Dave, breathing heavily, appeared on the bridge and said, "I think I can get her started. There is a nearly full tank of fuel on board from what I can tell from the gauges. How about up here? Can you handle it?"

Ryan looked back at him and said, "I don't think we have much choice. Yes, I can handle it once we get underway, but pulling out of this harbor won't be easy. It's pretty tight."

Dave glanced at Jackie and said, "How is she?"

"She's out. But I think it's just a bloody flesh wound."

Dave nodded, turned, and said as he left, "I'll get her going, and let's see if we can bail out of here. We need to move in a hurry."

Ryan nodded as he glanced down at Jackie and then turned back to the console. Shortly he heard the exhaust of the turbine engines as they started and settled into a reassuring whine. He hit the light switch for the console running lights and saw the engine instruments lit up, indicating normal operations. Fuel gauges also indicated nearly full status. The navigation system was going through some self-checks and would be up and running soon, but he didn't need that to get moving. It looked good. He turned off the instrument lights to reduce the chances of being seen.

Just as they were ready, a small squall hit the dock area, the wind picking up suddenly and rain coming down in a fury. Lightning struck nearby. Now they had to contend with the weather also but they were too concerned with getting underway and tried their best to ignore it.

Corey had returned to the dock and was standing watch in the downpour. He saw Ryan motion to him, and quickly removed the anchor ropes and hopped aboard. Ryan sat in the console and worked the joystick to begin maneuvering the large yacht out of the harbor. He backed it into a small side channel, then moved forward into the harbor proper and headed for the opening in the breakwater dead ahead. As they maneuvered into the channel, Corey shot out the breakwater lighting. Ryan marveled at the way the yacht handled—smooth and easy to "drive," and from the console he could monitor every system on the ship. It was truly a marvel of modern electronics and navigation systems.

Corey, dripping wet, returned to the bridge and bent down over Jackie. He replaced the bandage with one he had found in the galley. She started to moan as he tended to her. Ryan looked down, very relieved to hear her. Then they moved her to a more comfortable couch just off the bridge.

Thursday—August 4
Socotra Island Operations Center

Aban suspected that they had headed for the harbor and one of the boats tied up there. The guards at the pier and at the entrance gate weren't responding to radio calls. Nothing else made sense. They couldn't be anywhere else. There was disbelief in the control room. How could this be?

Muwaffaq alerted the sleeping response team in an adjacent room. It took several minutes for the team to get itself together and moving. They were an armed response team that was supposed to be able to get anywhere in the complex within five minutes of notification. It took more than five minutes just for them to get awake and moving. Armed with side arms and AK-74s, they raced out to their parked vehicles in the pouring rain, started them, and headed down to the harbor. As they crested the small hill toward the harbor, they could dimly see the yacht heading out through the breakwater. The breakwater lights had been shot out, but they could see part of the yacht in the dim light. They raced out onto the pier, saw the two dead guards, and opened fire on the now rapidly moving yacht.

As they passed through the breakwater, several trucks came screaming down the small hill to the harbor. The trucks pulled out onto the pier. Several armed men charged out of the trucks and opened fire on the now-distant yacht. A few of the shots ricocheted off the hull and Ryan ducked down. He pushed the joystick forward and the yacht increased speed significantly. They quickly left the harbor and the ayatollah's fire teams behind.

Abdul-Hakim, quickly taking charge in the control center from Aban and Muwaffaq, called the response team, and found out the yacht was gone and moving away fast. He hit his hand on the wall in frustration. That yacht could outrun anything they had ... and it was fully fueled and partially stocked in preparation for returning to the Chinese. He thought for a minute and then directed the response team to return to the operations center. They came back, bringing with them the two dead guards, who were placed in a side room. After what the ayatollah had told him earlier, he needed to think fast and get that yacht back. Without Ryan and friends still alive.

Corey appeared at Ryan's side with a cup of steaming coffee. Ryan hadn't even noticed that he had gone below. He took the coffee with a thanks. Corey then went to look at Jackie to see how she was doing. Corey quietly left. They were well underway.

Ryan used the intercom system and raised Dave. "Bridge to engine. How's it going?"

Dave responded, "Just ducky. This system is a wonder of modern electronics and propulsion. Once I figured it out, it is actually pretty simple to operate. Just turn it on and it waits for computer commands from your console. All I have to do is monitor it."

"Sounds good. If you think you can trust it, there is coffee in the galley. Do you know where Corey went?"

"Thanks, but I'll watch it for a while before doing that. Appreciate the thought. No. He was here for a few minutes but left saying he was going to look around a bit."

"Yeah. He was just up here too. Okay. Thanks. Be alert."

Ryan received a click on the intercom when Dave acknowledged his caution.

Jackie lay on the couch off the bridge. She slowly became aware of the movement of the yacht, and her head hurt terribly. What had happened? She was lying on her side, and slowly rolled over. Ryan heard the movement, set the controls for automatic, and quickly went to her side. He lifted her head slightly and caressed her cheek. She half opened her eyes and looked at him then around at her surroundings. She said, "What happened?"

"You took one on the side of your head. Pretty good crease, too, from what I can tell. Corey fixed you up until we can get some proper help."

She nodded slightly, winced at the movement, and closed her eyes. "Go do what you have to. I'll be okay in a little while.

Ryan then turned his attention to the stern and was watching for a patrol boat pursuit. The squall had passed and the seas were fairly calm. He was sure they would use one of the harbor boats to try and stop them. But nothing appeared on the very dark horizon.

The island's few lights slowly disappeared in the nighttime distance.

Chapter Forty-Seven
Chase

Thursday—August 4
Socotra Island Harbor

Abdul-Hakim gathered the response team together, called in two more security guards to replace the two that had been killed on the dock, and pulled Qasim, his primary security guard manager, aside for a conversation. Abdul-Hakim would accompany them, but Qasim would lead the effort to recover the yacht and dispose of the Americans. Abdul-Hakim was tired of the Americans, and they needed to be eliminated. He directed Qasim to take the larger patrol boat and overtake the yacht. The Americans were to be captured and then thrown overboard. The sharks would take care of them.

Qasim, almost six feet, with a bull of a chest, very strong arms, and dark, penetrating eyes, smiled at the thought. He had lost many good friends in the stronghold, and it would be good to strike back at these godless people. He nodded, then said, "We will do as you say. The larger patrol boat is fully fueled and has the Bushmaster. It will be able to stop the yacht. There may be some damage to the yacht, but I think that will be a minor consideration."

Abdul-Hakim just nodded and then motioned Qasim to get moving. It had already been over a half-hour since the yacht left the harbor. It was still very dark in the early evening, and by the time they could get everything together, it would probably be an hour since it had left. If the Americans had figured out how to use the hydrofoils, they would never catch them. Hopefully they hadn't figured that one out.

Qasim, intimidating and hard-tempered, gathered his men and loaded up in the trucks. Abdul-Hakim joined them, and they headed down to the harbor. They parked and ran for the large patrol boat tied up to the pier. Nazim, the helmsman on the patrol boat, was already idling the engine as the response team boarded. He motioned to the dock men to release the lines, they climbed aboard, and he slowly backed away from the pier. After getting aligned with the harbor breakwater entrance, he put the boat in forward and eased out

267

of the harbor. Once clear of the breakwater, he added power and they began to move out in the direction the yacht had taken. It would take a while to catch up with the yacht, since it had over an hour's head start on them and was out of sight over the horizon. He hoped they hadn't changed course, or they might never find them. And, as he looked at the night sky, at least the squall had passed by.

Another thought that Nazim kept to himself was that, with only about ten hours of fuel aboard, they might not have enough fuel to make it all the way out and still get back. While it was the largest patrol boat, it was still a local patrol boat, not meant for long-haul operations. The now man-heavy patrol boat, moving at close to thirty knots, was burning fuel very quickly. Assuming the yacht was moving a little slower, it would still be several hours before they could overtake it. Not a good thought. And if the people on the yacht were watching at all, they would see the patrol boat coming up on them from the stern even with all their lights off. Chances were very slim for a surprise attack.

The men aboard the patrol boat were anxious to catch the fleeing Americans. The two guards who had been killed were friends and coworkers. Revenge was a strong motive, and they knew they could do whatever they wanted with the Americans. Abdul-Hakim had said to eliminate them. As the boat was churning across the ocean waters, there was a good deal of talk about what they would do when they caught the Americans. Weapons were checked and some fired as they worked themselves up to a frenzy. Qasim quickly directed those firing their weapons to stop. He didn't want the sound to carry to the yacht.

Nazim watched this with some amusement, because he knew it would be several hours before they would be able to carry out their threats, and by then they would be quite tired out ... or possibly seasick. Most of these men had not spent much time on the sea. And the patrol boat was not a large ship ... it moved around a lot as the waves hit it.

It wouldn't take long to see who had their sea legs ... and who didn't.

Friday—August 5
Indian Ocean East of Socotra Island

It was now just past 12:00 a.m., and Ryan was enjoying the ride as they continued cruising to the east. Ryan had figured out the automated navigation system and programmed in Diego Garcia as a destination, even though it was a huge distance away. Using a satellite phone on the bridge, Ryan had been able to send a voicemail to Maria with their current status, satellite phone number, location, and destination. The yacht was responding as it should, and they were cruising quite comfortably at eighteen knots.

Jackie, slowly recovering and with a steaming cup of tea in her hands, was sitting next to him when he remembered the lipstick. He said, "Why did you slip this"—he pulled out the lipstick—"into my pocket?"

She looked back at him and said, "Did you open it?"

"No."

"Open it and check the edge of the cap."

He did and looked closely. The circular edge of the cap was razor sharp. He looked back at her, shook his head, smiled, and returned the lipstick to her. Quite a secret weapon. "Got it. Fortunately, I didn't have to use it. But good to know." And he smiled back at her.

Four hours later, in the dark of the early morning, the patrol boat, nearly silent, came up on their stern and hailed them. "Heave to and we will board you. Give up. You have no chance against our weapons." All of the men on the patrol boat had been warned to be silent. There was no other sound.

Startled and momentarily confused, Ryan looked around. Jackie yelled, and he looked in the direction she was pointing and saw the large patrol boat coming up from the stern on his starboard side. The boat looked like a cross between a fishing vessel and an armed attack boat. It obviously had a greater range than he'd anticipated. It fired a small mini-gun, and several rounds entered the water just ahead of the bow. It looked like there were around fifteen to twenty armed men on board.

He grabbed the binoculars off the console and looked in the dark at the attacking boat. Several well-armed men were reloading and preparing to fire the 7.62 mm machine gun. One was really excited and telling the others that the aim was off. But they were purposely firing in front of the yacht, not at it. It occurred to Ryan that they did not want to damage their own boat, just stop it and board.

Ryan looked over the side and saw the two main weapons the hailer was referring to. One was a machine gun around a 7.62mm size. That didn't worry him, since the yacht could handle that caliber with the onboard armor. It was the weapon in the back of the patrol boat that bothered him. A Bushmaster M242. The 25mm weapon could put a hole through anything on the yacht. And it could do it quickly. He was in a quandary. Hopefully his actions two nights before would work to their advantage. But he wasn't absolutely sure. He moved the joystick to the left to move away from the patrol boat. The boat just followed him. He moved the joystick forward to increase his speed, and they matched it.

"This doesn't look good," said Jackie, peering into the darkness.

The boat came abreast of the bridge. Ryan looked at it and hit the deck, yelling at Jackie to do the same. Just then the glass on the bridge erupted in a shower of fragments as the small machine gun opened up. The gunner knew the yacht had armor on the sides and couldn't be harmed by his weapon, but the bridge was vulnerable. He fired for what seemed like a lifetime. When he stopped, the glass was pretty well destroyed. Jackie, holding her head, picked herself up gingerly and, crouching, moved to the back of the bridge. Ryan crawled back up to the console and moved the joystick forward to increase speed. As the engines took hold, the patrol craft slipped slightly to the rear.

Dave called, "What's going on up there? I keep hearing gunfire and small explosions."

Ryan gave him a quick rundown as Jackie kept watch on the patrol boat. Corey was in the engine room also, and listened to the conversation. He then quietly left the engine room and went aft. Dave watched him go and shrugged, wondering where he was going.

Dave said to Ryan over the intercom, "Corey just went aft. Don't know why. Ryan, if we need to, don't forget that we have a submersible down here. There is a mini-sub and the moon pool. If they gain a foothold, let's bail out underwater. They can't follow us there, and the mini has room for all four of us."

"Thanks for the info. I'd forgotten about the mini-sub. It's getting pretty tense up here. Be ready for some action and quick changes in propulsion. I may need some more power. Stand by. If you see Corey, send him up to me."

"Will do." Dave, thinking about their precarious situation, looked over the turbine engine control console and found what he was looking for. Looking over one of the electronic control modules, he satisfied himself on its function. He was now prepared if they had to flee.

Ryan turned his attention back to the patrol craft. It appeared that there were quite a few men on board. All had side arms. One was at the helm, one was on the machine gun, several were at the rails, and the rest were back at the Bushmaster. None appeared to be concerned with concealment. They were all out in the open. The boat stayed off his rear starboard quarter and maintained speed.

Ryan watched as the patrol boat tried to get closer, but the boat was unable to get close enough to allow men to jump aboard. Ryan kept moving the joystick and kept avoiding them. Finally, the hailer again said to heave to, and he ignored it. His reaction must have frustrated them, because the 7.62 machine gun erupted, and the remaining glass in the bridge went flying as Jackie and Ryan hit the deck again. Ryan crawled over to the console and pushed the joystick forward to its max. He quickly felt the turbine engines come up to power, and the yacht surged forward past the surprised patrol boat crew. Ryan eased off the joy stick a bit, felt part of the stick in his hand and felt the yacht start to slow. One of the 7.62 rounds had damaged the joystick or its components. The engines did not respond to the stick inputs. And they were slowing down.

The patrol boat then surged ahead and eased up on the starboard side. Just as it got within about fifty yards of the yacht, Ryan saw a small smoke trail stream out from the aft end of the yacht. He quickly followed it and just barely saw the explosion on the cabin of the patrol boat. Ryan stared back at the source, and, on the stern of the yacht, partially hidden by the Sea-Doos hanging in their davits, was Corey. Looking at the aft of the yacht, he saw Corey putting down an RPG launcher and picking up another one. Corey lifted it to his shoulder and waited to see what would happen. The patrol boat slowed down and dropped off a further distance. Its cabin was blown away, but the engines were still operational. Corey took another shot with the RPG, but this time it missed. The patrol boat, apparently under manual control, surged forward, and they could see several men preparing to jump as it came alongside the yacht. At the same time, the Bushmaster was manned and aimed at Corey's position. Corey ducked away quickly from his exposed position in the stern. When they fired the large chain-driven gun, the barrel exploded and several of the crew were killed by the shrapnel. Ryan grinned in satisfaction. When they had been in the harbor the two nights before, he had managed to spike the barrel. The Bushmaster was wasted, but, while all this was going on, four heavily armed crewmen had managed to board the yacht.

As the yacht slowed down, Ryan called down to Dave and told him to open up the moon pool and get the mini ready. The four men were being followed by others as lines were tied fast to both boats. Corey was heading back to the main superstructure; he turned and fired at the intruders with an AK-74 several times, and then headed into the lower parts of the ship. Ryan and Jackie bailed out of the remains of the bridge and headed for the moon pool. The yacht had come to a full stop in the water. As they left the bridge, Ryan saw several more heavily armed men jump onto the yacht. It would be close. He fired and hit one of them. The rest quickly slowed down and took cover. Between Ryan and Corey, the yacht wasn't the easy pickings they had thought it would be.

They raced down the dimly lit passageways, ran into Corey, and kept running. Dave had the moon pool and the hatch to the mini open. He dropped the mini into the water and disconnected the umbilicals. They dove for the hatch, squirmed inside, and Ryan, the last in, dogged the hatch shut. Several men appeared in the passageway as they began to sink out of sight. Bullets pierced the water around them, and they heard a few ricochet off the mini's hull. Quickly they dove several feet, and the water slowed the hail of bullets to a noisemaker level. They had made it, but just barely.

While everybody tried to strap into seats, Dave manipulated the controls and they continued to dive and move away from the yacht. They had made it for now. Dave dove until the instruments indicated they were about one hundred feet down. He leveled off. Ryan was the last to get buckled in.

The mini-sub disappeared through the moon pool and was lost to view. Some burbling and water disturbance was the only indication the mini-submarine had been there. Abdul-Hakim, dressed in full combat gear, arrived on the catwalk overlooking the water and silently wondered what it would take to capture these Americans. They were slippery as eels. They were on the open ocean, no other boats or ships in sight, and they had lost the run for the Americans. He couldn't understand why they had been outrun again. His men had done all he could think of.

They had quickly left the harbor after the decision was made to pursue. The patrol boat was the fastest and largest they had. The Bushmaster gun had blown up when fired. He knew immediately that it had been spiked, but they had managed to still overtake the yacht and get aboard, even with the patrol boat's bridge blown away by the RPG. He had lost six men in the firing exchange, and the yacht, with only the four Americans aboard, had nearly escaped. However, they had succeeded in getting aboard, and were about to capture their quarry when Ryan and his friends took to the mini-sub and disappeared in the waters of the Indian Ocean. They had missed the Americans.

He looked to the heavens in silent prayer. Why was Allah allowing this to happen?

Chapter Forty-Eight
On the Indian Ocean

Friday—August 5
Underwater, Indian Ocean East of Socotra

Dave had the helm as they cruised at a depth of one hundred feet. It hadn't taken him long to figure out the controls, since much of the control system was a U.S. design stolen by the Chinese. He had worked on it as part of his job with Underwater Submersibles. He tested several of the controls and found it quite familiar, even though the various gauges were written in Chinese. He placed the mini-sub on automatic pilot, and turned to the rest to make sure they were all okay.

Ryan said, "Well, that was a bit too close. We just got out of there in time. Other than you, Jackie, anybody hurt?" He looked at each of them. They all shook their heads. "Good. At least we have that to be thankful for." Then he looked at Jackie, with her head swathed in a heavy bandage, and said, "Boy, you sure look like a poster child for the war wounded."

She just nodded at him and said, "We in the Marines have an appropriate response to that kind of comment ..." She gave him the one-finger salute while grimacing and smiling at the same time.

The whole group, including Ryan, chuckled at that.

After a few moments of thoughtful silence, Dave looked at all of them and said, "Well, now what? We're out in the middle of nowhere in this huge Indian Ocean and have this little submarine to call home for a while."

Ryan responded, "Yes. But at least we are safe for now. That was quite a crowd trying to get us a few minutes ago." He looked around as heads were nodding. "I think we need to get our wits together and see what we can come up with for a plan from here on out."

He looked around at the inside of the sub. It was small but certainly adequate for now, since it was designed for four people. They would need to see what supplies were on board and how long they could last. There might not be much, since the sub and the yacht were going to be returned to the Chinese for conversion.

Jackie got up and headed to the back of the sub, just a few feet away, and started looking around in small lockers. All she found were some bottles of fresh water and some small packets of reconstitutable food. She passed them around. None took a drink, since they all realized they might not have much water available for who-knows-how-long.

Dave said, "This sub has a lot of features we saw on the one we captured in the gulf last year. It isn't hard to navigate or run. It also has some communications capability I think we can use. Once we get out of range of the yacht, we can come up to the surface and see if we can get some help. We are actually near some sea shipping lanes here. We should be able to contact someone and get either a ship to help us or get the U.S. military to help. We'll just have to wait and see. In the meantime, I think we need to conserve any food or water that we may have."

Ryan looked over at Dave and asked, "Doesn't this sub have the capability of making drinkable water from the seawater?"

"Yes. But I'm going to have to figure out how, so I would suggest going easy on the water until I can do that."

Ryan, turning to Corey, said, "Where did you find those rockets you used on the yacht?"

"I wasn't being useful since you were steering and Dave was running the engines, so I decided to look around. I figured the yacht was really a form of warship and that they must have a weapons locker somewhere. I was right. It's located back near the stern, and had several automatic weapons and about a dozen RPGs, along with some miscellaneous flares and such."

"And you know, obviously, how to use them?" Ryan said with a slightly raising voice putting the statement into a question.

"Army Special Forces for six years. Then decided to get out and went to work for the State Department."

Ryan grinned. "Well, we have a SEAL, Special Forces, a Marine MP, and an underwater engineering geek here. If our friends on that boat had known that, it might have given them second thoughts." They all laughed.

Ryan nodded and turned to Jackie. "Are there any other supplies back there?"

She was still in the back of the sub, and looked around again. Moving some materials and parts around, she came across some additional food packets, but no more water. "No. There's nothing back here except a few more food items and, interestingly, there are some just barely out-of-date C-4 explosive packets. Since they're out of date, I guess they were going back to the Chinese."

Ryan thought for a bit. Dave was just sitting with his arms folded, glancing between the group and the autopilot navigation system. Jackie was still nosing around. Corey was just sitting ... staring out at the water through a viewport and thinking.

Ryan said to Corey, "You're being pretty quiet. Any ideas?"

Corey sat up straight in his crewman's seat and leaned forward. He put his hands on his knees and looked at all of them. They all looked back at him, wondering what the change in his posture meant. Corey, with a grimacing smile, finally said, "Yes. I think we ought to go right back up there and take that ship back from them. It's only been about fifteen minutes since we left, and a return would be the last thing they would expect. I recognize our tactical retreat was required, but I'm pissed off. I think we can do it. As you said. We have a Marine, a SEAL, Special Forces, and an extraordinary engineer. We can beat the shit out of them!"

Jackie and Dave looked at Corey thoughtfully and began smiling slightly. Corey was up for a fight and wasn't about to let these guys off the hook. They quickly realized he was right.

Ryan thought for a moment and then said, "You may have a point there. We guessed that there were about nineteen or twenty of them total, and there are four of us. Spiking the Bushmaster helped, and I'm sure your RPG helped get several out of action. Probably twelve to fourteen left. But if we can even the odds a bit more, perhaps we have a chance. That's if they don't get that yacht running and head back to Socotra. We couldn't keep up with them in this mini. They would just pull away from us."

Corey responded, "That's the way I see it too. I think we have a real chance, and it would solve our problem. But we need to move quickly, because they may take off on us and leave us out here to drift."

Dave looked over and just grinned at Corey and Ryan. "Ahh, yes. Well, that ain't going to happen anytime soon! As you said, Corey, I'm an extraordinary engineer."

Corey, Jackie, and Ryan looked at Dave as Ryan, looking at Dave sideways, breathed a sigh of relief. With a smirk, he said, "Okay, maestro, what did you do?"

Dave reached into his shirt pocket and drew out a small electronic-looking module about the size of a pack of cigarettes, with multiple copper connecting pins, and held it up for them all to see. "Guess what this is."

They all looked back at him, shook their heads, and shrugged.

"It is an electronic control module for the hydraulic moon pool doors. Without it, they can't close the doors. I unplugged it and stuck it in my pocket as we headed for the mini. And, since there is an interlock between the moon pool doors and the propulsion turbine electronics, they can't move. It's a safety measure built into their system. The moon pool doors have to be closed for them to actuate the turbine engines. Except for whatever the currents do, and they drift, they aren't going anywhere under their own power." He grinned and continued, "I thought it might be best if we made sure they couldn't move. It significantly increases our options for dealing with them."

Ryan, recovering from his surprise, clapped Dave on the back and laughed. "Man, you sure are a guy of many talents! I'll bet they are just beside themselves when they realize they can't move."

Corey did a small fist pump and Jackie just grinned. Jackie said, "Well, that certainly helps even the odds a bit, doesn't it? They are going to be preoccupied with trying to get underway, and we may actually be able to surprise them."

Ryan looked back at Jackie. "So I take it you feel we should take them on?"

"You bet. While there are just four of us, we would be going up against their numbers. But I'll bet they don't have anywhere near the training we have. They are probably just like the normal guards back in Socotra. Very little, if any, actual training. And none of it combat. While it won't be a cakewalk, we should be able to take them, or at least get the ship back and scare the rest of them off."

Corey was nodding. He added, smiling, "As I said, I think we can do it. We have a couple of weapons back here in a small metal locker. With a little tactical work, we should be able to distract them and get them as a group, or one by one, before they realize we are back. I agree with Jackie. With maybe a few exceptions, these guys just aren't trained for any type of formal combat action, especially at sea and in the dark. With the first explosion or shot, they are going to be ducking and should not be too hard to overcome. Our version of shock and awe." He smiled at the thought.

Ryan looked back at all of them, thought for a moment and said, "Okay. We actually don't have a real option here. While we could get out of the area, there's no guarantee we could run into anyone who could help us out in the near future. And this mini is purposely hard to see. Any large ship in the area could easily run over us and not be aware of it. Let's head back to their location, Dave, and on the way figure out how we are going to provide our own, as you said it, Corey, 'shock and awe.'"

Dave took a quick look at the navigation instruments and shifted the controls slightly, and they felt the mini accelerate, go into a slight bank, and begin climbing. Dave was smiling the whole time he was maneuvering. He loved this type of action. While he was small, he was very smart, and had an enviable capability of thinking well ahead of a situation and figuring a way out.

On the way, they had a lively conversation on how they might overcome the force they were facing. It only took several minutes before they were on the surface again and, in the near distance, they could see the yacht and the patrol craft tied together. Both were lit up in the darkness, and they could see workers trying to repair some of the damage to the two vessels. But neither vessel was moving.

It was nighttime, and the mini was nearly impossible to see, with a low silhouette and dark coloration.

Almost invisible. And besides, no one was really looking.

Chapter Forty-Nine
Yacht Recapture

Friday—August 5
Indian Ocean, East of Socotra

Abdul-Hakim was on the nearly destroyed bridge of the yacht. He was desperately trying to get both the yacht and the patrol boat capable of moving. They had succeeded in getting several repairs done to the superstructure of both boats, and some repairs were made to the navigation instruments. A temporary patch covered a medium-sized hole in the hull of the patrol boat from the RPG strike, but the patch was pretty fragile.

He had just been informed that the patrol boat could move under its own power now, but the yacht could not be moved until the moon pool doors were closed. They were too heavy to just disconnect from their actuators and, without the electronic module that was missing, they couldn't be moved. As a result, the turbine engines were currently useless.

They had missed their quarry, and now had to get the yacht in running order and back to the harbor in Socotra. It would take a while to get it all done, and they were sitting quietly in the water. Repairs to the bridge navigation equipment were being done, and the engine room would have to be manually operated if they could bypass the missing module. Then they could follow the patrol boat, itself heavily damaged, back to Socotra. He had communicated with the operations center and had received agreement. In several hours they would be underway ... hopefully.

Abdul-Hakim looked out at the dark ocean and wondered where the mini-sub had gone; probably miles away by now. They had no way of tracking it. It was frustrating to come that close.

After fifteen minutes of work, they realized the yacht turbines could not be used. As a backup, Qasim had finally been able to maneuver the patrol boat around to the front of the yacht, and they were going to try to slowly tow the yacht back to Socotra. It would be a very long journey, with close to one hundred miles to cover, and they didn't know what might

279

happen when water began to flow through the moon pool area. That part of the yacht, without the moon pool doors closed, was open to the seas, and there might be a flooding problem.

In his quarters on the yacht, Abdul-Hakim was very frustrated and disappointed that they hadn't been able to capture the Americans. With his crew, and the firepower they had, he was sure the Americans would be well underway elsewhere by now. The mini was capable of traveling long distances as long as they could recharge her batteries and, given the circumstances, could probably reach land somewhere within a few days or weeks. And there was always the possibility of a ship picking them up in the nearby sea lanes.

The two men he had down in the engine room were skilled in running the engines. The one that was in the moon pool area was also familiar with the mechanism for opening and closing the moon pool doors. But without the missing electronics module they were wasting their time. He had deployed five men to the patrol boat to get it underway, and had another three men at the front of the yacht trying to attach a line to the patrol boat through the anchor port. Two men were in the yacht's bridge area working on some of the radio gear. One man with some cooking experience was in the galley, cooking up a rice and fish mixture for the crew. And four men were spread out on the yacht as lookouts and guards. Abdul-Hakim felt quite secure that he would have no further problems with the Americans. His current major concern was getting the yacht back to the harbor in Socotra.

His thoughts were suddenly interrupted by an explosion, followed by a short round of gunfire on the patrol boat. The patrol boat rocked back and forth with the force of the explosion just above the starboard waterline and forward of the stern. Three of the men on the patrol boat were thrown into the water; two were limp and facing down, and the third was flailing his arms and screaming.

Abdul-Hakim raced from his quarters up to the yacht bridge. Running through the passageway, he ran into the man from the moon pool and one of the engine room men.

"What are you doing up here?" Abdul-Hakim asked. They both answered with frightened voices that they had heard the explosion and thought they might be sinking. Angrily yelling back at them, he told them to get back down to their assigned positions. They hesitated and then turned back.

Abdul-Hakim continued up to the bridge to see what had happened.

Jackie and Corey, floating quietly in the moon pool water, hearing and feeling the explosion, quickly crawled up the door supports and ran for the passageway they had seen the man use. They stepped into the passageway, heard running coming toward them, and quickly hid in a side compartment. A burly seaman went running back toward the pool, panting from the exertion as he ran. They quickly stepped out after he passed by. Jackie stayed behind and Corey followed the seaman. A few minutes later, Corey came back alone and nodded, and they headed up the passageway again.

Dave, in the mini-sub, was still on the surface with the hatch open when Ryan came back to the mini. He had placed some C-4 explosive on the stern hull of the ship, set a timed detonator, and retreated a short distance as the explosive blew up. Three men came flying off the boat as the explosion had its intended effect. From the water, Ryan shot the first man to stick his head over the gunnel. He dove underwater and headed out to a rendezvous with Dave.

Dave dogged the hatch and they headed for the moon pool where they had dropped of Jackie and Corey. Aligning with the center of the moon pool, Dave docked the mini and they both piled out on the run.

They headed up through the passageway that Jackie and Corey had followed. Passing a small room with the door open, they saw the body of the seaman, head at an odd angle and obviously dead. One less worry. Corey had done his thing. They were getting the job done.

Abdul-Hakim had reached the bridge and, looking at the damage to the patrol boat, realized the Americans were back. He turned to the man who had been working on the radios and asked if he had seen anything. The answer was no. He had been under the instrument console when the explosion occurred. But he had an AK-74 in his hands and was obviously ready for action.

Abdul-Hakim nodded and called down to the engine room. They had seen nothing. He called down to the moon pool and got no answer, even though he tried several times. Dread filled his thoughts. They were back … and somewhere on his boat. He turned to the other man on the bridge and realized he would have to take charge of the situation from Qasim. Calling to the skipper of the patrol boat, he asked for an update. Qasim reported that the patrol boat had been holed at the stern and could not make headway as yet. They were trying to make some temporary repairs and still look out for the Americans, but he only had himself and one other to do that. He needed more help.

Abdul-Hakim called to the sentries on the deck and directed two of them to help the patrol boat, and the other two to start an organized search on the yacht for the Americans. Abdul-Hakim did the mental math for the number of men he had. That put a total of seven of his men either on the patrol boat or in the water near it. Eleven men were left on the yacht. He knew there were four Americans, but didn't know where they might be. They had to be found and stopped.

Corey and Jackie had managed to find their way to the galley, surprised the cook, and disabled him with a knockout blow, ropes, and a gag. Jackie's head was really hurting, but she was gutting through it. They slowly proceeded up toward the bridge, where they found Abdul-Hakim and the two repair technicians. Skirting around the bridge without being seen, they looked over the side and saw the damaged patrol boat and one of the roving guards on deck below them. Ducking quickly, they looked for the other guard and found him shortly after in one of the lounge areas. Both of the roving guards were well armed and looked capable of using their weapons.

Deciding to stay together, Corey and Jackie waited for the guard in the lounge to move out. They waited in ambush and caught him, one low and one high, as he went through a glass doorway. His throat was cut before he could make a sound, blood spurting everywhere, and he went overboard. They then took on the other guard from behind, punctured his lung with a Ka-Bar, slit his muscular throat quietly, and deep enough to get both carotids, and threw him overboard. Two more eliminated. Between the explosion on the patrol boat and their actions on the yacht, the odds were getting better.

Dave and Ryan only went partially up the passageway and diverted into the small stairway downward toward the engine room, where the yacht turbines and the hydraulics for the moon pool were located. As they approached the mechanical room, they could hear the two men conversing. They slowly made their way to the watertight door and stopped so they wouldn't be seen at the entrance. They could not tell what the men were saying, but guessed that it was about the missing electronic module.

They were about to move into the doorway when they heard a slight noise behind them. Someone was walking very quietly down the passageway. They ducked behind some life support equipment and waited with tight breathing. Someone was moving in the hall in a very stealthy fashion. One person passed them by, and then another. Corey and Jackie with blood-covered clothes and very determined looks on their faces. Ryan hissed at them, and they both jumped a bit but made no noise. Both were armed with the .45s from the guards, and their bloody knives. They swung them around, but held fire as they realized who Ryan and Dave were. Ryan motioned for them to retreat up the passageway and into a small conference room in the middle of the yacht.

In the conference room, they were able to compare notes. Corey then went back to the engine room and listened for a moment as the mechanics continued their discussion. He came back and said they had been discussing the explosion and what it meant. They were totally unprepared to defend themselves or the yacht. No weapons. The four of them then went back to the engine room and disabled the two mechanics, who provided no resistance. They were mechanics, not warriors. They tied them up and gagged them. They had cleared the yacht, except for the remaining three crewmen on the bridge. After a moment's conversation and some brief planning, Dave and Jackie stayed behind in the engine room and began their work.

Abdul-Hakim was not aware of his almost total loss of control.

While the two mechanics watched from their position trussed up on the floor, Dave walked over to the electronics bay where the various engine controls and computers were located. He looked at the complicated panels quickly, withdrew the electronic module from his shirt pocket, and inserted the module into a small indentation in the face of one of the electronic cabinets. Several indicator lights on the control console lit up like a Christmas tree. They were operational. The two mechanics looked at each other, and one raised his eyebrows.

Corey and Ryan headed up to the bridge, being very cautious as they went. When they got to the starboard passageway to the bridge, they stepped calmly onto the bridge with weapons drawn and at the ready. At first they weren't seen, but then the repair tech working on the structure saw them and stopped working. His lack of motion and face caused Abdul-Hakim to look around. He started when he saw the weapons aimed at him, safeties off and ready to fire. The instrument tech, not hearing any conversation, backed out from under the console and also gave a start at the sight of the Americans.

Recognizing Ryan and Corey, Abdul-Hakim, slightly smiling, said, "Ahh. We meet again. This time it appears that you have the advantage over us, at least for now."

Corey said, "Yes, for now. Please step away from the console. Tell your two men to do the same."

Abdul-Hakim slightly nodded and said in Arabic to his men, "Be prepared. We are going to overcome these Americans."

Corey then spoke up, also in Arabic: "I don't think so. You will do as we say or you will end up in the ocean as shark food."

Abdul-Hakim was surprised, and his two men quickly complied with Corey's directions.

As the men moved, a low rumble began to permeate the yacht, and after a few moments the low whine of turbines, building up in pitch, could be heard. Abdul-Hakim looked at his men and then back at Ryan and Corey.

"So, you are not alone in this adventure of yours?" Abdul-Hakim asked.

"No," responded Ryan. "We are not alone." He glanced over the top of the instrument console and saw that three men on the patrol boat, and the three men on the bow of the yacht tending lines, were looking in their direction. It was obvious that they had also heard the turbines starting up. He looked at Abdul-Hakim and said, "I want you to wave at them and then turn away."

Instead, Abdul-Hakim yelled a warning to the patrol boat. Some on the boat reacted with alarm, and some had not heard him due to background noise. The radio on the instrument console came blasting on with a question in Arabic" "Is everything all right over there?" The three men on the yacht hopped over to the patrol boat to help them out. The lines remained attached between the two boats.

284

Corey grabbed the radio microphone and, speaking in Arabic, said, "No, everything is not all right. Toss your weapons in the ocean and stand back from the ship railings ... all of you." He watched as three men, two obviously wounded, figuring out the situation, complied and stepped back. Two others raised their weapons threateningly. Corey said, "I'm warning you, dump your weapons and back off." The two men began firing their small arms, which had no real effect on the yacht.

Corey called down to the engine room and asked Dave if they could move yet. Dave responded that they could, but not too fast as yet.

Corey asked, "How about in reverse? Can we move at all in reverse?"

Dave said, "Sure. What's going on?"

"I'll tell you in a few minutes. Just begin backing us up slowly."

Chapter Fifty
Final Escape

Friday—August 5
Indian Ocean, East of Socotra Island

A moment later, the yacht began to pull back away from the patrol boat until the towline connecting the two of them tightened. Then slowly, the patrol boat began moving backward as it was being pulled by the line. The line was too tight to be released. Corey said over the radio, "You either comply, throw your weapons in the ocean and back off the rail, or we tow you backward until that patch gives way or the hole in the stern starts to flood and you sink. It's survive now or drown in the ocean ... your call."

Abdul-Hakim looked incredulously at Corey and Ryan. He shook his head and said, "That would be murder. What do you think you are doing?"

Ryan looked at Corey with a small, tight smile on his face and then looked back at Abdul-Hakim. "Yeah. Right. You come out here fully armed and try to blow us completely out of the water, attack the yacht with everything you've got, and now you claim we are the murderers? Come on now, man. That doesn't make any sense at all."

Corey looked back at Ryan and said, "Okay, they've all complied. At least the ones we can see. What's next?"

"Call down to the engine room and have Jackie bring the mechanics up to the aft end where the small runabout is located. Then I want you to take these three down to the runabout, where Jackie will help watch all of them." He gave Corey some other instructions, and Corey led Abdul-Hakim and his two men to the runabout, picking up the cook along the way.

Jackie showed up with the two mechanics and watched as they swung the runabout out over the water on its davits. She said to Corey, "We closed the moon pool doors right after getting the turbines up to speed, and I was able to secure the mini-sub in its frame, so there won't be any restrictions on moving the yacht." Then she and Corey directed each of the men to get in.

Abdul-Hakim said, "But this small craft is only meant for four people, and we have six."

"Then it will be a little crowded," responded Corey with a satisfied smile.

They settled in as best they could. Abdul-Hakim asked, "Where are my other two men? They were on watch somewhere on the boat."

Corey briefly looked off in the distance, pursed his lips, looked back at Abdul-Hakim, and said, "They have been taken care of. You won't have to worry about them. They would overload the boat, but are no longer aboard."

Abdul-Hakim, looking sad, and very serious, said, "I understand."

Corey simply nodded just once in a curt motion. Then he turned to Jackie and said, "Watch these folks while I lower their craft to the water." As he walked around the end of the boat to the davit controls, he said to Abdul-Hakim, "And you, Abdul-Hakim, will stay here in the runabout along with your men as we lower you down into the water. You have no weapons and we have the keys to the runabout. We are going to set you adrift and notify the patrol boat. I am assuming they will pick you up. If not, good luck on your journey in the ocean currents."

Abdul-Hakim, holding on to the gunnel, just nodded as they were lowered down into the ocean waters. Glaring back at Corey, he vowed in his mind to get back at these Americans. They would regret the day they did this to him and his crew. When they hit the water, Corey released the davit lines and set them adrift.

Ryan used the radio to call the patrol boat and directed them to drop the towline. He reminded them that he still had Abdul-Hakim and several of their men. The patrol boat backed up slightly and the line went slack. A crewman on the patrol boat released the line. The patrol boat slowly turned to face the yacht.

Corey retracted the davit lines as Jackie headed for the bridge. When she got to the bridge a few minutes later, the towline had just been released and the patrol boat was swinging around. She hastily ran to the bow of the yacht and threw off the towlines so the yacht was free to maneuver. Then she returned to the bridge. She gave Ryan status, and he told the patrol boat to be looking for the runabout that had their men in it. He could see some animated activity on the patrol boat's damaged bridge as the yacht backed up slightly and swung around so the runabout became visible. Someone fired a few shots at the yacht as the two vessels separated.

Ryan ignored it and called down to Dave, "Can we begin to head out now?"

Dave responded, "Sure. We are all set to go. Just tell me when. Then I'll set it on computer control and join you up there. I'd like to know what happened!"

Ryan looked around as Corey joined them on the bridge. Ryan entered a set of destination coordinates to the northeast into the navigation computer, and told Dave to come up to normal speed and join them when he was ready. A few moments later, the yacht turned slightly to come to the heading, and Dave slowly brought the turbines up to cruising speed. The yacht moved out and away from the patrol boat as it was trying to retrieve the men in the runabout.

Dave came up after a few minutes and said everything was running well. Ryan gave him a quick rundown of what had happened. Dave just shook his head and smiled. He was inwardly very pleased that things had worked out as they had and that he had been an absolute key player in their success.

They had succeeded in regaining the yacht and getting away from the patrol boat. They were roughly one hundred miles east of Socotra and on a course toward Diego Garcia. Now what?

Ryan said, "Given this experience"—he paused to look all around at the horizon—"I think we need to set up some form of watch. I'd hate to have them come at us again. I don't think they will try, given the damage to that patrol boat and the shortage of usable men, but I don't want to risk it, either."

They all nodded. Ryan continued, "Dave, can you show Corey how those engines work so you two can spell each other off? And I'll give Jackie a good rundown on how the bridge works so she can spell me. I think four-hour shifts would work well."

Dave responded, "Sounds good to me. As I said before, the engines are pretty well computer controlled and not hard to monitor."

Corey just nodded.

"Jackie, you've been down in the galley. I guess it's really a kitchen on this yacht. But, anyway, is there any food down there?"

Jackie nodded. "Yes. There is some food, but most of it has to be reconstituted. They obviously didn't stock it for us. And there appears to be plenty of fresh water in the tanks."

"Okay. Good. At least we won't starve on this trek across the Indian Ocean."

They had all gathered on the bridge of the yacht. The turbines were running on auto under computer control, and they were cruising at a comfortable sixteen knots to the northeast toward Diego Garcia. Coffee was on hand for all, and they were in a fairly relaxed mood. The patrol boat that had caused them so much trouble was rapidly being left behind, and was now not visible at all on the vast Indian Ocean.

Ryan was comfortable in the captain's chair, and the rest were sitting on makeshift cushions and chairs. There was a pleasant warm breeze coming across the bridge from the broken side windows. The repairs that had been made by Abdul-Hakim's men included window replacements on the front of the bridge, so the wind caused by the forward motion of the yacht was not bothersome.

They all were silent for the most part as they enjoyed the relative peace and quiet. They were in their own thoughts as they began the long journey to Diego. Ryan wondered if the president was going to do anything to help them, and, if so, what. They were really out there, and he didn't know if there were any U.S. ships in the area. Most of the shipping in the sea lanes would be foreign-registered vessels.

Dave was looking out the shattered remains of the port window frames. He coughed a little, and turned to them. "I've said it before and I'll probably go to my grave thinking this, but I find this whole process very preposterous."

Corey looked over after his thoughts had been disturbed, and asked, "What's that, Dave? What do you mean?"

Dave responded, "Well, if you think about it, this whole adventure, and the whole thing with the ayatollah, is really quite odd."

Corey held up his coffee in a motion for Dave to continue.

"By that I mean, we have all these alternate forms of energy production available to us, and we continue to depend on oil with all its environmental and political problems. There is plenty of energy for everyone if we just make use of it. But no, we have to take the hard path in life. It doesn't make sense to me. The oil pollutes our environment both in production and in use. We are the only species on earth that intentionally destroys its own living environment." He stopped and screwed up his face a bit, then continued, "And I have to ask why. The answer is simple. It's greed. Money and power. The same thing that has plagued mankind for millennia. And I don't think, given the driving forces for greed, that we will ever change. But it really makes absolutely no sense. And eventually we will be brought to our knees over this."

Corey said, "Yes, you make sense, but humankind has never been a truly good steward of the environment. Oh, there have been some individuals that have made attempts at it, but for the most part, we are very shortsighted and don't look at the total picture. And even those that do look at the total picture and see the potential disaster are ignored by day-to-day concerns of the populace. It won't be until some actual disaster occurs before action is taken ... and then that action will only be stopgap. Mankind just doesn't change easily. And usually only through force does that happen. In other words, only when there is no other choice."

Jackie, touching her rough bandage, said, "I think, and don't blame me for being too cynical about this, that we will probably never overcome what you are talking about. Mankind has been so self-absorbed when it comes to money and power over the ages. The current crop of mega-corporations is just a recent manifestation of that same process. The big oil companies, with all their influence and infrastructure, just aren't going to fall over and go away. I don't think, short of a major political upheaval, they will ever be really held in check. They are simply too powerful due to money and greed. There are too many politicians, and not just in the States but worldwide, that are in their pocket in one form or another."

Ryan looked at the three of them and said, "Well, it's a good thing we sound like we are all basically in agreement. I'd hate to have us in a fistfight over this subject." And he smiled at the thought.

Dave continued, "I think it will come eventually, that is, some common sense in using oil. But it may come too late to help old Mother Earth avoid some significant changes." He stopped for a moment then said, "And some of that is already well underway. And in the meantime, we"—he looked around at everybody—"go through these types of troubles and problems to catch people interfering with the status quo. Somehow it just doesn't seem right."

They nodded, drank their coffee, and fell into an agreeable silence as they watched the bow wave slipping past the sides of the yacht.

There was an odd trilling sound from the bridge console. Ryan looked up at it and answered the satellite phone.

"Hello?"

"Hello, Ryan!" came a booming voice over the handset.

Surprised, Ryan responded, "Hello, Mr. President." He glanced over and saw the total surprise on Corey's face.

"I'm certainly glad to hear you are okay. You sound okay, at least. Is everything all right now or are there still some problems?"

"No, sir. We just chased some bad guys off and are sitting here figuring out our next move." Then he proceeded to tell the president what had happened and where they were planning on going. The president agreed with the plan and thanked him for a job well done.

Ryan then said, "Sir. We have a message from the ayatollah for you. He sealed it in an envelope and told Jackie not to open it, but that it was for your eyes only. Do you want us to honor that or do you want us to open it and send it via secure link to you?"

"Ryan, my boy! If I can't trust you and your gang of thieves, who can I trust? Open it and send it to me. Whatever it says, I can be working on it while you folks are enjoying your tropical ocean cruise."

"Thank you, sir. We'll have it on the way as soon as we can."

"Thanks again, Ryan. And take care. We'll see you in a few days here in Washington." And he disconnected.

Corey said, with some degree of awe in his voice, "The president? And we're going to see him in a few days! We're in the middle of the Indian Ocean. What's he going to do?"

Ryan looked around and shook his head. He didn't know what the president might do. What a day it had been.

"Don't know."

They opened the ayatollah's message to the president and read it. It said,

Dear Mr. President,
I am sorely disappointed in your actions toward my movement. The bombing of my stronghold and now the appearance of your spies in my compound cannot be tolerated.

291

With this note I am informing you that, with the exception of Ms. Conover, who delivered this missive, all of your spies have been permanently eliminated by my command. Any further encroachment on my compound and its surrounds will result in similar actions.

I intend to pursue my goals until they are met and the formation of New Persia is complete. Your interference in my efforts will lead to a constant escalation of activities on both our parts. To avoid this escalation, I require that you comply with the demands I placed before the world forum of the United Nations last year. Compliance with those demands will cause a cessation of my activities toward you and your nation's assets. Non-compliance will only lead to more "activities."

I hope you take the right course.

Allah Be Praised.

And it was signed by the ayatollah in Arabic.

After reading it, they scanned it into the bridge computer and sent it on to the president.

After reading the message, Ryan, Corey, and Dave all realized that, if Jackie hadn't come back for them, they would all be dead now. Ryan went over to Jackie and held her close. Then she backed off, looked at all three of them, and said with a smile, "Never question my intuition. If you haven't noticed, I saved your asses, guys!" Then she turned to Ryan and said with a wink, "Wait'll the president hears about all this. He'll be ecstatic!"

Corey closed one eye and looked at her, saying, "Yeah, yeah, yeah!"

And they all laughed as the tension and actions of the past twenty-four hours released.

Chapter Fifty-One
Rescue

Friday—August 5
Western Indian Ocean

In the early morning, dawn a U.S. Navy Black Hawk helicopter began a search pattern over the coordinates provided by the Pentagon Situation Room. From the yacht, which had no running or navigation lights from the fighting, Ryan and Dave, sitting in the now-breezy, almost windowless bridge, could see the helicopter begin a search pattern several miles to the northeast. Keying in the guard channel on their radio, Dave called the helicopter. In just a few moments, the Black Hawk was hovering over the yacht. After making sure the yacht occupants were not in any immediate danger, the Black Hawk crew dropped some supplies of water and food. Word was passed on to Ryan from the helicopter that help was on the way.

Two hours later, a ship appeared on the horizon and made its way to the yacht. It was a U.S. Navy cruiser, and as it approached their position, it slowed down to an eventual halt a hundred yards away. They had also halted the yacht and were sitting stationary in the water. A small lighter was dispatched to them.

After exchanging greetings and congratulations from the lighter crew, and welcoming a small Navy crew of specialists sent to assist in running and repairing the yacht, they cautiously moved the yacht over to the cruiser.

They finished watching the securing of the yacht, and Ryan, Jackie, Dave, and Corey were all escorted up to the ships captain's quarters.

Jackie was taken down to sickbay, where her gunshot wound was properly cleaned, two stitches put in, and bandaged. She was given antibiotics and cautioned, by the medic, to take it easy. She then returned to the captain's quarters and joined the others.

Commander Jack Anderson greeted them and asked them to have a seat while he had some food and refreshments brought up. He said, "Well, I don't know what this is all about, but you obviously had a problem out here and the folks in the Pentagon were quite worried about you. That yacht certainly looks impressive, and is, from first glance, worldwide capable. We received direction to drop our current patrolling activities and find you ASAP. The Pentagon was only able to give us some rough coordinates to search. While we're waiting for some food, can you tell me what this is all about? And perhaps begin with 'Who are you?'"

Ryan responded, "Sure. But where did you come from? This isn't a normal area, at least I don't think it is, for the U.S. Navy to patrol."

The commander chuckled a little and said, "Actually, it is an area we patrol. We are part of what is called Combined Task Force 150, and are charged with anti-piracy actions along this coastal area. A few years ago it was pretty busy, but it's fairly quiet now, but we are still out here." He hesitated and then smiled and said, "Okay. I've shown you mine, now show me yours."

Ryan told the commander that they were on a special assignment from the White House, working directly with the president. He then recounted some of the past events of New Persia and the recent actions of the past twenty-four hours, including their tasking to check out Socotra and their escape from the island. He added in the call from the president after they escaped in the yacht and the obvious reaction in the Navy to their situation.

Commander Anderson nodded and said, "Tasking from the White House! Well, that explains how we got tasked and why the urgency. So this has to do with the B-52 strike in Iran that I read about some time back on the internet."

Ryan said, "Yes. It turns out that the ayatollah, the primary target of that strike, escaped and has set up another headquarters in Socotra. It was our tasking to verify his location and current actions."

As they discussed the situation, sandwiches were delivered and they all helped themselves without any hesitation.

Jackie then said, "Commander, would it be possible to use your communications to call the White House? I think I need to relieve some people's minds there."

The commander said, "Certainly." He finished his mouthful of food, used his napkin, and called in a seaman. He gave the seaman directions to escort Jackie to the communications center. He then called the comm room and told them to make a direct call to the White House operator and follow Jackie's directions from there. Jackie left the others and followed the seaman to the comm center.

After Jackie had departed, Ryan turned back to the commander and said, "What's next? We need to get back to Washington and see what our next move may be. We also have to explain the various things we saw on that island. We going to Diego?"

The commander responded, "No. Not Diego, that's too far from here, at least on the surface. We are going to head north and join up with the aircraft carrier, the CVN *Lincoln,* that's on station just off the coast of Oman. From there you'll be flown back to Diego and then on back to the States. It'll be a long flight, but it is the fastest way to get there. And I wish you well on your mission. The yacht will be taken to Diego by the small crew we put on board today. I'm not sure what will happen to it next." He looked at the three men and continued, "From what I can remember, that ayatollah character is really something."

They all nodded in agreement.

The commander then introduced Lieutenant Knight, the weapons control officer. Lieutenant Knight would escort them to their rather Spartan quarters for the short period they would be aboard. Commander Anderson then excused himself. A few minutes later, they felt the cruiser change to a more northerly course and pick up speed. Jackie had returned from her visit to the comm center, and reported that the Oval Office was very relieved to hear of their status.

They were escorted to their quarters, where a change of clothing was provided. Since there were a few women in the crew, Jackie was accommodated with some new clothes also. They all took showers and freshened up. It had been a long and tension-filled day.

They gathered in the crew's mess, where there was coffee and soft drinks. Ryan wanted to discuss what they had seen and make sure they recalled, as much as possible, the details of the center and its capabilities. They sat at one of the tables and, using a borrowed tablet, listed what they had seen and what capabilities they thought the center had. The focus was on the capabilities and what a strike force would need to know. After an hour they decided it was enough, and they broke up to go back to their quarters.

Ryan took the borrowed laptop computer and reviewed several capabilities they had seen while on the island. The list was:

1. *Armed guards patrol the compound 24/7. Guard training is minimal.*
2. *Two of the ships in the harbor were ocean capable and worldwide capable. The yacht and the trimaran. There were three local patrol boats.*
3. *A satellite terminal was obviously there. The two thirty-meter antennas were installed on their pedestals but the operational status was unknown.*
4. *There were additional personnel as a response force positioned in the center for self-defense deployment anywhere in the compound.*
5. *Surveillance cameras were being installed but were not operational as of yet.*
6. *A warehouse in the harbor was full of offensive weapons ... RPGs, ARPMs, and small weapons.*
7. *Local populace, while appreciative of the compound, was in fear of some of the members and did not know what the compound was for.*
8. *The harbor entrance was open to the ocean waters.*
9. *No gun emplacements were observed.*
10. *The commercial airport was several miles away to the northeast. Capable of jet traffic up to at least 737 jets.*

Ryan then added a hand-drawn map of the compound showing the harbor, roads, gatehouse shack, operations center, warehouses, and the personnel housing complex.

He then took the information, loaded it to a borrowed flash drive, and gave it to the comm technician with instructions to send it to Admiral Watkins. The tech was a little overwhelmed at the level of the request, but did as asked.

Chapter Fifty-Two
New Persia Relocation Planning

Friday—August 5
Western Indian Ocean

Abdul-Hakim had succeeded in getting underway in the patrol boat, although it had taken until midmorning to accomplish the needed repairs, and was slowly making his way back to Socotra. They were taking on some water, but the pumps were just barely handling it. He was worried. It was very obvious that their location had been compromised, and they could well expect visitors soon. The U.S. government had already proven that they would stop at nothing to get New Persia and halt its activities. As the New Persia defense minister, he needed to plan how they were going to counter this threat to their Allah-given mission. The ayatollah had already made it very plain he would expect nothing less.

It had been a mistake to let the woman go; that much was now very obvious. The only way the men could have escaped was through her help. The guards at the gate and on the door had told them of her approach as they were guarding the compound entrance and conference room door. Abdul-Hakim needed to make sure the people he had, that were assigned to guard duty, regardless of location, had more training. In his mind, this was war, and they needed to treat it as such.

A woman had basically overpowered them, and New Persia was going to pay for it. If he ever got the chance to meet her again, she would not survive the encounter. His eyes narrowed at the thought. He looked out at the seemingly endless ocean, then at the deck, and shook his head at the shame of it.

He decided that they would have to make sure they had another emergency evacuation plan available so they could survive another attack. But where could they go and how would they get there? There would be another attack; of that he was sure. The Americans would suspect some form of escape, since New Persia leadership had succeeded in their escape the last time. It would be much more difficult to fool them again. He

297

would have to sit down with his advisors and figure this one
out. And he would have to listen to his inner thoughts this time.
He just knew the American task force moving into the gulf the
last time was "it," and he didn't act accordingly. It wouldn't be
the same the next time. He would be ready.

After several hours, it was past noon, the main island
of Socotra came in to view, and they moved around to the
southern approach to the center harbor. Slowing as they
approached the actual harbor entrance, passing between the
two breakwater prominences, they pulled into the pier and tied
up. Several maintenance personnel were waiting, and gawked
at the damage to the bridge and hull on the patrol boat. It
would take several weeks of repairs to get the bridge and hull
functional again, and many of the parts would have to be
ordered from overseas or manufactured on site. It would be a
major workload. Some of the men were from the island, and
they looked on the repairs as a godsend. It would provide them
with work for some time. Praise Allah! But their outward
appearance was stoic. They didn't want to appear happy over
their employer's misfortune.

Abdul-Hakim got off the damaged patrol boat as soon
as it had tied up to the pier. He headed immediately for his
quarters. Once there, he called Khatib to join him. After getting
some food, he sat down with Khatib, gave him a quick review
of what had happened at sea, and began discussions.

"Khatib. Obviously we have failed to keep our location
a secret. We need to plan on the possibility that the Americans
will strike again."

"I agree with you, Abdul-Hakim. What do you have in
mind? We cannot stay here for long. The Americans will
certainly try again." He paused and then said thoughtfully,
"Their pride will require it."

"Yes. But it will take them a little time. I think we need
to come up with another location, and this time I think we need
to keep it truly secret. I think the Americans found us because
of the communications links, and we need to figure a way
around that."

Khatib raised his eyebrows, thought for a few moments,
then said, "Of course. That certainly makes sense, and we were
very foolish to not realize it earlier."

Abdul-Hakim nodded. It had taken him a little bit of
time after the Americans showed up on the island, but he had

finally concluded that their communications links had been the problem.

Khatib then continued, "But where can we go? We have no place prepared, and we have very little time."

"Yes. You're quite correct. We need to find a place that can work temporarily until we can set up another center ... one without the communications difficulties."

Abdul-Hakim said, "Let us think about it for a few hours. Can you get with the ayatollah and see if he has any preferences? I don't want to begin selecting some possibilities if he has some biases we need to consider."

"Of course. I will tend to it immediately. When do you want to meet again?"

"Let's get together again in the morning and see what we can plan. I need some rest, but we both need to get our thoughts together, and perhaps we can come up with a viable action plan."

Khatib nodded, stood, slightly bowed, and left the office. Abdul-Hakim began thinking and pacing. There had to be a good answer, and he needed to be ready ... but how? These Americans were very persistent, and would take some form of action against New Persia.

As he was pondering the problem, he realized that they needed to get some form of warning if the Americans began moving toward them. The more time they had to react, the better, and an early warning or advisory would be of great help. But how? He puzzled over that question for several minutes, and even stepped outside to get some much-needed air. There had to be a way. Then it dawned on him. They had very capable support out there if they could just use it. New Persia did not have any capability for watching the Americans, but their Chinese supporters certainly did.

He hurriedly called Zhang Qiang and asked, "Have you got a few minutes? I have a request for you, and it is quite critical."

Zhang, taken aback by the obvious anxiety in Abdul-Hakim's voice, said, "Yes. Certainly. What is it?"

"Let me come over there and talk with you personally."

"Certainly. I'll be expecting you."

Abdul-Hakim hurried out of his office and down the hall to Zhang's office. He knocked lightly on the door and Zhang bid him enter.

Zhang said, "Okay. What have you got for me? You said some form of request. I assume you need our services, and quickly, from the sound of your voice."

"Yes. As you are aware, we have been compromised in this location. The Americans know where we are."

Zhang nodded in agreement. "And how does that involve us?"

"I, that is we, need to know as soon as possible if the Americans are coming this way. We have no capability for seeing their activities and whatever preparations they may be making to attack us."

Zhang's eyebrows went up slightly and he pursed his lips. "Ahh. But we do. And you want us to give you warning if they look like they are headed this way."

Abdul-Hakim, leaning forward, looked at the floor for just a moment and then back at Zhang. "Yes. That's exactly what I have in mind. I know you monitor their activities at various locations, especially in the Pacific and Indian Oceans. You may be able to see if they are forming some type of attack on us and give us warning."

Zhang responded, "I will look into it with my superiors. I take it you want the capability established immediately, or sooner, if possible?"

"The faster the better. And ... thank you."

Zhang looked back at him with narrowed eyes and said, "Don't thank me yet. It hasn't been done yet. I will let you know."

Abdul-Hakim then got up, bowed slightly, and left the office. He returned to his own office and took a deep breath. Hopefully, he thought, it would work and they would get adequate warning. If the Americans planned to attack ... And his thoughts drifted to areas he really didn't want to consider.

The following morning, Khatib and Abdul-Hakim met again, along with several other members of the support staff. They did not have much time, or at least that was what they thought. The Americans could show up at any time and they needed to get moving. It was a real case of constantly looking over the shoulder, and none of them liked it.

Abdul-Hakim briefed the request he had made to Zhang the previous night. They all agreed it would be a good. Khatib nodded and said, "That was a good idea. Regardless of what

300

happens, the more notice we get, the better, and the Chinese have a lot of capability in that area."

Khatib said, "I've given this a great deal of thought, and, while it may surprise you, think we should go back to the stronghold." Several in the room gave a start at that suggestion. He held up his hand and they silenced. He continued, "There are a couple of reasons for this suggestion. One, the infidels will never think that we would go back. Two, our training facilities are there and we can make better use of them. Three, we can set up couriers to run information to a communication center in Birjann or Zahedan and not give away our location. Four, it is still a good and defendable location. Five, our friends in Iran are not against our actions and goals. And six, our Iranian friends have begun to increase their military capabilities in that area. It is very difficult to attack that remote area, and the Americans know it." He stopped for a moment, then: "I think we should at least consider it."

Abdul-Hakim nodded. He hadn't thought of it and hadn't come up with anything better. He said, "A truly unique idea. I think it has possibilities, and you make a good case for it. Has anyone had any other thoughts or ideas?"

The director of operations, Ghanim, added, "Yes. I think we should consider moving to a larger city and getting ourselves buried in the middle of the hustle. It isn't hard to get lost in today's large cities, and, mixed in with other movements, it would confuse and make pursuit much more difficult. A large city in a Muslim country would be, in my mind, almost ideal. And the communications problem would go away, since we couldn't be traced, I believe, in all that comm traffic."

Abdul-Hakim nodded again in agreement. It had merit. And it would solve several logistics support problems. They could hide in the masses. He looked around. No one else spoke up. He asked again for input, and no one had other ideas. He looked at Khatib and asked, "What did the ayatollah have to say? Are there any restrictions in his mind?"

Khatib looked around the room. Then he focused back at Abdul-Hakim and said, "He doesn't want the influence of a large city on the movement. There are too many temptations and too great a risk of being infiltrated. I think that idea is out. However, he was not against going back to the stronghold, or to some other area that is remote and difficult to reach. Areas of Yemen and Oman could be considered, since they are also sympathetic to our cause."

Abdul-Hakim looked at Khatib and wondered if his influence on the ayatollah was part of this decision process. Khatib seemed to be very self-assured and confident. He wondered. Then his mind went back to the immediate problem. The meeting broke up and Khatib left Abdul-Hakim to his tasking.

Abdul-Hakim took the information Khatib had provided and, using some information gleaned off the internet, and some from his own personal knowledge of the Middle East, put together several options for the ayatollah to consider. There was always the possibility of returning to the stronghold, and that became option one. There were certainly drawbacks to that option, but Abdul-Hakim, since it had been mentioned earlier in their discussions, felt it might be a favorite. Option two would have them going to interior mountains in Yemen. This was an area of the world that was Muslim, had adversarial feelings toward the west, and would probably welcome them and the economic clout they had. Option three was similar, but located in Oman. While the government was not as anti-western, it was still Muslim, and the areas inland were very remote. He looked at potential city sites and discounted them. Ghanim had a point about communications and disappearing into the city, but the ayatollah had eliminated that from consideration.

He looked over the three basic options, fleshed out some advantages and disadvantages of each, and finished his presentation. Looking at the information he had gathered, he finally decided to recommend the Yemen option. The stronghold had been hit and was completely known. Oman was viable but not as friendly to their cause. He was quite comfortable recommending Yemen.

The decision was a tough one. And it would be difficult to implement on such short notice.

Chapter Fifty-Three
En Route Home

Saturday—August 6
En Route Home

The next morning, after a good breakfast in the chow line and conversation with several of the Navy people, Ryan, Jackie, Corey, and Dave were invited by Commander Anderson up onto the bridge. Once there, he said, "In a couple of hours we will meet up with the *Lincoln*. They are sending a helicopter over for you. The yacht and mini-sub stays with us and we will escort them to Diego Garcia. Our direction is to make sure no one tries to recapture them while going to Diego."

Ryan nodded.

Dave asked, "Where will they be ultimately taken?"

Commander Anderson said, "I'm not positive, but probably to Norfolk, where they can be studied and reverse-engineered. Both the yacht and the sub have some capabilities, my guys tell me, that we would be very interested in. The other possibility is that a team of engineers would come to Diego to study them. I just don't know yet."

Dave pursed his lips and said, "It will be interesting to see if these, and the ones we captured in the Gulf of Mexico last year, are the same. I think they are, but there may be some differences."

Ryan handed the commander his tablet and said, "Thanks for letting me borrow your tablet. I sent a preliminary report to the White House earlier. I've stored the information we need on a flash drive and will take it back with us. We really appreciate the hospitality. It's been great meeting you and some of your folks."

The commander nodded and smiled. "Well, it isn't every day that a ship gets to rescue people with the level of interest you have. And that yacht and mini-sub ... well, they're quite remarkable. Likewise, it's been a pleasure having you on board. I hope everything works out for you and the trip back home."

They then turned their attention to preparing to be airlifted to the carrier. Going back to their quarters, they gathered up their clothes and what few other items they had.

303

As they finished with that chore, they could hear the characteristic sound of helicopter rotors approaching. They were escorted by Lieutenant Knight down to the helicopter landing area on the aft end of the ship. Commander Anderson was waiting, and bade them goodbye as they walked out to the awaiting helicopter. Ryan turned around and saluted the flag before they were strapped in, and enjoyed a thirty-minute ride to the carrier.

After being welcomed aboard the carrier, they were escorted to "admiral's territory," where they were cordially greeted by the task force commander, Rear Admiral Jason Walsh, and then on to their temporary assigned quarters. They were informed that they would be flown out the next day on a carrier on-board delivery, or COD, aircraft for Mumbai, India, where they would fly commercial back to the U.S. A slight change in plans, but agreeable to them.

Sunday—August 7
Indian Ocean—*USS Lincoln*

The next day, after a good breakfast with Admiral Walsh, they were escorted to the flight deck, where a C-2AR Greyhound COD aircraft waited. Once seated in the rear-facing seats and belted in, they were "treated" to a catapult launch and on their way home. Several hours later they were in Mumbai and greeted by consulate personnel, escorted to the JW Marriott for the night, and provided with business-class tickets for a flight out the following day.

That evening they all met for drinks and light hors d'oeuvres, and Ryan asked each of them to meet in his room. He had made arrangements to have a speakerphone placed in his room, and wanted to call back to Washington to discuss future plans. They finished their drinks and went up to Ryan's room. Due to the time difference, it was late morning in Washington, D.C. They placed a call to the White House operator and were put through to Maria.

"Ryan. It's so good to hear from you. How are you and where are you?"

Ryan responded, "We're all in Mumbai and will be catching a plane in a few hours. Everything, for now, is fine, but we need to get back and talk with the boss. Is he available?"

"Mumbai? The old Bombay?"

"Yes. That's the old name for this city. Quite a place."

"Good to hear that everything is okay with you. Jackie too?"

"Yes, she's fine. She's still got a sore head from that near miss, but she's right here listening. Just as obstinate as ever, but she sure saved our butts. I'll fill you in when we get there."

"Just a second. I'll put you through to the president."

There was a slight pause and then: "Ryan! Man, you had us worried there for a while. I understand you are on your way back. What's your schedule?"

"Well, sir. We need to get back, and that will take a while but we leave Mumbai in a couple of hours. I'd like to meet with you day after tomorrow and discuss what we found out and see what you might want to do next. We can't talk about it over this line, but I think you get my drift."

"Sure thing. Jackie! Can we make that change in my schedule to allow Ryan and the rest of you to meet with me? After all, you do take care of my schedule, don't you?"

Jackie, somewhat taken aback until she realized he was joking, said, "Well, if you'd quit sending me out on these wild goose chases, it would sure help. I think we can probably arrange something. I'll have to check with Maria and see how badly you've managed to screw up your schedule. But we'll work something out."

Corey was looking on with amazement at this exchange. He didn't know the president, and the banter took him by surprise. Then, understanding the situation, he began to grin and gave Jackie a big thumbs-up.

Dave spoke up: "Mr. President, Dave Carlson here. We managed to get another yacht and its sub. Can't talk any more about it, but thought you might like to know that we are whittling away at them."

"Super news, Dave. No, I wasn't aware of that. I appreciate all you folks have done. I was briefed this morning on what was going on and am very pleased. You all sure showed your mettle. Admiral Watkins was impressed with your list, and especially the sketch of the compound area. Lots of good info there. Ryan, I'd like all of you to plan on dinner here after we have a discussion. And Corey, we'll need to talk about your next assignment. I don't think you can go back to Yemen. Be thinking about where you might like to go and in what capacity. Okay?"

Corey looked a bit stunned, but was able to utter, "Yes, sir. I sure will. And thank you."

"*De nada!*" the president exclaimed in Spanish. "Ryan, we'll see you and your gang of cohorts here in a couple of days. Have a good flight."

"Yes, sir. And thanks for all the help. That cruiser was a real life saver."

"Again. *De nada.*"

With that, they hung up.

Jackie and Dave were smiling at Corey. He was having a tough time adjusting to what he had just heard. He had gotten up from his chair and moved to the window. He had been recognized by the president of the United States; his boss's boss. And he had been invited to attend a discussion at the White House and have dinner there. His mind was just reeling. He turned around and smiled at his small audience.

Corey said, "You know. When they assigned me to help you folks out, I thought it was just going to be one of these routine touristy things, with a little back-country exploration thrown in for good measure. Maybe look around a little at the ayatollah's center. But man, was I wrong. This"—he waved his hand around the room—"is just something else. We get captured, escape, steal a yacht, escape on a submarine, get the yacht back and are picked up by the Navy, and now have this conversation with the top dog. You guys sure are something."

Ryan walked over to Corey, put his arm around his shoulder and said, "Yup! We're something, all right, and you helped save our bacon a couple of times now. Thanks for the help, and I think you'll enjoy the White House." He grinned, and Corey just grinned back. Jackie and Dave did the same.

As they tipped their drinks, Ryan looked over at Corey, who had sat down on one of the couches, and said, "Well, it sounds like the president is willing to step in and help you with your future career. While I know he just said it, do you have any ideas on what you might ask for?"

Jackie and Dave turned to see what the reaction might be.

Corey said, "I'm still a bit overwhelmed by all this. I'm going to have to think about it a bit. But I do have one thought that I'd rather keep to myself for now. I'm still thinking."

They all nodded in understanding. Ryan said, "I understand, and given the short notice and impact it could have, I'm sure it will take some time and thought. You have skills that most State Department people don't have, and those skills need to be considered in your decision. The other embassies in the Middle East, other than Yemen, can certainly use your language and physical skills. I'm sure whatever decision you make will be welcome. Good luck." And he held his drink up, saying, "Cheers."

They all clinked glasses and fell into more casual conversation. Then they all went down to dinner in a relaxed and pleasant mood.

Ryan and Jackie spent a quiet evening together with these friends. They were finally able to relax a bit and looked forward to getting home. It was a long flight, halfway around the world, but would be worth it to get home and back to some degree of normality.

Chapter Fifty-Four
Ayatollah's Decision

Sunday—August 7
Socotra Island Operations Center

Abdul-Hakim and Khatib sat down to discuss what they should do. Abdul-Hakim felt they needed to get off the island as soon as possible and establish themselves elsewhere. Khatib wasn't so sure. It had been a couple of days since the Americans had escaped, and nothing had happened. His contacts in Washington said everything was quiet, with just the normal Pentagon activity. Nothing big appeared to be planned, and midnight oil was not being burned. It was quiet.

Abdul-Hakim said, "Just because your contacts in Washington say everything is quiet doesn't mean we don't have something coming our way. They could very well be planning a strike and keeping it a very low profile. Just a few people in on it. That prevents leaks and could get the job done."

Khatib replied, "You're quite right. In fact, I'd be very surprised if they aren't planning something. But I don't think it will be real overt, like an invasion force, or even an air strike. They tried the air strike before and got mud on their faces. Yes, they took out the stronghold, but we survived. If they do anything, and they might not, it will be quiet and sneaky. I say they might not, because the western mind may tell them that we aren't worth the effort and that they have destroyed our movement. They don't recognize the patience that we have. And, of course, there is their national pride to consider. It's confusing, and we just don't know what they might do."

"Just the same, I'd like to see what the ayatollah would like to do. I can give him a couple of options and he can decide from there."

"Very well. I'll talk with him and set up a discussion for later today. Like you, I don't want to delay on this. If we have to move, we need to get on with it. If we don't move, we need to put together some contingency plans should the infidels show up."

Abdul-Hakim nodded in agreement and said as he stood up, "Fine. Let me know when we are meeting and I'll be prepared."

Later that day, Khatib came into Abdul-Hakim's office and said, "We have a discussion set up for 3:00 p.m. today. And he asked that I invite Salah, our technical lead, to be present also."

Abdul-Hakim nodded and said, "I'll be there."

They met in a small conference room just next to the ayatollah's office. Abdul-Hakim, as promised, was ready for several different scenarios and locations for presentation to the ayatollah. He presented them and then stopped. He said, "These are the options we have developed for you and your immediate staff to locate elsewhere. As you can see, none are near any large population centers. What would you like to do?"

The ayatollah looked back at Abdul-Hakim, then at Salah, and finally over to Khatib. He said, "For the moment, nothing. What I do want to do is eliminate, or nearly eliminate, all communications leaving this complex over our existing satellite connections. That's why I wanted Salah present for this discussion."

Salah looked startled, and got a quizzical look on his face.

Khatib looked puzzled.

Abdul-Hakim looked at him and said, "I don't understand."

The ayatollah continued, "The Americans are monitoring the message and communications traffic from here. If it suddenly ceases, or drops to a very low level, they may think that we have left. If we also send our trimaran elsewhere, they may see it as additional proof of our leaving. At a minimum it will confuse them, or put a question in their minds on what we are doing and, specifically, where I may be. It should cause them to hesitate until they can figure it out.

"We won't be quiet anymore, and we are still a force to be reckoned with. We haven't done anything of consequence since our work at Alaska and Heathrow. They may think we are getting complacent. So we will begin planning for another strike. This time in the Gulf of Mexico. But our communications need to drop off drastically."

Abdul-Hakim and Khatib both nodded.

The ayatollah turned to Salah and said, "How can we still communicate with our dispersed personnel without using the satellite dish at Salalah? Can we use some form of landline or other system ... even if it's slower?"

Salah, caught unawares, said, "Give me a couple of hours and let me look into it. There are no international landlines here in Socotra, or they're very minimal. But there may be another option I just thought of. I'll have to get back to you later today."

The ayatollah nodded in acknowledgment, stood, and said, "Until later, then."

Then he looked over at Abdul-Hakim and Khatib. He said, with a very cool tone to his voice, "Let me know the results of your planning." And he left the conference room.

Abdul-Hakim sat there in amazement, almost stunned. They weren't moving! He looked over at Khatib. Khatib was smiling knowingly. He nodded. As he nodded, he said, "I thought so. Rather than continuing to run like rabbits being chased by the wolves, we are going to go into the wolves' den and destroy part of it."

Two hours later, Salah came into the office where Khatib was working and asked to see the ayatollah. Khatib looked in on the ayatollah and told him Salah was outside. The ayatollah nodded and waved for him to come in to the office. He then asked, "I take it you have some good news for me?"

Salah said, "Yes, sir. At least I think so. We can't send a microwave signal to a landline location off the island because of the distances and no relay points. However, we can change satellites and not use the commercial ones monitored by the Americans."

"Whose would we use?"

"Well, if we can negotiate with them, we could use Chinese military communications satellites instead of the commercial satellites we have been using. They have several up there. The transmitter and receiving equipment for our thirty-meter antennas are now being installed and tested. With channel assignments and an adjustment to our antenna alignment and some of our software, a couple of their satellites can be in direct view. Changing the encryption of the data over those satellites will also make it much more difficult to intercept."

The ayatollah asked, "How long would it take to finish the installation and realign the antennas?"

"We have to run some test data back and forth, and that takes a little time. To finish the installation on the first antenna will take three more days. However, once we have the antenna frequencies and channel assignments, the actual antenna alignment with their satellites will only take a few hours, maybe less. A day at most. A total of four to five days."

The ayatollah's eyes gleamed. He would still be a force to be seriously considered by the western powers. He was sure his friends in the Chinese government could help with this simple request. He called Marid, his logistics manager, and explained what he wanted, and Marid hurried off. He didn't think it would be a big deal with his Chinese contacts.

Marid took off with his task in mind and headed straight for his office. When he arrived, he called Zhang Qiang's quarters in the western part of the center administration complex and made an appointment to see the Chinese representative early that evening. Then he called Salah and asked to meet him in fifteen minutes to discuss the details of what the ayatollah would require from the Chinese.

Salah joined Marid in his office.

Marid started the conversation: "Thank you for coming up with this possible solution to our problem, Salah."

Salah smiled and said, "No problem. We all benefit from working together. Now, what specifically do you need from me?"

They then spent two hours going over the details of frequency needs and potential frequency-hopping technologies, bandwidth requirements, transmission speeds, access requirements and capabilities, and specific satellite coordinates to accomplish their communications needs. Salah, using his tablet, was able to provide Marid with all the information he would need to discuss the request with the Chinese. At the end of the discussion, Salah added, "If you need my assistance, just give me a call. I know the ayatollah gave you this tasking, and you need to carry through with it, but if there are questions you cannot handle, I am available."

Marid said, "Thank you, Salah. We are all part of this team, and need to work together to see this New Persia vision come to pass, and even if we don't see it come to pass, our children will."

With those final comments, they parted, and Marid felt much better about his tasking. He was now prepared to meet with the Chinese representative and make his, and New Persia's, request.

That afternoon he met with Zhang Qiang and discussed the request for space and frequency assignments on the Chinese communications network. After some discussion, Zhang really understood what was behind the request, and thought about it a bit. They were already supporting this outlying organization with the ships and necessary logistics support, and now this additional need had arisen. And earlier, Abdul-Hakim had requested a spying mission on the Americans so he could be warned of a possible attack. How far would Beijing be willing to go? And this small, relatively speaking, movement needed the changeover for communications to happen within a week or so! Very difficult. But he would look into it and let Marid know.

Marid walked away from the meeting feeling far from satisfied. He didn't think the Chinese representative really understood their need, but he had no alternative but to wait for a result.

It would be a hard few days until the request was processed and either accepted or denied.

Chapter Fifty-Five
Presidential Briefing

Monday—August 8
Washington, D.C.

A day later they arrived at Washington Dulles. Jackie was driven home by the Secret Service, and Ryan, Dave, and Corey were taken to the Ritz for the night. All were quite tired from the long flight home, and needed the rest. They would have a meeting with the president the following day at 3:00 p.m., and agreed to meet with Jackie at the White House around 2:00 p.m. Corey would have to go through the security clearance process to get Yankee clearance for working with the president. It wasn't a problem, since he already had a State Department clearance, but it would take some time.

Tuesday—August 9
Washington, D.C.

The following morning at breakfast in the hotel, Ryan, Dave, and Corey reviewed the materials they had developed while still on the Navy cruiser. They made some minor corrections/changes to the materials as they sat having coffee, formatted the materials into a report form, and saved them on the flash drive. As they finished up, Jasper came in, grabbed a cup of coffee off the buffet, and joined them at the table.

He looked at the three of them, reached over the table, and said to Corey, "Hi. I'm Jasper. Understand you helped save these characters from a lovely forced vacation on that tropical isle of Socotra."

Corey, recognizing Jasper's name from earlier conversations, shook hands and said, "Well. We did have some anxious moments. I must say, it's been a while since I've seen the kind of action you folks seem to attract."

Jasper nodded and looked over at Ryan and Dave's shocked expressions. "Maria gave me a call yesterday and asked me to come up and attend the meeting you have set up for later today. You know," he said with a great big smile, "the next time you go gallivanting around the world and getting into

313

all these problems, I need to go along to help keep you straight. I'm really interested in what happened and what you found out. Next time this happens, I'll make sure I can go along. It seems, from what little we have been able to piece together, you sure had some fun."

Ryan started to laugh and then caught himself. "Yeah. Right. We really had a ball floating around the Indian Ocean in a little sub with no water and no food. You would have loved it!"

Jasper nodded, then got serious. "So what happened?" He carefully sipped his hot coffee and they gave him a quick rundown of the past several days' activities.

Jasper said, "So, in a nutshell, the ayatollah is on this island in an above-ground center. They have worldwide communications capabilities through an unregistered undersea cable system, a reasonable-sized harbor with some form of large catamaran, and some patrol boats. They have a state-of-art security system partially installed and a pretty capable defense head."

Ryan said, "Yes. And it appears that they have the run of the island, since they were able to get into our hotel rooms at will. I would suppose that, due to their economic impact, they can do pretty much what they want."

Jasper, Dave, and Corey all nodded to that comment. Jasper then said, "Well, given what you have said, and this defense minister's apparent skill, they know that we know where they are. If I were him, and given the strike on the stronghold, I'd be making plans to move again. Soon. If we want to get them, we'll have to move pretty quickly ... like yesterday."

Corey said, "I'd have to agree with that. What we saw on that island could be moved, but not without a great deal of trouble. I mean, all that comm gear with all the antennas and the security systems can't be moved in a day. Not to mention the weapons stores. It will take them a while to go somewhere. But it wouldn't take much too just move the ayatollah and a few of his henchmen. A couple of airplane tickets to somewhere is all it would take. I wouldn't be too surprised to see him in Tehran or some other major Muslim city as a temporary refuge until they can figure out something better."

"I think that will be a focus of the discussion later today," said Ryan, refilling his coffee from the table carafe.

At 2:00 p.m. a black Suburban picked them all up at the Ritz and drove them to the White House. Ryan, Dave, and

Jasper were admitted and went into the small security conference room while Corey was processed for his clearance. After a half-hour, they all walked to the Oval Office outer office, escorted by one of the uniformed White House police.

They came down the hall and into the outer office, where Maria greeted them warmly.

As she walked back to her desk, she looked at all of them and said, "Welcome back." Then, with a shimmer in her eyes, she said, "You know, when you guys are around here, we sure don't lack for action or interesting things to do. It gets pretty lively."

Ryan smiled back and said, "Yeah. I know. It's about time to calm things down a bit." Then he turned to Corey and said to Maria, "Maria, this is Corey Gaskins. He is with State, and really helped us out a lot. Corey, this is Maria Aragon, the president's secretary."

Maria came around her desk and shook hands with Corey with an appreciative and appraising look in her eye. She liked what she saw. She smiled, looked up at him square in the eyes, and said, "Welcome, and glad to meet you."

Corey looked at her, smiled, and said, "It's certainly my pleasure."

Jackie came walking in dressed very nicely in a light blue business suit with short heels. She walked up to Ryan and kissed him on the cheek, much to his surprise.

She said with a smile, "Well, we might as well make it public. Everybody here already is talking about us."

Ryan, caught by surprise, nodded and got slightly embarrassed. He laughed and said, "God. You're something. But I love you for it." She still had the patch bandage on her head.

Maria, surprised also, just grinned and said with an artificial huff, "Well! It's about time, you two!"

Another half-hour of small talk went by and finally Maria called them all into the Oval Office. The president was waiting at the small grouping of chairs and a couch. Ryan walked up to the president, shook hands, and introduced Corey. The president shook his hand and said, "Hey, Corey! Welcome to this little group of renegades." He smiled broadly then looked at the group and said, "Where's Jackie?"

Maria said, "She's gone back to her office to try and straighten out your schedule."

The president looked a bit dismayed, and said, "Go get her in here. She was part of all the action and I want her opinion as part of this group."

Maria smiled and left the office. A few minutes later Jackie came running into the Oval Office looking a bit unnerved. She looked around and took one of the chairs next to Ryan. The president looked at her and simply said, "Good." He obviously noticed the bandage, and made a show of shaking his head and frowning slightly.

The president looked at each of them quickly then turned to Ryan and said, "Okay. What have you got for me? Now that you had half of the U.S. Navy searching for you, and transporting you halfway around the world, there ought to be something to report." He smiled broadly.

Ryan then gave him a full rundown of the trip: what they had found, how they had been captured, and their escape with Jackie's critical assistance and wounding. Then he covered the yacht chase, the mini-submarine run, the recapture of the yacht, and elaborated on the support from the Navy.

After Ryan was finished, the president turned to Jackie and said, "Well, you did it again, didn't you? Saved his bacon." Then he continued with a gleam, "I'm sure glad you're on our side."

She blushed a little and said, "Well. He keeps getting into these little scrapes and somebody has to watch out for him. I guess I'm elected." And she smiled at Ryan.

The president looked very pleased. Then he got serious and said, "Okay. We have a situation. He continues with his ridiculous demands and threatens more actions. What do we do about it? Any suggestions from you experts?"

Jasper spoke up: "I mentioned to Ryan and company earlier today that we need to move on this information. If I was that defense guy, I'd be getting out of Dodge."

The president said, "I think you're right. It may be too late already. And he could have gone anywhere. We're back where we started several weeks ago. At this point we don't really know where he might be."

He turned to Corey and said, "Changing the subject for a few minutes, you really helped out on this adventure. I appreciate all the things you did. It's a good thing you had some knowledge of RPGs or this might have turned out quite differently. On the phone a couple of days ago, I suggested you

316

think about what your next assignment might be. Have you come up with any ideas yet?"

Corey, a little embarrassed over the praise, looked at the floor for a minute then looked at the president and said, "I would like to be placed on a special assignment."

The president's eyebrows went up and he asked, "Ohh? What do you mean?"

Corey looked at Jackie, Ryan, Dave, and Jasper, and then back to the president and said, "I think I can help in tracking down this ayatollah. You obviously have a group"—he looked back meaningfully at Ryan—"that is pretty well dedicated to getting him. I'd like to join that group until that mission is complete. Then I'd like an assignment somewhere in the Middle East where my language skills and knowledge of the culture can be utilized the best."

The president looked at him and then over to Ryan. He asked, "Your thoughts?"

Ryan said, "Sure. In fact, I had been thinking that maybe we needed to get a little more into this thing and organize an actual effort to capture the ayatollah. So far we have been working around the sidelines and seeing what he is up to since the stronghold strike. Perhaps we need to go ahead and actually try to get him and eliminate the problem that way. No major show of force; just a quiet disappearance. After all, the guy is just an international criminal. Let's deal with him that way. And Corey could be a great help in that."

The president nodded. In some respects it made sense, since the ayatollah was not a member of any government and the U.S. considered him a criminal. Just capturing him, putting him on trial, and sticking him in a regular U.S. federal prison for some of his crimes would take the wind out of the New Persia movement and solve the overall problem.

The president looked at Corey and said, "Okay. Let me clear it back through State, but consider it done. After all, you can't go back to Yemen, and State will have to find something for you. In the meantime, you'll be part of this quixotic crew." He smiled as he finished the comment.

Corey did a slight single fist pump and said, "Thank you, sir."

The idea of capturing the ayatollah had merit. But implementation would be a real problem.

Chapter Fifty-Six
Dinner

Tuesday—August 9
Washington, D.C.

After the discussion and meeting was over, the president excused himself and headed upstairs to relax for a bit before dinner. The crowd, with Ryan at the lead, went into a small conference room near the executive dining room and sat down on the leather couches. Drinks were offered, and the offer was taken up by all.

Corey, between sips of a beer, commented, "I never thought I would see this. I hope you"—he scanned around the room at each person—"don't object to my request to the president. I would like to be part of capturing this guy."

Ryan shook his head and said, "Not at all. We would like to have your help. The more the merrier. You have already helped us a lot, and we welcome your assistance." He smiled. "Corey, we may very well need your assistance and expertise with weapons before we are finished with this." He looked at each of the others and they nodded in agreement.

"Thanks. I appreciate the confidence," said Corey.

Jackie added, "And, in addition to your expertise, I may need help keeping Ryan out of trouble. It isn't easy for just one person to keep track of his misadventures." She winked at Ryan.

They continued with the banter for a short period and then refreshed their drinks. The president joined them for dinner. With him was a striking woman they all recognized. As they came into the room, Ryan and his entire group stood as the president said, "I'd like to introduce you all to my wife, Sarah." He turned to Sarah and said, "This is the group of adventurers" and he looked at each of them in turn as he used the term, then he turned back to her and continued, "who are solving our little problem with the New Persia movement." He then introduced each of them in turn, and she acknowledged each of them with a nod, a handshake, and direct eye contact.

She was very thin, with auburn hair, and had a smooth and nearly perfect complexion that would be the envy of models. She was about the same height in medium heels as the president, and had a very proud bearing. She certainly knew who she was. She reminded them of a slightly thinner version of the late Princess Diana. She was a very strong advocate for feeding the world and eliminating the waste of food throughout the world economies. Her other passion was improving the conditions of the poor. In both cases she had succeeded in getting support through Congress.

They waited as the president seated his wife and himself and then they all took their places. Food and drinks were served and they fell into a casual conversation. Sarah talked with each of them and was quite charming. Ryan, Dave, and Jasper had all met her before, but this was a new experience for Jackie and Corey. Both were having trouble eating due to nervousness. As the evening progressed, and the conversation was so casual, they were able to relax and enjoy it. By the time dinner was finished, they were quite relaxed and the discussion was easy.

A few minutes after finishing their food, Sarah got up, motioned for them all to remain seated as they began to rise, and said, "I have to beg your forgiveness, but I must excuse myself. It has been very enjoyable meeting and talking with all of you. I'm sure my husband has some additional matters to discuss with you, and I have some other matters to attend to. Please accept my apologies." She smiled, went over to the president, gave him a light kiss on the cheek, and said, "I'll see you later, dear." He nodded and smiled as she left.

Looking back as his wife departed, the president said, "Ryan. So far we have picked up the tab for your expenses but you have not been on any official retainer or contract. You've been doing all this, and placing yourself in danger, with no salary or compensation. I was thinking about it and would like to propose that you join my staff. Dave and Jasper also. Corey and Jackie are already on board. What do you think?"

Ryan was a little surprised at the request. There had been no discussion of it and he wasn't expecting it. He had submitted several expense reports through the system and had not really considered a position on the staff. Looking at the president, he asked, "What kind of position are you thinking of?"

The president replied, "Oh, something generic, like 'special assistant' or 'presidential representative' or something like that. Not descriptive of what you would actually be doing, but it would put you on the payroll and you wouldn't be working for free. I just think you need to be compensated for your efforts. If nothing else, you could work on a part-time basis and bill us hourly. Sort of like a consultant. How about it? Make sense to you?"

"Hmmmm. Yes. It would help out. The marina could use some additional cash infusion, and this effort is taking up a lot of time." He hesitated a few moments to think and said, "Okay. Tell you what. Let's do this on an hourly basis and we'll see how it works." He looked over at Jasper and Dave, and they both nodded in agreement. After a few more minutes of discussion, they agreed on a rate and it was settled. "Special assistant to the president." Ryan and company were on the U.S. government payroll.

Dinner was finished and they all enjoyed some dessert. The president then looked over at Corey and said, "Okay, Corey. I have talked with Kenton during our break"—referring to the acting secretary of state—"and he has agreed to turn you loose for the duration of this activity. You'll work with Ryan and the crowd. I expect that the bunch of you will get this ayatollah character fairly soon." Looking at the group, he said, "How you do it is up to you. I'm not going to take any direct military action, but the idea of capturing him and putting him in a regular federal prison sure is attractive to me. Great idea."

Ryan looked a bit startled. He said, "So let me make sure I understand what you are saying. You want us to work on our own, figure out where he is, and then snatch him back here for a trial and prison. Is that right?"

The president paused for a minute then said, "I think that we need to get this guy off the street. I could turn the CIA loose; that is certainly one option, and one I'd like to keep in reserve. But for now, I'd like to see what you guys can do. If you need help or assistance in transport or some quick manpower, Admiral Watkins will continue to be the contact point. You already have his cell phone number, and he's the one who arranged to get you back here, and can keep on doing it for now."

Ryan slowly looked at the others with his lips pursed. This one had come out of nowhere at him, and he wasn't sure it would work. He leaned forward in his chair and very slowly nodded. "Okay. We'll give it a go. Perhaps a small group like ours could be more successful than a large force." He looked at each of them and returned his gaze to the president. "And, in the process, you have deniability. I'd like to get with my people here and see what they think and how we might go about it. Then get back to you."

The president nodded and said, "That's fair. In the meantime, I may task the Pentagon to come up with a plan, just in case."

But the president hoped he wouldn't have to task the Pentagon. Too complex.

Chapter Fifty-Seven
Group Planning

Tuesday—August 9
Washington, D.C.

That evening, after returning to their hotel, Ryan called them all together in his room at the Ritz. He was a bit stunned over the turn of events that had occurred earlier that evening. Jackie joined them for the discussion. She was quite interested in what might be decided and what role she might play, both in planning and executing whatever they came up with.

Corey couldn't believe what had happened either, and was interested to see how this was all going to pan out. It seemed like the president had just about given them a carte blanche to get the ayatollah in any way they could. A real "special" operation. And Corey wanted to be right in the middle of it.

Jasper and Dave were likewise amazed. They were basically going to go undercover and see if they could capture the leader of this group and spirit him back to the States. In polite society it would be called kidnapping. In this instance it was called protecting your own and capturing an international criminal. They would be going after what they considered to be an international criminal, even though part of the world didn't consider the ayatollah in that manner. Either view was right and either view was legally questionable.

Ryan, after they all had gathered and found themselves a seat, began, "Well. I think we have quite a challenge in front of us. Corey and Dave, you saw the inside of that place and we all saw the office where the ayatollah spends his time. Any thoughts?"

Corey responded, "It was too easy the last time we were there. We could have walked right in there, just as Jackie actually did, and grabbed him. By now, I am sure they have activated all the security cameras and alarms. And if it were me running it, I would double the guards and patrols. Either that or they have bailed out for places unknown. Whichever way, this isn't going to be easy."

322

Dave added, "I agree. To use an old phrase, it won't be a cakewalk. And I'm sure that Abdul-Hakim character has put some additional safeguards on both the perimeter and the harbor areas. He won't want to be surprised by a return visit."

Jasper said, "Well, I wasn't there, but judging from your report, it is just becoming more fortified, and the ayatollah may not even be there anymore. It appears to me that we need to, somehow, find out if he is still there or has headed out. Logic would say that he's not there, but people aren't always logical. Otherwise we could be wasting our time. There may be a twist on this thing that we aren't considering."

Jackie then said, "Well, Jasper, I was there, and if it hadn't been for a couple of poorly trained guards, we might be talking a different story. If you want my opinion, and that's all it is, I think he very well could still be there. Sort of a reverse psychology. We think we scared him so much he bailed, so he figures that he will stay put."

Jasper looked back at her and shrugged as he said, "You could be right. We just don't know."

Ryan interrupted, "All very good points, folks. But also all speculation. I think that, for the meeting tomorrow with the president, we need to come up with some ideas on how to determine where he is, and then figure out how to get to him. An escape plan or backup for ourselves would also be helpful, but that can wait for now. Any ideas on how we can locate him?"

Jackie said, "One possibility would be for Jasper, since they wouldn't recognize him, to play tourist and see what he can find out. All of us are out, since they know who we are."

Ryan, Corey, and Dave nodded.

Jasper just sat there and thought a bit. He hadn't planned on being a lone ranger in this action. But it might be a bit of fun. He looked at the group and said, "Okay. How would we do that and what would I be playing at?"

Ryan said, "That island is just full of odd plants and strange formations. You could just be a tourist interested in strange places around the world. Sort of a rich individual explorer. Your story could be that you have been to the Galapagos Islands and found out about Socotra and decided to check it out. Nothing more."

"Yeah. I hear you. But how do I determine if the ayatollah is still there? Or if he's not, where he might have gone?"

Good question, and one the group didn't have an immediate answer for. They all looked at various parts of the room as if something might just jump out at them. No answer was immediately available. Nothing jumped.

Ryan said, "Don't know yet. I think we may have to wing this one. Perhaps one of the locals would know and slip information to us."

"Hmmm," said Corey. "We can try that, but we'd better be pretty covert. We don't want to tip anyone off."

After several more hours of discussion, the determination was made for Jasper to visit the island and just see what he could find out. There were too many questions that remained unanswered; the most important of which was whether the ayatollah was still there.

Assuming the ayatollah was there, they made preliminary plans for spiriting him off the island.

Wednesday—August 10
Washington, D.C.

Ryan called Maria the first thing in the morning. "Hi, Maria. Would it be possible to get a few minutes of the president's schedule sometime today? I need to brief him on what we have come up with for planning on the New Persia effort."

Maria responded, "How much is a 'few minutes' really?"

He could hear the humor in her voice but also knew she was serious. The president's schedule was always very tight, and they hated to overbook him. And that happened fairly frequently.

He responded, "Actually, about fifteen minutes should do it. That's assuming he doesn't change something or add to our planned effort."

Maria looked at the schedule and said, "Uh huh. Like he won't want to change something. I'll get you fifteen minutes just before lunchtime. At 11:15 a.m., to be exact."

Ryan was pleased. "Sounds good to me. We'll be there. And thanks for the help."

"*De nada*," she responded.

At 11:00 a.m., Ryan, Dave, Jasper, and Corey were all waiting in the anteroom for the Oval Office. They had a small presentation for the president and were fidgeting with anxiety while waiting. Finally, Maria invited them into the office and Jackie joined them there.

The president joined them on the couches. He said, "That was pretty quick. What do you have in mind?"

Ryan responded, "We plan to send Jasper in to see if the ayatollah is still there or if he has flown the coop. Assuming he is still there, because we think he might be using reverse psychology on us and staying put, we will then finalize our draft snatch plan to get him." Ryan then explained what they had in mind to capture the ayatollah.

The president's eyebrows went up as they described what they wanted to do. He looked over at each of them and said, "Sounds very risky. Do you really think you can pull it off?"

Jackie was shaking her head, and said, "Naaah. Common guys. Get real. As I said last night when we were discussing this, I have my real doubts. There are too many things that can go wrong. And then you'd be dead." She paused for a moment then added with a frown, "Literally."

Dave shook his head and said, "I really think we can do it. It won't be easy, but it's not impossible either. And the only other possibility is military, and we don't want to do that. Plus, going that route takes away your deniability if something does go wrong."

The president sat still for a moment and then said, "Okay. Let's do this one step at a time. Jasper, you go on your mission and see what you can find out. When you get back, we'll see about the next step. That sound okay to all of you?"

A moment's pause in the conversation occurred and they nodded in agreement. Actually, there wasn't much choice. After all, it was the president making the "suggestion" ...

Then the president added, "Good." He looked over at Ryan and continued, "But don't stop the planning for the grab. Get the details worked out while Jasper's on his vacation in case we have to move fast. And Admiral Watkins will be the contact for the support you'll need."

Ryan smiled broadly and said, "Yes, sir. Can do."

Jackie then added, "Well, since you are so determined to continue with this suicide mission"—she turned to the president—"could they get up-to-date satellite images of Socotra? There may be some changes we aren't aware of."

The president nodded and said, "Of course. We'll get them before Jasper leaves. Good suggestion."

With that, they stood, shook hands, and left the Oval Office with a charter to basically move out. They had taken fourteen minutes. Ryan stopped by Maria's desk and pointed at his watch as they left. She laughed and gave him a thumbs-up.

Chapter Fifty-Eight
Option Review

Thursday—August 11
Washington, D.C.

The president asked Maria to come into his office. She came in with notebook in hand anticipating some tasking. She was correct.

She took a seat in front of his desk and prepared to take notes.

President Martinez was standing by the window looking out at the lawn at some of the gardeners at work in the late summer flowerbeds. The grass had just been mown and the striping of the mowers reminded him of a golf course fairway. He smiled slightly at the thought and wished he could be on a course instead of in the office with all the chores and meetings he had to attend to.

He turned and smiled at her. "Thank you for all the help you give me." It was obvious he was in a sentimental mood.

She just smiled back and nodded.

He turned back from the window and sat down. "I'd like you to set up a meeting in here for this coming Monday with Mike in Defense, Kenton in State, Mark over in the CIA, and have Generals Foley and Fairchild, along with Admirals Watkins and Nelson, also. And ask Miriam Blacock to attend. We need to discuss, again, this New Persia situation and what to do about it."

She made a note as she nodded. "Do you want Jerry from DHS there too?"

He thought a moment and then said, "Yes. Of course. He has been involved in this since it started, so we had better keep him informed." He hesitated for a moment then said, "Thanks for the suggestion. It helps."

She nodded again. "Anything else?"

"No. We just need to get this resolved. Let me know the particulars when you have them."

She nodded again and then quietly left.

A short while later, she interrupted his reading and said, "I have it set up for Monday afternoon at 3:00 p.m. They'll all be here. Do you want me to plan on being with you?"

"No," he responded. "This will just be a discussion and there won't be any reason for a record of it. But thanks for asking."

She nodded and left the office.

Monday—August 15
Washington, D.C.

At a few minutes before 3:00 p.m. on Monday, the invited staff all gathered outside the Oval Office. Each was looking at notes from the day's activities in their own area of responsibility. They were not sure what might come up during the meeting, and therefore were just going to see what happened. No preparation other than their normal daily briefings on world events.

Maria, after checking with the president, walked them over to the door, and they all proceeded to enter the room and took seats on the various couches and chairs. The president was on the telephone with his back to the room and talking quietly with Ryan on some of the planned details. He turned around, glanced up, and nodded to each of them as he caught their eye upon entering. He finished his conversation, put the phone back on its recharging stand and came over to the group.

He looked at each person and then said, "Well. We missed the ayatollah the last time. We now know where he is, or was. Any of you have any suggestions on what our next move should be?"

Mike Detirro spoke first. "We missed him in his stronghold. Obviously they were prepared, at least some of them were, for a strike. I think, assuming we still want to go after him, that we need to make it a boots-on-the-ground mission and make sure we complete it. No questions. Somebody needs to take him out and be done with it."

General Foley, the chairman of the Joint Chiefs, looked at Mike and said, "I take it you really don't mean a full-out assault with your 'boots-on-the-ground' comment." Turning to the president, he said, "I agree with Mike that we need to make sure we are successful this time. And that would take eyeballs on the dead body. Not an airborne strike, but rather some form of surgical action by either the Special Forces or the SEALs ...

in his home territory, so we know, for a fact, that we get him. 'No questions,' as Mike said."

The president just nodded in understanding. The B-52 raid conducted over the southeastern deserts of Iran had taken out the ayatollah's stronghold and destroyed a good portion of his forces, but it had not gotten the ayatollah. The ayatollah had to be stopped, and the rest of the world, at least those who were interested, was just sitting back watching the action. There were other portions of the world community that couldn't care less.

Admiral Jack Nelson then said, "I think, since this new operation is located on an island in the middle of the Indian Ocean, that we need to plan on a SEAL operation to eliminate the new center." He looked around at the group. "The SEALs could be put ashore in the middle of the night, hit them hard and destroy all their command and control structures and facilities, eliminate their command personnel, to include the ayatollah, and withdraw. All within a few hours and under the cover of darkness. They can be inserted via ASDVs and recovered in the same way. A submarine can perform this operation with no difficulties. We have trained for this type of operation and can accomplish it quickly and quietly. Nobody would even know we were there except for the fact that the center would no longer exist."

General Foley said, "Well, it makes sense to take them out as soon as possible. The longer we wait, the stronger they will become and the harder it will be to get them." He looked around and continued, "Given the location of this new center, I have to agree with Admiral Nelson. I think it is a Navy show."

General Fairchild looked at the others and slowly nodded in thoughtful agreement. "Well," he said, "we tried the B-52s and that didn't get the mission done. I think I'd have to agree on a close-in strike on the ground and finish this thing off."

The president then looked over at Miriam. He raised his eyebrows. She said, "Well, it seems to me that we need to do something. As word has gotten around that he escaped the last try, our partners are questioning, behind closed. doors, of course, our capabilities to get this guy out of the picture. That's a bit of a problem, because these same partners won't help, at least not overtly. The Brits, French, and Germans have significant Muslim populations and are hesitant to help, at least on the surface."

Kenton then uttered, "Hmph. We didn't get him, and the world is being quite sarcastic in their comments to us." He looked at Miriam and then back to the president. "And some of it is not behind closed doors. I wasn't in favor of that action to begin with, and now we have to deal with the fallout. It isn't pleasant or easy."

The president was studying his hands on the table. He looked up as Kenton made his remarks but didn't say anything. He looked over at Admiral Nelson and said, "Do you have any more detail, or have you done any more planning on what you suggested earlier?"

"No, sir. It is just an idea at this point. However, we do have that capability for a SEAL strike from a submarine. It is silent and very difficult, with today's technology, to detect the approach to a target area. There's nothing on the surface and satellites can't see it. All very quiet. Using ASDVs to support the mission saves the energy of the SEALs, and they are much more effective. If you would like, we can do some preliminary planning for that specific location and come back to you in a week or so with some details."

Kenton then spoke up: "What's an ASDV?"

The admiral looked over at Kenton and responded, "An advanced SEAL delivery vehicle. Basically, it's a subsurface vehicle that can carry several SEALS and their equipment from the submarine to a beach or other target area. It rides on the back of the sub and can be deployed when the sub reaches a point for the SEALs to move out. It provides dry transportation, navigation help, and an air supply on the way in to an objective and then back out again. The SEALs ride in the vehicle and save their energy for the actual mission requirements. It also then provides a way out when the mission has been completed." He looked back at the president.

Kenton responded, "Sounds like a miniature submarine for close-in work."

The admiral looked back at Kenton and shrugged in sort-of agreement. His dislike of Kenton, with his frequent negative attitude, was just below the surface, and barely contained.

The president nodded at the admiral. "Okay. See what you can come up with on plans for a SEAL strike. Since this is on the other side of the world, I would assume that it will take a couple of weeks to get ready and get forces into that area. In your planning, set up a rough timeline so we have some idea when this could be accomplished."

Admiral Nelson said, "Will do."

The president looked around the room and then asked, "Any other comments?"

There were none, and the meeting broke up.

The president went to the Oval Office, sat down at his desk, and thought. He hadn't exposed the tasking for Ryan's group to the military planners just yet. He decided to see what Ryan came up with first. If it made sense to him, and it probably would, he'd let the Joint Chiefs know about it so they could support it. For now, he was keeping quiet. Besides, the military planning guys might come up with something that might help Ryan.

Chapter Fifty-Nine
Jasper's Visit

Tuesday—August 16
Fort Meade, Maryland

At Fort Meade, in Maryland, there is a whole forest of satellite dish antennas pointed at various locations in the sky. The National Security Agency is constantly on the lookout for satellite communications traffic that could potentially indicate future harm to the U.S. This monitoring activity is a 24/7 effort, with computer assist to indicate significant changes in activity. After the undersea cable link was confirmed, the island of Socotra had been monitored for some time through the New Persia satellite terminal in Salalah. A significant increase in the amount of traffic had been detected, monitored, and watched. So when the traffic dropped significantly this evening, and did not pick up again, a classified report was generated and sent to the Pentagon, CIA, and Homeland Security. The president was also briefed on it.

The president was puzzled. The latest photos of the island indicated that the trimaran was no longer in the harbor. Combined with the sharp drop in comm traffic, suspicions were raised. Had they left the island or was this some sort of ruse?

Wednesday—August 17
Socotra Island

Flying in to Socotra was an experience, since Jasper had to go through part of Yemen to do it. But since he was going in as an explorer on his own, the only requirement he had to meet was a visa from Yemeni officials. They were trying to encourage tourist traffic to the island, so it was not too hard to get the visa with State Department help. It still took over a week to get it, but he succeeded.

He flew down from Sana'a and landed at the relatively new, small airport. Commercial service to Socotra was available just twice a week, so he had to time it. But all went well, and he arrived with his pack and exploring clothing, including a camera and tablet, all intact. Using a local taxi from the airport, he then checked in to the Taj hotel and began looking around for a ride out into the small mountain range to the south. He wanted to go out first thing in the morning. The registration people behind the counter were able to connect him with a driver and vehicle. It didn't take too long, and he arranged for a ride at first light. He was alone. Nothing obvious.

The next morning, Jasper sat for a minute on the edge of the bed in his room. He had on khaki shorts and a bush-type short-sleeve shirt with multiple pockets and straps. His boots were a heavy cross-country eight-inch-high ankle style, given the rough territory he was supposedly going through. But they were comfortable and he was sure they would do well. He had on a very wide brim bush hat with the brim rolled up on the left—very natty—just what the wealthy world traveler would wear in Africa or any other rough hot-weather place. His clothing all fit and he was comfortable with the disguise. He added bottled water and some protein bars he had brought with him to the pockets. He also picked up a couple of maps of the area, including some he had brought with him that were satellite images, and a compass. And finally his camera, still in its case on his hip. He was prepared for the day.

The weather turned out to be fairly nice, with temperatures in the eighties and offshore breezes. It was a pleasant morning with the promise of a hot day later. The skies were clear, and humidity was just tolerable as he got up and prepared for the day's hiking.

He was on his way in a beat-up old Datsun. His guide warned him of a few of the plants and animals and left him on a trailhead taking him into the mountains. He was certainly noticeable on the trail. His size was quite a bit larger than the locals', and it marked him as a stranger to their land. He hiked for a couple of hours and came across several shepherds and their goats. With sign language and some pidgin English, they pointed out where he could climb and get a better view of the area. What he was really looking for was a view, if he could get it, of the compound. Then his long lens could be used to see the inside of the compound and any activity that might be going on inside.

Unfortunately, when he got to the promontory the shepherds had pointed to, there wasn't anything to view. More small hills and valleys, but no compound. He looked at the rough map that Ryan had drawn and realized he was several miles away. The guide mistakenly had taken him out to a trail that was going away from the compound. He couldn't complain, though … it would give away his real purpose. He would just have to enjoy the diversion as best he could. He looked at some of the dragon's blood trees, with the umbrella shape and red sap, and marveled at the uniqueness of the area. Then he settled down for a bit of rest and, after a short break for some bottled water and an energy bar, he began the hike back in to town. It would take a while, but he would make it after a few hours of walking. And while it was getting hot, he was enjoying the unique scenery and the otherwise pleasant weather.

On the way he was able to think about how he might get more information on the presence of the ayatollah. The locals probably couldn't help out, since the ayatollah kept pretty much to the compound, but he might be able to get some other information on the construction of the compound. After all, several of the locals had worked on building the compound, and would have some idea of how it was arranged and organized. And after thinking about it for a short while, he realized that the compound probably hired workers for such things as janitorial, repair, and food service. Even though they were a movement in the Muslim religion, they still needed those types of services. It might work. With the proper incentives—in other words, bribes—he might be able to get information on the layout of the compound and even whether the ayatollah was there or not. But he had to be cautious.

Sounded good. But how would he approach that idea? He was still supposed to be an explorer. Not a snoop. Who should he approach and how? If it turned out that he approached the wrong person, he could end up like Ryan had. Captured and held … or worse. He had to be very careful.

After several hours of walking—fortunately, he had good walking boots and a broad-brimmed hat—he approached town and the hotel. He climbed the slight stairs into the main entrance and went to his room. All was well and the room had been made up. He dug through some of his baggage and brought out the map that had been provided by the Yemen tourist folks when he applied for the visa. He looked at it and compared it to the rough map Ryan had drawn. He also looked at a copy of a satellite map that had been provided to him before he left the States. The satellite image showed buildings in the compound that were not on the tourist map. It also showed the harbor area with a couple of ships tied up. But no trimaran. The maps, of course, didn't show the ships, but the tourist map did indicate the harbor. It also had a notation that it was a restricted area and off limits to civilians. In other words, keep out. It also was a key item he wanted to look at, if he could figure a way to get to it without raising suspicions.

Jasper looked at all this information and shook his head. And he smiled. It would be quite an adventure, a great challenge, and most of all ... fun.

He could use a beer. But this was a Muslim country. They didn't have it. He went down to the front desk and walked up to the porter. The porter could only speak some English. Jasper looked at him, leaned to his ear, and simply said, "Cold beer?"

The porter, an older, smallish man with thin legs sticking out of his shorts, and arms to match, looked a little startled, and whispered back, "Muslim. No beer."

Jasper, much taller and probably outweighing him by 150 pounds, was disappointed, and looked back at the little guy. He cocked his head to the side and said, "I understand. But"—he held out two thousand rials—"you sure there isn't some around somewhere?"

The porter, looking around quickly, took the bills and said, "Room in few minutes." Then he disappeared through a doorway that said "Employees Only" over the door. Jasper went back up to his room and waited, looking out the window at the nearby sea. The blue of the water was a strong contrast with the faint blue-white sky. It was actually quite pretty. Too bad this country was so backward and so far out of the way.

A knock on the door. Jasper went to answer it and found a small plastic bag sitting on the hallway floor at his door. Nobody was there. In the bag was a six-pack of Budweiser! And it was quite cold. What a country! Jasper looked up and down the relatively short hall again, and there was no one in sight. He smiled to himself. The world was pretty much the same all over.

He went back inside the room. He popped the top of one of the beers and sat back to enjoy it. After his long day's fruitless hike, the cold beer really hit the spot. And he had found a source of beer in this out-of-the-way place.

He looked at the various maps again and an idea formed in his head. He looked at the satellite images and then at the tourist map. They didn't have the same information, but the combination of the two provided a pretty complete picture of the island and its features. He took another small swallow of the beer and thought some more. He just might be able to pull it off.

He put the remaining beer in the small refrigerator in the room. He would enjoy some more after he came back upstairs. He had noticed something when he had been downstairs, and he wanted to check it out.

He went downstairs, and some of the French workmen he had seen earlier were still there. There were only three left out of the six he had seen before, but he was suspicious. He had a hunch. He walked up to one of the Frenchmen and asked if any of them spoke English. The one he asked smiled a bit and responded that he spoke some English, and what did Jasper want? Jasper was pleased, and asked what the Frenchmen were doing on the island. He explained that he was doing some exploring, and wondered if they had seen any interesting things on the island other than the unusual plants.

The lead Frenchman said, "We're doing some work over in the compound, and we haven't had a chance to really look around the island much."

"What compound? There's nothing about a compound on the tourist maps," Jasper said with a sincere look.

The Frenchman said, "It's a compound of Muslims, but I don't know what they are doing here. It's pretty extensive, and we are installing some"—he hesitated for a moment— "electronic systems for them. They seem very concerned, on this outlying island, about security. Beats me!" He raised his hands and laughed.

Jasper looked at him with a puzzled expression. He said, "Security systems here? There's nothing but strange plants, goats, and old fishermen on this island."

"Yeah. But their boss, some ayatollah, is concerned, so they hired us to get the systems in and running. So, here we are."

"They have an ayatollah here? That's a pretty high rank for this desolate place."

The Frenchman looked a bit puzzled. "Well, they really don't have 'ranks' as we know them. But he does carry a lot of weight, and has quite a reputation." He hesitated and then continued, "Yes. And he and his head of security check out our progress quite regularly." He looked back at his men, and they waved at him to head out, making drinking motions with their hands. He looked back and said, "If we hear of anything interesting for you, we'll let you know. You here for long?"

"No, just a couple of days more. When I booked it I didn't think I would find much. I was right! But good luck on your work. It's been good talking with you."

"You too." And he left to join his men.

Jasper shook his head in amazement. What casual conversations led to. Now he knew the ayatollah was on the island and that the "electronic systems" were being installed by the French. He sat for a moment, then followed the Frenchmen up the stairs. He tried to watch to see what rooms they went into, but he had missed them.

Damn.

Thursday—August 18
Socotra Island

The next morning, after having some breakfast, Jasper put on his hiking shorts, boots, daypack, and hat, and headed downstairs. He approached the desk with the tourist map in his hands. He asked the clerk if the restricted area on the map was the same as the compound the French were working on.

She looked at the map and said, "Yes. The compound they are referring to is that restricted area. May I ask why you are asking?"

"Well, when I was talking with them last night I wasn't sure what they were referring to, and I don't want to go where I'm not supposed to. So I thought I would ask."

She smiled and said, "Good idea. You really don't want to go near the compound. They are very sensitive about their territory. Why, I have no idea, but the people around here, except for the ones working there, stay away."

"They have local people working there?"

"Oh yes. We have quite a few who are employed there doing various things for them." She turned as another customer came in. "I'm sorry. I can't talk anymore. Just stay clear of the compound and you will be fine." And she went to help the other customer.

Jasper watched for a moment and then turned and went outside. He approached the driver he had hired the previous day, pulled out the map, and indicated that he wanted to go to the other side of the island, starting out near the harbor, and work his way north. Away from the compound. The driver shrugged, went to the Datsun, and drove over to pick Jasper up. They drove over the hill and down past the main entrance gate to the compound, and then over to the beach area just north of the harbor. Jasper arranged with the driver to pick him up at the same location six hours later. The driver drove off and left Jasper standing on the beach with his daypack, food, water, and maps.

He looked back at the harbor and at the small part of the compound that was visible from where he was standing. He moved his glance away fairly quickly so anyone watching him would think he was just looking around. He had seen what he wanted. There was work being done on the harbor entrance. He wasn't sure what they were doing, but there were small cement mixers and workmen at the edge of the breakwater. Something was being installed or modified.

Chapter Sixty
Search and Spying

Thursday—August 18
Socotra Island

Jasper finished his walk for the day, having gone down the beach for several miles, seeing nothing of particular interest except for a couple of apparent Europeans sunbathing and reading on the nearly empty beach. It was tropically hot and humid. He went through a full liter of water as he walked, sweating along the way. He made it back to the beginning location and waited for a half-hour before the driver showed up. During his wait, he got out his field glasses and scanned the whole area, passing the harbor entrance twice, and very briefly, but he saw nothing of interest, and the harbor workmen had left for the day. It was a hot day, and they'd probably cut out early. He still wasn't sure what they were doing.

Back at the hotel, he went up to his room and got a precious beer, sat down, and enjoyed the coolness of the drink. At 5:00 p.m. he went down to the lobby with his maps and pretended to be studying them again for the next day's outing. His targets came in a little while later, and he followed the Frenchmen as they went up to their rooms. They were on the second floor and had a block of six rooms. He noted which rooms they had, and specifically the head of the group, and kept on going up the stairs to the third floor. He waited a bit then took the stairs back down to the lobby, sat down, and waited again.

Abdul-Hakim was satisfied that the security systems installation was progressing on schedule. He would be much more comfortable when it was in and completely finished. He wasn't an engineer and didn't understand it all, but the French company they had hired was supposed to be very good, and he had faith in their expertise.

They seemed to be quite efficient, and the installation would meet New Persia's needs for the compound security. Alarms, video cameras, and low-light cameras were all being installed, with a central control point in his security section of the central control facility. The ayatollah seemed to be satisfied also. While they had no worries about the locals, they were quite concerned about the Americans. Since the Americans now knew where they were, they had to make sure there was no attempt to capture or kill the leaders of the New Persia movement. The security systems would help ensure that no one could approach without them knowing it.

Abdul-Hakim had doubled the workforce he had available for security. All of the gate guards were now doubled up, so there were at least two on duty at the guard shack at any time. There were more frequent checks from central control, and he had two-man roving patrols moving over the entire compound all the time. When they finally got the cameras working, he could reduce some of the patrols, but he was nervous about it. There had been no apparent actions by the Americans, and that also made him nervous. What were they planning? They knew where the compound was located. What were they going to do? He was very anxious to see the various French-made systems installed and operating. He had suggested to the ayatollah that he and his staff go elsewhere for a period until the systems were operational, but the ayatollah had rebuffed him, and not in a nice manner. He could do nothing about that, but his comfort level was very low. And his anxiety level was very high.

An hour later, the French team all came down the stairs and headed out to a local restaurant. Jasper waited a few minutes to make sure they were gone and then headed up the stairs. He walked over to the lead Frenchman's room and checked the lock. It was an old-fashioned lock just like his. It actually took a key to open it. He tried it ... locked. And his key wouldn't fit it. He headed back down the hall to the stairs and climbed up one level to his room. He got a beer out of the cooler, opened it, and sat down to think about the situation. The outside windows were not an option, since they had no balcony and were on upper floors. Plus he was too big to be playing Spider-Man. But he wanted into the room, hoping to find some plans for the security installation. Probably not, but he had to try.

He sat there as daylight faded and darkness completely filled his room. He hadn't solved the problem when he went out to get something to eat. Following the porter's directions, he found a small restaurant and had dinner. Fortunately, he liked fish with rice, and that was basically all they had. It was truly a fishing economy.

He finished his dinner, walked around the town a bit, noticing that the various shops were pretty thin on merchandise, and then headed in to the hotel again. He decided to try and solve it in the morning, and went to bed.

The following morning, he was having a breakfast roll and coffee in the lounge when the French team came down, grabbed some coffee, and headed out to their rented vehicles. The lead caught sight of him, nodded, and proceeded out the door.

After a half-hour of brooding about it, he went up and looked down the second-floor hall. No one was around, and their doors appeared to be all shut and locked. As he went back to the stairs, one of the maids came out of a storage room and proceeded to the first room for work. She pulled her work cart up the hall, unlocked the room door, propped the door open, took supplies off the cart, and went to work cleaning the room. He looked at her, looked at the floor for a moment, and then went back to his room.

He waited for several minutes, got his laptop, and went down one floor to the target rooms. The maid was now in the room next to the lead's. He waited in the stairwell until she came out and entered the lead's room. He sauntered down the hallway, worked his way around the service cart, and walked into the room. She looked at him with a questioning glance. He looked at the briefcase in the corner of the room, pointed at his laptop, and walked over to the briefcase. She nodded and went back to her work cleaning the bath. He opened the briefcase and initially found nothing of worth, other than some company correspondence. Then he found what he was looking for. A flash drive. He put the drive in his laptop and copied the entire contents. It just took a few moments, and he removed the flash drive, put it back in the briefcase, and then put the briefcase back in the corner of the room. He smiled at the maid as he left the room, she nodded and smiled back, and he went up to his own room.

He fired up the computer again and looked at the files. Several were personal, and there was company correspondence also. A copy of the contract for the installation was on the drive along with ... detailed engineering specifications for the installation! He had what he'd come after, in spades! He took a second flash drive and copied the files to it. Then he hid the second drive in a compartment of his daypack.

His flight wouldn't come in until the day after tomorrow. He had to continue the act of being an explorer, so he went back down the stairs, out to the waiting driver, and took another tour. This time to the eastern beaches. He made the same arrangements and spent the day hiking along the beaches and hillsides. He met up with the driver and they headed back to town. He got back to the hotel, waved at the six Frenchmen relaxing in the lounge, and went up to his room for another beer. He popped a top and sat down. He checked that his laptop was still there. He powered it up and checked the files. All there. It didn't appear to have been tampered with. He breathed easier. He checked to make sure the flash drive he had copied earlier was still in his daypack. He had taken it with him on his hike, but was checking to make sure it was still there. Paranoia! It was simply too valuable to lose. He sipped on his beer.

After he finished his drink, he went downstairs, got a Coke from the desk, and looked around. He walked over to the lead Frenchman and shook hands. He asked, "So how's it going? I'm finding this island a bit of a bore from my standpoint. Nothing but beaches, some strange plants, and a few trails into the mountains."

The Frenchman responded, "Well. We're doing okay so far. Schedule is fine, and it's all going according to our plans. Haven't had a chance to get out and about, though, so I can't help you with any suggestions on your hiking."

Jasper nodded in serious understanding. "Thanks for the thought. I'm finding my own way around this place." He stopped for a sip of his Coke, looked at the Frenchman's glass, and realized it wasn't a soft drink. Even though in a plain glass, it looked like wine. He smiled at the Frenchman and said, "Where'd you find that? I've been looking around for some."

The Frenchman's eyes gleamed a little. "Just like any country in the world that has unpopular restrictions, there is a black market here. With the right contacts, almost anything can be bought. Plus, we brought some of our own in the equipment delivery containers. Boxed bottles in the middle of electronic modules aren't readily found, even if you are looking for them."

Jasper smiled and nodded. He'd been there before! He said, "Understand. Well, I have to get some dinner and have an early start in the morning. Enjoy your evening." He left the man standing there looking thoughtfully at his glass.

Jasper went out to the porch and met with the porter. He asked, "Is there somewhere that I can rent a small motor scooter? I want to wander around a bit on my own."

"Yes. I can arrange that. When do you want it?"

"Right now, if you can do it."

"Be here in half an hour and I'll have one for you."

Jasper was a bit surprised that he could do it that fast, but said, "Okay."

A half-hour later, he was back on the porch in long, dark pants and a dark blue shirt. The porter had a Vespa motor scooter for him. He signed the rental agreement, looked at the controls, played with them for just a moment, and then Jasper was off. He headed out of town as dusk fell. He returned to the southern side of the island, went past the guard entrance to the compound, and out to the beach. It was dark now. He parked the scooter in some bushes and left it. Pulling his hat down closer to his eyes, he hiked back across the rough ground until he was across the road from the guarded entrance. He sat down with a pair of night-vision binoculars and waited. He watched the guards on duty. After some time, he noticed that one of the guards was picking up a telephone or radio every twenty minutes. There was a routine going on ... the control center was checking every twenty minutes to make sure all was okay. They had obviously learned from Jackie's previous visit.

He continued his watch past midnight. The guards changed at 11 p.m. A new set of guards came down in a golf cart, and the ones now off duty returned to the compound in the same golf cart. But the twenty-minute check was performed regularly. They had a specific routine. The guards must change every four hours. The guardhouse was well lit both inside and outside. He could see cameras on a small pole next to the guardhouse facing the street entrance. Behind the guardhouse, the perimeter fencing, topped with razor wire, went off in both directions into the darkness.

He'd seen what he wanted to see. He quietly walked back to the bushes, retrieved the scooter, and headed back into town. He placed the scooter outside the porch and fastened the locking chain to it. He left a note for the porter and a thanks for the use of the scooter. He would have to tip him later. Then he went back up to his room satisfied with the night's adventure and findings, and made several notes on his laptop.

Friday—August 19
Socotra Island

The following morning, using his hired vehicle and driver, Jasper went over to the southern side of the island again. Workmen were installing moveable fencing and a large gate mechanism at the harbor entrance. He ignored them and went walking down the beach. He'd seen enough. He was just killing time until he could get out of there. He spent several hours hiking and then met up with his driver further down the beach. They took some back roads to the hotel, and he used the time for a bit of thought. He had found out that the ayatollah was here, security systems were being installed, they were blocking the entrance to the harbor, and some of the locals worked on the compound in menial tasks. From what he could see, there did not appear to be a large contingent of security personnel, just the necessary guards and a few additional security people for shift work and possible reaction to minor contingencies.

He got back to his hotel and he went up to his room. All was as he had left it in the morning. Boy! This paranoia was getting to him. Fortunately, he would be leaving in the morning and his little adventure would be over. He had two beers left and finished off one of them. He went downstairs and out into the main street, found a small hidden restaurant, had dinner, and went back to the hotel. He finished off the last beer, packed, and was ready to leave in the morning. He called down to the desk and made arrangements to be taken to the airport. Then he hit the rack. He was tired and anxious. Not a good mix for sleeping, which he had a lot of difficulty doing. Short of trying to get into the compound, he could think of nothing else to accomplish while he was here. And getting into the compound didn't seem possible. So a look at the pier and the trimaran were out.

It was getting late, but sleep just wouldn't come. He lay there with his thoughts. It would be a long day tomorrow, and the day after that. The flying time was extreme, since they were on the other side of the world from the U.S.

He got up and paced the room a bit. Then he powered up the laptop and began going through some of the materials he had copied from the Frenchman. The company apparently did a lot of foreign security work. There were several references to previous work and locations. The impression was that this company had connections in the Muslim world and were considered quite good. He looked at some of the engineering specifications. He could understand some of it, but felt Dave would be able to decipher it quite well. It was probably the most important thing he had accomplished during his visit. He powered the laptop back down and went back to bed.

He had finally tired himself out enough to sleep.

Chapter Sixty-One
Jasper's Return

Saturday—August 20
En Route to Washington, D.C.

The following day, Jasper caught the Felix Airline Boeing 737 and began the tiresome trip back to the States. He had accomplished his mission and was pleased with the outcome. The information he had gathered would assist all of them in planning a return trip to eliminate the New Persia movement. And New Persia wasn't aware of any of it.

He changed planes in Sana'a and flew into Paris, where he spent the night. From the hotel, he called Ryan and gave him a quick rundown on what he had found out, considering that the lines were not cleared for classified, and gave him his arrival schedule at Dulles.

After arriving at Dulles late Sunday afternoon, he went to the Ritz in downtown Washington, D.C., spent Sunday night there, and awaited Ryan's arrival later Monday afternoon.

Monday—August 22
Washington, D.C.

Ryan arrived at 3:00 p.m., along with Jackie, Corey, and Dave. After some quick late afternoon drinks, they had dinner in the restaurant and then met in Jasper's room for a briefing on his trip.

Jasper gave them all a rundown on the results of his trip. He used a hotel projector and the flash drive to show all of them the materials he had obtained from the French. Ryan was amazed at the detail he had gathered. Jasper gave Dave the flash drive containing all the information. Dave skimmed some of the information as it was briefed and said it appeared to be pretty complete. While some of the information was written in French, he was able to make out quite a bit of it. He had locations of the electronics, schematics of the interconnects, and locations of the command functions. He would get it translated and read it again to make sure he didn't miss anything.

When Jasper described how he got the information, they all just gawked at him, stunned. They couldn't believe it. People just don't do what he had done.

"You mean you just walked into his room and copied it in front of the maid?" asked Corey.

Jasper responded, "Yep. I couldn't figure any other way to get the information, and she didn't question me at all. In fact, when I went into the room I wasn't sure there was any information in there. I just took a chance."

"You sure did! She must have been intimidated by your size. And she wouldn't have known who the room was rented to," said Jackie. Then she added with a smile, "That took balls, Jasper." She shook her head, smiling, and then added, as she looked around the room at the bemused expressions, "Well ... it did!"

Ryan grinned at the comment, then said, "So you verified the ayatollah is still there, got detailed security information, including the name of the French company doing the installs, and saw the modifications they were doing to the harbor entrance. I'd have to say that you had a very successful mission. Way to go." And he walked over and high-fived Jasper.

Then they all drank to Jasper's success.

They had a prearranged meeting with the president set up for the next day to discuss what Jasper had found and to determine what the next course of action would be. Jasper and Ryan built some short briefing charts, added some information from Dave's brief review of the security information, and put the information on his flash drive. They would use it in the president's small conference room.

Tuesday—August 23
Washington, D.C.

Tuesday morning, everything was set up in the small conference room off the Oval Office. Maria had made sure coffee and a small selection of pastries were available, and they made good use of them when they arrived. Ryan brought the flash drive with the briefing materials and they checked out the computer that would be used with the projector. A few minutes later, Jack Harrison and Admiral Watkins joined them, shook hands, and began some small talk. Jackie joined them shortly before the president was due.

As scheduled, the president showed up, walking straight to the coffee pot for a morning bracer. He smiled at all of them as he got his coffee and then came around the edge of the table. "I can't believe what you have accomplished," he said. "What I understand you have done is way beyond what I could possibly envision." He shook hands all around and sat down at the head of the table.

The rest of them sat down and Ryan began the conversation: "Mr. President, I think we can best proceed with Jasper giving a short briefing on his recent trip to Socotra."

The president smiled and said, "Fine. Then we can discuss the next step." He turned and looked expectantly at Jasper. Jasper stood up and went through the briefing materials they had developed the previous evening. After he was finished, he waited as the president got himself another cup of coffee. Turning back to the table, the president motioned for Jasper to sit down, then he came back and sat down at the head of the table.

He looked at Jasper and said, "You just walked in there and copied his files? Right past the maid?" He smiled and added, "Remind me to never let you around our computers! That took a lot of nerve." He paused, and then added with a wink, "Cool. Thanks!"

He turned to Ryan and commented, "It sounds like quite a trip, and one that was very worthwhile. What do you propose for the next step?"

"We think we need to get with the Navy planners over at the Pentagon and see what their thoughts are. Then we can formulate a plan for getting the ayatollah back here. They may have some good ideas on how to get us on the island and back off again."

"How about that security system?"

Dave responded, "I'm having the specs, written in French, translated over at the language institute. They should be finished in a few days. I'm going to study them thoroughly and see where I might find some weaknesses. I'll work out some scheme for defeating the system. It was designed by humans and will have some flaws in it. I'll find them." grinned.

"How long is all that going to take?"

"Perhaps a week. Maybe a little longer. I may have to get some other experts involved, but I won't know that until I have the translated documents back."

"I see."

Turning back to Ryan, the president smiled over his coffee cup as he took a sip. "Okay. I know you better. You have some idea of what you want to do. Let's hear it."

Ryan leaned forward on the desk and clasped his hands together. His eyes met the president's. He said, "Yes, sir. We have discussed what we might do. As you will recall, you asked us to take this on and to avoid the military response. So, the bottom line is that the four of us capture the ayatollah and bring him back to the States."

The president took another sip and simply responded, "Yes ... and?"

Ryan continued, "So we have come up with a plan. It does still involve the military, but in a support role, and invisible to the New Persia movement." Then Ryan proceeded to lay out his plan to the president, Jack, and the admiral. Corey, Dave, and Jasper all nodded as parts of the plan were revealed. Jackie looked stunned at the details, but kept quiet. Given the current plans, she wasn't part of it.

Ryan finished, "We would like to talk with the Navy planners over at the Pentagon and see if all this is possible. If so, it's up to you to approve it, and we move on with some final details."

The president looked over at Jack and the admiral. "What do you guys think?"

Jack said, "I think you're nuts. The chance of pulling it off is very small."

The admiral, looking back from watching Jack, said, "It may work. Certainly the Navy support part of it will work. The rest is pretty risky. And most of it hinges on whether Dave can beat that system. That's the hardest part."

The president looked at Jack and the admiral. "The risk is high. But the reward is also high. I think we need to proceed as they have suggested and see how Dave's analysis turns out. We can do some of the preliminary planning, ship availability and so forth, and then reassess after Dave figures this thing out. Then a final decision can be made. And you realize that if it goes south, you are on your own. We will deny any knowledge of your activities."

Ryan said, "Fair enough." He turned to Admiral Watkins. "Can we get over to the Pentagon planners and pick their brains on this scheme?"

"Yes. I'll set something up for day after tomorrow. Tomorrow's too soon; they won't be available to respond that quickly."

Ryan nodded. "Good. We'll keep in touch with you. In the meantime, we'll continue to detail out some of the plans. Dave will be busy trying to figure out the electron flows."

The president looked around. "Fine. Gentlemen, I have another meeting. We'll get together again in a few days and see where we are." With that, he got up and left the room.

Jackie just shook her head. "I have to agree with Jack. You guys are nuts. You're just going to walk in and take the ayatollah for a ride. It won't be that easy." Her voice slowly went up in pitch and tempo as she spoke. She looked at Ryan with a plea in her eyes.

He looked down at the table for a moment then looked back up and said to his friends, "We have a lot of work to do. Let's get to it."

Jackie left to work on the president's schedule, Dave left to work on the engineering specifications, and Corey, Jasper, and Ryan stayed behind in the conference room. Using a whiteboard, they began planning the final details of this unusual mission. It would not be easy, and they had to make sure all the parts fit together ... and that nothing was missing. They also needed to put together, as part of the planning, a time schedule so everything would mesh up.

Using Microsoft Project, a program designed to capture all of the required events, they were able to begin the planning process. After several hours of work, they had detailed out a couple of hundred events that needed to be accomplished. They were then able to put those events into a time schedule and come up with an integrated plan.

Three days later, and after a thorough review of the engineering specifications, Dave went back to the language institute and retrieved some of the data they had translated. He went back to his temporary office in the White House. He spent several hours, into the early evening, going through the data and other schematic details in the specifications, looking for any weaknesses or possible ways of getting around the security system. While it was a well-designed system, it did have a couple of flaws, and he found them.

He sat back and thought about how they might actually defeat the system from an implementation viewpoint. What, physically, would they actually have to do to disable or defeat the system? His mind whirled. He looked at the schematics and installation drawings several times as he thought it through. There had to be something. Then ... he had it! He saw the weakness. They would be able to get around the security system. He thought.

Risky, but possible.

Monday—August 29
Washington, D.C.

Two days later, after another review with the president, they had approval to proceed.

General Newt Foley arrived at the White House not knowing what to expect. The president had called him over to discuss a sensitive issue, and he didn't know what that might mean. Always a nerve-racking situation, and one that he did not enjoy.

He approached Maria and then sat down. Maria notified the president that the general was waiting. After a few moments, the president came out, shook hands with the general, and invited him in to the Oval Office. They sat down on the comfortable leather couches.

The president said, "Newt, I'm sure you are wondering why I called you over here."

"Yes, sir. I am."

"I need to tell you of an operation that will begin shortly. An operation you know nothing about but may need to support."

Newt looked questioningly at the president.

The president continued, "Ryan McKenzie and his group are going to try and snatch the ayatollah and bring him back to U.S. soil for trial and prison. They will be starting soon and will need Navy support."

The general sat still for a moment. A mission completely outside the military was not unknown-after all, the CIA did it all the time-but this one was unusual and coming from left field at him. And it was coming at him from his boss, the president, who had obviously approved the mission.

"Why is it outside the military or, at least, the CIA?"

"Because I wanted it completely quiet and deniable."

General Foley certainly understood the deniability aspect and the politics involved. But it still grated on him that this critical mission was outside his control and influence. He nodded at the president's comments. Then he asked, "What type of support will they need?"

"I don't know yet. But I want the Navy to stand by for some classified work in the northern Indian Ocean. And it will be occurring fairly soon. I'll just have to let you know when they will need the help."

"Okay. I understand, sir. We will support as needed. Will I get the word through you for this?"

"No. Admiral Watkins will be tasking the Navy. I just wanted to make sure you didn't get it via the back door."

The general nodded. He looked at the president and said, "Thank you for that consideration. I'll just monitor the progress as things develop. Hopefully they will be successful."

"Thanks, Newt. I appreciate your cooperation and understanding."

"No problem, sir. And thanks for the heads-up." General Foley stood up, shook hands with the president, and left the Oval Office.

He softly said goodbye to Maria as he left. He found a men's room and just went in to wash his hands. He had to do something physical. He was seething in anger. A presidential-directed mission and he was just now being informed. Maybe it was time for him to retire. After all, he had over thirty-six years in, and maybe that was enough. The politics of this particular position were just about intolerable. But that was also something that he couldn't change. Part of life. He went back to the Pentagon ... not in a good mood.

Actually, he was really pissed off. But ... as a good soldier, he would support the mission.

Chapter Sixty-Two
Ayatollah Capture

Friday—September 9
Off the Coast of Socotra

It was now ten days after the president had authorized their planned actions. They were well on their way. To many people, the inside of a submarine would be a very claustrophobic experience. It takes a special breed of men and women to man these technological marvels. Close spacing and long periods of time underwater, with no surface contact, are difficult to tolerate, and the personnel assigned to these vessels are truly unique.

Flown out to the *Lincoln* and then helicoptered to the submarine two hundred miles east of the Socotra Islands, Ryan and his crew of three men were aboard. They had now arrived off the southern coast of Socotra and just below periscope depth. They were to take on the task of sneaking into the island underwater and trying to capture the ayatollah. If that didn't work, they were to make sure he did not survive their visit. It was a time of tension, anxiety, and anticipation.

Dressed in SEAL underwater gear, including dark wetsuits, various weapons, and scuba gear, they were to wait until late at night, process through the hatch, board the ASDV attached to the outside hull of the submarine, and head in to the southern coastline near the harbor. The ayatollah's quarters and center of operations were located just up a small grade from the harbor, and they hoped to arrive unnoticed, capture and disable him, and return to the beach, then to the ASDV, and then on back to the submarine. All without being seen. It was an audacious plan, but they felt they could pull it off.

Even though the trimaran was no longer in the harbor, the thinking was that the communication drop-off was also just a ruse. The general consensus of intelligence personnel, and the evidence from the signals intelligence, indicated that the ayatollah was still on the island. Satellite cameras had recorded an individual out on a resting area that appeared to be him. Abdul-Hakim had also been seen outdoors in conference with the ayatollah.

Jasper's visit to the island a couple of weeks earlier had led them to believe he was still there. One of the hotel personnel that Jasper talked with mentioned that the center, while appearing quiet, was still operating as usual. And Jasper's informal surveillance showed that truck and aircraft traffic supporting the center was at a normal pace. Of course, the locals did not know what the situation was regarding communications. That was being managed and operated by internal New Persia personnel.

So they had laid on the mission. Ryan, Corey, Dave, and Jasper would quietly invade the island and capture the ayatollah for return to the U.S.

It was audacious, and they were all quite worried. The defenses on the island compound were somewhat unknown, even with Jasper's visit. So they were going in with a hope and a prayer. The general theory was that just a few of them would be better than a whole force. There would be less chance of discovery at an inopportune moment, and less fuss. A significant force would be more detectable and would probably result in resistance and casualties on both sides. Bottom line: there would be fewer chances of someone being killed.

Saturday—September 10
Socotra Island—Southern Coast

It was 1:00 a.m. local time and the submarine was a half-mile off the coast and just at periscope depth. They were maintaining themselves as motionless as possible to lessen any surface disturbance, although there probably wasn't anyone around to detect it. Ryan and the others had put on the underwater gear, and one at a time they processed through the hatch and into the ASDV. Once all four of them had crawled inside, Ryan powered up the underwater navigation system, contacted the sub, and began preparations for separation. Coordinating with the bridge, he separated from the sub.

After departing, Ryan guided the ASDV downward slightly and then forward toward the beach. Following the navigation system, he guided the ASDV into a position several hundred yards off the beach and in about twenty-five feet of water. He powered it down, and it settled to the bottom as designed. They all detached from the ASDV, going on to their scuba tanks. They spread out into a close formation and headed in. Very faint flashing blue LEDs on their harnesses allowed them to see each other and maintain location awareness. The apprehension was high for each of them, since they didn't know what to expect at the beach. Armed patrols? Sentries? Something else?

Ryan was in just a few feet of water when he broached the surface carefully to look around. Just his head above water. It was dark except for some distant lighting at the breakwater, and there was nothing on the beach that he could see. Putting on waterproof night-vision goggles, he looked at the full length of the beach again. And again, nothing was in sight. All was quiet. Nothing, and nobody, was there.

He used the very small underwater LEDs to signal the others, and they slowly, like turtles seeking a nest, crept out of the water and onto the sand. They stopped to listen. Nothing but small waves breaking on the sandy beach. The road beyond the beach was dark and deserted of any traffic. The harbor was several hundred yards off to the right of them, and lights lit up the breakwater. No motion there either. It was almost too quiet. For an organization as vulnerable as New Persia, there should have been some security evident ... guards or patrols. It didn't feel right.

Ryan didn't like it. It had been several weeks since he and the rest had escaped. Abdul-Hakim must have planned some form of reception. Even though the New Persia group had indicated that they had left the island, it would just be prudent for the remaining defenders to put out some form of sensors or defenses should the U.S. try something. But nothing appeared in his night vision. Then again, he was thinking like a trained westerner. Perhaps New Persia was satisfied with their internal compound security systems and wasn't concerned with the beaches beyond their perimeter. But he still couldn't get over the feeling of concern. It was too easy and too quiet.

They scrambled up the beach and into some small, scrubby bushes at the edge of the sand. Stripping off the scuba gear, they all pulled out weapons and spare magazines, checked them, checked the Ka-Bar knives they wore, and put on the night-vision goggles. They repaired each other's camouflage grease paint on their faces and necks. They put on soft running-type shoes for quiet and quicker motion. Looking around, they still didn't see anything. No noises, no sounds ... just the quiet of the tropical night.

355

They spread out and headed over to the harbor entrance area, staying in the line of bushes and small shrubbery. Reaching the base of the breakwater, they slipped into the water and worked their way around the fencing, and ran right into more fencing. The harbor entranceway was blocked by underwater and above-water fencing that ran all the way across the entrance, eight to ten feet high. They couldn't climb it and they couldn't go under it. They retreated to the breakwater base.

Ryan whispered, "Well, Jasper, it looks like you were right. They have made some changes. We are going to have to figure out some other way to get into the compound."

Jasper whispered, "We'll have to go back the other way on the beach and approach the fence head-on. If we can get there, I'll cut through the fence and we can advance."

Dave and Corey nodded.

Ryan gave a thumbs-up and Jasper led the way back.

On the way, Jasper suddenly stopped. He had an idea. He quickly explained what he had in mind to Ryan. Ryan thought for a moment and then agreed to the move. Jasper led the way out to the location where he had observed the guardhouse while on his visit.

They waited until the shift change was about to take place. They observed the guards on duty make their report just as the replacement guards approached in the golf cart. Dave fired the invisible laser at the camera and saw it smoke slightly. The camera was out of commission. In the darkness they split up and, two from each side, silently charged from both sides of the guardhouse. The four guards were completely surprised and immediately overwhelmed. Knockout shots were given to each guard, and they were out in seconds. They trussed the guards together back to back and placed them out of sight on the floor of the guardhouse.

All four of them then headed in on the golf cart. They had less than twenty minutes to get in, get the ayatollah, and get out before the next report to the operations center was due from the guard shack. It would be tight. Dave, from his memory of the installation drawings, directed them over to a small outbuilding. He pulled out his small tablet and brought up a diagram. Right building. He quickly picked the lock and they were in. He took an LED flashlight and found the cabinet he was looking for. He opened it and found the tangle of wires and fiber optics. He put a jumper between two terminals. He unplugged two other connectors and rerouted a third line. He gave the group a thumbs-up and they left the building.

Racing to the main building in the borrowed golf cart, they approached a main door. Fifteen minutes left. Striding right past a camera, they boldly walked into the building. At this late hour, nobody was around. Dave had succeeded in disabling the cameras. They still captured the images, but the monitors inside the control center were now looking at earlier recordings, not the current images. And, with the disconnect of two terminals, the laser alarms were powered down. He had succeeded.

Thirteen minutes to go.

The ayatollah was sound asleep in his small apartment quarters attached to his office area. In the early morning hours, no one was up other than personnel in the operations center. The hallways were dimly lit for the night with just some small nightlights, and no one was around. Since they knew where his quarters were located from their previous "guest" experience, they rapidly approached the door to his office and quietly tried the handle. Locked.

Dave moved up and took a small tool kit from his pocket. Various picks. Corey looked over and whispered, "Aha. A man of many talents." Dave responded in a whisper, "One of my several hobbies." And he turned back to his work. He fiddled with the lock for a moment or two, picking out two of his locksmith picks, while the rest stood guard watching down the hallway in both directions, and after a moment of work the lock gave way. Dave put the picks away as Ryan slowly opened the door and looked in.

Dark and quiet. Nobody in, or even guarding, the office area. New Persia was obviously not worried about intruders inside the compound. They quickly moved into the room and silently closed the door behind them. Crouched down to reduce their appearance and silhouette, they looked around the room and moved over to the desk area. To the right of the desk was another door. They knew from the plans, and their experience, that it led into the ayatollah's apartment.

Using small red LED flashlights, Ryan and Jasper quietly went over to the door. Dave and Corey busied themselves looking at documentation on and in the desk. Jasper moved off to the side slightly, and Ryan, offset from the immediate front of the door, grasped the handle and slowly turned it. It made no noise, since it was fairly new. He turned it as far as it would go. He slowly opened the door as Dave and Corey interrupted what they were doing to watch. Nothing happened. Ryan opened the door further and duck-walked into the room. Jasper, doing the same walk, followed. Corey and Dave went back to their work.

There was a single bed with a large lump in it, a small dresser, a nightstand, and a small easy chair with a lamp next to it. There were no other furnishings in the room. The lump was a body. The ayatollah. The reason for their mission was right there. The critical moment was here. They both hesitated for a moment. Ryan motioned for Jasper to go around to the other side of the bed. Jasper nodded and began to move. The lump moved. The body turned over and was now facing Ryan. Eyes shut, with a slight snoring sound. Sound asleep. Hair unkempt, and the beard needed a trim. Ryan looked closely, but not too close, and verified it was the ayatollah. Now what?

Ryan pulled a small spray canister from his pouch. He motioned to Jasper to be ready. Jasper, in position now on the other side of the bed, coiled his legs under him, ready to pounce. Ryan held the canister up near the ayatollah's nose, waited until the ayatollah breathed in, and pressed the plunger. A short spurt of gas sprayed out into the ayatollah's nose. He gave a slight start and went limp. Jasper reached over the edge of the bed, turned the ayatollah over, picked him up, and, with Ryan's help, attached him to a harness on Jasper's back. Thoroughly trussed in the harness, the unconscious ayatollah was carried by Jasper into the office area. Dave and Corey had finished their quick look, made photocopies of several documents, and were over by the door to the hall.

Eight minutes to go.

Ryan led the way back out the door, and Jasper followed with the ayatollah on his back, then Dave and Corey. Corey very quietly shut the door and they proceeded down the hall and out into the night. They got into the golf cart that they had parked in the doorway area and headed back down to the entrance gate.

Seven minutes to go.

Once through the gate, they continued down the road to the line of bushes bordering the beach and their equipment. The darkness was a welcome relief, and they began to breathe a little easier. They were nearly there.

They unharnessed the ayatollah from Jasper's back and laid him out on the sand. There was still no alarm being raised in the compound. They handcuffed and foot-cuffed the ayatollah and connected the two chains together.

Time was up. Zero minutes to go.

Ryan took another canister from his small pack and sprayed it on the ayatollah. He became groggy as the antidote began to bring him around. He struggled a little against the restraints and finally realized he was trussed up. He opened his mouth to yell, and Ryan quickly shushed him, holding a Glock in front of his face. He could see the silencer screwed onto the barrel and the hole where a bullet would come out at him. He shut up.

Ryan leaned down to him and whispered, "Quiet. If you make any noise, we will shoot you. It doesn't make any difference to us if we take you back alive or dead. But it might make a difference to you." The ayatollah gave a slight start as he recognized Ryan. He nodded in understanding.

Ryan, Corey, Dave and Jasper all put on their scuba gear. The ayatollah looked puzzled. What were they going to do with him? While the ayatollah was still trussed up, Jasper came over and grabbed him, carrying him down to the edge of the water. He heard the waves and could see the water in the dim light of the stars and the breakwater lights. When Jasper set him facedown on the sand, the sand was gritty and he was immediately soaked by the warm ocean water. The ayatollah was scared—were they going to drown him?

Abdul-Hakim had been aroused from his sleep. The men monitoring the cameras in the center were suspicious. Something just didn't feel right, and the camera going down on the west gate bothered them. But none could leave the center. The monitoring was too important. They weren't authorized to activate the response team. Abdul-Hakim or Khatib had to do it. And the west gate was not responding to their calls. Abdul-Hakim looked at the monitors. He agreed. Something wasn't right. He looked at the images again. Then it hit him. Several outside lights were on in the images, and he knew they were currently disconnected for maintenance. He sounded the alarm, and several armed, groggy men hurried into the room. He put together the image problem and the camera outage. Someone had come through the gate and done something. He sent one runner to raise the ayatollah, and the rest of the response team he sent off to the west gate.

They raced outside and could see down the slight hill that the west gate was open. They climbed into their response vehicles and headed for the gate. Arriving, they roused and untied the guards and glanced down the road to the beach. It was pretty obvious that whoever had been here had headed for the beach. Two vehicles of men raced for the beach.

Corey heard an engine noise in the direction of the guardhouse. He hurried down the beach with a scuba harness and tank. He rolled the ayatollah over and quickly attached the harness to him. The ayatollah fought Corey. He said, "I can't swim and don't know how to use that equipment."

Ryan, aware of the engine noise also, quickly came over and said, very intensely, "It's obvious that your security folks are here. You will not be rescued. Now, there are two ways of doing this. We are taking you out to a waiting submarine. It is underwater a little over a half-mile out. You can either use this equipment or not. All you have to do is breathe in the mouthpiece. We are going to pull you through the water with the trusses on. If you choose to not use that equipment, you will still be towed underwater and drown. Whatever you do, you will be on that submarine in a short while ... dead or alive. Your choice. Am I clear?"

The ayatollah understood and was very frightened. But he nodded and let Corey finish putting the equipment on him. When the mouthpiece was put in place, he struggled a little until he realized he could breathe with it on. He calmed down a little bit and lay quietly on the sand at the water's edge.

Abdul-Hakim was trying to monitor what was going on. But all the alarms, including the lasers, were dead. The runner he had sent to the ayatollah's quarters had come back saying the ayatollah wasn't there. So where had he gone? He wasn't one to wander around much at night. Then it hit him. The alarms, the monitors, the ayatollah missing. They were under a very quiet attack!

And the ayatollah?

Kidnapped?

The vehicles came down the road at a slow pace looking for the intruders. It was dark, and all they could really see past the wild shrubbery was the slight edge of the water glowing slightly in very minor moonlight. They almost ran into the golf cart, but stopped just before hitting it. They turned on a spotlight and began sweeping the sand. Suddenly they stopped as they saw several individuals crouched at the water's edge, several hundred yards away. They gunned the truck engines and raced for the intruders. As they got closer, several of the men began to fire their AK-74s.

They radioed back to the operations center that they had found intruders on the beach.

Abdul-Hakim listened for a minute then grew panicky. Over the radio, he said to the team leader, "Are you firing at them?"

"Yes, sir. They are at the water's edge and we are using small arms as we get closer."

Abdul-Hakim was in shock. His men were firing at the intruders who had the ayatollah. They might hit the ayatollah! He nearly screamed into the radio, "Cease fire. Cease fire. The ayatollah is out there and you might hit him! Cease fire!"

He heard the order from the response team leader, in the background, being given to cease fire, and the firing eased off, with a few shots fired after the fact.

Chapter Sixty-Three
Dark Underwater Swim

Saturday—September 10
Socotra Island—Southern Coast

In a hurry now, Ryan and Dave entered the dark water and began to float. They waited as Jasper and Corey dragged the ayatollah into the water. All four of them then quickly placed their masks on their faces and made sure the air tanks and regulators were working correctly. Corey and Jasper grabbed the ayatollah's tank harness, clipped a strap to each side, and began dragging him through the watery sand into the low surf. Corey and Jasper, caught in the spotlights, hurriedly pushed the ayatollah into the surf. Shots began to pinch up the sand and water around them. Corey let go of the harness, as Jasper continued out into the low surf, and swung around with his SCAR MK 17 assault weapon firing off several 7.62mm rounds at the security forces.

The security men hit the ground when they realized they were being fired on. Several returned fire. Corey took a hit, spun, and fell in the waist-deep water.

Seeing Corey fall, Jasper let go of the ayatollah, crept back, and grabbed Corey's harness and swam out into the surf. Jasper made sure Corey's mask was in place and headed for deeper water as fast as he could, flippers churning. Corey was bleeding from a wound in the right shoulder. He was conscious but hurt, and only feebly swimming. Ryan swam back and grabbed the ayatollah and continued swimming out into deeper water, dragging the ayatollah after him.

Dave swam back to where Jasper was struggling with the injured Corey. He grabbed the MK 17 weapon, turned, and lay down in the surf with just his head and the weapon above water. Looking through the night-vision scope, he picked out an obvious target in the security forces and fired. The target spun and went down. He scanned over to the left and found another target and took it out. The security forces quickly realized they were under some very accurate fire, and disappeared behind anything they could find. In the process, their fire diminished quickly. Dave scanned across the bushes

362

in the distance, picked out one more, and fired. Another one down. Further scanning, he saw no more targets. He realized that the security forces had, for some reason, ceased firing in their direction. He didn't know why other than his accurate fire. Dave then slowly back-crawled into the surf until he could get further underwater. Then he turned and began swimming for all he was worth, putting his scuba mask in place as he went.

They were busy towing the ayatollah and Corey back to the ASDV when they heard a loud and obnoxious scraping and squealing sound carry through the water. Ryan looked back, but, of course, could see nothing in the darkness. Then it dawned on him that it must be the underwater gates at the harbor entrance being opened as the security forces were trying to track them. He moved deeper into the water and, through his underwater mike, said "I think that's the gates. Let's pick it up a little. I sure don't want them to catch us at this point."

They began kicking a little harder. Ryan triggered an electronic request from his chest pack, and the ASDV responded with a series of small high-frequency chirps. The signal and direction was indicated on Ryan's chest pack, part of his scuba harness. They modified their course slightly and finally found the ASDV where they had left it. In the darkness of the early morning hours, it was invisible, and the security forces wouldn't be able to locate it. The tracking beacon he had triggered led them to it. As soon as Ryan got in the ASDV, he turned off the beacon so the New Persia security forces couldn't possibly trace it. He also began powering up a small defensive torpedo just in case they needed it.

As they got to the ASDV, they heard one of the patrol boats' engine and screws coming out of the harbor. While it was still very dark, and the patrol boat probably couldn't see them, it might be able to trace them if any light were emitted. The others quietly, and without any lights, got into the ASDV.

They climbed in and secured the ayatollah. Dave and Jasper helped strap Corey in. He was conscious but obviously hurting. Ryan powered up the ASDV, lifted off the bottom slightly, and turned around. He waited until he heard the screws fading as the patrol boat was moving away from them in its search, and then started the ASDV on its trip back to the waiting submarine. Using a small navigation homing signal from the submarine, Ryan set a direct course, and they were quickly heading back out to the waiting sub. They had succeeded in escaping. And they had the ayatollah, alive and kicking.

The security response team was frustrated. They had found the intruders and missed them. They knew they had done some damage because they had seen one of the intruders hit, but no one was left behind. They didn't know who they were fighting, but, since they had returned fire, they were probably professionals. Two of their men were dead and a third was seriously wounded. But why were the intruders here?

The radio crackled, receiving a call from the control center. They radioed back that they had missed. The intruders had gotten away.

Abdul-Hakim was absolutely in shock. The ayatollah kidnapped from his own bed? And they had missed whoever had done it. Now what? He called Khatib, woke him up, and told him to report to the operations center.

This was not happening! The ayatollah could not believe that he had been kidnapped in the middle of the night from his bed and was now in the ocean on the way to an American submarine. In his worst nightmares he could not have envisioned this. He couldn't move. This underwater craft was very restraining, and the handcuffs and scuba harness held him tightly. His mind was a jumble of thoughts and fears. What happened to his security? Why hadn't they reacted to this intrusion? He looked about in the dark; he couldn't see anything except a very muted instrument panel in the front. He felt very claustrophobic. His mind whirled. Where were they taking him? What was to become of him? What would his staff do about his disappearance? Would he drown? Were these Americans going to kill him?

Ryan approached the awaiting submarine and sent out a low-frequency signal. He got a return indication on the instrument panel. He lined up with the mounts on the back of the submarine and positioned the ASDV using sensitive sonic transducers. Two SEAL scuba divers were in the water, and they locked the ASDV into place. Navy seamen came through the hatch and helped Corey first, getting him through the hatch and into the sub chamber. Once inside, Corey was hustled off to the medic. Then the crewmen helped the ayatollah untangle himself from the ASDV. Moving over to the hatch, they lowered him down into the chamber. Ryan and his group assisted in moving the ayatollah and stood by as he disappeared into the submarine.

Ryan stripped off the scuba gear, lowered himself into the submarine, and was able to step out into the interior. He looked around for Corey and the ayatollah. A crewman near him said, "Corey is in the medic area being treated. We removed the ayatollah's gear and he has been moved forward under guard. His trusses are still in place. He won't be going anywhere soon."

Ryan, still covered with camouflage paint on his face, neck, and hands, looked at the crewman and nodded. "Thanks. And thanks for the help with the gear."

Ryan headed to the medic, and found Corey under local sedation. The bleeding had been stopped and the medic was stitching up the wound. He turned to Ryan. "He'll be all right, but he'll have very sore shoulder for a while. The bullet went clear through. He was lucky nothing serious was hit."

Corey looked at Ryan and grinned. "Just my luck! But we proved ourselves pretty well." He grimaced slightly as a muscle spasmed.

"We sure did! Thanks," said Ryan. "I'll be back in a little while."

Jasper and Dave were looking and listening in. The three of them headed for the forward part of the sub. On the bridge, they found a still soaking wet ayatollah standing with Commander Morino. Commander Morino was studying his prisoner with very intense eyes. He turned as Ryan and the other guys approached. "Well. It looks like you managed to get him. Close to a drowned rat, but apparently not much worse for his experience. How's your buddy and what do you want to do now? I'd suggest we move out right away."

Ryan, looking at the ayatollah, said, "We need to get him some dry clothes and a little food. Then I'd like to talk with him. And he needs to be guarded constantly." He looked over at Commander Morino and continued, "The medic says Corey will be okay. That's sure a relief. I agree. I think we need to go ahead and move out toward our waiting carrier. The sooner we can exit these waters, the more comfortable I'll be."

Commander Morino nodded then looked over his shoulder and gave the helm direction to change course and speed. The submarine started to turn, and they all could feel it picking up speed. After a few moments, they could also feel it sinking to a lower depth and finally leveling off. Then there was no more sensation of movement. It was in a cruise mode heading north to a set of prearranged coordinates in the northern Indian Ocean.

Khatib was aroused from his deep sleep and hurried to the operations control center. He was not aware of any of the activity that had been going on. And it was now close to 2:30 a.m. He entered through the secure locks into the control room. Abdul-Hakim was in a state of near panic trying to learn what was going on. He was obviously in a state of confusion and was giving several orders to his personnel. Khatib looked at the monitors and could see nothing wrong. All the systems seemed to be operating and none were apparently down. Aban spotted Khatib and walked over to him.

Bowing slightly, he addressed Khatib: "We have a serious issue right now. While we are not completely sure as yet, it appears that the Americans have kidnapped the ayatollah."

Khatib's head snapped around to look at Aban. "What did you just say?"

"Yes, sir. We think the American commandos have just taken the ayatollah. He is not in his room and we cannot find him. There is evidence that there have been some intruders in the past hour or so, and we think they took him."

Khatib nodded quickly and moved over to Abdul-Hakim. "What is the status and where is the ayatollah?"

Abdul-Hakim, looking very disturbed, glanced at Khatib and said, "We think the ayatollah has been kidnapped by the Americans. My security forces are down at the harbor and they say some armed intruders there have gotten away. Two of my men are dead and one is wounded."

"But your monitors all look good. How can this be happening? Why didn't you see them coming? Where are the guards at the entrance?" he asked, leaning forward slightly with his arms outstretched.

"The monitors are playing a recording. How they did it, I don't know. The guards are knocked out and useless."

"I see. So your security system has been penetrated and is useless also. Is that not so?"

Abdul-Hakim looked back at Khatib, hesitated for just a moment, and slowly looked at the floor. Then his head snapped back up and he gave directions to the technical people to find the recording and get the system back running as it should be. Two technicians headed out for the central control facility where Dave had placed the jumpers.

Abdul-Hakim said to Khatib, "We will get it fixed. In the meantime, we need to locate and bring back the ayatollah."

"From what you have described, that's a tall order. The Americans probably have a submarine out there somewhere, and they are long gone with the ayatollah, and that's why the Chinese couldn't pick it up and warn us." He paused for a long moment, deep in thought, took a very deep breath of resignation, and then said, "Abdul-Hakim, come with me." He turned and left the control center.

Abdul-Hakim paused for a moment, thought a bit, and then followed Khatib. Khatib went back to the ayatollah's office and stood behind the ayatollah's desk. Abdul-Hakim followed him in and stood on the other side of the desk.

Khatib said, "Do you remember what the ayatollah told you just a few days ago? That failure again was not an option for you? That he expected you to make sure we were secure? That you were not to fail again?"

Abdul-Hakim looked at the ceiling, thinking, *This is hardly the time for this.* But as he returned Khatib's gaze, he said, "Yes. Of course I remember that conversation. What of it?"

"You have failed again. And this time really failed to the point we may have a problem holding this movement together. I want you to figure out how we can actually recover the ayatollah and do it quickly. We have no time to waste and the longer we delay the more difficult it will be."

Abdul-Hakim looked at Khatib. He realized that this was a matter of his own survival. He needed to get the ayatollah back and did not have a lot of options. He was gone and probably beyond reach.

He nodded at Khatib and left the room for the control center; his mind in turmoil. What could he do? He didn't really know ... and Khatib was very serious about getting the ayatollah back.

Chapter Sixty-Four
Heading Home

Saturday—September 10
Off The Coast Of Socotra

The ayatollah was given a change of clothing and some food. He was guarded and handcuffed as he slowly ate. He was then escorted into the execs quarters for a discussion with Ryan and group. Ryan, Dave and Jasper all waited in the cramped quarters. Corey joined them, with his arm in a sling, just before the ayatollah arrived under escort.

Ryan looked at the ayatollah and began, "Ayatollah Sarhardi, we meet again. You are being taken to the United States and will be held for trial before our federal authorities. You have destroyed several civilian and federal facilities, and you've downed innocent and unarmed aircraft murdering their crew and passengers. You are considered an international criminal by the U.S. Government and you will be tried for terrorism."

The ayatollah protested. "You invade my compound and kidnap me with no warning. You have no proof of what you say and the world will hear the truth from me and my people. I have nothing further to say to you."

Ryan looked back at him. He said, "You may not have anything more to say to me, but I have a few words to say to you. You attacked me in my home when Malik tried to kill me, and nearly succeeded. You tried again, through Ramiz, to kill me in my own home and failed again. You tried to kidnap a member of our president's senior staff and nearly succeeded. Your misguided efforts at forcing the world to your demands have resulted in your downfall. With you gone, I think your movement may very well be gone also. Your failure to negotiate your demands with anyone, in today's world, is just plain stupid. And has led to this action on our part." He stopped for a moment, then continued, "When we get back to the U.S. you will be placed in the hands of the federal authorities. There you will be held for trial. I don't know where that trial will be held, but I intend to follow it very closely. If I had to guess, you will spend most, if not all, of the rest of your life in prison."

Ryan then stopped, looked hard at the ayatollah, and got up and left the room followed by the others. An armed crewman guard remained. The ayatollah was still handcuffed and footcuffed. He wasn't going anywhere.

They gathered in the wardroom and, using a military laptop computer, developed a detailed report of their actions and results. For a change, a clandestine mission had been successfully accomplished. After reviewing, rewriting, and finalizing the report, they classified it "Top Secret". It was encrypted and transmitted to the Pentagon and the White House.

When the message was received in the Pentagon and the White House, it was immediately forwarded to the Joint Chiefs and the president. In both cases a sigh of relief happened and smiles and handshakes were very evident. Maybe now the major headache was over and they could get on with other pressing business. The president called Jackie in to the Oval Office and showed her the message. She sat down, covered her eyes and said a small prayer. Looking at the president she simply said, "Thank God. Hopefully it's over."

He nodded back and said, "Surely, let's hope so."

After several hours, and several cups of coffee in the wardroom, Ryan and his group were approached by the exec. The exec said, "We are nearly at the coordinates for the transfer. The *Lincoln* is standing by for your boarding and we are about to surface. You might want to get your friend ready for the transfer also." And he smiled at the 'friend' comment.

Ryan nodded and said, "Thanks. And thanks for all your help. Without it we couldn't have done this." Then, looking at Dave, Jasper, and Corey, who had joined them, he said, "I didn't think we had much of a chance to pull this off, but you all really pulled together and we did it. We can be proud of what we did, but unfortunately the world won't know about this little adventure. It will remain a secret just as most of the SEAL and Special Forces actions are kept quiet."

They all nodded at his words as he continued, "OK. Now I guess we have to get him over to the carrier. You heard the exec, let's get moving."

They all headed down the passageway as they felt the submarine tilt upward slightly as it surfaced. They, along with the armed guard, headed up to the bridge, went on through and up to the forward hatch where they would exit the ship.

They watched as the crew surfaced. Radio communications with the *Lincoln* set up the transfer process. A submarine crewman opened the forward hatch and they all climbed out onto the top deck of the sub. In the bright light of late morning, they were momentarily blinded. After a few moments they were then followed by the ayatollah being assisted by the guard and another crewman. A short distance away floated the massive aircraft carrier *USS Abraham Lincoln*. A small lighter started out from the *Lincoln* and headed in their direction. The submarine was still in the calm water as the lighter bumped up to the side and crewmen made it fast to the sub.

They all transferred onto the lighter. Just before stepping on to the lighter Ryan turned around, spotted Commander Morino on the conning tower, and gave him a splendid military salute. It was returned by the Commander and Ryan then stepped onto the lighter. An armed guard from the *Lincoln* was watching the ayatollah with interest. The ride back to the *Lincoln* was uneventful. The ayatollah was morosely staring at the floor of the lighter.

Once on board the *Lincoln*, Ryan and his group were escorted up to the bridge, where they met, again, with Captain Jesus Alvarez and Admiral Jason Bridgewater. They had met the captain and the task force commander when they were outbound on the mission. The ayatollah was taken to the on-board brig, where he was given water and then locked up under constant guard.

Ryan and his group were fed and enjoyed a hot shower and general cleanup. They spent part of the day just having some more coffee and discussing the events surrounding the capture between themselves. They also, for an hour, briefed the admiral on the mission and its successful conclusion. Then they were shown to some temporary quarters, where they spent the afternoon resting. The admiral was pleased at the results, and they spent the evening with him.

During the day they received a classified message from the White House, copied to the Joint Chiefs, of congratulations and thanks for a mission well done.

Sunday—September 11
Northern Indian Ocean

The next day a C-2AR Greyhound landed on the *Lincoln* with various supplies and mail. The ayatollah, with Ryan and the group, loaded up and were flown to Diego Garcia. There, a special mission C-17 took them on a very long flight to Andrews AFB in Maryland. Under guard at all times, the ayatollah was then transferred to the FBI and taken to a holding area for interrogation and trial preliminaries.

Several of the documents that had been photocopied in the ayatollah's office revealed some of the planning New Persia was developing for an attack on the Saudi oil terminals. Those plans were passed on to the Saudis for their information and action as deemed appropriate. There was also some preliminary planning for an attack on the British Petroleum oil facilities in the North Sea and their administrative facilities in Aberdeen, Scotland. This also was passed on to the British for their information.

Ryan's immediate mission from the president was complete. The ayatollah had been captured and would spend a good part of the next several years, or his entire remaining life, in a U.S. federal prison. Possibly a super-max.

Tuesday—September 13
Washington, D.C.

After returning to the States, Ryan, Jasper, Dave, and Corey met in the White House at the request of the president. Jackie joined them as they made their way into the Oval Office. The president was sitting at his desk as Maria opened the door and escorted them in. The president immediately got up and walked over to them, motioning them to sit on the couches and chairs around a small coffee table. There were some small pastries and coffee along with pitchers of water available.

The president looked at Ryan and the others on his team and said, "You really did a wonderful job out there. Ridding the world of this pest was quite an accomplishment, and I am grateful to you for it. It was quite a team effort, and you should be proud. The ayatollah will be standing trial soon, and it is only through your efforts that it will be possible. I would expect that he will spend most, if not all, of the remainder of his life in one of our super-max facilities." He looked around again and continued, "I would hope that, if I need your assistance again in the future, I will be able to call on you. I don't anticipate it, but would like to know your capabilities are available to us."

371

Ryan and the others just smiled and nodded as he spoke. Ryan looked around at his friends and said to the president, "I think I can speak for all of us and say we would be pleased and honored to help out, in any manner, should you need it in the future. Hopefully that won't happen, but you know the old saying, never say never."

The president smiled at this. He stood up and shook hands with all of them, and they departed the Oval Office.

Ryan looked at Corey and said, "Your pending assignment to Jordan. I would imagine it is quite interesting in that part of the world."

Corey looked back, smiling, and said, "Yes. I'm sure it is quite interesting. But not as exciting as chasing after the likes of the ayatollah. After all, the embassy duty just doesn't have the same pizzazz. It will probably be a bit on the boring side."

Jasper smiled and said, "Well, we can't always have the bad guys after us. Of course, over there, I'm not sure who the real bad guys really are. There's a lot of intrigue and backdoor dealing going on."

They all nodded.

Wednesday—September 14
Washington, D.C.

The next day, a press release was distributed to the media telling them of the pending trial of the ayatollah. No other information was released, and the world responded with a ho-hum reaction. Behind the scenes, the Brits, French, and Germans were pleased with the results, and congratulations were offered in the embassies.

Wednesday—September 14
Socotra Island Operations Center

Khatib, Abdul-Hakim and Ramiz continued developing their plans to return the ayatollah, and included finalizing the recovery of Kadar and the crew of the *Persian Desert*. They had the support of New Persia behind them. They had unfinished business to complete.

The author, Richard W. Barton, lives in Colorado with his family. A retired member of the US Air Force, and also retired from a major aerospace company, he spends his time on the golf course and climbing the trails and mountains of his adopted state. He can be reached via email at bartonrw1@gmail.com

www.ingramcontent.com/pod-product-compliance
Lightning Source LLC
Chambersburg PA
CBHW020238200626
46816CB00001BA/26